Silencio

L.A. BERRY

Silencio

Matador
9 Priory Business Park,
Wistow Road, Kibworth Beauchamp,
Leicestershire. LE8 0RX
Tel: 0116 279 2299
Email: books@troubador.co.uk
Web: www.troubador.co.uk/matador
Twitter: @matadorbooks

ISBN 978 1785890 994

British Library Cataloguing in Publication Data.
A catalogue record for this book is available from the British Library.

Printed and bound by CPI Group (UK) Ltd, Croydon, CR0 4YY
Typeset in 11pt Aldine401 BT by Troubador Publishing Ltd, Leicester, UK

Matador is an imprint of Troubador Publishing Ltd

*For Alan and my family – without them
this book would remain a dream.*

Sixteen

Mercedes returns home empty: with empty arms, empty womb, and empty of emotion. There is nothing left. The tears are spent.

Between the streaks on the glass, the reflection of a teenage girl stares back. Fingers appear in the image and play with a wayward ebony curl, but her hand falls from sight when the ghost of a baby materialises. Before she has time to stroke it, the mirage vanishes, and her focus drops to her lap.

'A boy or a girl?'

She sighs, and raises her eyes. A fog muffles the words and Mercedes' eyelids begin to close, but the woman tries once more.

'Is that your baby?'

At last, she hears the question and forces her eyes to meet those of her interrogator; she first nods, and then shakes her head. Her fingers tighten their clutch on the corner of the photograph, and she shrugs as she turns her face to the window, deaf to the drone of sympathy.

The engine grinds to a halt and Mercedes slumps into the seat, reluctant to abandon the sanctuary of the compartment. Other passengers disembark and, through the glass, she observes their progress along the platform. She is tempted to carry on her journey without a destination, but she prises herself out of the seat. A conductor blows his whistle as she negotiates the last step. The train gathers speed and creates the breeze that caresses her calves, then the world falls silent.

Mercedes aches for a sign of compassion from her parents; however, the vacant platform tells its story. She heaves the strap of the bag onto her shoulder and staggers; beneath the bloodstain on her blouse, the friction has left its mark. Outside of the station, she pauses and braces herself for the walk home; her route tracks the main thoroughfare of the town. Each step that she takes is leaden; her feet swelter in the winter boots that she wore on the day she left home, and every day since.

No one appears and her carefully prepared answers are not necessary. Hiding all signs of life, slats of wood protect her neighbours' homes from the searing heat of the afternoon sun. Unexpectedly, a shutter slams nearby. She risks a glance, but no one emerges and she resumes her shuffle, certain that she feels the darts of disapproving eyes piercing her back.

Hampered by the weight of her burden, progress is slow. Close by, the hoo-hoo of a hidden woodpecker seems to mock her and she quickens her pace when she realises that, before long, the church bell will sound four knells, a warning that afternoon siesta is near its end.

She yearns for a glimpse of Marie Luis, but when her eyes face upwards, her best friend isn't on the balcony. A new crack has appeared in one of the decorative tiles on the underside of the platform; nothing else has changed. Her banishment had been swift, with neither goodbyes nor time to confide in Marie Luis. She fears that her experiences have turned her into a different person, one whom her friend would struggle to recognise.

As Mercedes resumes her trek, the fleeting image of a new-born brushes her memory. Shaking away the vision, a rogue tear splays across her hot cheek; she brushes away the others before they are able to fall. She arrives at the orchards that mark the boundary of her family's estate, where the sound of a sluggish river encroaches onto her thoughts. Her bag explodes onto the ground in a cloud of dust as she stumbles over to the river's edge. The muddy bank sucks her knees as she scoops her hand into the bubbling water and raises it to moisten her lips. For a while she rests, lost in the memories of childhood play; a time when she and her friends sought escape from the burning sun in the cool fluid. A sigh escapes as she rises and turns her back on the reminiscences.

Her destination nears and her body trembles. She averts her eyes from the bullet-ridden wall of a crumbling stone building; in forty years, the rain has failed to wash away the tattoo of blood. The fresco ignites her imagination with its reminder of her persecuted forebears. Now she empathises with their anguish; any denouncement by family pierces the heart.

At the ancient door, embellished with elaborate carvings, she hangs back while she tries to control her tremors. On the other side, she envisages the accusing eyes of her parents. Her last sight of that door had been as her father slammed it shut behind him, and his wounding words could never be forgotten. Nor could they be forgiven.

'You are a whore! And a liar!'

His slap had left an imprint.

'José could not do such a horrible thing. He is like a son to me.'

He ignored her protests.

'You led him on. With your tarty clothes. Your painted face. I can tell you now that you will never bring your bastard into my house.'

She had been on the floor when he left; his last words echoed in her head long after his departure.

'Get rid of it! Go find a woman in the village to sort you out.'

Six months have altered Mercedes forever. Her teenage body now bears silvery lines that track the sides of her breasts and her still-softened belly. The soft rose tips of her breasts have reddened against the darker areola. Milk flows at the sound of a baby's cry. However, it is the unseen changes that are the greatest.

Rusty hinges groan as the door gives way to the thrust of her body. An uneven tile catches her boot so that she staggers into the jasmine-infused courtyard. She doesn't make any attempt to catch her bag as it falls, but remains motionless while she savours the cool shadows and the fragrance of her home. The emptiness disappears and suddenly she drowns in feelings; they threaten to explode when she confronts the vision of her mother, Esperanza, rocking back and forth in the well-loved wicker chair. New strands of white have appeared at the older woman's temples and, as the chair oscillates, her clenched hands betray her disquiet. They rest on top of the leather-bound Bible that covers her lap. Esperanza has another Bible that she carries to church, but this one contains the family records: births, marriages and deaths, written in the hand of the local priest for eternal preservation. As in every family, there are unfinished entries, during the bloody conflict of the civil war, the fate of some unknown. Pain sears through her chest as Mercedes catches her breath; another name will now be absent from the record.

'Mama?'

The hypnotic strain of the rocker's wheels on terracotta tiles is the only sound that challenges the silence, and Mercedes extends her palm; she can't hold it still.

'Mama? Please?'

Mercedes falters, unable to move without a sign. An eternity seems to pass and a pounding in her head becomes louder; then her mother speaks.

'You're back.'

The voice is familiar, yet not quite, with its harsh tone. Her legs wilt and her body teeters as she steps towards the chair. 'I've been so frightened. You don't know...'

Esperanza raises her palm and Mercedes clamps her lips, but she knows that she must try again. 'My son. When Sister Francisco told me...' Something grabs her voice and her lips freeze as her mother leaps from the chair; the only sound comes from the frenzied rocking.

'Wait, Mama.' Her words catch on a sob. 'Please let me tell you...'

Esperanza's back faces Mercedes and the bow of her head reveals that the brown mole in the nape of her mother's neck is also brushed with new whispers of grey. Mercedes' sliver of hope crumples when the older woman straightens and drags her sleeve across her eyes then turns to stare at her daughter with a blank expression on her face.

'Stop. No more hysterics. It is done.' Esperanza wipes her damp hands down the front of her dress. 'Your father will be home soon. He doesn't want any talk about this episode.' She points to the bundle, abandoned on the floor. 'Get rid of your things. And clean yourself up. Then, come help me in the kitchen.'

There is a metallic taste in her mouth and Mercedes touches her lip; when she pulls it away, her finger reveals the red taint of blood.

Before she passes through the doorway, Mercedes pauses to survey the bedroom. Two of the beds are in their usual state, piled with crumpled sheets and towels, and an array of jeans, blouses and underwear are heaped on the chair by the door. The corner bed is pristine, dressed with crisp sheets and a woven blanket. As she moves near, there is the scent of freshly washed linen and, when she catches sight of the pink rose at her bedside, her lips soften.

Her mother waits, but before she leaves the room, Mercedes pauses by the laden bookshelf and trails a finger along the worn spines. The fixings haven't given way to the erosion of the wall and, tucked between two of her favourite novels, Mercedes discovers her notebook, which bulges with wads of handwritten pages and her final school report. Señor Miguel's praise had been the excuse for a family celebration. *If she continues to write at this level, Mercedes will be a strong candidate for university entrance.* Now it is impossible to recollect her excitement as she scans the list of names on the reverse. At the top, with five red ticks by its side, *Universidad de Madrid* warrants prime position. Underneath each academy is a list of courses; the male-dominated ones eliminated with a thick black line. Next to *periodismo* she had drawn a golden star and she remembers the enthusiasm of her teacher. *Perfect. Journalism will give you all kinds of opportunities.*

The paper becomes a wrinkled mass that she lets fall into the waste bin as she leaves the room.

No one comments that Mercedes' plate remains clean. Every member of the family is in their place around the table; they share the chorizo sausages, chick pea stew and patatas bravas, all served from earthenware dishes stockpiled in the centre. Her stomach is full, even though she can't remember when she last ate a meal. Rosa, her youngest sister, sits at her side and, while the others eat and talk, Mercedes feels a small hand slip into hers. Rosa's cheeks flush and she beams when Mercedes whispers a thank you for the rose.

Her father doesn't acknowledge Mercedes; her recent absence is ignored. His voice projects over the others as he discusses harvests, money and cars with her older brother,

Sanchez. Inching down in her chair, Mercedes remains mute, unable to pretend that all is normal. Voices are familiar, but come from a distance. Her mother's chatter fills any silence; she speaks of her plans for the flowers at next week's fiesta when they will pay tribute to their dead relatives. There is one moment when Isabel, her twin if Mercedes had been born 11 months earlier, catches her eye but Enrique, the baby brother who shocked her parents with his arrival two years ago, drops something from his highchair and the connection shatters.

A full moon shimmers against the black sky and rays stream into the room as she sinks onto the bed. Her arms are heavy across her empty belly. On the wall above the mahogany bedhead hangs an image of the Virgin Mary, adorned with a piece of white veil from her first communion. She scrutinises the revered face and wonders at the experience they had in common, and whether Mary's parents named her a whore, albeit she protested her innocence. It seems impossible that the gentle mother had found the strength to survive long months of travel, to labour in a stable. Mercedes squeezes a pillow to her breasts; the pressure calms the ache. Had Mary loved Jesus from the first moment that she held her baby, touched his skin, and kissed his brow?

Mercedes isn't able to remember how long it was before her own dismay turned into hate, and then what changed it to love. Maybe it was when she heard a distant baby's cry, or perhaps while she was with another exiled mother-in-waiting, but a day dawned when she decided to embrace her fate as an unmarried mother. The disapproving nuns had been relentless in their efforts to change her mind.

'Give your child a decent chance. A child needs two parents.'

'You'll be outcasts.'

'You're unnatural. Why do you want to keep him? You tell us that you were forced; why remind yourself of that?'

At the end, the battle was futile and an outside force made the decision.

The ache eases from her limbs and Mercedes' eyelids surrender to the night. An image of her baby gate-crashes the peace when it appears against the backdrop of her closed lids, captured for her memory in that moment before he was snatched from between her legs.

'He needs help to breathe,' Sister Francisco had murmured as she left the delivery room carrying the bloodied bundle of towels.

That was the last time she saw him: a tiny being, covered in white paste and blood. Her baby's cry lingered, long after he vanished from the room. Etched in her recollection are those flashes from the moment of his birth: the shape of his head, the movement of his leg with its purple foot that escaped from the wrappings, and the tune of his muffled mews.

Minutes later, Sister Francisco had shown her the photo. Her baby, white. Eyes closed. Dead. His dark hair looked wet and clung to a bulge on the top of his head. When the nurse attempted to prise her fingers open and release the crumpled image, Mercedes had snatched it back and screamed at her to stay away as she held it against her heart.

There is a giggle and someone says 'shush' as her sisters push the door open; she turns her face into the damp pillow and feigns sleep. The sounds of chatter abate and soon their slumbering sounds echo around the room, a lullaby that soothes her tortured mind.

She wakes to her own scream, but her sisters don't hear her nightmare and they sleep on while she sits up in bed with her face in her hands. The mist is faded in her mind and disbelief hounds her sanity as she reaches under the covers to withdraw her treasure. She brings it close, wondering if she is mistaken. The photo is not the same image of her bald baby that is captured in her memory. Her heart begins to race, her skin becomes clammy, and she kicks away the covers; possibilities create chaos in her mind. Is some other woman the mother of that infant with his lifeless face, framed with the dark hair that exposes the truth? Why did the nun show her this photo? Her baby cried. Where is her baby? He's alive; of that, she is certain.

The collar of the nightdress is too tight and she flees the room, tearing at it with her fingernails. She is unaware of the lesions on her neck and does not feel the blood trickle over her skin as she seeks out a place in the orchard where she can give way to her fury. A nearby owl accompanies her lament.

Chapter 1

The gaze of the carved angel, Lucifer, nestled amongst the roses of Retiro Park, seems to follow her progress, and Mercedes shudders and averts her eyes as she hurries past his dwelling; his banishment into hell haunted the dreams of her childhood. She forces out the memory and heads for the haven that she has spotted ahead, a canopy of green branches that protects a metal bench from the sun's fire. She sinks onto the seat and lifts her curls onto the top of her head, securing the damp locks with a clip. She closes her eyes, allowing her chin to fall to her chest and the headache that has plagued her all morning eases as the tension ebbs from her neck and shoulders. For a few minutes, she is at peace with her lids lowered and her mind blank, but the scent of jasmine reminds Mercedes of her mother and the past. Tears gather and she tries to banish them with the back of her hand but the spectre of a baby floats at the fringes of her memories, a ghostly image that is her constant companion. The swaddling will have given way to football boots and jeans as her son turns ten, but Mercedes knows that she will recognise his face when she finds him, no matter how many birthdays he has celebrated.

Her hand reaches up to the knot of hair and curls bounce along her shoulders as she shakes away the musings. Moulding her back to the curve of the bench, she stretches her legs out onto the path while her fingers release the catch of the press pass, unpinning it from her lapel, and lower it onto her lap. No ring adorns her finger; no one has managed to break through the barrier that protects her emotions.

While she contemplates the morning's events, her hands manipulate the badge in a succession of somersaults, a dance in her lap. Chaos had reigned in the court waiting room with representation from all of the local papers and she had been one of many journalists in the crowd, dwarfed by the height of the men and overlooked by the interviewees. The hours spent in preparation of her questions had been a waste. Mercedes digs out her bottle of water and holds it against her hot cheeks while she tries to erase the memory of her impotence. The struggle to make her mark in her profession never eases.

A child's bubble of laughter shatters her daydreams and she peers under her eyelids as a woman chases her little escapee through the park. He negotiates the twists and turns of the path as it tapers down a slope to where it spills into the lake. The bronze Alfonso that stands guard at the shore-side dwarfs the child as he approaches and, with the water's edge in his sights, the infant accelerates. Mercedes steels herself, about to leap, when the woman cries out and pounces.

'Stop!'

The youngster launches himself in the direction of the marshy shore at the same time that the mother's fingers seize hold of his podgy biceps; the sobs disrupt her laughter as she thumps down onto the gravel path with her son imprisoned within her arms. The captive squirms against her chest and his cheeks seesaw as he avoids the battery of kisses, one after another.

Mercedes flops back into her seat; her heart misses beats as she stifles the eruption that simmers below the surface. When Sister Francisco carried her son through the delivery room door, she removed more than a baby wrapped in towels. Years of watching him grow have been lost and, although the pain has lost its raw edge, the ache is with her always. At times, resentment flares up and swathes her in bitterness. When that happens, she struggles to maintain the composed façade that she presents to the world.

An invisible rod holds her spine rigid as Mercedes keeps her face averted from the mother and child and reaches for her things; she refuses to sink into the dark pool of loss. The handle of her tote frays with a series of snaps and she clutches it to her chest before the weight of the contents completes the destruction. Her arms tighten, and she tries to squeeze the pain out of her heart while escaping the park and her memories.

When she exits the corner gate, she glances at the clock and turns right onto the boulevard: with only ten minutes before siesta ends, she picks up pace. Mercedes weaves through the sea of workers; the crowd thins as individuals enter buildings that line the pavement, home to some of Madrid's key businesses. She pushes through a gathering of debating employees that blocks the entrance to the newspaper's headquarters as the church bell chimes the half hour, a signal that the period for afternoon rest is finished. The marble wall cools her back when she leans against it to slip off the trainers and swap them for high heels. As she straightens, her fingers comb her parting to the side; someone mentioned that it makes her look more professional. Her shoes tap out a metronomic pattern on the tiles as she crosses the foyer to speak to Juanita. Her best friend is about to resume her position behind the reception desk but the chair gives way to her petite frame, gliding down with a hiss and coming to a stop when her nose is at desk level. Mercedes stifles the snort, but then her laughter resonates around the hall as her friend jumps up and kicks the lever underneath the seat. Juanita pumps with her foot, cursing the chair.

'This stupid thing!' The colour in her cheeks intensifies and, before resuming her seat, Juanita leans forward onto her arms and checks that it will hold her. Satisfied, she eases onto the perch. 'Keep your fingers crossed that I don't go down with a bump.'

Perhaps now is the time to tell her friend about the trick that Jaime plays when Juanita abandons her post; however, Mercedes decides to leave it for another day or two. It seems a shame to spoil his fun; nonetheless, she does feel a pang of guilt as she stretches across the counter to tug the end of Jaunita's ponytail. 'With that red hair, you look like you should be at school.'

Juanita's cheeks are on fire and she grabs her mane and holds it in front of her face with her eyes crossed. 'I hope I get used to it.'

Mercedes blows her a kiss and has one foot on the staircase when her friend calls out to ask if they are okay to meet after work. At first, she raises a hand to wave confirmation; however, she remembers the uncertainty in Juanita's eye and twists around to shout across the hall. 'It's fabulous. You look like a movie star.' Juanita's face lights up with her grin and Mercedes starts her climb, glad she voiced her thoughts aloud.

Four flights of stairs, two steps a time, lead Mercedes to the floor occupied by the paper's junior staff. Most of her male colleagues are missing from their stations and she squeezes between rows of desks that overflow with papers to her corner of the room. The neat desk stands out amongst the others; everything has a place in the drawers with the exception of her computer and the telephone, and she shakes her head when she observes the upheaval on top of the neighbouring workstations. She tucks the tail of her cotton blouse into her skirt, holding it so that it doesn't slip out when she leans to delve in the top drawer of her desk. Her fingers connect with her objective and she pulls out the buff folder of notes that she needs for the meeting. As she heads towards the conference-room at the opposite end of the building, she double checks the folder's contents. An 'occupied' sign hangs on the closed door and, when she stares through the glass panel, her teeth clench. The editorial meeting is underway, despite a number of empty chairs. Jorge stops mid-sentence, looks up and frowns as she creeps in. All of the men at the table watch in silence until she finishes sliding along the wall to a vacant seat at the far end of the table. She holds Jorge's gaze, ignoring the beads of sweat that gather above her top lip as she waits for him to resume his speech.

When the attention is no longer on her, Mercedes stretches her neck to glance over the shoulder of her neighbour but she struggles to decipher his scribbling. He winks, uses his pen to point to her headline, and jots *p-six-l* by its side. She chews on her lip as her shoulders slump; once again, her work has not made the front page. The curse escapes her lips before she can keep it back and, hearing muffled laughter, her eyes sweep towards the man to her right. The culprit, Orlando, is one of the recent recruits to the team and his hand covers his mouth but his eyes betray him as they crinkle above the crests of his cheeks. Mercedes can't help herself and rewards him with a grin but Jorge glares and she re-arranges her expression with an innocent shrug. The act doesn't fool her editor and his eyebrows meet in a single line while he studies her in silence. His scrutiny makes her squirm and she lets go of her breath when his attention returns to the papers in his hands. No longer under surveillance, Mercedes winks at Orlando and passes him a note behind her neighbour's back. *Who's been given the lead today?* He holds her gaze and nods towards the short tubby man who sits to Jorge's right side, eyes aglow as he hangs onto every word his boss speaks. Mercedes sighs. Of course, Pedro – the favourite.

'Do you have something to say, Mercedes?'

'No Jorge; nothing.' Her right hand covers her heart and then moves down to her tummy. 'My hunger never seems to be satisfied.' Everyone understands what she implies and several hands hide smirks. Jorge's mouth twists and his stare aims like a dagger at her head. She waits for the inevitable and sighs when he lifts a side of his mouth in a manner that always signals danger; then he dishes out his punishment.

'Take the Lopez article, Mercedes. On my desk, two days.'

Mercedes silences her curse and forces her lips to stretch into a smile until his eyes return to his notes, then her spirits sink. She could kick herself for antagonising the editor. Juan Lopez is a criminal boss known for his reign of terror over the local community and the police have him locked away in a secret location until his trial starts. His brother sends daily death threats to the witnesses, and it is unlikely that any door will open to a reporter, even a female one. It will be a miracle if she gets enough to fill her slot before the court case begins. There is no point in listening as Jorge allocates other assignments and his voice fades to a rumble in the background as she digs into her memory for the few facts that she knows about Lopez. Clothes rustle and chairs screech across the tiles, noises that signify that the meeting is over, and with four hours to the next deadline reporters rush to their desks, leaving Mercedes behind at the empty table.

Absorbed in her strategy to tackle the Lopez article, she meanders through the desks with her eyes locked on her folder. The round toe of a suede shoe appears at the periphery of her vision and her skin tingles as the owner moves close. Orlando shortens his steps to match hers but her eyes remain down; she struggles to neither wilt at his scent nor give a hint that her heart turned a cartwheel when he appeared. The gap between their bodies is non-existent and she is convinced that he must hear the pounding in her chest.

'And why were you so late for the meeting, Ms Cortes?'

His mimicry of Jorge is uncanny and makes her smile; her attention is still on her notes but a giggle gives her away and she looks up to acknowledge him. The current sparks and she misses her step as she drops her gaze to escape the brown depths that seem to unmask the secrets of her soul.

'An incident at Retiro Park. Some kid on the run from his mother. He was headed into the lake, and nearly made it too, the little terror.' Their steps, like their laughter, create a harmony, and she concentrates on the floor; her mind is blank as they stroll in perfect synchronisation.

'How did today's case turn out?'

Riveted by his odour, the silence extends until Mercedes breaks free of the spell and forces a reply. 'Not guilty. Can you believe it?'

'But what about the evidence? I was told that there were hundreds of witness statements.'

They halt and he listens while her hands paint the air and she repeats some of the testimony: wartime stories of people taken away, never seen again; freshly dug mounds of earth where shots had rung out a few hours before, the cover up with unspoken agreements of silence that have lasted lifetimes.

'Those old people were so brave on the stand. How could they let him go? It's a travesty. He should be in prison and instead, he stood outside that courthouse gloating. Those people have not received any satisfaction, it's as though their grief has no value.'

Mercedes doesn't hear Jaime approach from behind and she jumps when he puts his hands on her shoulders as he sidles past. Her tirade continues when she turns and he holds up his hands as he retreats.

'Okay Agustina de Aragón, I surrender. Calm down.'

Orlando chuckles as she mumbles an apology, then lowers

his head near hers, sending an electric shock through her body as she feels his lips touch the space near her right ear. 'As fiery as our Joan of Arc, aren't you?' Her cheeks burn and she steps away but she still hears his whispered question. 'What about Saturday? Do you want to come?'

Mercedes fidgets and prays that her colour soon returns to normal; romance isn't part of her long-term plan but each time he makes a suggestion, it becomes harder to resist. She has already fabricated excuses; last week, a trip to Juanita's family and the weekend before, work pressures. 'I'm sorry but…' The words stick in her throat. His eyes change colour as his chest deflates; he is not the only one who is surprised when she changes her mind and agrees to join him for a bike ride on Saturday.

Orlando's eyes sparkle. 'We could head up into the mountains. It will be cooler than the city.' Alarm bells go off in her head as his words tumble out with the arrangements. 'Fantastic! Let's meet at Atocha Station at 10?'

His enthusiasm is hard to resist and her heart leaps but she strengthens her defences and turns away with a curt, 'See you later.' *That man has the ability to wear me down*; she shakes her head as she grabs the back of her chair with a force that spins it on the rotary base so she has to leap on between its turns. In the desk drawer, Mercedes locates a folder filled with her reference notes and cuttings relating to current crimes and dumps the contents onto her desk; she flips through, searching for anything that will help with the Lopez article. Meanwhile, the computer groans through its start-up until she whacks it on its side and scribbles a memo to Jorge; he must do something about a replacement machine for her before it gives up completely. While she waits for her files to open, Mercedes jots down some questions and facts about the Lopez family onto a page in her notepad. The bustle of the office disappears as she becomes absorbed in her work.

An incessant ringing of the telephone breaks her concentration and papers explode onto the floor as she burrows to locate the handset. Bent over at her waist, she retrieves the sheets from where they have scattered below her desk. At the same time, she answers.

'Mercedes here. Speak to me.'

It is difficult to hear the voice over the background office noise. Muffled words wobble in her ear.

'Hello. Am I speaking with Mercedes Cortes? The reporter?'

The corner of a rogue sheet under her chair tempts her and Mercedes bends forward to stretch her fingers further, trapping it at the same time that she utters the confirmation; there is a note of victory in her voice.

'Ms. Cortes, I want to meet with you.' The caller is a woman, probably old; she uses the formal speech from a bygone period. *Not another crank,* Mercedes hopes as she mumbles words of encouragement.

'I don't know who can help. It's terrible. You must write about it in your paper.' Sobs interrupt the words. 'I can't keep quiet any longer. Other mothers need to know!'

Those last words intrigue Mercedes and she leaves the papers on the floor as she cups her hand around the earpiece. A tingle on the back of her neck forewarns that this may be a worthy lead and she tries to mask the predatory undertone in her voice. 'Will you tell me your name?'

'Carmen.' The whisper is audible, just.

'What do you mean, other mothers? Explain, Carmen.'

The silence seems never-ending but Mercedes waits, her instincts telling her the call is genuine. Carmen's accent is local, uneducated but polite; the woman probably comes from the northern outskirts of the city. After long minutes, Mercedes stares at the handset with frustration and she is about to voice some encouragement when at the same moment the woman mutters more words.

'Babies. Missing babies.'

Waves of nausea threaten to overcome Mercedes and the room spins as she scans around and looks for whoever is playing this malicious prank. No one in the office is on the phone nor displays any interest in her, and she turns her back on the others and tries to hide behind her arm. The handset slips within the sweat of her palm and she gulps for breath as she fights for composure. When the fuzziness in her mind clears, she chooses her words with care.

'I'm sorry Carmen. I'm still here. You took me by surprise. Whose babies? What makes you think that they're missing? When? Carmen, are you there?' The questions jumble in her head and she has to bite her lips together to stop the torrent. Mercedes counts every second of the pause; every so often, the sound of a laboured breath in the earpiece reassures her that Carmen is there.

'I don't believe that they died, no matter what they said. Maybe they were sold or were given away. There's too many. It doesn't make sense. I don't know but...' A door bangs in the background and Carmen exclaims, 'I can't talk now'.

'But why have you called me?' Anguish tarnishes Mercedes' question but the connection is lost; her eyes fill with tears as she stares at her white fingers locked around the handset. Little by little, her chest deflates as the air expires and she stabs at the telephone keys but is unable to reconnect the call; the hum over the receiver is continuous.

'Damn!' The outburst draws startled glances from her neighbours. She slams the phone down and her eyes dart around the newsroom as she strives to regain some sanity.

No one meets her gaze; each one of her colleagues appears occupied with the work on his desk. Five minutes is all that she is able to endure before she leaps from the chair and hastens out of the office; as she disappears, she shouts instructions over her shoulder to Jaime at the neighbouring workstation. 'If that phone rings, answer it and get a number. Tell her that I'll call her straight back. And come find me, I'm not far away!'

The cubicle door slams, wrapping her in solitude where she can release the knife in her chest and give freedom to her sobs. Carmen's call has opened the old wounds – areas that she keeps hidden. In those early days when she returned home to her family without her baby, she learnt that no one wanted to hear any accusations of hospital mix-ups. People of her town had grown accustomed to suppressing accounts of past injustices and persecutions after the civil war and a teenage girl's problem was one more issue that wore a shroud of silence. A hope that their reunion will occur one day burns like a fire deep within her soul but for now, her child is still missing and no more than a handful of people know of his existence. She is convinced that he is not dead and feels his presence, and absence, in every waking moment. Now an unknown woman has rekindled her faith, her hope, and her grief.

The tap water cools the warm tracks left by her tears and she inspects the mirror for tell-tale signs; some bluish shadows tinge the area underneath her eyes, otherwise it is her face that stares back. Its normality surprises her. On the way back to her desk Mercedes considers her next move. Jaime shakes his head and confirms what she already suspects. Without a phone number or last name, she has to rely on the hope that nothing stops Carmen from attempting another call. The bowels of the building hold the storage of the newspaper archives; if she looks amongst them, perhaps she will unearth some clues but it will be like trying to find one grain of sand on a beach without more detail. Mercedes taps the gnawed end of her pencil against her forehead and looks towards Orlando to ask for help but he is busy on the telephone and she changes her mind. The task can't be shared; she doesn't even know what she will be looking for as she heads for the stairs, resigned to aimless hours in the dungeon.

Chapter 2

Mercedes teeters on her toes and waves her hand in the air above the bodies. Black mould speckles the wall that faces her, and the smell of old beer and unwashed clothes can't be masked by the bundle of dried lavender. Suspended by a single nail from the wood beam, the fragrance faded long ago and it looks as though it has hung there for several decades. Wedged on all sides by the men who cluster close to the bar, she can't attract Felipe's attention. The extra few centimetres she gains with the high heels makes no difference and, when she realises that she is getting nowhere, she decides upon a different tactic. Mercedes crouches and pushes like a bull through the crowd towards the bar; she ducks under arms and around bellies and ignores the dirty looks she attracts along the way. A final thrust between two customers and she sprouts up at her destination where she yells at Felipe until he acknowledges the order with a grumble that matches his sour expression. The slovenly proprietor pulls a dusty bottle out of one of the terracotta semi-circles that line the wall to his left, and slams it onto the surface with a grunt. It's a miracle that the bottle doesn't break and she grabs it as she shouts the rest of her order at his back. A couple of fingers in a dismissive gesture indicate to her that he heard.

Two glasses and the bottle of wine cradle against her body as she fights her way back to the window table. Juanita is on the edge of her chair with the appearance of a rabbit ready to flee. A man, old enough to know better and mesmerized by her friend's chest, will end up sitting on her lap if he leans any further across the gap between the two tables. From the colour of Juanita's face, his words match his looks and Mercedes battles her way through the rest of the crowd until she is close enough to give him a rollicking; he drops his eyes and his mouth tightens as he retreats. It is too late to go to another tavern and Mercedes experiences a fleeting pang of guilt when she sits down opposite her friend and tries to make Jaunita laugh with a roll of her eyes while she pretends to stick her fingers down her throat. 'Don't think much of yours.'

'Funny.' Juanita sticks a tongue out but she does relax back in the chair and the invisible frame releases her shoulders.

'Felipe is an ignorant machismo toad. He deliberately looks over me and serves the men first. Maybe we should stop coming here.'

Juanita glances at the neighbouring table. 'You won't get any argument from me. There's a new bar down the road we could try next week. I hear that it's quite trendy.'

'The trouble is I'll miss seeing all these newsmen. Maybe one day they'll accept me as a serious reporter.'

Juanita gives her the look that says *in your dreams* and rolls her own eyes to the ceiling. The contortions of her friend's face make Mercedes chuckle but when she wags her finger, her tone is serious. 'You'll see. I give it ten years, maybe.' Her gaze sweeps along to the group of men from her office that fill one end of the bar as they share one of their regular chummy sessions and she wonders whether her belief is misplaced. A playful punch on her arm returns her attention to her friend.

'You will get there in the end. You'll see, one day they'll be climbing over themselves to be in your favour.'

'It's like having a personal cheerleader when I'm out with

14

you; I just hope you're right.' The glasses clink as they toast. '*Pimientos padrón* and *jamón* okay for you?'

'What? You usually save treats for birthdays.' Juanita's eyes narrow. 'Is there something that you haven't told me?'

'Of course not, you know everything.' She concentrates on a chip on the rim of her glass, her comment isn't quite true. 'I just feel like a splurge.' Her eyelids close against her friend's scrutiny and she tilts her head back as she sips the wine. To end the silence, she explains that she wanted to give them a treat but the excuse sounds feeble and she gives up, aware that her behaviour seems at odds with her norm. Through spidery eyelashes, Mercedes can see the hint of unease in Juanita's face as her friend reaches across the sticky surface to touch her clenched fist.

'Are you okay, Mercedes? Money on food instead of clothes, that's a rarity. Has something happened?'

Amongst the swirls of rosy fluid in her glass, the outline of a baby forms; when she rubs her eyes and looks again, the image has dissolved and there is only wine. That phone call from Carmen earlier has left her out-of-sorts and having had time to think about it, she finds it hard to believe that the choice to contact her is co-incidental. It could be a hoax but that possibility upsets her even more than if it is genuine. The open face of her friend tempts her and she weighs up how much to reveal; the past is a secret that is securely locked inside and she hasn't spoken of it since she left her family home at eighteen in pursuit of a new life in Madrid. The past has passed, and bears no resemblance to her present; the private search for her child is the only thing that she carries with her from those days.

'Mercedes, let me help. You're my best friend. I can see that you're sad. Is it your family? Have you heard something?'

Mercedes cools her cheeks with her palms. It would be

impossible to admit, after all this time, that her family aren't the villains in her story. The white lies gave that impression when she spun those years ago during her early days in Madrid, but then she was fuelled by anger; people who loved her should have trusted her belief that her baby lived. How can she confess now that her own stubbornness is the reason behind her self-imposed exile? There is no way for her to take back the hateful words that she spat out as she turned her back on her family. Now that she is older, she can see that they were trying to ignore the past and get on with life, like most who had lived through the war.

The moment is opportune and Mercedes draws a breath, but before she begins her revelations Juanita interrupts. 'They are your family. You should see them.' A look of cunning appears in her face. 'Mama agrees with me. I could contact them for you?'

Something contracts in her chest and Mercedes snatches her hand back; she tries to imagine the havoc that would bring to her life while she pretends that she needs her fingers to raise her glass. An invisible wall seems to separate the women and their silence smoulders; neither of them knows how to break it until Felipe delivers their tapas and they both reach to pick up the same pepper. Juanita lets her take it and gives a half-smile, but her tone is careful as she asks whether Mercedes wants to come to the family home for the weekend meal.

She leaps on the opportunity to lighten the atmosphere between them. 'Oh, I forgot to tell you. Orlando asked me to bike into the mountains on Saturday.'

It works and the smile widens until it reaches Juanita's ears. 'Hurray! What happened to the hard-to-get, "I don't want to encourage him" line?'

'It's not a date, Juani. That man won't take no for an answer.'

'And you have to make the sacrifice.'

It is obvious that Juanita isn't going to be convinced by her protests so she tries to change the subject. Her friend isn't ready to let go now that she has started.

'I don't know why you have an issue with him. A guy like him doesn't come along that often. He's good-looking, intelligent, and he's kind. In fact, he's the perfect man and best of all, although God knows why, he seems to be really into you.' Then she raises the glass of rosé into the air and starts humming a wedding march, to which Mercedes sticks out her tongue and reminds her that they have always said there is no such person as the perfect man.

She pinches another hot green pepper by its stem, pops the charred bulb into her mouth and changes the subject. 'Now this is perfect.' Her mouth tingles with the combination of sea salt and chilli fire.

'Mama will be disappointed that she won't be seeing you this weekend. She's prepared suckling pig.' Juanita runs her tongue over her lips. 'It's Antonio's saint day. Most of the village will be there. Can you believe my little cousin is thirteen?'

'It's crazy. He was little more than a toddler when I first met him; now he's nearly a man. Do you remember the day that he put the spider on top of the bread? I don't think I've ever seen your mother so angry. The image of her chasing him with her mop kills me.' Mercedes' guffaw draws the attention of the old men at a table in the corner and they interrupt their game of draughts to give the women the evil eye. Their grumbles carry across the room and she mouths an apology in their direction but when she turns her back on them, she smirks and comments on the dangers of interrupting a man's game. 'I love your mama; she is so good to me. Tell her I'll come next Sunday.'

'I bet that I come back with a parcel of food for you. She's always complaining that you need more meat on these bones.' Juanita tries to pinch some flesh on her arm.

'Stop that.' She slaps her friend's hand away. 'Don't tell her I'm going out with Orlando for the day. She'll be planning the wedding before I know it and you know she won't give me any peace.'

It is a few hours later as they are about to separate outside the tavern when Mercedes divulges a rare insight into her family. Juanita loses her balance on some uneven cobblestones and tumbles hard onto her knees and Mercedes squats to help her off the ground. When her friend is back on her feet, she keeps an arm around Juanita's waist until the shaking stops. Although her friend nods when Mercedes asks if she is okay, it is clear that the fall has shaken her and she isn't able to blink away her tears. Mercedes hands over a handkerchief and then kneels onto the ground so that she can brush the gravel off Juanita's knees. Some pieces have lodged into the reddened skin and she takes care not to hurt her any further as she picks out the tiny stones. Her own eyes glisten and she tilts her head to look up into her friend's face.

'I remember twisting my ankle badly when I was a little girl. My poor dad had to carry me home on his back. It took hours and he pretended that I weighed nothing, but it was two weeks before he could walk normally.'

'Come on, I'll get the rest out when I get home.' Juanita reaches down for Mercedes' hands and helps her up from the crouched position. When she hugs to thank her, Mercedes feels overcome with homesickness and sags into the comfort of her friend's body. Then she sighs and begins to pull back but Juanita stops her as she catches Mercedes' face between her hands and cradles it before she kisses both cheeks and pushes her away.

'It's a good thing you weren't my age.'

'He still would have done it, I guess. Then of course, not now.'

'Why not? You're his daughter, things can't be that bad.'

The uninvited memory has drained her energy so she can't be bothered to answer; her hand is a lead weight that she waves before turning away. A few metres along the path, Mercedes glances back and notices that her friend stands as though frozen. She shouts to tell her to go home and not worry and when Mercedes reaches the corner and checks again, Juanita has faded amongst the night-time shadows of the narrow alley.

Chapter 3

The waiter's query forces Mercedes to relinquish her surveillance of the street as she twists around to answer. Three times he has returned to the table; each time the sun has moved a little higher in the sky so that now she squints into its midday rays.

'No more coffee, I won't sleep tonight.' She screens her eyes with a clammy palm and returns her gaze to the street. Aware that a moment can change a situation, she extends her neck to inspect both directions for new arrivals. The wheeze behind her chair informs her that the man hasn't left yet; no doubt he believes a date has stood her up. In a way he is right, she has been here for hours and with a final glance down the road, she surrenders and demands the bill.

The watch face attracts her attention and she checks again, even though the minute hand has hardly shifted since the last update. An hour too early for the meeting, she appeared before the storekeeper of the adjacent shop had lifted the blinds and while the café chairs towered in stacks chained to the wall. The waiter had dragged over a chair and delivered her first coffee with a grunt; she was surprised that the cup didn't shatter when he slammed it down in his rush to get back to the serving hatch and his cigarette, burning as it balanced on the edge of a worktop.

At her left elbow, on the plastic table alongside some crumbs from her toast is a cup tattooed with coffee foam, baked solid from the sun. Her chair is at an angle so that she can observe the approaches from both junctions. From the front row seat, she has watched the morning activity of the locals. Early in the day, many business people hurried by, briefcases in hand, soon followed by gaggles of women who disappeared into the market on the opposite side of road. Chains of children filed past the front of the café with their hands linked, filling the air with a chatter of excitement. En route for some school trip, a wave of sympathy swept over her for the teachers as they struggled to retain control. Dogs danced along the pavement, most tugged at their leads but one owner dragged his stubborn mutt – its pitiful whine and miserable expression made her chuckle. New mothers with bruised eyes pushed fashionable prams and old men with belts holding up their bellies shuffled past, but through it all her notepad remained untouched. The observations flicked in and out of her mind, momentary impressions of no importance.

There was still no sign of white hair held with a mother-of-pearl comb.

'How will I recognise you?'

The call had come finally on Thursday afternoon, just as she was about to descend the staircase on her way to siesta, and she had been tempted to ignore the taunts of the sound. Her conviction that Carmen would try again had waned over the days. Nevertheless, before her foot touched the second step, she gave in to the noise, ran back and snatched up the handset.

'Ms Cortes?'

The familiar voice made her stomach twist and she grabbed the edge of her desk as she whispered *'thank God'* before she flopped into the chair. 'Yes, Carmen, I am here.' There was a catch in her voice when she uttered those first words; her hours of searching hadn't unearthed any clues to the elusive identity of the woman.

'There isn't much time. He'll be back soon. I don't want him to hear.'

'Who? Your husband?'

'It doesn't matter. Shall we meet?'

Below the words, *husband, fear*, and *why,* Mercedes had scrawled the details of their arrangements.

The notebook, pages covered with the questions that she had prepared, lays abandoned alongside the crumbs of her breakfast. As the waiter approaches with the bill, she picks through the coins in her purse and tries to delay the moment of her departure. While her head is down, a woman sneaks alongside and when Mercedes lifts her eyes, she starts as though the arrival is unexpected.

'*Buenos dias*. Señorita Cortes?'

The woman could pass unnoticed. She is frail, almost nondescript in her dowdy attire, and the journalist can't see the avenging angel drawn by her imagination. White threads mix with slate-grey hair in a knotted twist that sits at the nape of the folded neck. The clue that Mercedes has been on the lookout for, an ornamental comb with mother-of-pearl domes framed in rows of tiny pearls, is lifting out of its anchorage and is in danger of falling out of the hair. An impulse draws Mercedes' hand towards the adornment, but before her fingers connect her intention falters and she lets her hand fall back to her side. Carmen's age is impossible to guess; years of sadness and hard toil appear to have left many criss-crossed lines in their wake. A glint of humour shows behind the milky lenses of her eyes and Mercedes flushes, breaks off her inspection and stops making assumptions about the woman's past. She steps closer to salute the tissue-thin cheeks and when she puts her face near, there is the scent of her mother; lavender and rose, which touches emotions deep-buried.

She remains on her feet while Carmen wobbles and lowers into the chair; the table rattles long after she releases her grip. Eventually, Mercedes uses her foot to trap the table's stand and halt the sound. Curiosity is on hold while they place their order for drinks but all the while she observes and appraises her companion. Sweat glistens on the older woman's upper lip as she fumbles through a plastic supermarket bag until she utters a cry of triumph and withdraws a rectangular packet. Holding one end between gnarled fingers, she flicks a wrist and the concertinaed folds open to form a colourful arc. To Mercedes' delight, Carmen touches one edge of the fan with the fingers of her other hand; *I want to talk to you.* It has been years since she has seen anyone use the language of the fan; when she was young, her grandmother taught her the art of the secret communication. Carmen's mouth loses one or two of its creases when she sees that her message is understood, and she rotates her wrist and wafts air towards her face.

'Oh, how beautiful.' Mercedes reaches out to touch the piece of art, glorious in its detail of minute images of graceful ladies in ball gowns who rest their fingers on male shoulders covered with epaulettes; the couples are trapped forever in the moment of their dance. Wooden sticks support the ends of the painting, carved with intricate swirls and twists that allow glimpses of daylight.

'It was my mother's. And her mother's before that, so it is over eighty years old.' Carmen points with her index finger, the swollen joints creating a crooked line. 'See how it's torn here. The original lace is delicate.' An invisible weight presses on her shoulders and adds years to her old body. 'I thought that I would pass it on to my niece.'

The note of loss behind the words can't be overlooked, but Mercedes is eager to get to the point of their meeting, so she mumbles an appropriate response and reaches for her notebook. The waiter interrupts with their drinks and, by the time he disappears, the fan has vanished. Carmen's hands shake as she fights to take hold of her glass and Mercedes suppresses her impatience as she attempts to put her at ease. 'This café was one of the first places I found when I moved into Madrid. The city seemed so big and I was terribly lonely. The owner reminds me of my friend's father, they are both gentle giants.'

'Where do you come from?'

The answer comes to her lips but then her guard goes up and she finds a way to change the subject. 'Why did you phone me?'

'You won't put my name in anything you write, will you?' Carmen leans over and clasps Mercedes' hand. 'You must promise.' This isn't the first time that she has had such a request, but most people worry a neighbour will find out that they have betrayed a confidence or that they have broken some pact of silence. Carmen is different; the tone in her voice resembles fear. When Mercedes reassures the old woman, some of the furrows disappear between her eyebrows. While she sips (the aroma of the coffee masks the sour sewer smell that is worsening with the heat) Mercedes studies the woman. Carmen has withdrawn into a private world, with her gaze locked on the streams of condensation that trickle down the outside of her water glass. What secrets lay behind the faded eyes, what harrowing memories does she harbour? That generation don't speak openly of the past but, through her work, Mercedes has learnt that many have experienced pain and loss. While she is busy with suppositions, Carmen begins to speak in not much more than a whisper.

'My home is in the outskirts of the city, not far from Aravaca. I was born there, in my grandmother's bedroom. The house became mine when she passed away because I nursed her in those last few years when her mind went. My brother was furious, he thought that it should have come to him, but that wasn't her wish. It created trouble, but I got it in the end.'

Mercedes' heart sinks as she steals a glance at her watch; it's going to be a long afternoon.

'When I was little, Aravaca was a village, not part of the city at all. Everyone knew everybody else. I had many mothers, and even more aunties. The villagers looked after each other. We little ones played in the street, late into the night and without a care, while the adults packed into the bars. The sound of their voices always seemed to rise above ours; it rumbled around the main square and down the alleys wherever we went, and was a noise that we trusted.'

Her voice trills as she relates how the adults were always talking about families or about jobs or about the government; and then, she sobers and describes the way things changed with the talk of rebellion. No one was frightened to show passion then; that came later. The women would argue with their voices and the men with their fists. When things grew heated, all of the little ones would scatter and hide until the adults found them, huddled together for comfort in one of their many secret places.

'Back then, packed like sardines in our childhood shelters, we trusted our childhood comrades.'

Every so often Mercedes nods, but her attention wanders as she seeks a way to be polite, to persuade Carmen to forego the saga and to come to the point of their meeting.

'No, they weren't really angry at first, just passionate.' In a flash, the woman returns to the present as she seeks something behind Mercedes' eyes. After a pause, she looks down at her clenched hands. 'Funny how things change, isn't it?' She waits for Mercedes to nod before she continues. 'It was a wonderful time but–' the words catch in her throat and for the first time,

Carmen stumbles as she speaks of the past. The sigh articulates her grief. 'Things changed and it became difficult to know who could be trusted. You must know tales about those days. Even families divided as they made the choice of which side to support, neighbour against neighbour, brother turned on brother.'

This isn't unfamiliar but even the war stories of her father had held no interest for the younger Mercedes. She pulls at a thread in her skirt until it causes a run in the material. Irritated – it is one of her favourites – she lifts her head to ask what the story has to do with missing babies, but Carmen is in full flow.

'I was born a rebel. "My little matador" was my father's nickname for me. They all said that I should have been born a boy. Always fighting. Always in trouble. My mother once chased me to the other end of the village to rescue her red cloth; it was the perfect cape for pretend bullfights.' A glimmer of the spirited youth shows in the sparkle of Carmen's eyes. 'Mama told my father that he would pay a high price for encouraging the tomboy in his daughter.'

Blue veins transverse her eyelids, lowered while the woman inhales her past; Mercedes hesitates, but knows that she must interrupt the reminiscence otherwise the tale could go on and on. 'And then? You grew up, but how did that bring you here, to speak to me about things happening to babies?'

Carmen wags a finger and warns her to be patient. 'Yes, I grew up and pretend bullfights gave way to romance. The boys didn't want to play anymore.' Some ancient secret pleasure makes her flush. 'Not the childhood games anyway. And so, at last, I became the daughter my mother wanted. She made sure that everyone realised I was the youngest Fiesta Queen ever elected and made me parade all over the town in my costume. It took her hours with the needle to repair the antique embroidery on my shoes; she said that they must be perfect to match my dress.'

When she smiles, there are still signs of 'the looker' that Carmen says she was and, imagining a mass of curls past her waist and the dark eyes of youth, Mercedes suspects that the woman was indeed a beauty. Carmen's voice drones on as she describes sitting for more than two hours as her mother weaved the ear plaits. The description of the headache touches a place locked away in Mercedes, the sensation of pain when her own mother did the same and she exclaims, 'My brothers made fun of my tears when Mama twisted the coils and secured them with my grandmother's jewelled pins. I thought that she was going to stab me. I can still remember the way the black mantilla swished around my shoulders; she fixed it with a tortoise-shell comb that erupted like a mountain from the top of my head.' It surprises her, this happy memory. It has slept until now, hidden in the collection of the unpleasant ones, and a glow seeps through her body. Then the ugly caw of a crow breaks the spell as Carmen nods.

'You can't get rid of a rebellious nature. It lingers; maybe stifled, but it is always there, bubbling below the surface and waiting to explode.'

Carmen's eyes and words seem to unearth the secrets of Mercedes' adolescence, in particular when she describes the way she felt when she met a boy from another village: the racing heart and a stomach too crumpled to tolerate food. Anger floods her as she thinks about the tainted memories left in José's wake when he stole her innocence. She pushes them out of her mind and cools her cheeks with her hands.

A pile of confetti grows in front of the elderly woman; the remains of her serviette. 'He was the most handsome boy I had ever seen; dark and mysterious. I was smitten from the moment I first saw him, and would have followed him anywhere.' Another napkin splits apart and, when Carmen follows Mercedes' eyes, she seems surprised at the mound of

27

fake snow on the table. She collects the pieces together into a ball and squeezes it in the palm of her hand. 'He broke my heart.'

The woman gives her a sad grin and plays with a ring on a chain around her neck. 'No, you misunderstand; he would never leave me, not by choice. We were soul mates, brought together by God. For a time, we were happy. We ran away to find a priest. My parents were furious and refused to speak to us for months, but they came around in the end, when they saw how he looked after me. It was later that they began to worry.'

She bows her head and lowers her voice to tell Mercedes about the rebel, her husband. She took up his cause and together they attended protest rallies and demonstrations, speaking out against the government. The table rattles when her clenched fist comes down and she rubs the red mark on her hand with a grimace. 'We were blind. And young. And innocent. We didn't understand the dangerous game that we were playing. Both of us paid dearly for that.' She shrinks low in the chair and moans; her upper body slumps forward, her chin falling to her chest, then her hands cover her face. Watery pearls seep between her fingers until, with a stuttering sob, the hands fall away and, finally, Carmen talks about a baby.

'My first daughter was born in Salvador Clinic, the one in the centre of Madrid. We were living in a new flat. "Rehoused to a place of safety", my family said. "Enemies of the state", people called us. Friends told me that we were lucky; we were still alive. We thought that we were lucky. Then.'

Salvador. Mercedes stiffens, stunned by the familiar name; her mind fills with a ghostly image of Sister Francisco walking out of the door, carrying the bundle that contained her son. Mercedes went to the clinic to search for information about her child. It was not long after she came to study in the city but she unearthed nothing. A member of the staff, a battle-axe wearing the uniform of a nurse, told her that her baby's grave is unknown and unmarked, and advised her to forget about him and get on with life. Now the hairs on her arms stand on their ends but she keeps her silence when she sees the pain in the aged eyes. Instead, she places a hand on Carmen's arm.

'I never saw her. They took her out of the room the minute that she was born. We never found out where. Minutes later, I was ordered to go home, now that she was dead. I didn't believe it. How could my baby daughter be gone? I heard her cry.'

The world spins as Mercedes is overcome with a sense of déjà vu.

'For months I saw her everywhere: in the street, in the market, even in other women's arms. I guess I went a little crazy. People kept telling me, "don't worry, you can try again". I wanted to hit them. How could they say such a thing? As though I could replace her.' A moan of pain interrupts the flow of her speech; it isn't the memory, but the clamp of Mercedes' fingers around her hand that triggers the sound. Carmen massages the bloodless digits while she speaks of their joy and fear when they discovered that she was expecting once again. She recounts a saga of endless days of prayers and lit candles behind Diego's back. He wasn't a believer but Carmen said enough for them both in her prayers for another little girl. 'And God answered me. I will never forget those few moments of joy when I held her. And then my agony as I held her again when she was cold. As cold as the ice in winter. Two babies gone in three years. It was too much. I lost my mind.'

Mercedes sits on the edge of her seat and nearly abandons a decade of censorship to express how well she understands. Before she gathers the courage, Carmen clutches her chest. Her tone is incredulous as she tells of the woman in their block of flats who betrayed them, and how Diego was taken away in the middle of the night.

'Her words were lies, but no one cared about that and, because of her cruelty, I lost Diego as well. I thought I would die from the pain. I wanted to.'

During the evenings, Mercedes' parents whispered about similar events, which she overheard when she was supposed to be asleep. Anticipating the outcome, she pushes her lace handkerchief into Carmen's hand before she asks about Diego's fate.

'No one returned once they were taken. Well, a few did but they were never the same. I never found out where they took him. My friends made me hide until things settled. Gunshots echoed through our dark shelters every night and, with each boom, I would say a prayer that he was alive. Later, when I knew more, my prayers changed; I just wanted him to die quickly, without suffering.' She wipes her hands on her skirt as though erasing the evidence of her fallen tears. Unable to wait, Mercedes begins a question about the babies but the old woman ignores her and shakes her head. 'They don't reveal all of the facts to you young ones. Forget the past, my friends told me. We have to move on.'

Her voice escalates to a louder pitch and a man at a nearby table glares in their direction as he warns them to be quiet, muttering under his breath about hysterical women.

'How can I forget? They killed my Diego. I can't forgive.' Her furrowed lips tremble and Carmen sighs that it all happened in the distant past.

'You mentioned a husband when you phoned.'

'I remarried.' The passion melts away and Carmen's eyes go dull. 'He's solid, not excitable at all. So unlike Diego, but I was a marked woman and needed protection. 30 years we've been together. I guess he's a good man; he's loyal anyway.' Her voice is flat and it is obvious that Carmen's heart belongs to the lost love of her youth. 'And we had a boy and a girl. They have their own families now.' She reaches into her bag and pulls out a well-thumbed photo. 'Look. Beautiful, aren't they? Four grandchildren, all of them perfect.'

It is impossible to see any resemblance to Carmen in the stiff faces, but Mercedes understands what is expected. She compliments them and asks their names.

'Thank you. You're kind, but I know they aren't of any interest. We must talk about the reason I phoned. There's been a cover up of what really happened to new-born babies who died at Salvador. I hope that you can expose the truth.'

Chapter 4

Shockwaves strangle any response, her heart and stomach gallop to the same tempo. Mercedes gulps and tries to recover her voice. 'What are you talking about?'

The harsh question upsets Carmen and she focuses on the waiter, who has come alive during the midday rush, dashing around with trays of food and drink. Then she says that she first realised it when her niece, Marie Luz, got into trouble ten years previously. She looks up to see that Mercedes understands the meaning of the term, but the younger woman keeps her eyes fixed on the ashtray and blames the afternoon sun for her rising colour. When Carmen returns to her tale, Mercedes lets go of her breath.

'We were like this.' Carmen holds up crossed fingers. 'I know it's wrong but she was my favourite of my sister's children. The others were terribly naughty but she was a good little thing. When she was tiny, her mother became ill with measles, so Marie Luz lived with me until her mama recovered. Three months I had her; my own were out of nappies by then. What a precious thing she was; petite, with curls that sprouted out all over her head, and the longest eyelashes I have ever seen. Like a beautiful doll. She was shy, always hiding under my skirts. She called me *mam-tia,* mama and aunt combined you see.' The lines deepen at the sides of her mouth and she dabs it with Mercedes' lace handkerchief. 'When her time was near, her parents sent her to a clinic for unwed mothers. The church arranged it. She spent a night with me before she left. She knew that once the baby arrived, there wouldn't be time for our chats.'

Resigned to another long-winded account before the woman comes out with any facts of interest, Mercedes half-listens as Carmen describes how her niece defied the gossips with the decision to keep her child. 'Marie Luz taught herself to sew and made miniature socks, bonnets, nighties; everything a baby needed. She even hand-sewed the nappies. Once she had accepted the situation, my sister helped her; I would arrive to find them, side-by-side on the terrace, with their heads buried over their work. They wrapped every item in tissue to store in her special box. It was Diego's storage box; I had covered it with painted red roses for her seventh birthday and filled it with clothes for her dolly.' Carmen pulls a worn piece of cloth from her handbag. As she unfolds it, debris sprinkles on to the table, the broken petals of a dead rose. Carmen rubs the material against her cheek. 'I made this snuggy out of a piece of my wedding dress for the baby.' Her eyelids close while she holds it to her nose and inhales.

Someone shouts to the waiter and she looks up; recognition dawns when she sees Mercedes staring at her and she folds her memorabilia, placing it on her lap where she guards it with a cupped hand. Her voice hardens as she badmouths the married Don Juan, well known for playing away from home. Before she becomes lost in another monologue, Mercedes stops her mid-sentence with a question about the reaction of her niece's father.

'He spent his free time carving a cradle, and he defied the local gossips and escorted her to church every Sunday. It must have been killing him inside but he stood with her, and no one dared challenge them.'

Mercedes burns with envy but Carmen misreads the

33

reason for her discomfort. 'Sorry, I am close to the point of the story. When you become old, you get lost in the memories. Our family would have loved the child, but it wasn't meant to be. My niece arrived home the day after it happened, unable to speak with grief, and went straight to her room to lie on the floor at the side of the cradle. She didn't cry, she didn't move. Her mother couldn't get through to her. No one could.'

It was two weeks later, as Carmen took her turn on guard, that the inhuman wailing started. The elderly woman puts her hand to her throat with a whisper that the story could have been hers, and a chill runs through Mercedes' body as she listens to an echo of her own past. Another bereaved mother, but this one was able to hold her cold baby. Marie Luz described an icy stiffness, which penetrated the layers of swaddling. 'She asked the staff why her baby was frozen but her questions made them angry and, when she wouldn't be quiet, a doctor forced her out of the clinic. Her parents thought that a cat was scratching to come in that night, but when her mother opened the door to chase it away, Marie Luz fell in.'

Children playing nearby fill the void with their laughter and Carmen tilts her head to listen before she goes on. Tears stream unchecked down her withered cheeks. 'She was only twenty-one when her mother discovered her, hanging from a tree. It was a special place, one that she loved, next to the swing that her father had made for her when she was a little girl.'

For a while, neither woman speaks; each is lost in her thoughts.

'She is at peace now.' Dried tracks on Carmen's face glisten in the sunlight. 'My brother and his wife never recovered. They are with her now.' Carmen's hand draws a cross in the air as she glances up to the sky. Then her lips tighten. 'I haven't been able to forget her description of the baby. It wasn't cold.

The word she used was frozen. Why would a new-born baby be frozen? It doesn't make sense. At first, I hated Him. How could God take our babies?' From under her cardigan, she extracts a gilded chain, from which hangs a simple cross. She lifts it to her lips, kisses it and mouths 'I'm sorry' before she slides it back to its hiding place. 'Then I realised that He wouldn't punish the innocent. I didn't know why He wanted our babies at his side, but I tried to accept it. However, the words of Marie Luz give me nightmares. There is no sense in them.'

Carmen's flat voice dismisses the collection of days that made up the years afterwards; there is a note of excitement as she speaks of a chance meeting with someone from her past. However, Mercedes wiggles back in her chair and feels a twinge of misgiving as the woman's tale seems to lose credibility.

'It was a strange co-incidence. I was in the city to buy a dress for my nephew's first communion. My husband was in a bar – he hates shopping. While I was in El Corte, trying to decide between two that I liked, Lola tapped me on the shoulder. I don't know how she recognised me because the last time I saw her we were as big as bulls, both expecting our first in the same week. I never saw her again after I lost my baby. When I came back, she was gone and, to be honest, I was glad; the sight of a new-born would have killed me. In my struggles, I forgot about her.'

Mercedes feels like a pawn in some wild fabrication as Carmen leans forward and almost sings when she bursts out. 'Her baby was born in Salvador as well! And, she was told he had died!'

Mercedes focuses on the blank page of her notebook as she tries to shake off her unease. Juanita is forever reminding her that she is hopeless at hiding her thoughts so she knows her disbelief must be all over her face.

'After that meeting with Lola, I started wondering why our babies didn't survive so I began to seek out other women from those days. The names were easy to remember, but many have disappeared over the years. Sometimes they did manage to escape. Names changed. And I had to be careful. Not everyone is proud of their past.'

'How did you track them down?' Accusation colours the question and Carmen appears puzzled by the challenge.

'Mama always said I had a good memory. Three of our friends were still in their original villages; our generation hasn't moved like yours. Each told me about a mother who lost her baby in Salvador. Some local women refused to go there to give birth.'

The end of Mercedes' pen is no longer round but chewed to a flat pulp and she mumbles that the co-incidence seems bizarre. Carmen misunderstands her insinuation and replies that the babies seemed to disappear from mothers who were considered social outcasts.

Then Carmen reveals why she decided to contact the reporter. 'My husband mentioned your name when he was reading one of your articles.' She flushes and admits that she never learnt to read. 'My niece tried to teach me years ago, but my husband didn't like it. He's a stickler for the old ways and doesn't think that women need to read or to write. He was so angry when he found out what Marie Luz was doing that I thought he might put me in hospital. The men wound each other up at the bar so that they were as tight as springs when they arrived home. Women were getting above themselves and he didn't like the idea. Maybe he thinks I'd leave if I could read and get a job; he wanted to burn my reading book so I hid it. It was an old one of the children's.

'"A woman's place is in the home".' Carmen's mimics a man's voice. '"If she doesn't push out babies, then we won't have children, and who will feed us when we are old?"'

Eager to get on with some research, Mercedes makes polite conversation while she waits for the bill. 'Many men agree. At work, they give me any rubbish assignments. My editor thinks that I should cover fiestas and do a column for housewives.' Her laugh is curt. 'What do I know about housekeeping? I went to university. For my degree, I studied politics and law, not sewing and cooking. What a waste...'

The rant comes to an abrupt halt when Carmen performs an odd dip to one side and pulls up the collar of her cardigan to cover her face. She refuses to look up, and all that Mercedes sees are two men ambling along the street. When they are less than a metre away from the end of the table, she overhears their debate about who will be victorious at the afternoon's bullfight. There is nothing sinister and, dumbstruck, she gawps at Carmen; the woman's head remains down and her shoulders tremble. Keen to figure out the trigger for this reaction, Mercedes focuses on the street and catches one of the men staring at her with an intent that makes her squirm. He doesn't look away until she outstares him, then he nods at his companion and they carry on down the road. Their shadows follow their bodies, elongated thin patches that remain on the ground until they turn the corner. Finally, Carmen peers over her collar, her eyes prominent against her pale skin. Her voice breaks on the whisper as she unpeels from her crouched position. 'Please help. I can't stay. He'll kill me. I'll phone again.' Warm breath moistens Mercedes' ear when Carmen leans in to kiss her cheek.

'Be careful.'

With a furtive glance in the direction of the men, Carmen scurries off in the opposite way. Lost for an explanation, Mercedes watches the solitary figure until she turns to the right and disappears out of sight. Now all the players have vanished, Mercedes wonders if she has been a support act in a drama, and irritation replaces her bewilderment.

On the other hand, it is hard to disregard the panic in Carmen's voice when she issued that warning.

Chapter 5

She shouts at Orlando's back but her words blow away in the wind; the gap between them widens as her legs struggle to keep to his speed. A rogue breeze soothes the heat of her face for a second but it isn't enough to dry the damp on her brow. The incline steepens and her breaths labour, so she doesn't try to say another word until they reach level land. Without the pressure on the pedals, the burn eases from her thighs and the searing chest pain disappears, and she is finally able to remember that there is enjoyment in the exercise. She watches the sculptured muscles at work when Orlando stands up on his pedals, then he turns to speak and catches her eyes on his backside. He grins and her face turns redder.

'How about a break?'

'If you need one. Of course.'

His laugh booms at her answer, it fills the air between them. He crouches forward into a sprint and Mercedes begins to regret issuing the challenge as she tries to ignite her legs once again. A call for mercy is on her lips when his bike tears up the gravel and he turns to the right. Man and machine disappear through a gap in the pine trees.

'Thank God,' she whispers; each breath is now tortuous and her muscles demand rest. The narrow path snakes through a corridor of trees and exits onto a cliff shelf where ahead an imposing vista displays like a landscape masterpiece. In the distance, there are the strata of white-topped mountains, and below a valley stretches out. Coloured gold by the crops, it fills the expanse between the alpine landscape and their viewpoint. Just visible are clusters of white blots and, when she squints, she makes out that they are the white buildings of the small towns that crown the foothills. The commotion of the stony earth under the wheels of their bikes is the only sound that disturbs the peace of the setting.

Orlando skids to a halt and contemplates her with a satisfied smile while she approaches. 'Any clever words for this, Señorita Reporter?'

She glides alongside, puts her feet to the ground to brake, and perches on the crossbar; she is relieved that her legs still have enough strength in them to keep her upright. The vision distracts her from the pain when she leans forward onto the handlebar. 'This is incredible! And the air, I love that smell of pine.'

His face betrays his pleasure as he looks deep into her eyes; it unnerves her so that her heart misses a beat. He must see the discomfort in her expression, because he turns his face to the sun and suggests that they find some shade. They leave their bikes propped against the trunk of a hefty pine and carry their panniers towards a flat boulder that rests under a fern canopy.

'A table fit for a queen.' The preparations are fastidious as he irons out every crease of the gingham cloth that he spreads across the improvised table, sets out plastic cutlery and paper plates, and then covers the surface with containers. They create a kaleidoscope of colour, packed with green and black olives, a rainbow salad of peppers, carrots, tomatoes and bite-sized chunks of Manchego cheese. The wasps start to gather, attracted by the scent of the garlic and olive oil dressing, and he swats them away as he peels off the cling film that covers a plate of *jamón*. He is like a magician and she can't help teasing him.

'Is there wine in that small bag as well?'

He crosses his fingers and winks as he says, 'Abracadabra! Now that's what every picnic needs.' Pretending to dig deep into the bag, he extracts a bottle of rosé and two glasses.

'Okay, I'm impressed.' Overcome by an impulse, she reaches forward to touch his arm, but pulls back at the last minute and tucks her hands under her thighs to keep them in control. The action amuses him and it is clear that he knows the effect he has on her when their eyes entangle. She battles to break the entrapment.

Free at last, she struggles to calm her rapid breaths; it comforts that the pace of his breathing is faster. A cloud covers the sun, the air cools a little and the spell is broken. Mercedes looks for something to do. 'I can't let this go to waste.' She lifts an olive and watches the sky-dance of the martins as she nibbles around it. 'I'd love to be able to fly above the earth. Wouldn't it be wonderful to have this view every day?'

Desire oozes out of his eyes, which aren't on the birds when he agrees with her, so she quickly changes the subject and offers him a plate with her gaze locked on their hands. His stare drills into her curls but when she won't acknowledge it, he takes several slices of *jamón* and toys with the food, pushing it around his plate as he gives monosyllabic responses to her chatter. The dense atmosphere thickens until Mercedes acts; a playful push and he falls onto his side as she dashes into the woods. 'I bet you can't beat me to that tree.'

Needles crunch under her feet as she flies past the trees and pushes herself until her breaths burn in her chest again. There is a scuffling sound as a small animal escapes from her path and then the sound of heavy footsteps approach. Orlando shoots past. During the second that they are side-by-side, he exposes his teeth in a wide grin. He doesn't give her a chance as he surges in front and, when she reaches the tree, he is

41

leaning against it with his arms folded across a puffed-out chest. 'Taking a walk?'

The taunt reminds her of competitions she had with her brother when they were children. Spurred on by the challenge, she musters her strength and pushes him again. While he recovers his balance, she races back to their start point. 'Catch me if you can!'

Flat on her back on the ground, she hides her fake yawn with a hand as his shadow spreads over her body. She pretends to snore but can't hold back her giggles when he flops down beside her.

'Cheat. You are a ruthless woman, Mercedes.'

'Anything to win, Orlando. I always do get my own way you know.'

Through cracked eyelids, she watches him turn his face to the sun. His reply is barely audible when he murmurs. 'So do I.'

Her body is rigid, held fast by the proximity of Orlando's slumbering form. Hairs on her arm stand erect as they stretch for contact with his and she is aware of every movement he makes during his dream journey. Without a sound, she twists her head to the side, so that she can watch as his nostrils swell and collapse with the soporific breaths. Each time he exhales, the air escapes his mouth with a popping sound, and she almost gives in to the desire to place a fingertip there and feel the vibration of his lips. Instead, she moves her hand so that it lies next to his and turns her eyes to the cloudless sky, watching the birds in their synchronised movements. Hypnotised, her limbs relax and she drifts to their patterns.

Something endeavours to disturb her but she fights it; she longs to keep her dream family with her, but in a trice they disappear as the image drawn by her sleeping imagination fades. The sky above is sapphire when her eyelids flicker to let in the daylight. The ache in her muscles transports her back to the present. The sun is in the west and, although it remains warm, the intensity has lessened during her escape into the fantasy world. When she rises onto her elbows, Orlando is clearing away the last vestiges of their picnic and she jumps up with an apology.

'How long have I been asleep?'

'Hours! Don't worry, you didn't snore too loud. You didn't wake the lions anyway.'

When she jerks the strap of her bag onto her shoulder, Mercedes misjudges the weight and swings it so that it thumps her in the middle of her back. 'Ouch! Funny man.'

They are silent until she is in the middle of fixing the pannier back on her bike, and he asks, 'Heard anything from the mystery woman yet?'

She swivels towards him and tells him about the meeting with Carmen the previous day. His questions probe for detail and she appreciates his skill but edits her description of the encounter to a few lines. Wondering what he will make of it, she explains the odd manner of Carmen's departure. 'There was something about those men that frightened her off.'

'Sounds intriguing. What were you discussing?'

As soon as she says the word babies, he loses interest and changes the subject. She wonders if she should elaborate but it feels as though the moment for revelation has passed. When she mentions that she hopes Carmen will phone again, he makes a throwaway comment.

After a final tug to check the strap of the pannier, she returns to help him with the clearing up and makes him laugh with her jokes. Orlando shakes the tablecloth and she steps close to help; he misunderstands and opens his arms. They tempt her, more so with the smell of his musk aftershave, but she wrenches her body away before she loses control and keeps her gaze moored onto the ground as she pretends to check for missed items. There is a smile on his lips, as though he guesses how close she was to giving in to his embrace, and her tongue is dry as she turns to take hold of her handlebars. His hand indicates that she should follow as they push their bikes into the undergrowth; plants skip across the spokes of the wheels in a serenade of brushing sounds. When they emerge onto the path that will take them down, Mercedes groans and lifts her leg over the crossbar. 'I'm moving like an old woman.'

'I don't think so. And, if you were old, I do know that you wouldn't get away with those shorts.'

She tugs the cuffs of the legs down and tries to cover more of her flesh; she had spent a few minutes debating whether to wear them earlier. On the other hand, she can't help feeling pleased at his comment. 'I may have white hair one day, but I'll never give up my shorts.'

'I'd love to stick around to see that.'

Pleasure surges in her chest and Mercedes escapes, telling him how lovely that would be as she pushes off on her bike.

The wheels of their bikes whizz as they wind around the hairpin curves of the mountainous road and her feet travel in a blur, redundant on the pedals as they spiral out of her control. Ahead is the skyline of Collado Villalba, where a wall of towering apartment blocks hides the more traditional town centre. The train station is on the other side of the town and, from their elevated position, can't be seen amongst the sprawl of buildings. Mercedes slows down to scan the countryside and spots several small towns and villages dotted in the green waves of hills; the concrete jungle of the city feels like it exists in another world. The low sun shines on a reservoir, the rays rebound off the glistening water and she blinks to clear the moment of blindness caused by the glare.

Orlando coasts by while she is lost in her observations; his laughter trails on the wind and he raises his hand in the air to capture her attention. She abandons herself to the freedom of the hill as she pushes off and her laugher accompanies his sound. Strands of hair whip her face when her ponytail band begins to slide out and she releases it, giving in to pleasure as the wind rushes through her mane. There is a prick of regret when the run ends and he pulls over to a layby, but she obeys his instruction and accepts the water bottle he offers. Once replete, she hands it back to him and watches a blood vessel pulsate in his neck when he tilts his head back. Then she turns to view the panorama. A blob of white erupts from a canopy of green trees but she can't quite make out the detail of the structure and points it out to Orlando. 'What's that in the distance?'

'The Valley of the Fallen.' His lips compress into a single line. She is surprised that he managed to get any words through them, and he avoids her eyes with his jaw rigid and teeth clenched.

'That structure must be the cross. I remember someone telling me about it at uni.' She tries to chip away at the invisible barrier but her rambling bounces off his rigid back. 'He said that thousands of political prisoners from the civil unrest are buried there.'

'Not just prisoners.'

Her friend told her about that as well so she nods. 'And of course there's Franco's tomb. A friend of Juanita's father went to see it last year.'

A hiss oozes through his teeth as Orlando turns his back on the monument and crosses his arms over his chest. The silence is uneasy; she makes an effort to relieve the tension and

45

tells him that Carmen's first husband was a rebel. 'I wonder if that is where they took him.'

With a thunderous expression and a few sharp words, Orlando explains that his grandfather and two uncles also disappeared during those years. 'My parents have searched for years for their bodies, but nothing has come to light. My mother was a toddler and my dad not much older, otherwise they may have vanished as well. It wouldn't surprise me if my relatives are below those foundations over there. It is said that many lives were lost during its construction.'

'Maybe there's a record of prisoners' names?' Her words fall into the air and there is no reply as he leaps onto his saddle in a single movement and sprints down the hill. It is rare that she swears but as she tries to catch him up during the descent, she lets rip.

He is outside the entrance to the train station, the toe of his shoe grinding into the concrete and, when her bike skids to a halt alongside, he offers a boiled sweet and mumbles an apology. Mercedes shrugs and takes the token, glad he hadn't been within earshot of her tirade.

'Any water left?' Plucking the bottle out of his hand, she drains the last few drops. While she drinks, he lifts the curls away from her damp neck with the lightest of touch. She keeps the bottle at her lips so that the moment lasts longer.

'Thanks for mine.' The humour belies the sting of his words and she shakes the empty bottle with a grin.

'Sorry.'

'*No pasa nada*. It doesn't matter. There's a machine inside, I'll go there.'

As he makes his way across the terrace, his dark head rises above the throng of passengers that gathers under a cloud of cigarette smoke as they wait to go through the gate onto the platform. She follows his progress until he disappears to the other side of the building. She thinks back to the strange monument and its disturbing history; the impact on people is worth more research, especially given Orlando's reaction. Absorbed in her thoughts, she doesn't hear him return and jumps when he touches her elbow.

'Our train's here.'

His presence triggers a heat inside that confuses her thoughts and she turns her attention to helping him manoeuvre the bikes into the carriage. Once they take their seats, she attempts to apologise for reminding him of his parents' sorrow but he interrupts and explains why the topic makes him seethe.

'No one talks openly about the past. It's the fear of retribution, I guess, but all my family wanted was to honour their dead loved ones.'

He turns his head to the window and she stares at his profile. She wonders if she has missed an opportunity to tell him about the wall of silence she has encountered in her own search for someone.

A jolt alters the rocking motion of the train and wakens Mercedes on its final approach into Atocha station; the pillow that she nestles turns out to be Orlando's shoulder and she keeps her eyes closed for an extra second. Unnerved by the desire to remain nestled against his body, she withdraws into the corner as he stands to lift down the panniers from the rack overhead. He places them on the floor, ruffles her hair, and says, 'Let's go sleepyhead, time for home.' The stiffness in her legs makes her groan and her hand reaches out for support. He keeps hold of it, long after she is steady.

'I've thought of a solution; you need more exercise to stop them getting worse. Let's go dancing tonight.' His eyebrows move upwards to form two pyramids and seem to challenge her as he continues. 'That is, if you want to?'

The words are out of her mouth before she is able to censor them. 'I'd love to, but I'd better warn you. I can dance the night away; and I mean all night!'

In a dodgy disco type of move, Orlando does something strange with his arms and legs around the middle of the platform. She scans the station and looks for anyone who might recognise her. At the same time, he does a twirl and assures her that she will love his moves.

'I can't wait.' She pulls on his sleeve and pleads. 'Please stop.' They move along the platform to the station exit and she tells him that everyone said she was the best dancer to come out of her hometown in generations. 'But I haven't danced Flamenco since living in Madrid, so I may be a bit rusty.'

At hearing her choice, he screws up his nose. 'Oh. Not quite what I had in mind but okay, I know a place where they play some flamenco music, if that's what you'd like.'

They arrange to meet in Chueca at midnight and go their separate ways. Away from the power of his presence, reticence replaces her enthusiasm and she recalls the hopeful glint in his eyes. If she is not careful, his charm will seduce her and break through her shield.

Chapter 6

Ten minutes remain before she has to leave and there are four dresses discarded on top of her bed and a fifth in a crumpled heap around her feet; she can't make a decision. Dressed only in her underwear – a set of lacy frills with the shop labels still attached when she found them pushed to the back of the drawer – she inspects her reflection in the long mirror and wonders what he would make of her naked body. Even the thought sends a quiver low into her pelvis, and her nipples try to erupt through the material of her bra. She puts those thoughts aside and picks up the scarlet dress embroidered with black roses. It has a black lace trim around the elbow-length sleeves that matches the lace border of the elasticated shoulder-line. Nervous that it exposes too much bare flesh, from the curve of her neck down to the swell of her bosom, she pulls it up over her cleavage but it slides back in its original position. Knee length flounces, divided with identical lace, separate into layers that sway when she moves. Initially passed over because of the way that it clings to her body, she realises that nothing else will suffice for a night out with him. She stabs a coral comb into her curls and checks her eyeliner for smudges before performing a swirl for the mirror. That will have to do.

'You're looking pretty tonight.'
Señora Vega is on her perch – a plastic chair that has seen

better days – at the side of the entrance to the block. Mercedes smiles at her neighbour, a sombre spirit in widow weeds; the timeworn woman has never missed a night guarding the door. Other residents issued warnings to Mercedes on the day she moved in. *Beware of that Señora Vega, she's a bit touched. Every night she waits for her son to return, it will take a miracle for him to rise from his grave.* Although she hasn't time to spare, Mercedes makes her accustomed stop to have a few words with the grieved mother.

'Thank you. I'm meeting a guy. Do you think I'll do?'

Señora Vega kisses her fingers and blows an imaginary kiss, then the vacant smile descends once again as she turns her head and peers into the dark.

A lilt is in her voice when Mercedes sings, 'I'm going dancing,' but the huddled figure stares into the distance and has already re-entered her imaginary world, so she completes the pirouette for her own pleasure.

The corner where they have arranged to meet is within sight. Orlando is looking at his watch and hasn't caught sight of her yet, so she pauses to survey him for a minute. One leg crosses the other as he rests his back against the rusty lamppost with his arms crossed over his chest. An open-neck white shirt clings to the muscles of his shoulders and upper arms, and black trousers expose the shape of his waist and skim his hips and legs. Physically he could crush her, but in the greatest danger is her emotional wellbeing and, for a moment, she considers turning back.

Too late. He whistles, and she sashays in his direction.

'Wow, look at you.' His index finger makes a twirling sign and she obeys the command; the skirt revolves around her bare legs as it produces a kaleidoscope of red and black. To her ears, her giggle contains the excitement of a teenager and she covers her mouth, but he grabs her hand and leads her into the narrow alleys. When a couple of girls they pass try to catch his eye, she locks their elbows together. He tilts his face down with a grin and she flusters as she focuses ahead, under the impression that he knows what is going through her mind. More husky than it usually sounds, his voice whispers into her ear, 'Not bad for a country girl.'

There is little space between their bodies as they travel through the dark passageways and the sparks destroy her ability to think of clever conversation. The heels, sexy but higher than she is used to, catch in the cobblestone paving and when she topples, he puts an arm around her waist and tucks her against his body. They stop at a weather-beaten wooden door with neither a sign nor a number on the outside and she raises her eyebrows at Orlando.

'Listen,' he says. A muffled mix – the plucking of guitar strings and beating of drums – is just audible. 'They are just starting up.'

As though on cue like a magician, a doorman materialises and Orlando hands him some coins. The uniformed man's hand takes the offering but his eyes are busy as they travel the length of Mercedes' body and stop to linger on her bust. Orlando establishes his claim and pulls her to his chest with a glare that halts the inspection. When they enter the club, her eyes need time to adjust to the dimly lit room but Orlando keeps hold of her hand and guides her through the crowd towards the bar. Smoke and fog camouflage the detail of the venue, but she notices that a DJ set-up occupies one corner of the room and customer booths butt along the perimeter. When a girl at the bar, too pretty for comfort, turns to speak to Orlando, Mercedes pushes forward and touches her lips to his ear. Without a word, she reclaims his attention, and the rival shrugs as she turns to seek out another prey.

They slide into a vacant booth and he shifts forward so that their knees connect. The fan she pulls out of her bag and flutters in front of her face does nothing to cool her body's reaction. The heat builds inside until she springs up from the chair and moves to the centre to find a space amongst the dancers; each performs a pantomime, sometimes as an individual, but more often as one of a pair who face each other. Many of the dancers are older; experts state that maturity is necessary to achieve greatness in the style, and indeed, her favourite performers are the age of her parents. Her body sways, gently at first as it finds its rhythm, then it undulates to the music and she immerses herself in the trance with her palms clapping an echo to the beat. Bending her back into the dance's classic crescent shape, she twists and turns, and maintains the proud grace that defines the talented dancer. Around her, pairs of feet stamp the tiles in time to the tempo as the music quickens. She speeds up so she doesn't lose the *duende*, the spirit of evocation.

It surprises her when Orlando appears opposite; he dances in his own space but mimics her movements, and everything and everyone fades into the background as they weave. Passion glues their eyes to each other and she increases the speed of her heels, challenging him to match her pace. He doesn't disappoint; his feet fly and equal her beat as they circle each other, moving in perfect symmetry. The magic continues until the DJs change and, with a new man in charge, the Flamenco sound disappears. Mercedes aches with regret that it has ended when the music brings a new style of dancer onto the floor. Orlando bows in front of her and she tries to hide her pleasure when he says, 'You win.'

Back in their booth, he orders more drinks, then crosses his arms and studies her with interest. 'You're amazing. Where did you learn to do that?'

'Thanks. People do dance outside of Madrid, you know.'

Their heads close, to hear above the music, they talk about nothing of importance, however their conversation mesmerises Mercedes. It is the way he traps her eyes with his when he speaks. He pauses and tilts his head back as he drains his glass and his neck tempts Mercedes' lips, an area on his hairline between a few tufts. She forces herself to look away. That piece of flesh and its wisps of hair have stolen her concentration and, when he asks the name of her hometown, she nearly tells him the truth. Then her stomach turns over and her invisible guard returns. Aware that her eyes might betray her confusion, she hides them as she bends to loosen her shoe straps until the blood flows into her feet again and they throb and pulse in a rhythm that matches the music.

Instead of an answer to his query, she distracts him and asks if he knows how to access local birth records of forty years ago. The reply dashes her hopes as he describes the lack of organisation in the system, suggesting a clinic's own paperwork may be more reliable. When he delves into the reason for her enquiry, Mercedes pretends to be investigating birth rate trends and changes to the subject of shared university experiences. It makes him laugh aloud when she describes some of her own escapades; the story of a bat flying around the girls' lodgings one night and bombarding their hair is his favourite. It transpires that he was a mischief-maker in his youth; his sense of humour landed him in all kinds of trouble. He tells some of his own stories and Orlando demonstrates a side to his personality that she likes, and wants to know better.

The sun's rays thrust upwards from below the horizon into the pre-dawn sky as they exit the building to the shrill wake-up songs of the birds. Mercedes turns to say goodbye but Orlando steps forward so that the sides of his arm, hip and leg fuse with hers, banishing her conscious thoughts. Unintentionally, her face tilts up to him and his breath warms her lips. Just before their breaths mingle with the meeting of their lips, she closes her eyes against the tidal wave that threatens to sweep her away. It is a relief when his lips finally fix onto hers; they are a perfect match and, when someone moans, it takes her a while to realize that the sound is hers. Before she drowns, Mercedes stiffens and thrusts him away, with her handbag clutched against her chest as she stumbles backwards. Eyes dart everywhere to avoid connecting with his. She has nothing to give him; her love is earmarked for her son.

'I can't.'

Before he has time to answer, she rushes to where the alley exits onto the main road. When she steps around the corner, she can't resist the temptation and looks back at his lone figure. The impulse to run back into his arms nearly overpowers her, but she wins the battle. As she heads home, it is with an inkling that she may have lost the chance of something precious.

Chapter 7

The white porcelain moon is a shallow bowl prominent against the black sky and it lies ready to catch the falling stars as Mercedes crosses the hospital boundary with the evening visitors. At the sight of a bench to the right of the entrance, she lowers to perch on the edge of the seat and waits until the fluttering in her chest calms and the sour taste clears from her mouth. She feels no need to read the name written above the door; she could never forget the Salvador Clinic. The arrivals are diminishing, and she must act soon if she is to escape detection, so she stands and strides towards the doors with a mask of confidence.

Mercedes enters, and the doors hum together and trap her inside. Her memories cripple her for an instant and she reaches with a trembling hand to the wall for support. The tiles cool her burning forehead as she tries to think rationally, but the memory of her baby intercedes and she regresses to her sixteen-year-old self. A warm breeze wafts her cheek when the doors open to admit another visitor; he stops at her side and returns her to the present when he puts a hand on her shoulder. She reassures him that she won't collapse, and forces herself to exercise control over her emotions as she marches through the foyer.

Little has changed in ten years. Signposts swing on metal strings suspended from the ceiling and indicate directions for the various departments; the letters have faded and, in some cases, even disappeared. It doesn't matter to Mercedes because the red route to the maternity unit is tattooed in her memory. Faded to pink now, it leads her along a corridor that she last travelled in the company of a woman whom she considered her protector. Later, when she needed support, the woman had revealed her true character and left the young childless mother abandoned as she found her own way home.

Black clothing, the colour worn by the bereaved, is the disguise that she has donned to help her to avoid unwanted attention. No one notices when she sinks onto a vacant seat with her face hidden in her hands. Doctors in white coats and nurses in black habits hurry past, without pause, and Mercedes watches through her fingers as the daytime activity abates. Behind her legs, shrouded by the ankle-length skirt that she wears, is a canvas overnight bag. It contains a partially eaten bread roll and an empty carton of orange juice, both stashed underneath a floral nightdress. If anyone should ask, she is ready to produce the sleepwear that a fictitious ill relative had requested.

Time is slow while a new life fights to make its appearance in the world and Mercedes keeps her hands clamped over her ears. Nevertheless, she is unable to shut out the relentless screams, which shatter the peace of the midnight hours. They penetrate the soundproofed walls. A lifetime has passed since she was the woman labouring behind the swing doors opposite to where she now sits. Hours later, the onset of growl-like groans indicates that the culmination of the unknown woman's labour is imminent. A final bloodcurdling cry severs the voice mid-flow.

Everything stops around her as she waits. Mercedes hears the whimpering mew of a new-born and the invisible vice around her body releases. She melts into the chair and the thumping in her chest lessens until she can no longer feel the labour of her heart. Beads of sweat sting when they fall into her eyes. She mops them up with the back of her hand and the pain eases, but her cheeks still glisten with the remnants of her tears.

The world is peaceful now that the ordeal has finished and Mercedes waits, with her chin tilted forward onto her chest and her face concealed by the curtain of her hair. Another disguise rests on her lap; a book wrapped in yellow paper – a gift for a nameless patient – topped with a twist of green ribbon. Although perfect when she left home, the taped seam has fallen apart, crumpled by the agitation of her fingers. The lightening of the sky signals that morning is near and, in the distance, there are sounds that warn of the hospital awakening. Soon she won't be able to hide in the dim corridor.

Her limbs tremble with weariness as she gathers her belongings and the gift catapults from her lap onto the floor. The noise it makes as it lands shatters the quiet and echoes along the corridor. At the same time that she bends to pick it up, a draft of air caresses her ankles; someone prises open the door opposite and it makes a swish as the wheels of a trolley emerge. In their trail, she catches sight of plastic overshoes that support the body of a ghostly vision. The only colour in the sea of white swaddling, apart from a splatter of red on the gloved hands that steer the moving table, are florid blotches around the eyes. The metal top is laden with crumpled sheets drenched with birth fluids and stainless steel instruments that make a tune as they rattle together in kidney-shaped bowls. When the trolley stops midway through the door, Mercedes watches in morbid fascination as a red river spills like an undernourished waterfall over the edge of the shelf and forms a pool of blood on the floor. The nursing sister doesn't notice; she issues instructions back over her shoulder to an assistant.

Mercedes remains a statue, her stony face a mask for the

internal torrent, as she waits for the nurse to act. She holds the pose until the squeak of the wheels fade as the trolley vanishes through a door along the corridor. The door hisses as it latches into the seal and, no sooner has the midwife gone out of sight, Mercedes launches across the corridor. Before the gap closes fully, her fingers curl over the edge of the door and hold it open. She listens, but there isn't any evidence of anyone else nearby so she prises the door open a little wider and peers through into the labour unit. Muffled voices are audible, but her target area is deserted. She must not delay any longer.

The counter opposite is an imposing structure. It reminds Mercedes of the barricade that employees in the local post office hide behind while they deliver their indifferent service. Papers and folders litter the surface; at the rear and lower down, Mercedes can see a desk cluttered with several large books, two telephones, stationery, a thirsty plant and an open box of chocolates. The area is deserted and she knows that her time is limited when a woman's cries penetrate beyond a pair of closed doors – one of three that face the desk – and a voice announces the urgent need for a doctor. The open door of the third room allows a view of an empty bed, prepared for a new occupant, so she deduces that the new mother and her baby must be behind the second set of closed doors.

Although it is not necessary amid the other sounds, she holds her breath so that she makes no noise as she dashes to the workstation, disobeying the warning and no-entry signs plastered on the door's panel. She sprints to the far side of the desk and, when she arrives, holds onto the solid structure and hesitates. No one appears to investigate the drumming noise that booms out of her chest. Then the cry of a new-born baby rises above the other sounds and threatens to crush Mercedes' spirit and intention with its reminder of her loss. Overwhelmed by the awareness that she hasn't any idea where to look for information, and of the futile nature of her efforts, she turns around to make her escape. As she takes a step away, her eyes settle on two faux-leather covered books. They are stacked one on top of the other, and massive, so wide that they cover a third of the desktop and she suspects that they are weighty even when held with two hands. Impressed into the tan cover of the top book the word 'Deliveries' is written in gold italic letters; the space underneath contains the current month and year penned in black ink. Her tongue wets her dry lips as she slides a trembling finger under the solid cover and turns it to reveal a printed page of columns, complete with handwritten information. Underneath headings are the recorded details of name, address, date of birth, sex, birth weight... The handle of a door clicks and her stomach twists; she is out of time.

By the time the nurse opens the door fully, Mercedes has stepped away from the desk and portrays a puzzled expression as she stares around. Dark brown eyes flash at the sight of the intruder and the white rectangle gauze sucks in to clutch the lips underneath; it fills like a balloon when the woman tries to speak. Glove-puckered fingertips struggle to grab the lower edge of the mask and eventually pull it down to expose a mouth pursed with an invisible stich.

'What are you doing?'

Mercedes presents her wrapped parcel to the nurse. 'I'm looking for my friend, Rosa Martes.'

'Get out of here! This area is out of limits.' She draws attention to the sign on the door. 'Can't you read? Go!'

The flap of wings chases Mercedes through the swing doors to the accompaniment of a scolding, which continues as the doors latch together. Her apology is offered to the wooden barrier and an empty corridor. She scuttles along the passage towards the main entrance with the expectation that a hand will clamp down on her shoulder at any minute but without hindrance, she makes it to the main vestibule. In the far corner, there is a vacant chair alongside a water dispenser and, ignoring the sensible option of completing her getaway, she takes a chance, knowing that it will give her time to recover her wits and consider how those books could help her.

Her brain buzzes, the lack of sleep forgotten, ideas flitting through her mind. She doesn't notice the old man as he lowers into the adjacent chair until he grunts, '*Buenos Dias*'. After she acknowledges his greeting, she follows the path of his eyes; the material of her skirt is in a tight coil between her fingers and untwists like a spring as she lets go. Her hands iron out the creases and then her attention wanders until it settles on the busy waiting area for patients at the opposite side of the foyer. Four porters chat in a group, then one breaks away and grabs hold of the wheelbarrow handles of a tin trolley on wheels. With the intent of a racing car driver, he pilots it out of the reception area into one of the many cavities of the building. As he disappears from view, Mercedes turns her attention to the ferocious woman in charge of the reception desk who manages to ignore every person seeking her attention. When the telephone starts to ring, the receptionist allows it to carry on, and it echoes on and on around the foyer until Mercedes is tempted to scream out the command 'pick it up'. Eventually the sound stops and the woman shrugs, then it starts again and this time she snatches up the handset and listens.

A shadow crosses her vision and she shifts so that her eyes follow the progress of the man in the buff-coloured overall of a hospital porter who has emerged from the nearby corridor. The bulge of his neck and arms remind her of the weight lifters at her gym as he pushes an open pram-like trolley; the basket teems with folders. When he parks his vehicle alongside the reception desk, he speaks a few words to the dragon and plucks some folders from the tin bucket to shove into her outstretched hand. Several records tumble from her grip but he doesn't jump to her aid; instead he grabs a handle with one hand and makes a dismissive gesture behind his back with the fingers of the other one. An idea takes shape in her mind and Mercedes crumples the plastic cup, lobbing it into the overloaded bin before she sets off in pursuit of the man and his trolley.

Stalking the man through various departments, she observes how the records travel around the hospital. The door labelled '*Authorised Personnel Only*' brings her to a standstill and the minutes tick by as she stands sentry until the appearance of a security guard forces her to leave. When he draws close, she presses a handkerchief to her eyes and keeps her head down as she shuffles towards the main entrance. Halfway out of the door, her heart drops when a man's arm reaches around her body, until she realises that he is trying to return her handkerchief that had fallen out of her pocket. Words of thanks catch in her throat when she sees his eyes, unusual in a nation of dark-eyed people. Green seas harbour the pupils, bottomless pools of black, and she breaks from their hold and stutters her appreciation. His mouth smiles but the expression in his face makes her shiver. When she releases herself from his power and turns away, her forehead is damp with perspiration and, although it is obvious that the colour stems from contact lenses, the dead expression in the cold eyes leaves her uneasy.

The morning sun reawakens her as she leaves the concrete façade of the hospital in her wake and tries to calculate how many coins she will need to persuade the porter to become her ally. Manuel, according to the badge he wears, may be the exact person she could use to show her the whereabouts of the old delivery records. And with luck, those documents will reveal information about Carmen's niece's baby, and perhaps the fate of her own son.

The flashing green light signals permission to cross the road with the crowd. When she steps off the pedestrian crossing up onto the pavement, the back of her neck tingles and she pauses to glance back. Not far behind, she spots his head above the crowd; sunglasses hide the eyes but she can feel them watching her body and something flurries in her stomach. The feeling continues, even when she has claimed a seat on a bus and stares along the aisle at the driver. She tries to shake off the disquiet when the woman in the next seat draws her attention to someone on the other side of the glass. His sunglasses are in his raised hand and, as the bus cruises past, he smiles. Something in his expression reminds her of a villain in one of her teenage novels. When the woman asks if he is her husband, Mercedes denies it with a shudder and closes her eyes so that she doesn't need to respond to further questions. There is no reason behind her fear but she doesn't breathe normally until the front door of her flat is locked behind her.

Chapter 8

Two weeks have passed by since her visit to the clinic and Mercedes has convinced herself that the stranger's interest in her was a fabrication of a tired imagination. Today there isn't a whisper of a breeze in the cloudless night and every window in the flat is folded back on the brass hinges as far as it will go. The wooden shutters are tucked into their reservoirs at the top of the window frames, where they can't interfere with stray breezes, and overhead in the middle of the ceiling the fan hums as it whirls at top speed. Drums, guitars and screeching voices join in a crescendo, all followed by silence that is almost painful in its sudden arrival and forces her back to the present.

Care is required to avoid trampling the papers in her path as she crosses the room to the stereo. A plethora of documents erupts from the floor between two recliners; she stretches over the mound to press the plastic button and eject the tape after it finishes its rewind. Her fingers flick through her collection and create their own clicking melody as she tries to locate one of her favourites by Enrique. All of the current music is stored alphabetically in two drawers of a pseudo-wood unit; she has filled numerous shoeboxes with once-loved music that she can't bear to part with. She slides her selection into the tape player, with a finger ready to press the stop button if the ribbon clogs, but it works and she relaxes into the Latino sound, swaying her body to the rhythm. The pace picks up and she sings along to the pop song while performing some salsa dance moves. She looks up and meets his eyes, crinkled with amusement; she flushes as her singing and dancing come to a halt.

Orlando's presence shouldn't be a surprise. He arrived earlier that evening when she made her call for help, but he fits so naturally into her home that, for a few minutes, her guard lowers. A light shines in the far corner of the room and the orange glow illuminates the contours of his body. He reclines on the fluffy rug, which she normally keeps near the entrance to her flat, and his head and feet extend over the edges of the short piece of fake fur; his sprawling form fills most of her living room floor. A patchwork cushion is scrunched up and cradles the back of his head. Earlier, he threw it onto the floor as he lowered into her favourite chair, with a complaint about women and cushions. He had been working from the chair but declared a 'time out' for a rest and flopped onto the floor. His dark curls spread over the quilted padding to create a halo effect around his face, but the look in his eyes is not angelic and makes her burn as she focuses on a crack in a floor tile.

The discomfort is replaced by niggles of worry about the number of papers and boxes strewn around the room; she has given a promise to the porter, Manuel, that she will return everything by the next morning and there are still five boxes to attack. Her concern must show in her face because Orlando levers onto an elbow and offers to help return the load to the clinic. His proposal warrants a hug but the thought of that closeness discomforts her so she settles for the offer of a drink with some nibbles. While collecting things from the kitchen, she shouts as she tells him about the porter's warnings of the risk involved.

'He'll be punished if anyone discovers he's given me access to the archives.'

'I suppose he could lose his job but I still think you paid

him too much, considering how many of the books are missing. And I certainly don't believe what he told you about documents disappearing during the troubles. If they were important, I would understand it, but who would want to destroy old birth records?'

Glasses in one hand and a bottle of white wine in the other, Mercedes comes back through to the lounge; she stumbles, halted by the vision of the T-shirt stretched over his chest. It allows her to witness the display of his muscled torso, and muddles her thoughts so that she has to force her eyes to relinquish their hold and return to his face. He stares at her, she flusters and tries to remember the question. There is no doubt that he is aware of his effect on her by the way that he grins when he gives her a prompt. She flushes and shakes her head as she muses aloud.

'Who stands to gain if the records vanish?'

The music fills the silence while they both think, but neither can come up with an answer and after they finish their snack, Mercedes resumes her position on the floor in the clear area amongst the boxes. With a sigh, she puts her hand into the half-empty one to her left and withdraws another ream of approximately 50 sheets of aged paper. Two punched holes once held the sheets in their original binder, but now twine laces them together in date order. The porter informed her that he collects the papers every six months from the wards, delivers them to the archives for permanent storage, and the staff re-use the faux leather binders she saw in the Maternity Unit for the next batch of recordings.

Thick tape seals the join between the lid and box and Mercedes uses a kitchen knife to slice through it. After they finish examining the contents of each box, Orlando re-seals it and places it in the corner. Large black letters identify the contents, *Hospital of Salvador Delivery Book Record,* in addition to some dates, on the cardboard sides. The writing on the papers is legible in most instances, except when the ravages of time have obliterated some of the detail. She works her way through the box of 87-88; when finished, the sheets fashion a tower on the floor as they wait to be returned to the container. Each parchment bears a watermark, which Mercedes believes is unique to Salvador, and she has discovered that some similarities exist between the oldest documents and the more recent. The date and time of a baby's entry into the world, the condition upon birth, the sex and weight of the new-born, and the parents' names are listed on all of the documents, old and new.

'Are you remembering to make a note of the stillbirths?'

He gives her a look as he slams down the paper in his hand and she makes a silent vow to bite her tongue next time. 'How can I forget when you remind me every 20 minutes?'

Enrique sings about never forgetting, and Mercedes tries to ignore the dig as she joins in a duet under her breath and reaches for another page. After a few minutes, he asks her what her best friend thinks of the woman's story.

'Does she agree with me? You've got to admit that the old lady's story is far-fetched.'

She had been ready to confide in her friend on the day following her hospital stakeout, but she couldn't bring herself to spoil Juanita's excitement that day; the guy she fancies had finally asked her out. Since then, the days have passed and so has the opportunity to speak about it with her friend. Curious about his statement that Carmen's tale sounds false, she questions him further but the foundation of his theory is a hunch and so she dismisses it with a grunt as she returns to her immediate task. Orlando isn't ready to give up on his challenge and comments that there is little sense in the way that the woman ran off. Her teeth grind in frustration as she looks at the number of boxes left to work through; while he talks, his pile doesn't decrease. Aware he is here as a favour and can leave when he has had enough, she tries to control her irritation and make him understand what happened.

'Whoever those men were, they terrified her. She did tell me about an occasion when her husband nearly hit her; maybe they are friends of his. He didn't know she was meeting me.' Silent while concentrating on the next sheet, when she places it on the completed pile she pauses to remember the meeting. 'I'm sure that she's legitimate, no one can fake that kind of emotion. The grief, it wasn't just her words. She actually shrunk in front of me.' Her attention turns to the next document and she mumbles under her breath. 'It was real.'

Her senses are on alert and seem to buzz in the silence as Mercedes' attention goes between the papers that she reads and every shuffle that he makes. Half an hour passes and she strikes gold with a cry and waves her find in the air. 'I've found it; the record of Marie Luz!' His bewilderment is obvious and she moves to his side to point at the writing. 'Carmen's niece. This must be it. Look! The date, her age, everything is right.'

'Don't get excited. Wrong outcome. This baby was alive. Look at that column.'

The bubble deflates, and then grows again until it threatens to burst, as she absorbs the implications of the detail on the document. Carmen had said the girl held a dead baby and was told her baby hadn't survived despite his first cry. However, she described an icy feel to the child in her arms and Mercedes is convinced that a baby would not turn cold so soon after a birth. The record she holds may prove that Carmen's accusations have some foundation, and at least one newly delivered mother was deceived with a switch of infants. The conviction that her son survived his birth strengthens with the find, until Orlando interrupts her joy with a theory and a suggestion that makes her hand itch.

'Maybe the niece gave the baby up for adoption. And then found that she couldn't live with the guilt.'

Instead of berating him for his inability to empathise with the young mother's feelings, she goes into the kitchen on the pretence of more drinks. It is as though his words have ripped something in her soul and she keeps her back to him so that he can't see the pain in her face. By the time she returns with the glasses, her emotions are under control but her palms carry the imprint of four half-moons from her fingernails.

With a forced smile, she faces Orlando and, at that moment, the open door of her bedroom grabs her attention. For the first time since he arrived at her flat, she is aware that he is a witness to her intimate sanctuary and, as though her embarrassment projects a supernatural power, the grey jacket she discarded onto her bed when she came home from work earlier begins a steady slide towards the floor. The red spaghetti-strap top that she wears suddenly feels too revealing as her nipples react to the erotic thoughts that dash into her head. A butterfly clip traps her curls high on top of her head and exposes the bare flesh of her shoulders. The few tendrils that have escaped do not provide any cover; she resists the urge to undo the restraint to allow the rest to fall and give her a cloak to hide her skin.

As she moves towards the bedroom door, she catches sight of her reflection in the cheval mirror that she picked up at the market last year. Coral toenails, her favourite summer colour, seem conspicuous in the open-toe sandals that poke out underneath the hem of her fawn trousers. Her matching lipstick has faded and her lips have returned to a natural colour, blush pink, the same shade as her cheeks. She places her cool hands on her face and wonders whether they will always overheat when Orlando is in the room. Grey smudges of mascara have created shadows under her eyes; she rubs the darkened lashes absentmindedly while at work, but the remnants of makeup don't cover the lilac puffiness that has been ripening during the past four sleepless nights. His eyes burn into her back and she puts aside the worry about her appearance as she pulls the door to and turns around to face the room.

Two boxes remain untouched, so in another couple of hours they should be finished. As she resumes her place on the floor, it is with a silent resolution that after she has returned them safely to the porter, she will treat herself to a whole night of sleep. A gape of her blouse reveals the mounds of flesh above her bra when she leans across for the next document, and Orlando flaunts a cheeky grin when she places her hand to block the view. The look in his eyes adds warmth to her cheeks but is forgotten when she studies the sheet. Her heart begins to race and she hands him her find. 'I've found something. Look, halfway down. This smudging, here.'

'It looks as though someone's tried to erase some of the writing. Can you decipher what it says?'

She takes it back and holds it in front of the lamp so that the light reveals some indentations of the original marks. 'Someone has changed these numbers. That looks like a 9. I remember this! It's part of a score given to babies in the first few minutes. A good number means the baby is healthy, I think.'

'But here it states that the baby didn't survive.'

They take turns to look at the sheet from every angle but neither can determine any other detail of certainty and eventually Mercedes puts the sheet aside to start on another one. The discovery has alerted them and they look for similar defacements on other records of that month's deliveries. Those of the subsequent month appear untouched so she returns her attention to the affected pages, laying them out side-by-side on the table and studying them until her vision begins to blur. Intuitively, she senses that there is something she should notice but she can't pinpoint it so she rests back, stretches her arms and rotates her shoulders. When she glances down, the answer is obvious. 'Look at this. All of the erased entries had the same nurse in attendance when the baby was delivered.'

'Clever girl. Let's look at some of the older sheets and try to discover when she started working at the clinic.'

The name only appears on six weeks of records and then it vanishes, but Mercedes has noticed something else while she skims through the sheets of that year. Every so often, an entry is marked with a tiny circle in the column where the author has written the fate of the baby; in each case, the child did not survive. The rustle of clothes as Orlando stands up breaks into her train of thought. 'Oh no, you can't leave! Not when we are finally getting somewhere.'

'The game starts in an hour and it will take me that long to get there.'

He has given up so much time already but she ignores the guilt and pleads with her eyes until he names her 'ruthless' and replaces his ticket in his back pocket. Lowering her head to hide her triumph, she escapes to the kitchen for a virgin bottle of white wine and a packet of crisps, slipping the corkscrew into the waistband of her trousers before she heads back in his direction. Slumped in the chair, he surveys the redundant ticket but, upon her arrival, crumples it and lobs it towards the bin. She wants to tell him to go but when he gets up to help he doesn't relieve her full hands; instead his fingers touch the bare skin at her waist to withdraw the corkscrew and the words are forgotten as her body jumps to attention.

Her gasp explodes into the room; he ignores the sound, impales the cork and tops up their glasses. Their fingers meet when he passes her the glass and she retracts as though burned, turbulent inside like the swirling wine in the bowl of her glass. The eddies dissipate before she feels able to disguise her emotions and looks up but his eyes are closed, the lids aflutter. Inside of the glass he holds between two fingers, the wine is on a slope and threatens to spill over his trousers, so Mercedes reaches out to rescue it. When she takes hold of the stem, she notices the ink tattoos on the end of his fingers, evidence of the evening's work. Back in the sanctuary of her recliner, she tries to continue working through the final box of records. Her eyes detour frequently and there is an aura of peace in the room as she watches him doze.

He is still unconscious when she secures the lid onto the box and moves to the table with her notebook, where she divides a blank page into columns and begins to organise the data. Every fact goes into a titled column and, as she records her findings in related groups, the significance of the discoveries becomes more apparent. The number of women admitted to the clinic equals the number of babies recorded as born; the discrepancies appear afterwards. The total of live babies that leave the clinic doesn't match the register. Babies identified as stillborn on the birth register later reappear on the discharge records she found in the final box. In many cases, these babies left the clinic for an unknown destination. For a few minutes, she stares through the figures before she makes a decision. Tuesday is free in her diary and she draws a line through the morning in order to visit the office of civil registration. There she will be able to access the official death records, and possibly the burial records, and try to match some names and dates. Logical answers will not be found in the hospital records amidst so many discrepancies.

Lucid thought disappears as the aroma of Paco Rabanne invades the air around her body and Mercedes freezes as Orlando edges near. His presence warms the side of her neck and she catches her breath as his fingers gently gather a bundle of her curls to move them to one side. The ball of lead in her stomach explodes and sends quivers to the ends of her toes when she feels moist lips make contact with a perfect spot. His mouth lands on the sensitive area where the curve of her shoulder sweeps into the nape of the neck; she didn't realise that area existed until now. Too many senses are on fire and she closes her eyes when his lips travel along her shoulder, giving herself up to the fleeting impression as they touch her skin. He reverses the route and each flurry on her body echoes a beat inside of her heart. She turns her face and lifts her lips to his, but the satisfaction is short lived as an ache builds inside and her body demands more, forcing her to twist and reach her arms to gather him around the neck and weld their bodies together. His hands span both sides of her waist and nearly meet when they lift her from the chair; her feet dangle as he transports her to the settee and, as though she is made of precious glass, he lowers her onto the cushioned seat. During the few seconds of separation before he joins her, she is bereft, and then his weight presses on her body so that she no longer feels abandoned. His mouth commands possession of hers and renders her helpless so that she is unable to resist the tease of his tongue. Meanwhile his broad fingers stroke her clothed body and, underneath the fire, her skin cools a little as he pulls up her blouse and exposes her bare midriff. Light fingers cross her belly, like soft butterfly wings that dance across her flesh. The muscles tighten in her abdomen when his hand discovers a path that commences near her belly button and leads to the area over her heart, between her breasts. It isn't a direct journey; instead he tantalises as he traces from one side of her abdomen to the other with feathery touches. She traps his hand when it reaches her heart but doesn't have the willpower to detain it for long.

A call for mercy is on her lips when a ferocious banging

from the neighbour's door brings the glorious torture to a standstill. For a second she believes that the pounding comes from her heart but when the neighbours' voices rise to vent their anger at each other in yet another domestic, she surfaces from the dreamland. With that comes the awareness that she is in danger of falling for the man's touch and her guard rises. She stiffens and his hand stops and hovers briefly before it resumes its caresses. The spell is broken and his weight is now a trap, her arms are pinned and her lungs desperate for oxygen. She tries to press her palms against his chest but his bulk does not yield and, mute with panic, her trust in him evaporates. Aware that her strength is fading, and she won't be able to push for much longer, Mercedes bends a knee and levers him away. The liberty is short-lived as his weight collapses back onto her and forces out her remaining breath. She succumbs to the deep-rooted nightmare of her past, transported back to the moment when a different man's body trapped hers. They are José's eyes that she sees in the face above, mocking her in his triumph, and Mercedes opens her mouth to scream for help, but no sound emerges. The face of her baby son replaces José and inspires her to fight for him, and she yanks an arm free and batters Orlando until he rolls to one side.

She gulps for oxygen, her mind releasing the past, and turns her attention to the man who remains in a crumpled heap on the floor. Dismay accompanies the reality when she catches sight of his air of defeat but there is no time for explanations. Orlando springs from his position, snatches his jumper from the chair and speeds out of the front door. Although she calls his name and tries to explain, the door swings on its hinges and her words tumble into empty space. Cool air rushes into the room and she wrenches her top over the exposed flesh as she runs to the landing; the staircase is empty and the only sound is the slam of the entrance door as it echoes up the stairwell.

Even the neighbours have ceased the braying as she pulls the door of her flat closed.

A section of her hardened heart shatters as she slumps against the wall and hope rouses her as she dashes to a window. Orlando has vanished from the street below and she thumps the glass with her fist; she takes a second look when she notices a man sheltering in the doorway of the tobacco shop. He is too tall and his hair is the wrong colour; angry tears cascade down her cheeks and she begins to haul on the pulley to lower the blind. A screech of tires, followed by the crunching of metal, makes her raise it again but her help is not required. Something niggles in her memory and she takes a second look at the man in the doorway. He has his head bent forward as he lights a cigarette so his cupped spare hand hides his face from her scrutiny. A red glow from the burning stick reflects onto his face as he glances up at her flat and she remembers when she last saw him. Although she can't see the colour of those eyes, they are pointing in the direction of her window. Goose bumps erupt on her arms and she steps out of sight, lets the blind fall and re-checks the lock on her front door. Later, when she settles down in her bed, she makes certain that her telephone is within reach and she tosses for hours before she enters a nightmare world, accompanied by a green-eyed lover.

Chapter 9

'What's this rubbish?'

Jorge glares as he waves the printed page in front of her face and her good mood disappears. Prepared by her expectations, she looks up with a blank expression. 'I have proof.'

'I don't care if the president himself gave you the information. This is not going in.' He crumples the paper and throws it onto her desk before he storms off in the direction of his office. 'Write the assignment that I gave you or it will be your last for this paper.'

Oh well; it was worth a try, Mercedes decides as she gathers some folders together and shoves them into the bottom drawer. She will come back to them later, refusing to give up now she has uncovered some evidence. Jorge's decision isn't a surprise, as all of the staff know that his friendships have a major influence on the content of the paper. Some of her colleagues believe his favour is for sale for the right price, and at least one of the clinic doctors, who she named in the baby exposé that Jorge just crushed, is a member of his circle of friends.

The alternative piece, about the recent improvements in family healthcare, doesn't require much effort and she has it ready for his inbox within the hour. Her correspondence is up to date so she has some free time to review her folders and no one takes any notice as she lifts the top one out of the drawer and returns it to the surface of her desk. Nonetheless, she makes certain that the contents aren't on view to onlookers. She opens the cover to a page complete with columns of names that she has transferred in from her notes, forming the hub of her current research; each of the entries marked with the little circle in the original record is on her list. Pedro yells from the other side of the room and breaks her concentration. 'Pick up the damn phone, Cortes!'

His boorishness is insufferable and she glares back as she lets the phone continue ringing. Finally, she picks up the receiver and a voice commands that she come into the post office to clear out her box, as they can't fit anything else inside. Two days she has waited for a response to the appeal she inserted in this week's local paper; it nestles in the personal column at the back, between an offer of handyman services and one of satisfying massages.

Female journalist is investigating maternity services and wants to speak with women who gave birth to a stillborn baby in Salvador Clinic during the years 1980-1990. I guarantee that I will protect your confidentiality in this sensitive issue. Reply to box no 473, Calle Palos de la Frontera 6.

With Jorge nowhere in sight, Mercedes grabs her opportunity to sneak out of the office, muttering the excuse of an interview as she leaves. She has to sprint in order to arrive at her destination before it closes for the siesta and is out of breath when she enters the building. Rows of square metal doors line the wall to her right as she enters the *correos*; the post office box that she was allocated is at the end of the second row. When she inserts the key into the unit and pulls open the door, a multitude of envelopes spills out and falls to the floor. They drift in all directions and she squats to retrieve them as she scoops them into her shopping bag. The cloth handles drape over her shoulder and she stands to turn towards the exit. At the edge of her vision, she spies a pale pink envelope that has blown further than the rest and caught in the corner of the building. She salvages the message and tucks it safely in her bag with the others.

Heading towards the door, she has to skirt around the queue of customers that snakes from the one open service point. Wedged between a woman as wide as she is tall and a be-whiskered ancient who mashes the filter of his unlit cigarette between his teeth, she glimpses a man who causes her to stumble. At that moment, she hears a symphony of clinks behind her as something falls to the floor and shatters, claiming her attention. When her glance returns to the queue, she is unable to see the green eyes anywhere. A disgruntled worker, with his broom in hand and his eyes on the clock, pushes her out of the way and, in a loud voice, accuses her of creating the mess, ignoring her claim of innocence. The bristles of the brush push over her leather shoes and she threatens him with the cost of replacement as she points out the youngster responsible and struts away. It is over 30°C outside in the sun but the coincidence of seeing those strange eyes in the post office makes her feel cold as she leaves the building behind.

To navigate around people while they hasten home during the siesta period is similar to the negotiation of the slalom on the winter slopes, and she uses the same techniques to avoid collisions in the mass that bundles her in the direction of her flat. Her eyes flit in every direction on lookout but, when she arrives at her building, she is convinced that no one has stalked her. Alert to onlookers, she feels blindly and wiggles the key into the lock of the entrance security grates; the door gives way and she squeezes her body through the gap and closes it in one movement. Peering through the iron grills that protect the occupants from intruders, she observes the faces of passing pedestrians; the man with the distinctive eyes is not amongst them.

Worried that her reaction was extreme, she turns and stares up into the dark stairwell but, for once, she is tempted to enter the safety of the lift. Her fist punches the temporary light switch on and, before it times out, she rushes up the stairs to hit the switch for the next flight. By the time she arrives outside her apartment, the stitch in her side has her doubled over as she tries to steady her breaths. Once inside, she bolts the front door and deposits her bag onto the chair as she moves to the window. Below, a couple entangles in an embrace, a woman walks her dog and two men converse, but there is no sign of the man with the catlike eyes.

'Get a grip, you're developing a phobia.' Speaking the words aloud helps and she marches into her bedroom, grabbing the bag of post from the chair as she passes. She tosses the bag on her bed, drags a chair over to the wardrobe and walks her fingers along the top of it until they make contact with an empty cardboard box; it previously held the shoes on her feet. Her fingertips manoeuvre the box to the edge until it slides down into her arms. With it comes a shower of dust, which settles over her like snow, tickles her nose and makes her sneeze. Not all of the envelopes will fit into the box and she dumps the first load on the kitchen table before she returns for the remainder. There must be over one hundred envelopes and before she starts, she grabs an orange from the ceramic fruit bowl and ambles over to the window. Hoisting the blind, she stares out as she peels the fruit, observing the normal street scene below. Cracking the window allows a cooler breeze to break up the stuffy air, clear her head and banish the phantom stalker; he is a creation of her emotions, they have been in turmoil since her meeting with Carmen. The party music of her samba tape helps to expel the rest of her dark thoughts; she turns up the volume and dances over to the table of correspondence.

The choice is a lottery so she picks the top envelope and slides her finger between the gummed seal to discover a single leaf of paper folded in half inside. There is neither a name nor an address on the sheet, just a date of fifteen years ago. The other side is also blank and, when she discards it into the box, she prays that the next one offers her more information to work with. Sure enough, the next white canvas contains two sentences written in black ink: *Maria's baby born 12/8/1975. Never came home.*

Light refracts on the bevelled edge of the window, a prism that creates a rainbow, inching down the wall during the time she works through the mound. Fine red lines appear on the edges of her fingers and she soothes their sting with a lick of her tongue. It is a temporary relief as more appear, requiring similar attention. Sometimes an envelope contains a letter, sometimes a slip of paper with a name and date. Few of them offer an address, an order, *no contacto*, is the first line scrawled across many of the messages. The content of a single envelope may differ but each exposes common experiences and describes them with similar phrases: *unforgotten loss, enduring grief.*

By the time she allows the final envelope to flutter to the floor, an ocean of discarded envelopes and tear-stained sheets of paper surrounds her chair. Some of the stories date back many years, long before the timescale that she specified in the paper; each one has left its impression. When the clock sounds its first peal and she lowers her hands from her cheeks, her fingers are damp; the marks on the papers did not all fall from the eyes of the authors. The church clock finishes its series of chimes and reminds her that she must return to work but she is slow to rise, reluctant to part company with these soul mates. The afternoon's toil has helped to dispel some of the fog in her mind and left her with a renewed clarity. One letter, in particular, has offered her another path to pursue. On her way back to work, Mercedes pops into the train station and purchases a return ticket to Burgos for the day after tomorrow; a woman who lives in the city of the pink cathedral is willing to talk with her about what she calls 'dubious adoption agencies'.

'I didn't expect that many replies.'

The first to arrive, Juanita has seized one of the outside tables at the café. The establishment is run down but it is convenient and only a few metres away from the office. Mercedes glances at her wristwatch; they have time for a second espresso so she signals to the waiter. Voices hum on all sides of where they sit, with every table occupied for the 'second breakfast'. She sits on the edge of her seat, unable to relax, aware that Orlando is at a nearby table with his back to her. Four of their colleagues are with him but he is the magnet for her eyes; they keep returning to a curl that spills over his collar. When she hauls her attention away from him for the umpteenth time and returns it to her friend, Juanita isn't quick enough to hide her interest.

'What's that look for?'

Juanita tips her head towards the men's table. 'What happened between you? One minute you're both love-struck, and now you won't even acknowledge each other.'

She squirms in her chair and her eyes fill as she tries to explain that she couldn't do what he wanted but Juanita gets the wrong impression and threatens to kick him where it hurts. Then she touches Mercedes' arm with an unusual pinching at the sides of her mouth and her voice soothes as she probes. 'Did he try to force you?'

Her eyes sweep down to the floor, then to the table at

their right, then down again, until finally she looks into her friend's face. 'Nothing like that.' She doesn't want to bad-mouth Orlando. 'It was just,' the words stick and she clears her throat. 'Now he thinks I'm a tease.'

'It was too soon for you. He'll understand that if you explain.'

She shakes her head and finishes her coffee in silence, the memory of his face as he stormed out of her flat tormenting her.

'Give him a chance.'

A coffee moustache decorates Juanita's top lip and Mercedes doesn't want to discuss Orlando anymore, so she forces a smile and indicates her own lip with an index finger. The hint works and Juanita laughs, clearly relieved the mood has lightened, as she wipes it away. Afterwards she extracts a cigarette from the near-empty packet at the side of her cup. The flame from her lighter almost sears her eyebrows when she leans over it; her bosom rises as she inhales and falls and a cloudy ribbon escapes through her lips. A snakelike pattern weaves into the sky as Mercedes sighs, recalling the article that she wrote for the health section recently; if she reminds Juanita of the warnings, no doubt, her friend will have a retort ready.

'Are there any interesting ones?'

The question comes out of the blue and she needs a second before she realises why Juanita asks. 'Lots.' She checks the neighbouring tables for eavesdroppers, and lowers her voice as she shifts closer. 'Too many. Every day I collect another bagful. How can there be so many lost babies? And over so many years... Some stories originate fifty years ago.'

'Mind letting go?'

White fingertips poke out from beneath Mercedes' grip and, with an apology, she opens her palm to set them free.

'Sorry, I get carried away but this story is bigger than I originally thought.'

'I don't think I want to hear anymore. It's upsetting to think of all of those poor mothers and lost babies.' Juanita has her hands over her ears.

'But that's the problem, Juani; no one wants to hear about it.' She tries to suppress the irritation in her voice, she doesn't want to distress her friend but inside she seethes. It is common to her society; the tendency to overlook what is obvious to see but unpleasant to acknowledge. As quickly as it arose, her irritation with her gentle friend vanishes and she changes the subject, telling Juanita about the woman in Burgos, who she is meeting the next day.

'That's a trek. I hope the story is a good one and it's worth it.'

'It should be. Some scandal with adoptions but she wouldn't tell me more.'

'What's that got to do with stillbirths? That's what you're writing about, isn't it?'

Metal screeches over tiles as some of their neighbours stand to leave and the noise distracts Mercedes; the grunt she makes could be either an agreement or not. The link is unproven and she gulps back the remainder of her drink, pushes her chair back and glimpses a final time towards Orlando before she leaves. She tries to disguise her sorrow when he keeps his back to her but Juanita takes her arm and draws her close. They walk in time across the road and, when they enter the offices, Juanita offers to take a day off to come to Burgos, adding that they could shop after the interview. She considers the suggestion but declines with a shake of her head. 'You could be hanging around a long time.'

Blinded by the night, the woman suppresses a scream of triumph when her fingers reach the bone handle of her father's heirloom. Used by him to strip the animal skins that now decorate her walls, it rests on two hooks above the fireplace. Her fingers tremble as she lifts the knife out of its position. Then she grasps the handle and turns to plunge it into the broad chest of her attacker. Warm fluid gushes from his body and showers her, his scream expressing anger as well as pain. She doesn't linger but feels for her escape path along the wall. Her neck snaps when he grabs hold of the skirt of her dressing gown just before she reaches the door handle. She makes her final mistake when she presses down on the handle and allows a trickle of light to illuminate the room. Realising the error, she slams it shut but she has delivered what he needed and his laboured breathing is next to her ear when—

Someone knocks her elbow as he walks along the aisle of the train and she loses concentration; her eyes leave the page and survey her fellow travellers. Most of the passengers wear business attire and she checks her chiffon blouse and khaki chinos. Maybe a suit would have been more appropriate but it's too late to worry. She pops a mint into her mouth in the hope that it will help to mask the odour of aftershave and musty clothes that emits from the man in the adjoining seat, making her feel nauseous. Worn patches shine at the elbows and knees of his suit, and the cuffs of his shirt are frayed; she is convinced he is on his way to an interview because she has noticed him studying the same document since they left Madrid. Every so often, he closes his eyes and recites some data as he beats his pen against his briefcase, a hint of perspiration dusting his lip. He opens his eyes and notes her interest, but she ignores his attempts at conversation and studies other passengers.

A man, seated next to the aisle and three rows ahead of hers, comes to her attention. His dark hair and bushy eyebrows are thick and coarse, highlighted with grey, and he wears a black suit with a nondescript tie. He detects her scrutiny and unfolds the newspaper on his lap, holding it open so it hides his face from view. She recognises his face but can't remember if it was from the platform in Madrid when they embarked or elsewhere that morning. An elderly woman leans across the aisle to offer Mercedes a grape and she gives up on the memory. The flesh is sweet, from her own vines the woman tells her, which sets off a long-winded description of the garden, the family and the row with the neighbours. The revelations continue until she disembarks at the last stop before Mercedes' destination: Burgos.

The exit signs lead her to the vestibule at the front of Burgos train station and she stands for a minute with her head back and eyes directed upwards to the impressive arches. She hears church bells and realises that the hands of the station clock both point to 12:00. Her route takes her past the city's best-known landmark, the pink cathedral that looms above the walkway. Dazzled by its majesty, she is reluctant to walk by without stopping, but the quarter-hour chimes and reminds her that her meeting takes place in fifteen minutes and she has to locate her destination.

Although she is alert to the name, Mercedes walks past the entrance of the bar without noticing the small ceramic plaque that announces its presence. The pedestrian street takes her away from the semi-circular row of ornate buildings that forms the heart of the shopping area, and eventually she reaches a junction. When she consults the city map in her bag, it shows that she has walked past her destination so she heads back to her start point; this time, she counts the building numbers until she reaches number seventy-six.

Precisely on the half-hour, she locates the entrance. It feels as though she has spent most of the last few months at meetings arranged in bars and she breathes in a supply of clear air before she pushes open the door, her hand ready to wave away the thick haze of cigarette smoke that spills out. Women occupy most of the tables inside and the accumulated sound of their daily updates is deafening. She loves the fact that groups of women always find something to discuss, whether it is their child's behaviour, or the meal they will put on the table that day, or one of the many annoying things their husbands have done. Her entrance attracts some attention from the men propping up the bar; dark eyes inspect her to the mumbling rumble of '*Buenos dias*'. The hubbub of voices diminishes while Mercedes surveys the room from the door but no one waves her in. When she is no longer an object of interest, the vibrant discussions resume at a pitch that bounces around the tiled interior. The *tabernero* is in the middle of an argument with a customer and gesticulates with windmill arms so that ash floats like snow from his half-finished cigarette as it arcs through the air. An ember lands in the hair of the customer, but he ignores the smouldering and continues his rant until someone bashes him on the head to put it out.

Mercedes weaves between the tables to the bar. When she gets there, she has no option but wait until the two men break off their fun. The coffee looks to be a good one, dark and thick, and she carries it to a table near the entrance so that she can observe new arrivals. The drink is so bitter that her eyes water, so the first image of her contact is blurred. The taller of the two women has tried to disguise the age of her hair with a vibrant red dye, whereas her companion has given up the battle with her own salt-and-pepper mane. Matching court shoes and handbags complete brightly coloured outfits; *no widow weeds for these two*, Mercedes observes as she signals to them. One of the women goes to the bar and the bartender jumps to attention when she issues her order, whilst her companion steps over to Mercedes' table. Younger than the press archive photos made her seem, the woman resembles a kindly aunt, but Mercedes knows of the grit that lurks in the personality beneath the façade. Señora Ferrer is renowned as a local campaigner against government corruption and her voice has been effective in facilitating the downfall of several high-ranking officials.

'Señorita Cortes?'

'*Encantada*, Señora Ferrer.'

As she kisses the air to the right of the woman's ear and inhales the aroma of rose, Mercedes catches a glimpse of the man from the train; his hand gives him away. Two thirds of his ring finger are missing and the gap is on show as he holds the same newspaper he was reading earlier. Their eyes connect and, when he realises that she has seen his face, his focus travels elsewhere.

'Shall we sit?' Her female companion tilts her head at the chairs, but then she notices the direction of Mercedes' gaze and also scrutinises the man. The older woman remains on her feet while she waits for an explanation.

'That man, I think I recognise him from the train.' The smile is an act and she turns her back on him and shrugs. 'Maybe I'm mistaken.' Still uneasy, she steals another glance over her shoulder but is reassured to see that he is settling his bill and she twists back to face her companion. The door bangs as the man leaves and she tries to banish him from her mind so that her complete attention goes into the meeting. The niceties take seconds and Mercedes gets to the point with a referral to the letter. 'You replied to my advert because I mentioned Salvador?'

'Yes, when I read it and saw that name, I knew we could help each other.'

'Your answer was the only one that didn't describe personal loss, but the depiction of your experience at the orphanage intrigues me. Do you think there's a connection between it and my search for the bereaved childless mothers?' When the woman indicates she is on the right path, Mercedes gives her a condensed summary of her investigation; the protection of her sources and their confidentiality is vital and her description of the meeting with Carmen contains sparse detail. 'Since then, I've discovered discrepancies between the records of the Madrid clinic and the official register of births and deaths.'

Señora Ferrer listens without interruption but her eyes are alert and seem to penetrate Mercedes' expression. The younger woman senses that her suspicions do not need explanation. At the mention of the register, Señora Ferrer frowns, looks around and raises her hand to her mouth to hide her words.

'Salvador is the link. Forget the official paper. Population records aren't worth the paper they're written on.' A shadow darkens her face and commands attention; her friend has appeared at the side of the table. The movement of her head is so slight that Mercedes nearly misses it, but Señora Ferrer glances in the direction the other woman indicates and, when she looks back to her friend, both nod as they make a silent pact. The woman moves a chair and sits facing the room; Señora Ferrer introduces her by first name with no explanation of her companion's role.

'We may not have much time, so I'll be brief. An orphanage near the city keeps babies for a few days before they are sent elsewhere. I know for certain that there's a connection with Salvador.' While Señora Ferrer speaks, the other woman's eyes cruise the room and occasionally her hand moves to Señora Ferrer's arm, with a signal that changes the topic until a squeeze of the fingers encourages her to continue. Mercedes can't identify the reason for their caution and the behaviour seems bizarre. Nonetheless, their eyes remain alert and, if a passer-by comes near, the conversation changes from orphans to food and fiestas. She has barely had time to scribble in her notebook when again the hand touches Señora Ferrer's arm;

this time her spirits sink because they stand to leave. As she makes a salutation against Mercedes' cheek, Señora Ferrer whispers in her ear. '*Cami de las rotas, numero 7*. One hour.'

They go through the door with their arms linked at the elbows and their heads close, chattering as though friends. Before it has swung shut, a stocky man in a worn shirt and patched trousers stops the door with his palm and leans his head out. He turns to look to both sides and moves outside but, before the door hides him from view, she notices that he steps to the right and takes the same path as the women. As she finishes her drink, she takes a glance at the city map in her bag; the '*cami*' is minutes away. A sinister atmosphere has seeped into the bar; she turns at every innocent noise, and decides to escape the gloom and explore the city until the hour has gone by. The brightness of midday outside is a shock after the dark room and, now that she is amongst the pedestrians, things fall into a normal perspective again. She walks at a leisurely pace along the row of shops, with frequent pauses to window-shop, giving her an opportunity to check the glass for any followers. One simple meeting has triggered numerous questions that clutter her brain and give her a headache that threatens to turn to a migraine before the day is over.

Shade falls in her path – the cathedral – and reminds her that Juanita had mentioned that she must look inside at the chapel frescos. The stone steps that lead up to the entrance have been worn smooth under the footsteps of pilgrims and visitors over many centuries, and she has to keep her eyes on the ground so she doesn't misjudge the uneven surface. A stick taps the ground behind her with an aggressive beat and strikes her calf, forcing her to one side to allow an old man, held upright by his carer, to pass. Unable to move anywhere for the moment, she strives for patience as she waits out the man's laborious ascent. When her route is clear and she is about to move again, someone pushes her in the middle of her back. She wobbles on the narrow step, struggling to keep her balance. A hand tugs at the strap of her bag and tears it out of her possession and, before she has time to recover, footsteps clap as someone runs down the steps. Frozen by the unexpected assault, it is a moment before anger swamps her and she sets off in pursuit of the thief, without caution. At the base of the staircase, she pivots her head to both sides and spies a faded denim leg and sneaker disappearing around the corner to her left. The youngster runs fast, but Mercedes won races as a teenager and her killer instinct resurfaces as she pushes as hard as she can. He is less than twenty metres ahead when she comes around the bend and her open bag flies in his wake, depositing contents along the cobblestone path. Her pink leather wallet explodes as it hits the ground and coins pirouette in opposite directions; she stoops to rescue it but doesn't waste valuable time on the change. That momentary pause is enough to lose sight of him and, by the time she takes the next corner, the alleyway is empty. She doesn't stand a chance of catching him now, and she stamps her foot and turns back towards the cathedral; she can't believe she has been so careless. Her mouth widens when she notices a black handle hanging from a rubbish bin. House-keys, chequebook, make-up; it's all there. Her notebook is gone but it was a new one and came into use that morning, so the few scribbles are fresh in her memory and it is not a great loss.

With the shoulder strap draped across her body and the bag tucked under her arm – she will not be caught a second time – she returns to the steps of the cathedral. There isn't enough time for a visit so she gets out her map to check her route to the *cami*. A boy claims her attention, nine perhaps but no older, his hand joined with the hand of his mother. He wears football kit and, as they pass, Mercedes tries to imagine her son in his place. It is impossible to summon that vision without knowledge of his face, and her heart swells as her eyes follow the pair.

Her observations come to an abrupt halt as her glance alights on a man, the one who left the café after Señora Ferrer, now posing as though he waits for someone. A prickle travels up her spine; she is convinced he has followed her, and for a moment she debates her next action. A tutor once advised her to confront problems and she straightens her shoulders, walking straight to him. She nearly deviates from her course at the hint of malevolence in his eyes but he walks away while she is steeling herself to issue a challenge to him. Relief swamps her; she feels that she has had enough excitement for one day, although she is puzzled why her investigation has stirred up a nest of strange men who seem to follow her.

The area is quiet and allows little cover for a pursuer, with no trees and most buildings opening directly onto the *cami*. A car, millimetres from the walls on either side, displays dents and scratches all over its bodywork; it amazes her that anyone would try and drive along the narrow route. Nothing distinguishes number 7 from the other frontages with the exception of a sliver of light, visible through a gap in the front door, propped open with a statue. Her knuckles tap lightly at first but when her second, and louder, attempt doesn't bring a response, she opens the gap a little more and peeks inside.

Stone clad walls form the borders of the empty courtyard and she inches through the gap until she is inside. Before she goes further, she turns to snap the catch of the door into place, hoping that she will hear the creak if it opens again. It doesn't appear as though the other woman has arrived and the sound of Mercedes' steps echo in the vacant space as she moves across towards a door on the far side. This one is ajar as well and she takes it as an invitation to enter, but when she steps into the silent room, no one comes out to greet her. She stands, flummoxed, as she considers what to do.

In the hallway ahead, something white lies on the surface of a mahogany chest, and she steps forward to look. The envelope has her name printed across the front so she picks it up and, although her fingers itch to tear it open, she slips it into her waistband for later. It is thick, padded as though the contents are folded inside, and the paper edge of the envelope scratches against her skin, it is too big for her pocket but she doesn't trust it in her handbag any longer. Before she leaves, Mercedes tries the handle of the door that separates the hallway from the rest of the building; it refuses to budge. Fed up with games of intrigue, she slams the door behind her and steps into the *cami*.

On board the train returning to Madrid, her travel companions are a woman a few years her senior, who travels with her twin daughters. Mercedes relaxes; the only threat that they pose is to her head with the noise of their nattering. Paper bags, stuffed into the racks above them, bear the names of well-known clothes stores and their conversation includes a detailed critique of each one. Headphones help to lessen the impact of the shrill voices and she closes her eyes, thoughts dancing in her head to the music on her Walkman. The rough edge of the envelope is a razor against her skin, but she doesn't dare remove it from its safe place.

She rests her ear against the front door of her flat and listens before she enters; nothing seems amiss but she wants no further surprises today. The light switch is next to the frame and she reaches in to flick it on before she steps inside. Her blue slippers are still at the side of the door; her hairbrush is on the occasional table near the mirror; everything is as she left it in the morning. Only when the bolt is in place on the front door does she let go of her breath.

The energy drains from her body when she sees that there is no flashing light on the answerphone and realises that Orlando hasn't tried to leave a message. Her legs give way and she sinks into a nearby chair, her elbows planted on her thighs and her eyes shut. Flashbacks compete for her attention as she tries to make sense of the day's events; the pain over her hip suggests that she is going to have a massive bruise where she bounced off the wall in pursuit of the thief. All she wants to do is crawl into her bed, but the slam of the neighbour's door returns her to the present and, as she straightens in the chair, the rustle at her waist reminds her she still has work to do. The wad she withdraws from the envelope consists of various papers and Mercedes separates the newer leaves from the thin parchment sheet, brittle with age, which harbours between. The first line of the new pages addresses her by name.

Chapter 10

Dear Mercedes…

Our meeting came to an abrupt end, and I apologise that I didn't have time to explain but, as you will have discovered, my work has upset powerful people. I am always on guard and worry that you may also be in danger. You must be careful if you continue with this investigation. The people involved have no scruples and won't hesitate to rid themselves of anyone who threatens to expose them.

My story begins 15 years ago when I volunteered to help at an orphanage in Burgos. My children were in school and the hours suited. When I first started working there, I loved it and found it satisfying to give children without parents a little care and affection. There was no heating and little food, and the nuns who lived there starved themselves in order to feed their charges.

Three months after I arrived, on a winter's day, I was searching for blankets to put on the beds of the older children and, desperate, I went to search inside a building we never used. A padlock was on the outside and, when I climbed onto a wall to look through the window, I saw that the room contained rows of baby cots. The policy of the orphanage was 'no babies' because the sisters said they needed special attention and took too many hours off the staff. I assumed the baby equipment was in storage, a leftover from the past. As I jumped off the wall, the director happened by and became agitated, threatening to throw me out. I begged to stay and the nuns supported me so he gave in, but I know he watched me thereafter. Curious about his reaction, I kept my eyes and ears open as I worked, and was convinced the man was hiding something.

A year later, I transferred to work with the younger children and I entered that building again when I was ordered to work with the tiny ones. Babies arrived, occupied those cots for a few days, and then disappeared. Most were young, days, even hours old. There is nothing like the smell of a new-born and I was thrilled to look after them. I assumed that most of the mothers were single and unable to keep the child. Sometimes the baby was only with us for a few hours, barely time to change the nappy and give a bottle before he left. It shocked me that there were so many, even though the sister in charge told me they would be going to loving families. I made a note of the sex, name and weight of each baby for my own records in addition to the date of arrival and departure and I noted the birthdate or unique marks. No one knew about my record, not even my friend Inéz, because I did it as a private reminder of all of the beautiful children. I knew somehow that I should keep it quiet.

My journal filled with the details until I decided someone should investigate why so many mothers gave up their babies. It was difficult to know who I should approach so I brought Inéz in on my secret. Her reaction was not what I expected; she became agitated and came up with excuses about the excellent reputation of the orphanage. My notebook disappeared less than a week later from the pocket of an overall I left in the changing room. Sister Asunción made me leave with an order to keep away.

The memory of those orphan babies has haunted me all this time. I know that they weren't born in the local hospital; one arrived wrapped in a blanket stamped with the name of a clinic, Salvador.

The buzzing of the entry phone wakes her and Mercedes surfaces from a dream of rows of nuns with babies in their arms marching along an endless road. She drags a scatter cushion over her head and tries to drift off again but whoever is at the front entrance persists. The papers drop from her lap onto the floor and she stumbles to the intercom.

'Aren't you awake yet?'

At the sound of Juanita's voice, she comes to life and checks the time. It is nearly 11am and she has forgotten that they have a tennis court booking.

'Give me five minutes.' On her way to the bathroom, Mercedes pulls off yesterday's clothes and, within minutes, she has the racket-bag in her hand and is ready to walk out of the door. To her left, as she exits the building, her friend stands with her back against the wall, both hands trying to lengthen the hem of her tennis skirt. With reddened cheeks, she grabs a hand and pulls Mercedes behind her body.

'I couldn't stand there much longer. The comments were disgusting!'

Mercedes' glance dips to thighs barely covered by the white skirt, and she smiles as she raises an eyebrow. 'Can you blame them?'

During their walk towards the sports centre, Mercedes describes the meeting with Señora Ferrer and tells her about the orphanage; she skims over the pickpocket incident and makes no mention of the man who followed her, that will worry her friend unnecessarily.

'Those poor children. I don't know how anyone could give up their family. Mine is precious to me.' The hurt is unintentional and, when she notices the pain in Mercedes' eyes, Juanita rushes to apologise. 'Of course, everyone's situation is different. I'm sure you have good reasons why you don't see your parents.'

Her heart misses a beat and, for a brief moment, Mercedes fears that her friend has guessed about her secret child, but when she realises that Juanita refers to her parents, she tells her to forget the slip of her tongue. Nonetheless, the sour taste lingers in her mouth for hours.

They win by two games and celebrate their league promotion with a glass of cava. The men who were playing on the next court are in the bar and Mercedes points out that the good-looking one has his eyes fixed on Juanita's legs. Although she pretends to act demure, Juanita turns slightly so that he has a better view. Mercedes notices two red circles have deepened on her flushed cheeks and her friend's eyes keep returning to the man. For twenty minutes she waits for one of them to act, then Mercedes decides enough is enough, and sends Juanita to the bar for a top up of their drinks. The man steps to her side, engaging her in conversation and Mercedes grins as their bodies lean towards each other. Juanita returns with their drinks and a date for the next evening, her face alight like a lottery winner.

Late that afternoon, Mercedes manages to finish Señora Ferrer's letter to discover the woman never made much progress in her efforts to unravel the mysterious origins of the babies.

> *Each time I come close to an answer, I encounter a wall. The director of the orphanage refuses to answer my letters and the sisters think I am employed by the Devil to betray them. An editor at the local paper was interested, but he never published the article and when I tried to contact him, he was unobtainable. Mercedes, when I read your advert and you mentioned Salvador, I contacted you because I know that something is wrong, and I can't get any further. Maybe your*

position on a national paper will give you the power to expose the truth.

You must be careful; it may be dangerous. A car almost ran me down, I was robbed and attacked twice, my house was fire bombed, and I've had to change my phone number because of threatening calls. All of these incidents may be due to some of my other crusades but it started when I tried to go public about the babies. The police say that they can't do anything without names. I don't believe that, maybe they have been warned off by someone.

Included is a document I discovered last year. It's a fragment but it should help. If you need to contact me, please go through my sister in Guadalajara. Her address is below. Please don't reveal it to anyone and use it only in an emergency.

Salu…
Marga Ferrer

Mercedes places the letter on the table at her side and reaches for the parchment; the yellowed paper crackles as she moves it over a light so she can read the faded writing. The script resembles a piece of art with arcs and scrolls that finish in trails of indigo ink as thin as a strand of hair. The letters are cramped and Mercedes struggles to decipher where one word finishes and another begins. The light emphasises a watermark impressed into the sheet; it may be a crest but is ill-defined, and so she is unable to identify any detail apart from what appears to be the wings of a bird in flight. After a while, defeated by the conundrum, she applies herself to the content of the document.

… struggle to find inner peace. Your words of wisdom have helped me to understand that it is our duty to give these children

*of God an upbringing to prepare them to serve and obey Him.
I accept that the children will benefit if they are raised in a
better environment, but it is my belief that we are going against
His wishes and the natural order of life. My heart tells me we
should try to encourage the parents to repent of their sin, giving
them a chance of everlasting life and the opportunity for their
children to stay within the bosom of their families. I pray that
you will forgive me, but I cannot live with the guilt and am
leaving to seek outside conf...*

Even on the second occasion, the content leaves a sensation
in her stomach that is similar to one after an overindulgent
meal. There are no clues to the identity of the author in the
envelope, nor has Señora Ferrer given any hints as to whom it
might be. She gives up the pointless surmising and places the
papers in the same box as the messages recovered from her
post box. Another to-do-list fills several pages of her notebook
by the time she finishes.

After recording her plan, she rises from the chair and goes
to the dresser in her bedroom. She slides open the middle
drawer to stare at the tissue-wrapped item inside. With two
hands, she lifts it and cradles it against her heart as she carries
it through to the lounge table. Age has left the tissue friable,
so Mercedes takes care as she unfolds each side of the package
until she reveals a scrapbook lying in the middle of the cream
lawn. She wipes the tip of her finger on her trousers and uses
it to turn over the cover to a title page; under the hand-drawn
picture of a baby is a date, the black ink now faded to grey.
Sentences merge with each other, fuelled by her passion in
those early days, and the first few pages team with passages
that describe her pregnancy and the day her son was born.
She wonders if she should tear out the pages from those first
dark days at home, when she produced cartoons of miniature

boxes decorated with crosses. On one page a Devil wears the white coat of a doctor, and on another horns decorate a nun's headdress. They are the scribbling of a teenager distraught with grief. As her sanity returned, Mercedes filled the pages with photos and a diary of her life, a record to give her son when they reunite. After some soul searching, she included an image of her family with each name written below. For ten years she has kept the record for her child, but it's been twelve months since she wrote her last entry; her enthusiasm has been put to test. The developments today inspire her to take up her pen and start a new entry.

A few weeks ago, I received a phone call that renewed my faith that we will reunite one day. It has led to new discoveries and I now believe that you were taken from me in the delivery room to be given to another family. This journal will show you that I never give up hope that…

Chapter 11

When she inspects her hip in the mirror, the purple extends down her thigh and she winces as she touches the area over the bone. The bruises to her arms are trivial by comparison and she selects a long-sleeved blouse and some loose trousers to hide the injuries. If she doesn't sit on the wrong bit, no one at work will guess, and she adds an extra half-spoon of coffee and two heaps of sugar to her cup to mask the taste of the painkillers. While she sips her drink, she stares out of the window at the daily life beginning in the street below.

Two old men wearing flat caps and woollen jumpers despite the heat leave a trail of white haze from the cigarettes hanging from between their teeth as they shuffle along the path. A neighbour's child, Felicita, her school uniform already adrift, hops over cracks and jerks her mother's arm as she leaps. Mercedes' eyes go to a window, facing her from the next floor down in the building opposite; Vincente has been moving his furniture again and the position of the sofa looks much better than it did. Then she bursts into giggles as she notices he is not wearing pyjama trousers and his bits and pieces are on view. He looks up and catches her spying, waving an acknowledgement before she has time to pretend that her eyes are directed elsewhere.

While a slice of bread toasts under the grill, she squeezes the last of her oranges. She rubs the toast with a clove of garlic – on the turn but it smells okay – and adds a spoonful of the tomato and oil mixture that she keeps in the fridge. Her normal routine is to watch the headlines while she eats her breakfast; she reads the full reports later at work. This morning, another prostitute has been found dead by two young boys as they played in a park, the third one in as many weeks – the press are naming the killer 'The Ripper' after a famous case in London. A politician pontificates about extra funding for schools that may or may not happen in the next year but it is good publicity during an election year. The footage of a movie star tripping on the red carpet at her film's premiere makes her choke on her juice.

Breakfast complete, her finger is on the power switch when she hears the name of her road mentioned in connection with a violent burglary. Hypnotised by well-known images, she sits to watch the on-site reporter outside of her building as he points to the façade and gasps as the camera zooms in for a closer look at the window on the floor above hers. As Señora Vega returned from her nightly vigil on the front step, she disturbed the perpetrator inside her flat. He left the woman in a critical condition. Fortunately, the neighbour spotted the open door and went to investigate. The latest statement from the intensive care ward describes her condition as serious but stable. The thought of the old woman injured and alone in her flat punches her in the stomach and the ghoulish voice of the reporter vexes her so that she scolds the screen as she presses the off button. She decides to drop by the hospital with a box of Señora Vega's favourite, Valor chocolates, and adds them to her shopping list. Now late for work, she rushes to get dressed.

Before she sets off downstairs, Mercedes double checks that the lock is secure on the front door. In the foyer, several neighbours have gathered to discuss the crime and one blocks her route to ask whether she heard any noise during the night from the flat above. There is no room to squeeze past, and she sighs and looks pointedly at her watch, mentioning that she is on her way to work. Expectant eyes expect an answer.

'I didn't hear a thing. And I was awake most of the night, so the thief must have walked on his tiptoes.'

'Haven't you heard the latest? That's the strange thing, the police say it wasn't a robbery. Nothing is missing from the flat.' It surprises her that the neighbour is able to whisper, because the conversations with her husband that Mercedes overhears most nights always take place at full volume. 'The policeman says he may have gone into the wrong flat!' The woman turns puce, about to burst, and is ready to start jumping up and down – or have a heart attack. Her daily vigil at the flat window has not yielded anything this exciting in years.

One of the other two, Señora Perez, a resident with ten children (packed like sardines into three bedrooms) turns pale. 'Why does he say that?' She shivers and looks up the stairwell. 'Which flat do they think he was after?'

Someone's nephew, an ambulance man, has overheard rumours and his mother telephoned her sister to pass on the gossip. The puce is nearly purple now as the woman relays her knowledge. 'A strange man has been seen hanging around this street and the tobacconist says he has been watching our building.' Behind shining eyes, Mercedes sees her brain whirl as she tries to work out who should have been the target. 'Maybe Señor Alegre? People say he loved his guns when he was younger. And he didn't use them on animals.'

Mercedes is sure the woman winks as she spreads her malicious tale. The suggestion that the assault was on the wrong person bothers her while suspicions take root and her eyes scan the stairwell above. Her goodbyes are brusque as she steps outside and stares at the window above hers. It would be an easy thing to get wrong, and the warning mantra of Señora

Ferrer plays like a broken record in her brain, all the way to the office. Distracted by her search for phantom pursuers, when a commuter brushes against her she jumps with a cry that startles them both; he backs away as though she is crazy.

Once inside the sanctuary of the office building, she surveys the world through the protection of the lobby's glass windows, but not one monster appears. She feels like a fool and, too depleted for the stairs, enters the lift and rests against the panel with her eyes closed. The undersides of her lids are stained with images of the frightened Carmen and the broken body of her neighbour and don't allow sensible thoughts. Her eyelids spring open and she watches the numbers change instead.

The doors slide apart and Mercedes steps out of the lift into normality, drawers clanking, chair wheels rumbling and computers whirring. There are no villains lying in wait as she walks towards her desk, even Pedro doesn't qualify. As her chin goes up, she vows to banish the demons and concentrate on facts instead of fantasy. *Find Carmen*. The to-do list grows. Her trust in Carmen's motives is on a downward slide and after three weeks of no contact, tracing the woman has become her top priority. Mercedes feels to the back of her top drawer until her fingers disturb a ball of fur, the teddy bear, a 10th birthday present from her mother; he swings from the ring that holds a set of keys. One of them gives access to the drawer where she stores her private things at night. Today the key doesn't twist in the lock and the drawer is open slightly. It's normally the last thing she does before leaving work, and she wonders if she forgot to lock it on the evening before her trip to Burgos. Everything is in its correct place when she pulls the drawer open and below several documents and a small collection of photos lies a thin buff folder labelled 'Carmen'.

Engrossed in reviewing her notes and looking for clues

that may lead her to the woman, Mercedes doesn't hear Orlando approach. Her stomach flips when she recognises the fragrance. His words come from a distance when he speaks.

'*Hola* Mercedes.'

The aroma evaporates and she looks up; her eyes stalk Orlando, but he is stepping into the lift and her heart falls into her stomach, becoming a lump of stone. He lingers in her senses, leaving her unable to concentrate. Suddenly she springs from the chair as she decides enough is enough and races after him. The doors of the lift bounce apart when she sticks her foot between them and steps through before they shut once again. He shifts away from her and she takes a deep breath before she lays her hand on his sleeve.

'I am sorry, Orlando.'

'Forget it. Your feelings were clear.' He inspects the ceiling with his arms crossed. She tries to tell him there are things that he doesn't understand, but he pulls his arm away from her touch.

'Please let me explain.' With each floor, her opportunity to make things right erodes, so she blurts out her words without censorship. 'I like you. Very much. It's just...' An invisible hand clutches her around the throat and she hangs her head; so much for her resolve.

In the same moment that the doors release them from the cage, Orlando mumbles that he will give her ten minutes to explain later. She stays in the lift and rides back up to the office. Jaime comments on her grin when he joins her at the water dispenser, asking if she has won a prize. With a shake of her head, she turns away, but he grabs her by the arm and tells her that he is covering the crime in her building.

'Have you heard about your neighbour?'

The undercurrent in his voice prepares her for grave information. She groans at the latest news from the hospital that her neighbour may never walk again. The feeling of responsibility may be unfounded, but the nausea stays with her for the remainder of the day. Her interest in writing up the report on a business fair, her assignment, has waned and she stares through the words on the computer screen until Jorge's voice interrupts her thoughts as he calls for silence. Mumbles of the people around her desk fade and the background noise dwindles.

'Something big is going on at the town hall. You and you, get your butts down there as quick as you can.'

A repeat of his order is not necessary as Mercedes has her bag over her shoulder and is on the stairway before Jorge turns back to his office; an opportunity to report on significant news is a welcome change. She skips down the steps and Roberto catches up with her on the first landing. His camera bag bangs against the handrail and he jumps two steps at a time in his efforts to maintain her pace until he clutches his side, barely able to speak when they reach the town hall.

Back at the office, Roberto sorts out photos while her fingers flutter across the keyboard and she summarises the disgraced politician's career that culminated in an arrest for fraud that morning. When she presses the save button and her heart returns to a normal rhythm, she stretches her arms above her head, enjoying the feeling of a job well done. Then the phone rings.

'It's on its way Jorge.'

The voice is not the one she expects.

'Ms Cortes. It's Carmen.'

She grapples around her desk for her pen and a piece of paper.

'Thank God. Are you okay? I've been worried.'

The voice interrupts. 'I have to be quick. They watch me.'

'Who? Wh…?'

'I'll explain when I see you. The corner bar, in Calle Moreno. Tomorrow, 10:00 am.'

'You left in such a hurry—'

She might as well have saved her breath; the crackly voice is substituted by the continuous buzz of a broken connection. Reluctantly, she replaces the handset and, although futile, she stares at it and wills it to ring once more. The address is in her diary but she isn't likely to forget as every word of the conversation is imprinted in her memory. A tap on her shoulder causes her to flinch and move her gaze from the telephone to Jorge who stands at the side of her desk with a printout in his hand. His eyebrow rises to a point.

'Whoa, tiger. What's got you wound up?'

His eyes assess the situation but she composes herself and shrugs off the question with a change of subject. There is an uneasy pause, then he gives in and they spend ten minutes going over issues of accuracy in her article. The hairs on her arm stand on end – they often do when he stands close to her shoulder – and they don't return to normal until he leaves with the final edit in his possession. Something about the man puts her on edge and she shivers as she watches his progress across the office but she forgets about him when she looks at her watch and the sight of the time spurs her into action. Although she is late for Orlando, this time she remembers to lock her drawer.

He is already in the bar with a half-empty glass of beer and his feet tap a manic beat on the tiles. When she closes in on the table and observes the look in his eyes, her smile freezes and an invisible muzzle subdues her greeting. Silent, she lowers into the chair opposite him. Fire burns in his eyes, she is not sure whether it is anger or some other emotion, and his mouth doesn't give anything away. She can't tolerate the hush any longer and explains that she is tardy because she couldn't get away from Jorge. He doesn't look up and remains mute as she reaches for his hand but he moves it so that his arms cross over his chest. Her own hand joins the other on her lap and ties imaginary knots.

'Orlando, I want to explain why…'

'What are you two whispering about?'

Jorge is immune to the daggers that come from her eyes when he drags up a chair and joins them. He shouts across the terrace to the waiter for a beer and a second round of drinks for them. The cloud disappears when it becomes clear that he has done her a favour as Orlando winks with a shrug and his expression softens. Later, as they return to the office alongside Jorge, who gives them an explicit description of the fight between his girlfriend and his wife, Orlando whispers a question in her ear. She looks down at the floor and nods, and has to fob off Jorge when he comments on her sudden high colour.

A cloud of rose fragrance drifts behind Mercedes as she leaves her flat, wearing a new silk skirt that kisses her thighs. When she is outside, shivering in the night air, she considers going back to change. It is the sexiest item of clothing she has ever purchased but, on recollection of his face in the café earlier when she was late, she keeps walking to the restaurant. The head waiter leads her to a table in the corner. Orlando's eyes seem to strip off her clothes and it strikes her that she would feel sexy in a tent in his company. When she takes her seat, her body leans over the table and he inspects her black lace top; one of her favourites, it skims her bust, moulds to her body and reveals how her trim midriff tapers into her waist. The skin tightens in the crevice of her bosom at the look in his eyes and she lifts her hand to cover it, but his appreciation pleases her and so she fools with her necklace instead. When he stops staring at her breasts and their eyes meet, his grin shows her he has read her mind.

Wine breathes in the decanter, impressing her when she recognises the name on the label of the bottle by its side; it is a favourite of Juanita's dad and costs at least half of her weekly wage. He buys it at a special bodega and her friend says she knows a boyfriend is a success with her father when that wine appears. A single rose lies across her plate. Her heart performs a cartwheel at the sight of the gesture and she brushes her finger over the petals while Orlando and the waiter discuss the own-goal of the football player who sits at a nearby table. There is no room in her stomach for food, even though it has been hours since she ate anything, and she asks Orlando to choose for her. As they sip the wine, they hold a polite conversation until she becomes uncomfortable. When their food arrives, she pushes it around the plate with her fork. Meanwhile she drums up the courage to broach the taboo subject.

'I need to explain about the other night.'

He cuts her off, shaking his head. 'Don't bother. You weren't ready and I shouldn't have tried to push. Forget it.'

'You don't understand…'

'I didn't stop when you told me to. It wasn't fair to you.'

She longs to touch his hand but he is too far away. He seems to look inside her head and moves his chair close so that his breath warms her cheek; it sends her heart into palpitations. When he speaks, his voice croaks.

'Please forgive me.'

Food passes her lips but she doesn't taste a morsel and, when he suggests that they skip dessert and go to somewhere more private, she struggles to answer. His arm around her waist takes her wobbly weight and when he tucks a curl behind her ear she teeters into his body. She giggles and blames the effects of the wine but all the sounds around her melt away as his fingers brush her earlobe. When they move to caress her cheek, her breath stops, and his eyes lock with hers as his hand cups her chin and tilts her face to his. Soft lips meet with hers, she sighs, and the world stops turning. It starts again with a wallop when she tastes his tongue and her mouth opens of its own accord as he strokes and probes. The cradle of his hands around her face vanishes, he finds the bare skin of her waist and she melts with a groan. Some youngsters jeer and one sings a childhood tune about kissing in a tree and love; she remembers that song from her own adolescence and joins in with the chorus. The teenagers cheer and dance until Orlando takes a step in their direction and they scatter. The smallest one halts at the corner to wave before he disappears after the others, Orlando laughs as he opens his arms for her. Within his secure circle, she lays an ear against his chest and listens to the beat. It speeds and she feels his body stir.

'Come home with me.'

The doubts have disappeared but the consent inside her head comes out as a whisper. He beams at her answer and his hand takes possession of hers, the connection almost scorching her skin as he leads her on a journey she barely notices. It may be a few hundred metres or more. However far, the distance is too great and the minutes too long, yet it is neither far enough nor long enough and soon he fumbles with some keys and Mercedes almost swoons with the comprehension that things are beyond a point of stoppage. There is an exclamation of triumph as the door opens against his weight. He pulls Mercedes into a recess and presses her against the wall. The length of his body flattens along hers and when he pulls back, her lips feel swollen and her chin sore where his stubble has marked her face. She wants more and tempts him back. His hand makes snakelike movements as it explores new territory. He finds a path beneath her top, fondling the naked flesh until she pushes him away so that she can breathe. Despair dawns in his face and he slumps against the wall by her side, but she touches her mouth to his ear and his sorrow evaporates.

'We must go somewhere private. Which one is your flat?'

It would be easy for Mercedes to fall in love with the delight that spreads across his face. The pounding in her chest has nothing to do with the climb when they arrive at a flat entrance identified with a brass '6'. The security light has timed out and she gives silent thanks that no one can see her as she waits for him to open the door; her bra is exposed and the zip is undone at the back of her skirt so that it has slipped down onto her hips. A mirror faces them when they enter the flat and her hand automatically lifts to tame her hair, the task cut short when his arms scoop her up and carry her through to his bedroom.

As though handling a precious item, he lowers her onto the mattress and keeps her wrapped in his arms as he claims the place at her side. There is a moment when she could stop him; instead, she tries to meld his body to hers. His weight, as it moves on top of her, is a welcome load, but he notices that he is crushing her so he shifts onto one side. Her arms now free, she opens each button of his shirt, one at a time, until she arrives at those trapped below his trouser belt. His gasp makes her pause briefly to catch her breath before she pulls to release the buckle from its fastening. The muscles in his abdomen harden and, although he groans as though in pain, he presses her hand lower and she continues her manipulation until the clasp parts. When her fingers slip inside the waistband, he breathes in and tightens his belly, allowing her more room to explore. The edge of her nail catches on one of the downy hairs and her hand rests as she mumbles an apology, but the

110

urgency in his voice encourages her to continue. Then, his hand imprisons hers.

'Wait.'

An eternity goes by after she obeys the command, his fingers on hers, then he shudders and his body relaxes. Even the muscles in her face remain rigid during her vigil, but he surprises her and levers her onto her back. There isn't a part of her body that he doesn't stroke: her face, her neck and her body with a slowness that tantalizes her. Finally, his hand reaches her breast, only for a second and then it's gone; the next time she is aware of his fingers, they fiddle with the hook of her bra and he achieves his goal, her bosom springing loose of its bindings. Saturated with the desire to feel his touch on her breast she moves a hand, but he finds the way to her nipple without help and ignites a gush low in her pelvis. Her hips tilt upwards but his hips block the way with a tell-tale hardness straining to escape from his trousers. Once more he separates from her as he presses his palms into the bed and lifts his torso, seeking the answer in her eyes to his unspoken query. Mercedes nods, her thighs already parting to receive him and, in that moment, her heart ceases to remain hers alone.

Chapter 12

The fur makes her sweat and she kicks the blanket away with her foot; a cry of pain jolts her awake. The unfamiliar sight that meets her eyes holds her rigid and she does not dare breathe while the man at her side grunts and rolls to the other side of the bed. When his snoring resumes, she stares at the ceiling as the memories of the previous night chase away all other thought. Her mouth begins to ache with smiling and she eases onto her side and inspects the downy hair that covers his shoulder blades; the temptation is too strong and she stretches her hand towards the feathery surface. It hovers so that her palm doesn't disturb his flesh and her heart turns as hairs tickle the inner surface of her hand. Desire erupts deep inside of her pelvis, her muscles tighten, she would love to bring him back to consciousness but exercises restraint. It is like a hunger that can't be appeased and she knows that if he wakes and pulls her into his arms, she will welcome him despite the rawness between her legs. Under cover of the sheet, she moves her fingers to touch the swollen area; it is a different sensation from the one cemented in her memory following José's brutal assault. Something melts inside of her as she watches Orlando sleep; he will never know the demons he has exorcised.

Pressure on her bladder warns that she must vacate the temporary paradise but she shelters a little longer next to the human warmth and looks around the room, overlooked in the urgency of the night. Not one item of clutter is in sight, the décor is austere with a neutral colour and bland furnishings. A collection of sporting trophies on two shelves and a poster of the national football team break up the monotony; Orlando lives in the archetype of a bachelor pad. While she slept, he picked up her clothes from the floor and they are now folded and stacked in a neat pile on top of the chair in the corner. A section of the living area is on view and she glimpses the armrest of a chocolate-coloured settee and the motionless blade of a ceiling fan. Elevating onto her elbow to look further, Mercedes dives back under the sheet as she realises that the window gives the neighbours opposite a full view of the bed. Crouching out of sight, she slithers out from under the covers and scurries to the pulley; the shutter falls with a clamour that makes Orlando fidget, but his dreams don't release him yet.

The discomfort can't be ignored any longer and she tiptoes out of the room to begin her search for the bathroom. As she passes through the living room, she notices a collection of photos in a cluster on top of a travel-chest, something to look at when she returns. An inner voice urges her to explore the contents of the bathroom cupboard but she stops herself and instead picks up the bar of soap in the shower tray, holding it under her nose. Its fragrance is Orlando and she nearly steals it to keep a piece of him at home, then she comes to her senses and returns it to its proper place.

The shape of the mound in the bed is unchanged and she knows that she will toss and turn if she joins him, so she unhooks his t-shirt from the door. It comes to her knees and, clad in her makeshift nightdress, she settles down on the settee. Photos cover the coffee table near her knees and she lifts the smallest frame in the group to inspect it in more detail. A baby sits unaided on a knitted white blanket and shows two new teeth as he smiles up at a woman who obviously adores him. The photograph doesn't reveal her face but there is a toy in her hand and joy radiates from the image. She guesses that the child is Orlando, the woman his mother. A different still captures the same woman, younger and holding a bouquet of flowers in one hand with the other trapped beneath the arm of a young man at her side; neither of them smiles as though the day is the happiest in their lives. A photographer has caught the same couple, a decade older at least, as they pose in a public garden. She smiles with her mouth but her eyes are those of a beaten animal and the sullen man's fingers grip her upper arm. Seven children of different ages stand at either side of them and eventually she makes out Orlando; he rests against his mother's knee and her arm drapes over his shoulders, pulling him to her leg. She has noticed his voice soften when he speaks of her and the tenderness between them shows in that gesture.

One photograph is at the back, excluded from the intimate family ones, in which a group of five young men pose at the front of a stone *finca*; some tools nestled at the corner of the shot indicate that it may be a farmhouse. Each man has his arms draped over the shoulders of his neighbour and they stand in a semi-circle, the tallest of the men at the centre. Her eyes don't linger there; she is interested in the man at one end of the group, the man who she believes is Orlando's father. In this exposure he looks to be the youngest, a teenager of sixteen or so, and although his jaw shape is the same as his son's, his father's features are coarse and less appealing. He does not look at the photographer; instead, he stares with awe at the soldier in the middle. Uniforms are an enigma for her and she does not recognise the service or his rank, but on the right side of his collar is a pin bearing an emblem she has seen recently: a dove with its wings spread. Its appearance here strikes her as one of those strange co-incidences and she returns the photo to its place but something niggles her about the face of a youngster at the other end of the bunch, and she takes a second look. She has seen a more recent version of that face and waits for inspiration but is unable to drag up the elusive memory.

Everything flies out of her mind when the mattress squelches and alerts her that Orlando has emerged from his sleep. She puts the photo back on the table and returns to his bed with a flame in her belly.

The breeze wakes her as it kisses her naked leg and she reaches blindly to grasp the edge of the sheet; it fills like a balloon and floats over her head. She tries to drift off again but something prods her in the back, impossible to ignore, and she slaps it away. It refuses to move and she turns over, opens her eyes, and comes face-to-face with Orlando.

'Finally. I've been waiting.'

'What's the time?'

He ignores the question, gathers her into his arms and makes her laugh as he nuzzles her neck. Touched with a pang of regret, she pushes him away.

'Leave off. You've had your lot.'

A chuckle betrays his hurt expression and she fights off his hands as she swings her feet over the side of the bed. The sheet becomes a toga that wraps around her body and covers from her breasts to her knees; the blind is up but she is ready for onlookers this time. Her watch is on the bedside table, alongside the other jewellery that she removed when she realised she was here for the night. She is still drowsy when she glances at the display; the realisation is a shock and words that she rarely uses stream from her mouth as she bolts towards the bathroom. Orlando's laughter reverberates along the corridor as she grabs her clothes en route. At the bathroom door, the billowing train falls to the floor like a discarded bridal veil and, in less than five minutes, she returns dressed in her clothes of the previous night. Her cardigan, buttoned to her neck, disguises the low cut of the top and she can't do any more to make it appropriate for a daytime meeting. The black coffee, pressed on her by Orlando who states that she must have a hot drink at least, scalds her tongue and she sips while trying to repair last night's make up.

'That'll have to do.'

When she turns to say goodbye at the door, it is with sadness at the realisation that their first night has disappeared forever. He tightens his embrace and whispers against her lips.

'Tonight?'

The sensation surges in her pelvis once again and she nods an answer against his chest. Her legs, though weakened by the thought, carry her through the door. She does not dare look back; his face has the power to turn her around.

Groups of young mothers, congregated for their morning catch-up over coffee, occupy most of the outside tables but a table for two becomes free near the door. She dashes to claim it and, ten minutes ahead of schedule, orders an orange juice and unfolds the newspaper. The headlines suggest the right wing leader will announce the party election manifesto and she reads a few paragraphs of the article until a shadow darkens the paper. The smile of welcome freezes midway as a giant glares down at her. He whispers, but every word is clear.

'Consider this your warning. The next time you won't be so lucky. No more baby questions, or else.'

His vehemence stuns her and she squeezes her eyes to shut out the vision, then her anger ignites. About to spit a response, her eyelids shoot open but he has vanished, without a sound, in the same manner that he arrived. The coins she throws down rattle over the edge of the table and fall onto the stone pavement; some roll in her direction as she sprints after him.

At the junction, she halts; he has disappeared and she kicks out at a lamppost, frustrated that, although his intimidation only lasted a moment, it was enough to rattle her. The threat confirms her research into the lost children worries someone and the story may be more sinister than she first realised.

With a full heart, she resumes her seat in the bar and withdraws the photo from her bag. 'I'm getting closer.' She kisses it, returns it to safety and waits, without hope, for Carmen.

An hour after the arranged time, she gives up and returns to the office. Concerned for the safety of the woman – threats from men like that giant could give someone of *her* age a heart attack – she craves a message, but Juanita shakes her head. She nibbles her fingernail to the quick as she considers how to proceed. Her spirits sink when she realises it is time to revisit the Salvador Clinic.

Chapter 13

To her left, certificates embossed with gold decorate the wall in black gloss frames alongside many photographs of well-known individuals shaking the hand of the man who sits opposite. The size and design of the ornate desk attests the position of power that its user holds in the organisation. The collar and lapel of his white coat both show signs of wear; a stethoscope drapes across the back of his neck and dangles along the sides of his charcoal tie. The man squints through round glass circles, connected by a thin piece of gold and perched halfway down the slope of his nose. She expects them to slide off the bulbous end at any minute. It doesn't surprise her that she failed to recognise him in the photograph at Orlando's place; in that year, the youth was gaunt. His cheekbones had long since disappeared when she first encountered him ten years ago and today, his dark hair is gone and a bare round patch tops his head. The colour must have faded at the same time that the lines in his face started to embed roots. His girth is twice what it was on the day he barked orders at the sister who looked after Mercedes while she was in labour.

She fights to control her irritation as the man ignores her and reads a paper on top of the folder on his desk; it's as though she doesn't exist. Her rounded tummy presses onto her bladder, the sharp edge of the prosthesis destroying any jot of comfort, and Mercedes wiggles to one side in her seat as she seeks a better position. Bushy eyebrows rise at the sound of her activity and his tongue clicks as though annoyed. Maybe he believes she should remain motionless until he gives her permission to move. It will destroy her plans if he discovers her disguise at this stage, so she lowers her lids to hide her amusement.

A shelf behind the doctor's desk claims her attention as her eyes wander in search of a diversion while she waits. Yet more photos of the man compete for a place on show; some hang at the edge of the precipice and appear ready to tumble at the slightest encouragement. The tiny woman who features in a few of the photos must be his wife. Two young men and three girls, in various stages of development, pose at her sides and it seems that all of them have inherited their mother's slight build and, sadly, their father's nose. Outnumbering the family stills are more images of the doctor with local celebrities; he isn't shy about showing off his influence and connections. Bored with the repetitive subject matter, her eyes flit over them and return to a photo that sets off a queasy bubbling inside as she recognises the three men in the image. A young version of the doctor stands in front of a country house arm-in-arm with another young man who has matured into a local political heavyweight. The man on the opposite end of the group makes her heart race and nausea build.

For several weeks, she has shared the bed of that man's son. The face of Orlando's father has some attractive features, such as the dark eyes of his son. Although the shape is similar, his father's eyes appear lifeless, without the warmth of his offspring. His pursed mouth destroys any beauty as he poses for the camera and his attempt to smile appears to have taken an unusual amount of effort. The connection between the three men in the image puzzles her and she tries to remember the detail of the photo at Orlando's flat. She has yet to find a tactful way to ask Orlando about the relationship but this evidence cements her determination to tackle the subject when they meet later that night.

The doctor still has his head down and, fed up with the wait, she opens her mouth to speak. At the same time, he closes his folder and, without apology, regards her with a half-hearted smile. After he removes the cover of his pen and places the nib on the paper, he speaks.

'What can I do for you, my dear?'

The undertone to his words belittles her; *the man is a chauvinist, there is no question about that*. The impression of his character threatens to erase the demure smile she practised for hours in front of a mirror to get right. Her eyes drop to her hand that rests on top of the fake bump and she provides some bait, ensuring that he sees her touch the naked ring finger. Caught by the hook, his mouth twitches and he pretends to adopt a sympathetic expression but not before she spots his interest. His pen makes some marks on the paper, which he underlines with two bold lines.

'No one will talk to me. My mother won't look at me. They were mad enough when they found out and, now that I want to keep my baby, they have sent me here to Madrid.' Her practice ensures the delivery is pitch-perfect. 'I'm all alone.'

Podgy fingers interlink across his chest as he gives her his attention and she continues to spin her fairy tale. She constructed it to tantalize.

'I need to register at a clinic to have my baby; he's nearly ready I think.' Mercedes weaves into her tale a move to the city and her solitary state and the doctor is unable to mask his scrutiny. His eyes would frighten her if the story were true. There is a vulture-like quality in his attempt at compassion.

'Are you sure that is what you want for your child? To be an outcast, without a proper family. We could help to find a loving home for him. To find parents who can afford to give him the best of everything.'

Now she has caught his interest, she begins to reel him in and allows him to witness her performance of indecision. She makes the first blow with a comment about the terrible rumours going around about safety of the clinic.

The brandy fumes force her to recoil when he leans forward over the desk; there must have been a good measure in his morning coffee. 'Malicious people talk, what have you heard?'

Her fingers twist the handkerchief in her hand into a coil and it is ready to spring free as she times it so her next words deliver their impact. The man's eyes flash when she suggests that people say they allow babies to die. With the first inkling of doubt in his expression, he searches her face, then leans back with his hands behind his head.

'Evil gossip! Would we be allowed to stay open if my clinic wasn't safe?'

Her damp palm sticks to the leather side of her bag so that it pops when she releases it to move her hand near the front pocket. Her fingers hover but don't go further; it isn't the moment to show her final card. Enunciating each word, she runs her palm over her tummy and talks about her fears for the baby. 'Isn't this what any mother wants, to do the best for her child?'

Time is limited and soon he will catch her out; the man is not stupid and an examination will uncover the truth of her costume. Her eyes stay away from the couch, covered with its paper sheet, against the wall beside his desk; it waits for her body.

'What will happen when I come in to have my baby? Will you deliver it? Do the same nurses work with you all of the time? What are their names?'

The pounding in her chest beats with the tick of the clock and she tries to be patient. One name is all she needs but he is on guard and takes his time to answer. Hope fades. An open drawer of the filing cabinet may hold answers, but her brain reels as she thinks of ways to get him out of the room so she can look inside. A female dragon was guarding the outside desk when she arrived and an idea grows of a way to get rid of both of them at the same time. Suddenly he gives her a gift, the names of two nurses who have worked with him for the last thirty years; women of the church, who better to trust, he says. While he goes on about their expertise, she sits on her hand to prevent a punch in the air as she recognises a name from her past. The triumph is short-lived and his eyes burn with suspicion.

'You recognise those names. Why?'

One glance at those files will be enough and, inspired, she clutches the belly with a groan. She observes his reaction underneath her eyelashes as she prays he will give her the moment she needs. Nothing happens and she begins to doubt the success of her ploy, planning an escape instead. Medical instinct takes over as his fingers feel for her pulse and, before he has time to make an assessment, she says that she must lie down, asking for a glass of water. He levers his bulk out of his chair and makes his way towards the door as he points to the couch.

'There. I'll go for a monitor and ask the receptionist to get you a drink.'

There is no time to wait for the door to close and she rushes to the cabinet. Her eyes fly over the labels on the tabs; the dragon maintains an efficient filing system that makes her task simple. Meaningless medical terms mingle with subjects such as receipts and payments but all are in alphabetical order. Her eyes bounce over the coloured steps until they arrive at a familiar name, the orphanage in Burgos. The drawer comes close to amputating her fingers as a hand reaches around her body and slams it shut. Fury splutters in her ear and she withdraws her trump card, a faded photo that she holds for him to view as she turns to face him. His cheeks turn the colour of her favourite berry jam.

'Who are you? Why are you here?'

The venom pushes her back and she is not convinced he will stop the momentum of his fist, but it tumbles when it is a breath away from her face. She doesn't falter and the image remains on display.

'This picture is of a baby born here ten years ago. You told me that my baby was dead, but that wasn't the truth, was it? This isn't my baby, is it?' The room is too small to contain the volume of her accusations. 'Where is my child? What did you do with my son?'

Doctor Ramón doesn't wait for the end of her accusations, hurrying outside to shout at the receptionist; she is on the phone to security as Mercedes pushes through them and dashes towards the stairs. No doubt they will guess that she will head for the nearest exit so she climbs to the next level and takes the elevator to the top floor. The doors open and she follows the sign to the restroom. Inside a toilet cubicle, she releases the straps that held the bulge against her stomach; the indentations on her skin are the only signs that remain of her pseudo pregnancy. A silk scarf hides her hair and she pops out the coloured contact lenses. Her eyes are red and gritty but she ignores the sting as she lines the rims of her lids with black; she finishes off the look with red lips and a pair of glasses. The mirror reflects an older, more sophisticated woman that she hopes will take her past anyone looking for a young pregnant girl. A plastic shopping bag contains the pseudo bump instead of the suit jacket on her back and she holds her breath and steps into the corridor. The lift bell sounds, the door opens and she prepares to run as two men in uniform step out and survey the area. One speaks into a walkie-talkie as she presses the button for the ground floor.

A mechanical voice asks, 'Have you found her?'

'No. We'll check outside.'

'Make sure Reception know she isn't to be let back in. Doctor Ramón says she's crazy…'

The doors cut off the remainder of the conversation and she steels herself to walk through the main reception area; she hopes they expect her to use a less visible exit. Her hand protects the dictation machine in her jacket pocket, in case she has to run, but the only thing that follows her is the lens of a security camera, which does a slow sweep in its regular inspection. Praying that the disguise is adequate, Mercedes dips her head and joins a family as they cross the threshold. She proceeds to the bus stop, getting on the first vehicle that arrives; it doesn't matter where it is headed. She claims a seat at the back and as she lowers into it she catches sight of a security guard as he emerges from the building. His head swivels and shakes as he speaks into a radio and goes back into the hospital. Eyes closed, she rests her head back and plans how to get hold of those files.

Chapter 14

Someone slides an arm into the crook of Mercedes' elbow and makes her start. When she turns around, ready to let rip, it is her best friend who has crept up on her.

'You're jumpy.'

The expectation of arrest at any instant has been with her for days and she squeezes her friend's arm, blaming a horror film the night before. Mirroring Juanita's stride, they walk as one as they leave the building. They haven't spent much time together since the explosion in her relationship with Orlando and she tries to assuage her guilt with a suggestion that they go to her flat to make paella.

'I'll make it like Mama used to when my family visited my aunt's holiday home on the coast.'

'Sounds good. Do you need any ingredients?'

'We'll pick up some veg and make do; after all, it's a peasant dish. How was your date?'

Her laughter grows until her stomach aches at Juani's descriptions of the night. The relentless campaign of her friend's mother had worn her down so that she finally agreed to meet the good catch, a friend's son with a good job and lots of money. Juanita had been dreading the evening all week.

'He'll be another waste of time.'

Apparently, it went as expected and one disaster followed another during the meal at a famous restaurant, so it surprises her that they have a second date planned for tomorrow night.

When she tries to hide her reaction, Juanita spots it and slaps her arm.

'Stop it. It's a date, that's all. Enough about me. What about you and lover boy?'

Even the sound of his name during a conversation with her friend raises her temperature and she avoids Juanita's eyes as she admits she has seen him most nights this week. It isn't quite a lie; the truth is she has slept every night at his place during the past three weeks and even has her own cupboard space in his wardrobe. In a short time, he has become the second most important person in her life (her baby will always hold the first place) but she suffered a meltdown yesterday. For some unknown reason, words spilled out of her mouth of the need for breathing space; where they came from, she has no idea and, if she could, she would gladly rephrase the suggestion. Of course, his kiss was lacklustre when she left his flat this morning.

Her friend is the only person who is privy to their relationship; Mercedes isn't ready for the next step of sharing it with their colleagues. This morning, they walked into the building with an invisible wall separating them and he failed to look back at her as he stepped into the lift. An abnormal ache in her chest has plagued Mercedes all morning but she isn't ready to confide her disquiet about their future, and fortunately Juanita changes the subject.

'That baby article you wrote, did it really happen?'

'That the woman's baby was taken away because she was single? Sadly, yes.'

'You're amazing! Wherever did you find her? You made me cry when I read her story.'

'Through a contact, Señora Ferrer, the woman I met with in Burgos; the one I told you about, from the orphanage.' A touch of irritation flares as she remembers the meeting with her editor the previous day. 'Jorge was fuming because the director of the orphanage telephoned him in a huff and threatened the paper with police and lawyers and all that. Now, he's after my blood.' Too late, she remembers her vow to keep her problems to herself, and now Juanita has a worried expression on her face so she tries to alleviate her concerns. 'Don't worry; Jorge has to support me on this one, he approved the article.'

'Please be careful, Mercedes. Bad things happen to journalists who upset the wrong people.'

She attempts a show of nonchalance but Mercedes is aware of the truth behind her friend's words. Her joke is terrible and makes Juanita groan but succeeds in lightening the gloom. Arms linked, they wander and chat as they look for a market stall that has not dismantled for the day, where they select fresh vegetables to add to the rice and leftover meat. Still engrossed in their chinwag when they arrive outside the apartment block, her friend holds the shopping while Mercedes roots in her handbag for the keys.

As the key releases the door and she reaches for one of the carriers, she freezes. Two young men across the road attract her attention and she realises they've been in the same place every time she's come by for a change of clothing on her way to Orlando's. She thought they were tourists, definitely not Madrilenos with fair hair and towering height, lost in the maze of Madrid's alleys. Today they make her uncomfortable. Each displays biceps with tone that is only possible to achieve through hours in a gymnasium, but neither looks to be out of his teens. They stare at her face, and one nods to the other as she steps through the open door. She gestures to Juanita to be quick, breathing a sigh as the lock engages behind them.

'What's up with you?'

She begins to climb the stairs as she considers her response but her friend persists and she gives in. 'Those guys across the road, they give me the heebie-jeebies.'

When she catches up with Mercedes in the flat, Juanita is gasping and unable to speak; she flops down on the settee and closes her eyes. Mercedes is at the side of the window looking down onto the street.

'Lock it, will you?' She notices the colour of her friend's cheeks and brings her a glass of water. 'Sorry.'

'You. Are. Crazy.'

'Wait until your breathing is normal before you moan.'

Satisfied that Juanita won't collapse, she goes into the kitchen and starts the preparation for their lunch. The telephone rings and, when she picks it up, Orlando speaks and her legs give way so that she has to grab onto the worktop. In the background, Juanita makes smooching sounds when she hears Mercedes say his name. Covering the mouthpiece to hide her laughter, she sticks out her tongue and faces the opposite direction. After they each ask how the other is, there is silence. Frustration in his voice indicates that he wants to get beyond monosyllabic replies, but neither can offer the words of apology and when he hangs up, she bangs down the handset. Arms wrap around her from behind and she allows her head to fall onto Juanita's shoulder for a second; then she straightens her spine and tries to laugh it off.

'Men. Come on, let's get this meal on the go.'

Side-by-side, they return to work in the kitchen and before long the pan of rice mixture bubbles over the gas flame. Glasses full, Mercedes pours the remainder of the bottle of white wine into the paella, her special ingredient she calls it. While they wait a final 10 minutes for the rice to soak up the remaining liquid, they sit with their bare soles facing each other across the top of the coffee table. The doorbell sounds and Mercedes jumps up, catching the newly opened bottle with her foot. It hits the floor and explodes in a fountain of shards and fermented fluid, a river building in one of the grouted channels. Tucked around her waist is a tea towel, her makeshift apron, which she throws down onto the mess before choosing a safe detour around the danger.

'Just a minute.'

One hand fiddles with the lock while the other wrings wine from her skirt. She is already turning back to the room as she pulls open the door.

'Hello, Ros—'

The greeting breaks off as she throws her weight against the door, but one of the men wedges his toe inside so the mechanism can't engage. Every ounce of her strength keeps the door in place and she waves her hands and shouts to Juanita to get away. Her friend springs up and mentions the police as she sprints towards the telephone. Mercedes manages the raspy start of a scream when a sweaty palm clamps over her mouth and her voice becomes impotent.

'Don't scream. We don't want to hurt you.'

We! She rolls her eyes to the side, trying to locate her friend but she is out of her sight. A man imprisons Mercedes, one arm locked around her waist while the other hand keeps pressure on her mouth. The face of her attacker is not detectable;, but opposite stands one of the two men from the street. His face is not that of a villain. He wears a worried expression and, when he meets the fury of her eyes, he smiles apologetically.

'Get off of her!'

A blurred being streaks across the room and, unable to shake off her straightjacket, Mercedes observes the shadow of something crash down close to the young man's head. He moves out of its trajectory just in time and turns to face her friend with open palms.

'Stop. We come in peace.'

The loosening of her captor's grip enables Mercedes to bend her knee and prepare for a kick at his scrotum. Her foot is ready to go when he speaks.

'If I release, will you keep quiet for a minute and let me explain?'

On standby, in case it is a trick, she inclines her head and his fingers ease their pressure on her lips. She inhales and prepares to scream but, at that moment, she realises that their attackers are boys – younger than she first thought – resembling frightened children rather than hardened criminals. There is no vicious intent in either face and she relents, giving him the opportunity to speak. His arm keeps her close as he half-carries her over to the sofa; his partner-in-crime escorts Juanita and indicates that she should sit at her friend's side. When the boys step back, the women huddle together, locking their fingers while their legs quiver in rhythmic harmony and they wait for their assailants to drag two kitchen chairs across the tiles. Juanita's escort doesn't sit down straight away but says something to Mercedes. His words don't make any sense until he mimes the action of sweeping the floor, then she understands that he wants something to clean up the broken glass. *Abnormal behaviour for a criminal*, she thinks, and her heart stops its attempts to burst out of her chest. His trainers were navy a long time ago, now they are a blotchy grey; a bizarre headline about killers in trainers flits through her mind but neither boy looks capable of killing an insect. Mercedes tries to summon a smile for Juanita.

'Please don't be afraid. We aren't here to hurt you.'

The accent is foreign and he clearly struggles with the rolling sound of the double 'r'. Curiosity takes over, and she raises her eyes from her knees, runs them up his jean-clad legs to the denim shirt and finally to his face; the skin of his forehead crumples as he looks at her with concern. His eyes appear almost green against his olive-toned complexion, and topping it all is a mop of blonde curly hair with dark roots that could do with a trim. He isn't unlike the boys she sees on the pavements of Madrid, still awkward in their new adult bodies. During the inspection, the boy's teeth play with his bottom lip and his white knuckled fingers curl over the joints of his knees. In clumpy sentences, he attempts to deliver an explanation.

'I'm sorry. We didn't understand how frightened you would be. I'm Robby and this is my friend, Sam.'

Sam recognises his name and grins at her from his post on the side-line, where he sits in one of her kitchen chairs. She wants to demand that he puts it back in its rightful place but he utters something that sounds like '*hola*', the Spanish word for 'hello', and his hands tremble, so she holds onto the rebuke.

'We're American, from the States.'

'I know where Americans come from.'

'Of course. Sorry.'

'And don't keep apologising. It won't make this better. Jumping on women. Do they teach that in your country?'

'Yeah. No. Sorry.'

Juanita's shoulders are a plank of wood beneath her arm and Mercedes holds her tongue, rather than upset the current truce.

'We're from the mid-west, a little town in Ohio.'

He repeats the name twice but she can't pronounce it and has no idea of where the place is. The sound at the end elongates into a nasal twang so his accent sounds different to the few American visitors she has met in Madrid.

'*Oeeo.*'

'Yes, it's a state in the middle of the country. Like *Castilla y Leon* in Spain.'

At last, he says a name she recognises and she motions for

him to continue. Before he speaks to her, he says something to Sam who nods and points his thumb up.

'He can't speak much Spanish.'

Enough is enough; she doesn't care whether the boy can speak her language or not, that is no excuse for such behaviour. Leaping to her feet, she stabs her finger at Robby's face, coming to a halt just short of his nose.

'What the hell do you want? Moreover, why force yourself into my flat? How did you get in downstairs?' As if water released from a dam, the questions pour out, even though the only person in the room wearing a blank face is Juanita. Once her tirade runs out of steam, she draws a breath and repeats the questions slowly, striving for calm as she enunciates each word. Both boys hold their palms up and shrug their shoulders and, on the third effort, she speaks as slowly as she can. When her words make sense, Robby interrupts and attempts to explain.

'We didn't break in. I could see your flat from the outside, but didn't know which number it was and I pressed all the buttons until someone let us in. Once we got inside, we figured out which floor you live on. Yours was the first door we tried.'

The explanation sets her off into another tirade about irresponsibility and terrifying women; their faces redden under the attack. Pulling at the hem of her skirt, Juanita whispers a warning to take care but, now that she has begun, Mercedes can't hold back. The boys, no longer ogres, shrink, looking sheepish with their heads drooped as Robby mutters apologies into his chest.

'We didn't think. I just wanted to speak with you, to find out what you know.'

Arms across her chest, she is a fighter facing her opponent. Out of the corner of her eye she sees Juanita perch on the edge of the sofa as though ready to take flight at any second.

'It's simple, if you let me explain. We were hiking through

the Pyrenees a few days back and stopped in a mountain restaurant. There were some newspapers and I read your article about the single mother who had her baby taken away. We came to look for you here in the city because I think that you can help me.'

'Go on.'

'My mother, actually she was my adoptive mother, tried to tell me about something during her last few days, before she passed away. Some of it was gibberish; there was talk of an angel in Spain who sold me to her. I thought that it was the morphine but afterwards, when it was over and she'd gone, Dad admitted it wasn't all fantasy. Apparently, she had been desperate for a child and, by the time they realised it wasn't going to happen, the legal agencies informed her she was too old to adopt. A friend from their church couldn't stand to watch her agony and offered to put my parents in touch with someone who could help.'

Mercedes drops onto the sofa beside Juanita with a sudden need for something other than her legs to take her weight. There is a catch in her heart as she listens and understands how young Robby is; he's a boy who has lost his mum twice.

'I found a paper amongst my mother's things when I was looking for my birth certificate, an adoption certificate, anything that could tell me who I really am. This thing looked official, stamped and all that. My Spanish teacher translated it.' There is a pause while Robby is distracted by a memory, and then he smiles. 'I always wondered why my mother insisted on those classes. Maybe she knew that one day I would come to Spain to search for my roots.' Three sets of eyes avoid watching Robby when he covers his face with his hands. He can't stifle his sob and Mercedes reaches forward to stroke his hair but, before she makes contact, Juanita grasps her hand and shakes her head.

'It was a contract. An agreement of silence. Nothing else. Signed by my parents. I don't know who else signed it. Didn't recognise the names. My father refused to tell me. He's been angry since Mom died and gets worse every day. Anyway, he told me to forget it, saying it would only cause trouble if I tried to find out. They were warned to keep the secret and weren't supposed to tell me I wasn't their natural child; Mom shouldn't have said anything. It was a condition of the adoption.'

For the first time since she tried to be a heroine, Juanita speaks to the boy. 'I can understand that a woman who gave her baby away would not want to be discovered later. Maybe she kept it a secret from everyone.'

Her friend's theory makes Mercedes' chest fill until she is unable to breathe, but Robby doesn't notice. He nods and explains that it was more than that. His father was terrified and went on about the consequences. 'But it's like an itch, I have to know more; who I am and who my people are.'

Her own son might say those words one day and, when he describes the places he has searched, she is impressed with, almost proud of, his ingenuity; although young, there isn't much he hasn't thought of. He managed to track down a birth certificate but it was of little use as it turned out to be counterfeit. The longer he spent investigating, the more nervous and withdrawn his father became. Then his father started to disappear for long periods; first for a few days, then for a week or more, until eventually he was hardly at home.

'He didn't want to be implicated in what I was doing.'

Sam's words are incomprehensible but his support and agreement need no translation. The sentiment is clear and their unspoken communications give her some insight into their relationship. This friendship is similar to hers with Juanita and that knowledge tears down the last bit of her resistance to their intrusion into her life. Robby describes his depression as each enquiry led to nothing; he had no room in his head for anything else and, when it was obvious he was going to fail his senior year, the school principal suggested time out.

'My exams have been delayed until next year and I came up with a plan for a grand European trip. I would see different cultures and my teachers thought it would be great for understanding history. Sam insisted on coming with me and my father was so eager to get rid of me that he offered to pay for us both. He didn't come to the airport, but he did give me a full wallet.'

In halting Spanish, Sam manages to complete a sentence. 'I graduated last year and had time before uni. I couldn't let this guy have all the fun, could I?'

'Yeah, but the fun is over now mate. It's time to find out who I really am.'

A loud rumble from one of the boys' stomachs erupts in the silence and Mercedes jumps up with a hand to her forehead.

'I forgot the paella! Come on, Juani, let's get these boys some food.'

Her friend's mouth falls open and Mercedes feels the glares on the back of her head as they leave the room. The minute that they are out of earshot, she demands to know whether Mercedes has completely lost her mind. Her grumbles about the wisdom of supping with thieves last the entire time they spend preparing a platter of *jamón* and bread. When the food is on the table, Mercedes calls the boys through and, although they protest at her kindness, they follow the example of the women and dig into the cooking pan with their forks.

Soon, only the *socarrat* remains, the toasted bits stuck to the pan, which the boys leave until they notice the women scrape it off and eat with relish, commenting that it is the best bit; they follow suit. The women are familiar with a midday meal that lasts for at least an hour but the others shovel the food into their mouths, as though this is their first decent meal in days. Meals at home with her brother are a distant memory but Mercedes observes them and decides that it must be normal for boys of this age.

'That was ace,' Robby says and stands while he starts to collect the plates.

Another expression that baffles her, but she sees in his face that it's a compliment and tries to explain about the rice.

'It's a dish from Valencia, an area along the east coast, and has always been one of my favourites. Traditionally it's cooked over an open fire, but obviously we can't do that here. Sometimes when you walk along the roads in that region after a fiesta, it's possible to see the remains of the cooking fires, especially in the coastal towns where they hold a lot of fiestas!'

Her descriptions of some of the quirks of the fiestas intrigue the boys and they fire questions at her. When she tells them about local people jumping over fires and the deafening sounds of the firecrackers during the daytime *mascletas*, so loud that they rattle windows, Sam raises his eyes in a silent appeal to Robby.

'If we have time, okay, we'll try to hit one. For now, grab some plates.'

They insist that she and Juanita relax while they sort things out. While Sam washes and Robby dries the dishes, they entertain the women with stories of their travels; the Eiffel Tower is a favourite sight thus far. Their tales inspire Mercedes, she would love to travel to other countries. She is lost in the excitement of their adventures when Juanita points to her watch and bursts the bubble.

'We're due back at work.'

As they collect their things, she proposes to Juanita that the boys stay at the flat until she finishes work, but her friend tells her she is stark raving mad and reminds her that, a few hours ago, these boys were intruders. The four unlikely friends travel down in the lift together and Mercedes arranges to meet them at a bar near her office later.

'By that time, I'll have figured out a way that I can help you, Robby.'

He nearly crushes the breath out of her when he hugs her but most of the moisture in her eyes comes from a different pain as she thinks of her own boy.

Chapter 15

Ideas compete for her attention and Mercedes disregards most of them as impractical or impossible. At the end of a sleepless night, the sun comes up and she jumps from her bed, still in a quandary about how she can help Robby. His command of the language is adequate and she has directed him to the official records but she doesn't have much hope for their value in his situation, and fears that he will be chasing a mirage. In the bar last night, she and the boys talked about it for hours until they came up with a plan of action. It saddens her that it is unlikely to give the boy the answers he seeks.

Today she must return her focus to her own investigations; the door is already half open when she remembers she is not alone. Slipping a t-shirt and jogging trousers over her see-through nightie, she picks her way through the clothes, rucksacks and legs strewn across the lounge floor until she reaches the kitchen. At first, her movement is stealth-like, but the two heaps remain immobile, so she bangs the cupboard doors as normal. While she chews her toast, she watches for signs of life but the bodies are immune to the noise of her morning routine. En route to the shower, Mercedes shakes the mound of linen that camouflages Robby; she doesn't stop until a grunting voice assures her they will be ready by the time she leaves for work. The hot water of the shower helps to wash away her muzzy head, a hangover of poor sleep, and while she drip-dries, she debates whether she should tell Juanita she changed her mind and offered them shelter.

Robby intends to spend the morning in the public records office and Sam, the art fanatic, is going to the Prado; Mercedes arranges to meet them outside the museum at 2pm as she leaves them at the bus stop. Already late, a crowd of onlookers obstructs the pavement while watching the antics of a tourist; the stranger has driven his car into a pedestrian area and has not yet discovered how to make his escape.

As she enters the office from the stairwell, Mercedes wishes she could turn back, but there is no way she can avoid Jorge. He stands at the side of her desk looking as though he has eaten bad fish, and taps his finger on the surface as he monitors her approach.

'I'm pleased you finally decided to grace us with your presence.'

A clever retort comes to her lips but she manages to seal them before it escapes, forcing an apologetic smile in its place. He rants while she assumes her position at her desk, but when he receives no argument, he leaves to find someone else to scold. A pile of post has come in overnight and most of it goes into the bin. Amongst the dross, she finds an envelope that breaks up the tedium of daily correspondence.

Carmen asks that you meet her on Friday at midday, inside the café in Retiro Park.

She feels uneasy as she wonders who penned the message for the woman unable to read and write. Nonetheless, the appointment goes into her diary with a note to reschedule the interview with the head of the Homemakers' Organisation; Señora Gomez's flower arrangements will have to wait. Jorge emerges from his office, surveys the room and his eyes skim past her but as she is the only reporter available, he dictates an order.

'Get a statement from the head of this school. We've had a tip-off he is covering up a drug ring operating amongst the kids.'

The initial enthusiasm wanes when she studies the map; the American boys may have a long wait outside the museum as the school is in the suburbs.

Hoards of people on the local train wear community scarfs around their necks in support for their representatives in the fiesta parade that takes place later in the afternoon. She avoids the front carriages where the passengers press against each other in the aisles and instead steps in through the last door. The only vacant seat is next to an elderly priest and she tucks her skirt close so she doesn't intrude on his space. It may not be reverent but relief fills her when he acknowledges her greeting and immediately settles to doze and leaves her to concentrate on her list of questions about the alleged drug ring.

Later, when she catches him reading her words from beneath hooded eyelids, she slams the notebook shut and glares until he closes his eyes. His disapproval hangs around like a rain cloud but she refuses to allow him to intimidate her and reads her novel, ignoring the childhood conditioning. When he stands to disembark, he gives a theatrical sniff and flounces along the carriage to the exit.

The train stops at two more stations before she steps out onto the platform in an unfamiliar suburb. The route to the school weaves through an old section of the town, past shops selling religious artefacts and cafés packed with tourists. Alleys crisscross with more alleys and she begins to feel like Alice in the maze as she consults her map. Something metal on the shelf of a shop display reflects a ray of sunlight into her eyes and temporarily blinds her. A silver trophy is the culprit but it is the item on the shelf above that captures her attention: a brooch, a religious medal imprinted with the symbol of a dove, its wings spread in flight. The last time she saw this emblem hovers at the fringes of her memory but is beyond her recall, the detail an elusive thought that agitates in her mind as she walks the final few metres to her destination.

At the school a procession of children – they look about eight years old – snakes through the main gate and she stands to one side to wait for the end of the line. Two boys are involved in a play-fight that could tip into something more, until a reprimand from the teacher at the rear converts them into angels. When they parade past her, one of the boys pulls a face and she can't hold onto the burst of laughter. The smile is still on her face when she enters the school.

The interview with the head teacher is exacting; the man is an expert at manipulating his answers. When he shows her to the exit, she has less than two pages of notes and not enough information to complete more than a couple of paragraphs. For a few minutes, she remains at the front of the building and stares at the artwork that hangs in the windows, until a mother pushes her out of the way, providing inspiration. A parent may be able to fill in some of the gaps, there must be a mother or two at home who live near the school. She navigates the row of identical houses to the right until she reaches number 26; children's toys litter the tiny area at its front. The woman who answers the door displays a fresh bruise that hides an eye, a baby on one hip, and a toddler that hangs on the other leg. She looks horrified when Mercedes introduces herself as a journalist. The door slams as she speaks and the end of her introduction falls on a plank of wood. While she deliberates whether she can make do with the information she has, a woman carries a half-empty bag of rubbish out of the adjacent house; Mercedes suspects the bag is a sham and, sure enough, the woman stops for a gossip.

'Stranger around here?'

Mercedes nods and keeps quiet. The woman is itching to talk.

'You won't get much out of her. Keeps herself to herself.'

'Hmm.'

'Moved here before them two was born. Her and the gorilla she's married to. Only here two months, and a baby appears out of nowhere.'

'What do you mean?'

With eyes full of glee now she has a captive audience, the woman can't wait to go on.

'Not one of those two hanging on her now. The eldest. He's at school. There's no way that child is theirs, no matter what they say. Flat tummy one day and a baby the next, they must think we're all stupid here. No baby hides that well!'

The woman may be a nasty piece of work but Mercedes could kiss her. The simplicity of her reasoning delivers a solution to one of her puzzles.

'The kid doesn't even look like them.'

A window opens with the crashing sound of metal and a woman's voice yells out into the street.

'Stop talking about me, you witch. I'll give you one if you don't shut your mouth.'

The gossip shoots inside her home, the rubbish bag still in her hand, and her door slams behind. The next time Mercedes sees her, the woman peers through the wrought iron grates that secure her windows.

'And you can push off or I'll get my husband after you.'

Mercedes doesn't wait for a second warning. The dodgy school is already a problem of the past; she is on a mission to locate women who surprised their neighbours with new offspring. The challenge will be to encourage people to betray their neighbours' secrets.

'Damn!'

The dilemma is driving her mad with no obvious solution. Neighbours will not talk about each other, people prefer to keep their silence and there doesn't seem to be a way to tease out the stories of unexpected babies. All the women in the building seem to know of one until she demands facts, then their memories go dim and the details dissipate like cigarette smoke. This morning there is an unusual hush amongst her colleagues and she checks her watch – an hour before she needs to be at the café. Every minute drags in her muddled mind and she tells Jaime she is off to do an interview; maybe the change will help her to find clarity. On the way out, she pauses for a quick word with Juanita, who looks at the clock with a remark about early siestas.

'I'm meeting Carmen so keep your fingers crossed she makes it this time.'

At the door, she twists around and asks Juanita if she wants to go shopping the following day.

'What about Orlando? You two are supposed to be back together.'

'We agreed to have occasional nights to ourselves and I've seen him every evening this week. He's off to see the game tonight with friends and no doubt they'll hit the town later. If we shop during the day, perhaps you could come back to my place and we'll have a girly night, do our nails and things.'

'As long as no strange men turn up!'

'The boys have moved on. I think they're in Italy now.'

'Was Robby disappointed?'

She nods. 'I was too. It's a shame I couldn't do more. Never mind, are you coming or not?'

'I'm skint until payday but I guess there's no harm in looking.'

'I'll meet you at the front of the *centro comercial* at 10 am.

We'll start in Juteco so I can get my make-up. Then we'll hit the clothes.'

'Okay, but remember, me look, no buy!'

She hides her smile until she is outside. Juanita says the same thing every month.

There are homemade pastries in the display cabinet and Mercedes is about to give in to the temptation when Carmen arrives, out of breath, her face masked with a fine sheen. An accident in front of her bus held up the traffic.

'I wasn't sure you would still be here.'

The woman fidgets in a skittish manner; she locks and unlocks the catch on her handbag half a dozen times after choosing the chair with its back to the café. Her eyes flit to every table before they settle back on Mercedes.

'We don't have much time. I need to finish…' her voice trails away as the waiter pauses for their order and she waits until he is out of earshot before she continues. 'It's my husband. His friend says I shouldn't talk to you about personal things.'

'What business is it of his?'

'They don't tell me their secrets. My husband told me I was causing trouble. They watch me all the time. Today I've pretended I have an appointment at the doctor's; my husband hates anything to do with women's problems.'

'Trouble for who? Why are they worried? It doesn't make sense.'

Carmen stutters incoherent words as her eyes dart around the café. Mercedes' eyes follow her lead, she scolds herself and returns her gaze to her companion; it is broad daylight and the biggest threat comes from the fleas on a stray dog hunting for scraps under the tables. Carmen starts her tale as though someone will amputate her tongue at any minute, the words running into each other.

'Several months after my niece died, her mother received a note from one of the trainee nurses at the clinic. It came with a pile of post, I thought that it was a condolence letter and my friend read the first couple of sentences to check before we allowed them to see it. The first side of the page was about God's side and sympathy; it was too soon and I couldn't listen to anymore, so it went into the box for later. If I had let her read the rest, then maybe...' Her voice falters and the furrows at the sides of her mouth deepen. 'When I went through my sister's things after she'd passed on, I found it. I'm certain she never knew what it said. If she did, she wouldn't have given up.'

Her pleated hands unfold the correspondence and Carmen explains that it contains a revelation. They discovered it when her daughter read it to the end as she helped her mother decide which documents needed to be kept. It turned out to be a letter of confession that the young novice had written; she wanted to give Carmen's sister some consolation after the loss of her daughter.

'She wrote that she hoped it would comfort my sister to know that he lives. When I first heard those words, I thought she meant that the spirit of God lives, but Marga pointed out she had written 'he' as though he was human, not the Almighty. The capital in that one letter changes the meaning of the word, you see.'

The women grasp hands as Carmen's face lights up with excitement. The hope is infectious.

'Her child is alive.' For an older woman, Carmen has a strong grip. 'He's out there, that's what she tried to let us know.'

During the lectures in her early days at university, the professors explained that the basis of news investigation begins with fundamental questions, so Mercedes controls her eagerness. She must handle this new information in a balanced manner and find out the answers to who, when, what, where, how and why. Her spare hand controls the twitch in her leg and she tries to curb the flare of hope at the chance of unravelling the truth, but she can't ignore the links with her own story. It comforts her that others believe their child lives and this may turn out to be proof.

Cool fingers tighten on her hand and interrupt her musings. 'You'll help find him, won't you? I just want to know he is safe.'

'Have you told the police?'

The woman's body deflates, her opinion evident in her face, and Mercedes understands. In the past, her own accusations were ignored and she was treated as if she was a crazy bereaved mother. She racks her brain but, for the moment, can't think of another official avenue. Carmen's head and shoulders disappear into her shopper – a tattered wheelie bag that has seen better days – there is a muffled cry of triumph, and she emerges with a piece of paper. She looks around first, ignores the outstretched hand and shoves it underneath the table onto Mercedes' lap. When Carmen rises to leave, a weighty drape seems to fall over her, the heaviness adding more years as she mutters that he'll expect her home soon. The farewell is cursory, she shuffles a few steps, and then stops and looks back.

'I forgot to tell you, Marga said there's a signature.'

Mercedes spreads out the paper on her lap; to label it a letter is an exaggeration, it is little more than a note written on a scrappy piece of lined paper. She skims to the end for the signature but her attention diverts to an indentation of something moulded into the sheet. Even held up to the light, it's hard to make out what it is. She thinks there are some letters that separate a sequence of numbers.

'This is a serial number.'

The man passing her table gives her an odd look and she glances around but he is the only person who hears her words. Once again, the old woman has vanished without leaving a contact number but she doesn't have time to smoulder as a breeze lifts the note from her lap and it tumbles along the pavement. Everything else becomes irrelevant as she leaps and traps it beneath her foot before it can disappear forever. Bits of gravel and an imprint of her shoe don't obscure the script and she quickly reads the content before anything else can happen. It is a short piece of writing, the lines that offer sympathy preceding the stark announcement on the back. The words mesmerize her: 'he lives'. Marga and Carmen have judged it well, no nun would write that in error. Difficult to decipher as the letters of the signature compress and fuse into one long scribble, she studies the paper from every angle until she decides that the first part of the name is 'Maria' and the next component begins with a 'J'.

There is no more time to devote to it; in two hours she has to meet the deadline for her article and it requires polish. On the lookout for Carmen as she returns to the office, she thinks she catches a glimpse, but the multitude of people on the pavement swallows the shadow.

It is gone midnight when Orlando gives her a final kiss and she shuts the door to her flat. Although she would love to crawl back into bed, she perches on the settee and takes one more look at the note. During her contemplation, she rubs aloe vera into a rough patch on her chin; she has grown to love the reminder of his stubble against her skin. There had been the usual debate before he left – he wanted to stay the night, but when she reminded him of her intention to get up for a run before the sunrise, the quandary had a solution; his bed is a temple that he likes to enjoy on Saturday mornings. She giggles aloud in her acknowledgement that he deserves his rest. That thought is forgotten when she makes out another letter. Maria J…s. The 's' comes at the end of the second name, she would be willing to bet a lot of money that it is the name of the son of God and writes out Maria Jesus before putting the puzzle aside. Twisted sheets remind her of bodies writhing in the bed and she opens the window to cool down while she repairs the damage.

Chapter 16

She never seems to arrive on time these days and Mercedes sprints through the shopping centre, flushing when she sees Juanita checking the time on the overhead clock. Her friend waits outside the beauty store with her arm in a strange position and, for a moment, Mercedes gets the impression that she has injured her shoulder. Then the 'Bijou' bag hiding behind Juanita's back becomes visible and she is laughing as she nears her friend, peers and taps the carrier bag, causing the things inside to rattle against each other.

'What's this?'

Juanita's colour deepens as she surrenders and holds the bag over her heart. 'The cutest necklace and earrings jumped out at me. I just had to have them.'

'No money, eh?'

They enter the cosmetic emporium and walk arm-in-arm through aisles filled with an invisible fragranced cloud towards the make-up area in the far corner. Both sample various colours of their favourite brands until she makes her choice. Juanita sighs as Mercedes goes to buy the same beige she always wears.

'I think this one is darker. The ones at home make me look like a ghost.'

'You don't know how beautiful you are.'

Juanita's palms cradle Mercedes' face and she doesn't release her until she accepts the compliment. The flush stretches down onto Mercedes' chest as she stuffs change into the back pocket of her jeans and stomps through the exit before the shop girl laughs any louder. Juanita chases, catches up and pulls Mercedes' arm into the nest of her elbow as she plants a kiss on her cheek.

'You are.'

Although the words aren't meant to be overheard, Mercedes catches them and their warmth touches her heart. Juanita didn't intend any embarrassment and Mercedes returns the kiss and suggests a coffee break. They saunter along the corridors until they arrive at the *chocolateria*, and Juanita salivates at the window display until Mercedes gives in; her friend needs her weekly fix of a sickly drink and churros. She doesn't understand how the girl remains so slim; the one thing that Mercedes won't eat during the daytime is chocolate. Once started, she will eat it non-stop and grow into a fat doughnut. Instead, she sips a black coffee and watches with envy as her friend dips the end of the first doughnut finger into the thick chocolate and places it between her lips.

'I don't know where it all goes.' She shakes her head at her friend and when a dribble of chocolate runs down Juanita's chin, she dabs it away with a tissue. No sooner does she sit back than the interrogation starts, digging into her relationship with Orlando.

'I do like him. Yes, he stays sometimes. No, I don't know if it's serious.'

It is uncommon for her to be evasive with her friend but she feels an alien desire to protect the intimacy of her fledgling love. Fortunately, the questions come to a halt when a good-looking man walks into the café and creates a diversion. Two sets of female eyes follow him as he walks to the counter, gives an order, and claims an empty table. A girl with model looks enters soon afterwards and, as he waves, the friends catch each other's eyes and sigh. Mercedes narrows her eyes as she ponders about Juanita, time to tease her friend about her date the previous night.

'Is he the one?'

The question leads to a soliloquy about his attributes that continues until they leave the café and head up the escalator to the next level of the shopping centre. As they step off the moving stairs, Mercedes pulls Juanita by the hand to look at a perfect splash of colour.

'Look at that, isn't it pretty? I would love a new scarf.'

Juanita tries to stop her but Mercedes will not be deterred.

'How many wraps do you need? I'm surprised there is room in your drawers for anything else.'

Materials puff like balloons as they fill with air and Mercedes tries on one scarf after another, each a different colour and length. The assistant hovers, her face glowering with suspicion until Mercedes settles on a sky blue one. The young girl manages a smile. There is a silver thread running through the trim that Mercedes loves and she loops her purchase around her neck with the tassels hanging over her shoulder. When she spins, it swirls around her body and reminds her of the material that belly dancers wear on their hips.

'Mercedes? Where have you gone?'

Someone clutches her arm and she looks down, shocked that her limb quivers under Juanita's hand. She realises that her friend is the one shaking her arm and brandishes her head from side to side to clear the fog that distorts reality. The scarf stall is still in sight, but the shadow that emerged nearby and transformed her into stone has evaporated. Flesh puckers between Juanita's eyebrows and her lips compress into a tight line as she waits for an explanation.

'A man. I thought I saw a man.'

That isn't enough to appease her friend and Juanita is silent as she waits for more.

'It's to do with something I'm working on.'

'It's that Carmen, isn't it? What is it with that woman? I've never seen you like this.' Comprehension dawns and Mercedes watches the rose fade from her friend's cheeks. 'This man you saw, he frightens you?'

The temptation to bare her secret and soul nearly wins but she can't bear to burden her friend and tries to shrug it off as nothing of importance. With a change of the subject, she cajoles Juanita with the suggestion that they visit the jean shop. Unusually, a silence lies between them as they walk in that direction. The normal nature of their friendship blossoms again when they stand in front of the shelves and survey the piles of denim trousers, laughing at some of the way-out styles. In the changing room a growing heap of ditched items surrounds their feet until Juanita finds a pair that doesn't make her bottom look too big or her thighs too chunky.

'Two pairs! You told me you had no money.'

'I can give up food for a week, but never the perfect pair of jeans. Besides, the black ones will be great for a night out. Come on, let's celebrate.'

A trendy café recently opened in the centre, which Juanita suggests they try; it's not cheap but she's heard good reports on the food. The place buzzes and they grin at each other at the entrance while they look for a vacant table. It is a fount of black, silver and white, buzzing with the voices of the crowd of fashion setters. Juanita points at a table that comes free and, when seated, the girls compare opinions on the different styles customers are wearing while they wait for their order. Before long, Juanita wants to delve into what happened in the mall and she probes for an explanation. Mercedes glosses over the frequent appearances of the man as co-incidence, but her friend knows her well and pinpoints the reason for her unease.

'When did you first notice him?'

Scooting around the question for a while, she gives in to her friend's persistence and confesses that it was at the Salvador Clinic. Like a dog with a bone, Juanita refuses to let go of the subject until Mercedes relates the discoveries from her research. She can't bring herself to admit that the root of her interest lies in her experience with her own baby, anxious she will encounter disapproval from another loved one when the truth of her illegitimate baby comes out.

'Let me get this straight, you think someone has been taking new-borns from the hospital? What do they do with them?'

Expressed in those words – like the theft of equipment or an item of little value – the theory sounds implausible. Mercedes experiences a moment of doubt but she steels herself; even if she can't fully trust Carmen, she can't deny what has happened in her own life. The look of revulsion upon Juanita's face as they discuss the theft of babies disturbs Mercedes and she regrets not leaving her friend in ignorance. That gentle nature seems tainted with the exposure of the evil and she has to explain; it's unfair to leave things in limbo for her friend and she holds a finger to her lips as she lowers her voice.

'I managed to get into the doctor's records. Nothing adds up.'

'What do you mean, his records? Even I know he didn't just let you go through them. They're confidential.'

As though under a spotlight, like a child caught in a naughty act, she keeps her eyes on the floor and squirms in her chair.

'Mercedes, did you break in?'

There is no point inventing another lie, Juanita knows her too well.

'Are you mad?'

'Don't worry, no one saw me.'

Everything bottled up inside gushes forth when she leans forward to trap Juanita's hand with hers. 'This is big. It isn't just a few babies.'

Juanita's voice squeaks. 'Not a few!' Mercedes gestures so she lowers it to a whisper when she continues. 'How many?'

'I don't know, maybe more than a hundred.' It's a random guess but it wouldn't surprise her if it's close. 'I have found evidence it's been going on for years.'

'You haven't answered my question. Why would someone take a baby?'

'To sell. I think that's what they do with them; to childless couples, I guess.'

'But surely their neighbours suspect? Bellies grow, women look pregnant; they don't just suddenly come home with a baby one day as though they've picked one up at the market.'

'Exactly! That's what I'm investigating. I don't know the detail of how it works yet, but Señora Ferrer, that woman I met in Burgos, told me some things about an orphanage. I think it may have been used as a temporary nursery before they were sent to new homes.'

Tears spill onto her friend's cheeks and Mercedes feels like joining in now that their day out has been ruined. She attempts to repair the damage with some bad jokes but Juanita's lips force a smile as she tries to be polite. Clearly haunted by the story, she returns to the subject time after time and they are unable to regain the light-hearted atmosphere that accompanied their roaming earlier. It isn't long before they decide to call it a day.

As they pass the security guard on their way out of the

centre, Mercedes looks twice. Although standing inside the complex, he wears reflective sunglasses that disguise his eyes and she shivers when his head follows their direction. One of his hands holds onto something in his front pocket while the other hand swings a bunch of keys and the clanking resounds off the tiled walls. The action hypnotises Mercedes but she doesn't realise she has stopped until Juanita touches her arm and asks if she is ill. She strives to keep her tone blasé when she answers, reluctant to upset her friend with more bad stories. Now that she inspects him more closely, he isn't wearing the same clothes as the shadow she saw earlier and convinces herself it's a different man, banishing stupid concerns from her mind. Juanita claims her attention with another question.

'The American boy at your flat told us he comes from a Spanish family. Could he be one of these babies?' Her face screws up as she voices her thoughts aloud. 'No one would know if a baby was sent out of the country. It's not like an adult with a job and community around him. He would be missed.'

'Exactly! But how do you get an infant out without papers?' Mercedes jumps in with her response.

'False ones, maybe. Do young babies need papers?'

Mercedes shakes her head, then nods, but she doesn't know which answer is correct.

Juanita stands still, closes her eyes and offers some suggestions. 'It would be obvious on a plane. Maybe the border with Portugal or France. That would be easy enough. When my parents drove us up to France last year, we were in the country for nearly an hour before we realised that we had crossed the border.'

'That's it! Thank you.' Mercedes' chest muffles the sound of Juanita's laughter as she jumps up and down with her friend in her embrace until Juanita demands room to breathe and pushes her away.

They separate at the bus stop with plans to play tennis later. When Mercedes steps in to kiss her goodbye, a rush of love for her friend floods through her and she removes the scarf from around her neck and drapes it over Juanita's shoulders.

'Here. You have it. It's your perfect colour.'

'But you said that you loved it.'

'Yes, and you'll carry a little piece of my love with you when you wear it.'

Kisses land on Mercedes' hand until she breaks away with a plea for mercy. 'Okay. I get it. Go on. Get home. See you later.' As she walks away, her friend tosses the scarf over her shoulder and preens in front of the glass wall of the shelter before disappearing onto a bus. Mercedes steps onto her own bus, the cloud no longer dampening her spirits now her friend is smiling again.

Chapter 17

Arms and legs suspend in the air but the cushion under her body disappears all of a sudden, and she falls at the speed of a meteorite heading for the earth. Mercedes tries to scream but she chokes as her heart moves into her throat from her chest and pulsates at the pace of a racehorse. A building comes into view, its roof flashes by and she clenches her eyes shut just before she crumbles into pieces on the pavement that hurtles in her direction.

Her body stiffens in a spasm and she wakes, the dream cut off forever in the second before she hit the earth.

A sour taste remains in her mouth as she watches the moonbeams dance between the shadows on the wall; their performance soothes her unsettled mind. As she adjusts her legs, a weight shifts on her lap. An empty wine bottle rests on its side, suspended in the hammock between her legs that the blanket has created. The room swims when she adjusts her head, bringing back unpleasant memories of the twenty-four hours of hell she endured on a ferry two years ago. The plate on the table at her side overflows with spent matches and scrunched paper tissues; at least she didn't burn the place down when she tried to light the fire. Hazy memories of the night flit into her consciousness and replace the remains of her nightmare. Even though she eases herself up, a vice tightens around her skull, causing her to moan aloud. A photo frame lies face up on the floor beside her left foot. It must have fallen off the coffee table during the night and she bends to retrieve it but the movement triggers a wave of nausea. Leaving it for later, she collapses back in the chair with her eyes pinched as she waits for the spinning to stop. After the world stops turning, she raises one eyelid and tests the daylight before she blinks the other one open.

Mercedes could paint the photo on the floor from her memory. Everything is a shade of white – the blanket, the surroundings, and the tiny face – all white. When held close, it is possible to make out the darker shade of closed eyelids and, below them, a button that is a perfect nose. If the lips were pink, they would be a rosebud but it is hard to appreciate the shape with the absence of colour. The hair shows on the baby in the photo but no reminder of her own child is necessary; there was none on her baby and the top of his head was bruised, damp, and speckled with blood and a waxy white paste. In the blanket cocoon, the child's hands and feet are not on show but if she closes her eyes, she can picture those of her son, so tiny that all four together would fit into the palm of her hand. One additional thing the photo never captured was the lifeless feel of his body. This likeness is not of the baby she remembers, but she has learnt to make do, and treasures the image as it gives her some solace.

Blood rushes into her head when she pushes herself out of the chair. She wavers, holding onto the table edge until the room stops its spin. Then she picks up the frame and kisses it as she replaces it in the drawer. Her progress through the flat is careful and when she sees herself in the bathroom mirror, she sends Juanita a message by telepathy, wishing for a less painful start to her day after the indulgence of the previous night. The bottle of painkillers is on the top shelf of her medicine cupboard and, although the whole bottle couldn't ease the pain in her head, she settles for the recommended dose.

The memory of the night is a blur; a jug of sangria after

their game led to a decision to go for a night on the town instead of the girly night in. Her alcohol limit is usually two but when she came home during the early hours of the morning without Juanita – who had an early start and didn't want to disturb her – Mercedes was feeling high, not ready for bed.

The empty bottle drops into the bin as she vows there will be no further sessions like that for a while. The telephone rings and she rushes to turn down the volume before the sound splits her head in two. She hesitates to be certain that she won't collapse before she picks up the receiver and grunts.

'It must have been a good night.'

Laughter explodes like thunder inside her head and when she asks him to turn down his voice, Orlando teases until she holds the receiver away from her ear and threatens to hang up.

'Did you win?'

'Huh?'

'Tennis. Yesterday.'

Her answer that she thinks they did but can't be certain sets off his booming once again but eventually he runs out of steam and suggests a walk, saying that the fresh air will help to clear her head. Her protests that she needs to hide in her bed for the day elicit no sympathy and finally she gives in to the pressure.

'I want to hear what the old lady had to tell you.'

Immediately she wants to clam up, blaming her reluctance to discuss Carmen on her sore head and queasy stomach. Instead of a response, she changes the subject and asks where they should meet. She slips the phone back into its cradle while he is in the middle of giving her unsolicited advice for recovery after a night out, and holds her stomach as she stumbles to the bed, pulling the sheets over her head to block out the world.

The headache has waned into a dull throb and she manages to keep down some toast. Juanita's phone switches to the answer machine and Mercedes remembers she is out at her parents' for the day; it will be at work on Monday before she is able to clarify what happened the night before. Under the hot spray of the shower, she lathers her body and hair as a mental battle goes on, one side urging her to hold on to Carmen's secrets and the other voice reminding her he has given her no reason to distrust him. A pool of water saturates the rug under her feet while the debate continues outside of the cubicle. Her wet skin cools and she begins to shiver, then she makes her choice. With a rough towel, she buffs her body until her skin buzzes. The sensation escalates as she imagines what they will be doing later.

Her red blouse goes well with her jeans but when she examines her reflection, she replaces it with a black one that has a deep v neckline and lace panels, which give a hint of the flesh beneath. Red lipstick improves her pallor and a final check in the mirror reveals little evidence of the night's excesses. When she climbs down the stairs, she feels like a martyr but revives somewhat with the first breath of fresh air.

The temperature is perfect, between the extremes of summer and winter, and she moves across the deserted streets of the city with unfamiliar ease. Many Madrilenos are at the coast for the bridge weekend; the saint day on Monday gives a three-day break so the five-hour drive is worth the effort. She considers a second look at the details of the flat in Gandia that Jaime tried to tempt her with last winter; a place near the sea would allow her to escape the city heat but it would be a struggle without a salary increase.

Usually people sit on the fountain wall and block the view of the three naked goddesses, but today one man stands there as he observes the water explode into the air and shower down over the marble figures. The toast crushes in her stomach and her heart flutters at the sight of him. She pauses to enjoy the anticipation, then he turns and opens his arms. Her ear presses against his chest so she hears the gallop in his heart. Isolated in their intimate circle, she isn't aware of the spray as it dampens their heads, nor the dogs that play at their feet. She does hear the air enter his chest and the rush as it blows out through his mouth, in harmony with her own breath. He leans back a trace and looks into her face; she loves his eyes but has to adjust to a sense of loss.

'Hello beautiful.'

The words caress, his voice thick with lust, and the muscles tighten in her pelvis. She falls against him as her legs melt a little more.

'I missed you.' Her words slip out, not what she intended to say, and she tries to defend them, which sounds worse. 'It must be 24 hours at least.' She hates that her voice sounds so needy and tries to blag her way out of it but everything she says worsens the impression. She changes the subject completely and tries to describe what she remembers of the previous night instead. Orlando pulls her to his side, drapes his arm over her shoulders, and whispers that he missed her as well. Their hips weld together and they stride along the path in unison.

The light bulb on the landing needs replacing so she feels her way along the walls until her fingers touch the door of her flat. After fiddling with the key, she pushes open the door, hits the light switch and dispels the gloom. Enrique's love song replays in her head as she waltzes into the room and twirls until she is dizzy. After her head returns to normal, she writes a memo to the maintenance man; it is not a harsh reprimand on this occasion, nothing will ruin her good mood. The red flashing light of the answerphone claims her attention and when she punches the play button, Juanita's voice fills the silence.

'Mercedes. Are you there?'

The message stops her halfway across the room, and she turns to stare at the machine. The words end abruptly with a peculiar tone of urgency, as though there wasn't time to wait for the answer. Her friend is at her parents' house for the remainder of the fiesta weekend and rarely telephones from their place, so it must be important and Mercedes debates what she should do, – dial the flat in Madrid, or call Juanita's parents. It's after midnight and she doesn't want to worry anyone, and her clean sheets look inviting. As she undresses, she consoles herself that Juanita would have tried again if the call were urgent. She decides that if her friend hasn't phoned in the morning, she'll ring Juanita's parents before Orlando picks her up.

Sleep overcomes her as soon as her head sinks into the pillow but nightmares haunt her night and, an hour later than normal, the birds wake her. Panic sets in and, ready to jump to get ready for work, she remembers it is a fiesta day and there is no rush.

She puts her novel aside when the hour is reasonable to ring Juanita at her flat. Once again, the call goes straight to the answerphone and she lets her know she received the message. Then she tries the family home but that call also goes to the answerphone and she feels oddly on edge as she stares at the handset and wills it to ring.

Throughout her morning routine, the sense that something is wrong swells with her unease, growing each time she fails to get through to her friend. The feeling that she made a bad decision to leave things overnight intensifies and, in her final message, she urges Juanita to call and let her know she is all right.

Orlando notices straight away that she is concerned. 'Do you have any idea what she wanted?'

'Not a sausage, but her voice sounded odd.'

'What do you mean odd?'

Words can't describe the intonation and she settles by saying that her friend sounded frightened.

'We can stop by her flat and check things out, if you wish.'

Her eyes light up, then she peers into his face and shakes her head. He has talked about this day for weeks and, if they call at Juanita's, it will be impossible to get to Salamanca for the start of the concert.

As they step on board their train, she can't rid herself of the feeling that she should have agreed to his suggestion. Orlando loses himself in a magazine but she can't concentrate on the words in her book and wriggles in her seat until he tells her to go for a walk to the buffet. The journey takes less than an hour and when they arrive, they have time for a short stroll around the university where they amuse themselves looking for a frog, carved long ago into the ornate façade of the historic building. The concert isn't her choice of music but Orlando knows every song and sings along to the words, so she is glad that they came.

When they return to Madrid, he tugs her hand and leads her in the wrong direction for either of their flats.

'I know you won't rest until you've checked she isn't lying with a broken leg, unable to reach the phone. If she's not there, we'll leave a note.'

There is no reply from the flat's entry-phone bell; she continues to press until Orlando persuades her she has tried long enough. The neighbour doesn't answer his bell either, and she gives in and pretends that posting a note in the box makes her feel happier.

They go to his flat and, after making love, she lies next to

163

his comatose body, watching the sweat evaporate and the rise and fall of his chest. Sleep evades her and the worry is like an itch that keeps her alert. Dawn is breaking before she manages to slip into a state that mimics slumber, a repose filled with nightmares and villains.

Chapter 18

Tuesday morning is the end of the four-day weekend and Juanita still hasn't returned her calls. Mercedes' eyes automatically swing towards the reception desk as she enters the building, but it is unmanned. She must be poorly, but in the years that she has known her, Juanita has neither overslept nor missed a day of work. A wave of urgency floods her and, desperate to get to her office phone, she forgoes the stairs and attacks the lift buttons to prevent the doors closing. They separate and she steps through with a nod of apology to Pedro, standing in the corner with a Styrofoam cup in one hand, his leather briefcase in the other and a horrified expression on his face. She doesn't know what she has done to deserve that response and turns her back on him to stare at the graffiti engraved into the metal panels of the cage.

'Are you okay?'

She whips around to face him, struggling for a connection with his eyes; he looks everywhere but into her face.

'Why?'

The word bursts forth, an accusation she attempts to soften with a smile. He stares at the floor while a surge of red changes the colour of his neck and ebbs up to his cheeks. Fed up of waiting for an answer, she crosses her arms over her chest and leans against the cold metal; her shoe heel taps on the floor and the sound echoes around the box. Pedro is intent on observing the numbers as they light up in turn during the ascent and when the seven illuminates, he clears his throat as though he has made a decision and steps to her side. Before she can evade his embrace, an arm goes across her shoulders and she doesn't know whether to kick him in the groin or to scream for help. Her knee pulls back and is ready to strike when he asks a question that warns of impending doom.

'I didn't think you'd come in today. You haven't heard?'

Juanita! Strength seeps from her body and leaves her with no power to push him away; her legs give way and her stomach threatens to expel its contents when his stricken eyes finally link with hers. The light performance continues overhead and Mercedes wants to poke the red button, compelled to stop the inevitable, as the premonition of disaster overpowers everything else. She isn't aware of the doors opening, or when Pedro takes charge or, as they reach the first vacant chair, his hands grasping her upper arms and pushing her down with instructions to stay put. The order isn't necessary; she is incapable of doing otherwise. He steps a few metres down the corridor and, as he passes a colleague, she overhears him issue an order about privacy, then he pulls up a chair and sits down on the outside of her bubble. The man she used to mock for his lack of sensitivity leans forward and gently takes her hand. She knows what is coming will change her life forever by the drops that glisten in his eyes. He tries to muffle her screams of pain as he rocks her against his chest.

Shady figures tiptoe around a room that is dense with its silence. At times, someone clears a throat nearby; Mercedes is in a vacuum so he might as well be a million kilometres away. No one matters other than her friend, and whenever anyone appears with a fresh cup of coffee and some meaningless platitude, she has to enter another dimension before she lashes out. How long she has been in the room, she has no idea. Pedro is no longer with her, he fled from her fury. She can't tolerate him being in the same room; his voice has left a permanent scar. Her fingers scrub at tear marks, damp speckles on the leather arms of the chair, and the friction burns their tips. She welcomes the discomfort, any pain to befuddle that agony in her heart.

Juanita is gone, discovered in the early hours of Sunday morning face-down in the water at El Retiro Park. Scarred forever by their discovery, a young couple were looking for somewhere romantic to finish their night when they found her. Pedro told her the young man tried his best, but it was too late. The police who first attended the scene thought she had drowned, but then they saw the mark around her neck. Mercedes' imagination cannot rid itself of images of her friend, dumped amongst the lakeside weeds with lifeless eyes staring down into the depths of the dark water. Caught in the thorns of a nearby rose, the police found the shredded remains of a sky-blue scarf with silver thread; it hung on the branch, of no further use to the killer.

The police officer asks for her help but she can't; her voice stops working and, even though she realises it is important for her friend, he demands too much of her. A woman enters, a female officer who cajoles and then bullies, but she remains mute. No one understands. In her career, she strings words together to tell stories, but there are no words for this tale of horror.

Her memory replays that last vision of Juanita as she walked away to the end of the boulevard after their night out. Still dancing as she disappeared from view, over her dress she wore a jacket, a hand-me-down that once belonged to Mercedes but suited her friend better, and the new scarf.

Her gifts.

Her clothes.

The guilt burns. *It should have been me.*

★

On the façade, where the roof pitch juts up from the building, an artist has sculpted a family of matchstick figures that walk towards a rainbow. Mercedes guffaws, but the sound is a bitter croak and no one could misinterpret the sentiment. A crowd gathers outside the building, a craven of crows in their mourning outfits. Huddled together in a private circle, the family protect the shrunken woman almost lost in its centre. She is barely recognisable; gone are the florid cheeks and warm smile of her friend's mother. In their place are crevices at the sides of her mouth and gorges that contain her red, swollen eyes.

Someone is brave enough to approach the circle. The man wears black but has dry eyes and, when his mouth moves, he points to the entrance. Mercedes gasps when she comprehends his job. The bereaved mother begins to slump to the ground, but her husband catches an arm and shouts at his son to take the other, so that between them they keep her upright. Her feet drag along the ground as the men take her inside and a knife stabs Mercedes' heart when she notices the price label still stuck to the soles of the black shoes.

As one, the members of the congregation follow the family inside, but Mercedes' legs refuse to move until Orlando steers her with gentle pressure on her elbow. When she emerges on the other side of the door, she can't take another step, transfixed by the vision of the polished wooden box that erupts out of a bed of flowers. The fragrance makes her nauseous and her weight sinks against her boyfriend's body. His arm tightens around her waist and a whisper urges her to place one foot forward. The music of the organ sounds forth a melancholy beat for their slow march to the end of a bench packed with colleagues from the paper. There is a screech as the organist hits a wrong note and, for the first time since she sat down, Mercedes lifts her gaze from her knees. Her attention does not waver from the sight at the front; the box is too small to hold all of the being that was her friend. Her breath catches on the sob because there is nothing that is big enough to hold who she was in Mercedes' life. The poster-sized photograph on the easel at one side of the altar is a sterile image of her friend. The professional hasn't captured the joy in her eyes or the vibrancy in her face. It was taken the previous year at the insistence of her friend's mother, to complete a family series. Juanita thought it made her look stern and hid her copy in a cupboard at home; Mercedes had reassured her it wasn't that bad, but her friend refused to put it on display.

In fact, she can't understand most of the choices made for the final celebration. White and yellow flowers tower out of vases that come halfway up the walls in the four corners of the room. Why did they choose lilies? Juanita disliked them intensely, full of complaints about the orange dust that taints everything as it settles. She even had a nickname for them – 'beautiful fiends' – because she said that despite their delicate appearance, they left behind an ugly stain. A chanting begins as the priest commences his prayers, and she traps her hands under her thighs as anger threatens to burst out of her mouth with scorns for the god who allowed evil to win.

'Are you okay?'

His arm stifles her with its weight and she ducks away from the burden; his protection oppresses her, one more thing that fuels her anger. Most of their fellow mourners have departed and new cars arrive, also filled with people dressed in black who emerge from their transportation and walk as though an invisible load cripples them. She lingers on the drive, in a place where the cars have to swerve around her, not ready to take leave of her friend yet, fearful of that final step. There is no answer for Orlando when he asks where she would like to go. In her mind, she screams out 'nowhere' but her voice remains silent. A faint odour of wild rosemary and lavender impregnates the breeze that strokes her cheeks; it has no power to soothe her sore eyes and broken spirit. At the edge of her vision, she detects an oasis. A few trees protect a patch of green grass from the sun and her body obeys the feet that carry her to the edge of the shade. At the far end of the area, a stone-clad entrance marks the start of a path into a village of white monuments. Orlando's footsteps echo behind hers on the cobblestones as they travel under the arch into the city of the dead and in procession, wander along gravel roadways that separate the ancient tombs and mausoleums, with the occasional halt while she reads an inscription. There is some comfort in the realisation that her friend won't be alone with the many young spirits in this place to keep her company.

The adornment on top of one of the older plots particularly impresses her; a carved woman kneels on a plinth with her hands palm-to-palm and swan-like wings cast along the shape of her back. It is the joyous piety in the face as it tilts towards the heavens that captures her attention. Below the white marble is a second block that bears an inscription alluding to the earthly sisters who celebrate the woman's summons to the deity's side midway through her fifty-first year. On first glance, Mercedes overlooks the engraved area at the upper corner of the stone; it has eroded over time and all that remains are a few gashes in the marble. However, when she slips her hand into Orlando's and they turn to leave, something flickers in her memory and brings her to a halt.

'What is it?'

Her eyes close while she tries to capture the elusive apparition but it is out of reach, so she turns back to the memorial and seeks the trigger again. Something tantalises at the margins of her conscious, and although she wipes away the grime with a handkerchief, the full picture won't form. Running her finger over the surface, she traces a curved line that could belong to an animal head; she can't be certain and the rest of the image has eroded over time. A cloud covers the sun and, without the warmth, she shivers. Orlando insists she needs rest and she allows him to take her hand and lead her to the exit. When they reach the main road, she drops his hold as he tries to pull her towards a waiting taxi.

'I need to be alone.'

His face betrays his struggle when he finally agrees with her decision. 'Are you sure? You shouldn't be on your own tonight.'

Her fingers loosen the imaginary scarf that tightens around her neck as she puts more distance between them. He steps closer and the noose constricts; she tears at her throat.

'No! I can't breathe.' Rejecting his open palm and offer of sanctuary, she escapes in the opposite direction, to seek the dark solitude of her flat.

Chapter 19

A bell is under siege and, despite the pillow over her head, it won't go away. Yesterday was the same. And the day before that. How many days has that sound haunted her?

'For God's sake, stop. Someone answer that door!' She screams the order but who cares? No one is here to obey.

Bbbring. Bbbring.

Incensed, she slings the cushion across the room and, as it flies, the edge knocks the tower of dirty plates from her coffee table onto the floor. Pieces of china fly in every direction, a snowfall of ceramic, and she stares at the configuration with a sigh. In an ideal world, she would hop up and sweep up the debris; instead, she closes her eyes and rests her head back on the cushion. She really can't be bothered to make the effort.

The bell continues its torment.

'I can't take anymore.'

A bottle tumbles from her lap as she shoots up, and the sound makes her pause as she considers her bare feet. She decides, *what the hell*, and ignores the pain as she walks over the top of the fragments to the speaker.

'Go away!'

That should get rid of them, she smirks as she slams the handset back onto its hook, but the ringing gets going again before there is time to turn away. She snatches the handset and screams into the mouthpiece.

'Leave. Me. Alone.'

Red footprints paint the floor as she returns through the glass lawn and throws herself face-down on the sofa to bury her face in the cushion. In the relief of her dark world, she carries on her conversation with Juanita, reminding her of the day they spent together in Segovia. Five minutes later, someone hammers on her front door; the noise doesn't stop, dragging her back from her pretend world.

'What do you—'

The door flies open and hits the wall with a resounding crash. Rage extends through every part of her body, but when she sees the face of her visitor, it melts away. Certain that she has finally lost her mind, she can't take in the presence of the young woman; it's been ten years since she has seen the beloved features of her sister and she never thought to lay eyes on her again. For a moment, she stares at her and quenches her thirst, then her heart swells and the bubble that has isolated her from the world ruptures as she collapses into Rosa's arms.

Her gaze fixates on Rosa's face; a blink will be too long to lose sight of her. Every so often, even though they snuggle side-by-side on the settee, she reaches her fingers and touches Rosa's flesh in a different area to remind herself that this isn't another nightmare. Orlando tidies the flat around them. The dirty plates have disappeared and the floor smells of pine, all signs of the footprints erased. His first task after he escorted her sister inside was to treat the damage to her feet; they sting but he painstakingly removed every sliver before he wrapped them in lint bandages after yielding to her refusal to visit the emergency clinic. He seems satisfied that the floor is safe and disappears into the kitchen to reappear moments later with a platter of bread and cheese.

'Eat. You can catch up afterwards. You need proper food; ice cream isn't enough.'

He shakes his head as walks away with the dirty bowl and leaves them to tuck into the cheese while he prepares a tomato and avocado salad in the kitchen. Her protests that she is full go unheeded and he stands over her until she clears her plate. Meanwhile, Rosa nibbles at a piece of cheese and refuses to speak until her sister holds her tummy and cries out for mercy. When he joins them for coffee and tells Mercedes she is allowed to ask her questions now, she smirks; this control thing will have to stop soon but, for now, he has dragged her out of the anguish so she doesn't protest. Her eyes soften when she speaks to her sister. 'Why are you here? How did you find me?'

'It wasn't hard to figure out. You were always going to do well and I knew that my best chance was to search for you at the big papers. I watched each one from the outside in rotation until one day I saw you coming out of the offices with the receptionist.'

It sounds simple but it has been weeks since she last ventured out to work, and even more since she and Juanita left the building together. 'Why didn't you approach me? How long have you known where I was?'

'Long enough. When you left, I couldn't bear the thought that I may never see you again. Once I knew you were safe, I was content to watch. There was a lot of anger at home in those days and I didn't know if you'd want to see me. I'd visit the city every couple of months to check that you were okay.' She squeezes Mercedes' hand. 'I'm proud of you. Why didn't you come home?'

'What else could I do? Mama and Papa made it clear they didn't want to listen to me.' She glances at Orlando but he isn't eavesdropping and seems engrossed by the sports section of the paper. 'They never believed me. It was driving me crazy. I had to get out.'

'Do you know how much they regret that it got out of control? Mama misses you.'

'Not Papa?'

Rosa ignores her query and changes the subject. 'I came up to the city a few weeks ago and waited where I usually do outside of the ABC building, but you didn't appear with the others. I had this strange feeling that there was something wrong so I stayed with a friend overnight and went back to the offices the next day, and then the day after that. My husband needed me at home and I couldn't stay any longer so I left, but I couldn't stop worrying and, the following week, came to the city again. Eventually, I stopped one of your colleagues and asked if he knew where you were but he wouldn't tell me a thing, until I pestered him to the point when he gave me Orlando's number.'

The sound of his name makes him look up, their eyes connect, and her heart misses a beat. 'And he brought you to me.'

His eyes soften as they smile into hers, and he puts the paper down and comes over to stand behind them. 'You need your family. I don't know what happened between you all in the past, but it's time to move on. You two have lots of catching up to do.' He leans over the back of the settee until she feels the light touch of his lips on the top of her head. 'I'll come back tomorrow morning, darling. Be ready to come out with me.'

When the door clicks into the latch behind him, Rosa looks as though she is melting. 'Where did you find him? You have nabbed the ideal man.'

It is dark when Rosa leaves to catch the last train home, with a promise that she will stay overnight on her next visit. She won't walk out of the door until Mercedes promises to eat and look after herself.

'I've turned a corner.'

Rosa's arms hold onto her as though she is frightened to let go. 'Don't forget that we love you.'

'I don't doubt it. What would I have done without you and Orlando?'

Mercedes rests her forehead against the door after her sister leaves, suddenly cold in the silence and aware her departure has left a gaping hole. Her nose heats up and tears well, a dark void threatening to pull her in once again. She turns to face the room, notices the bowl of fresh fruit that has replaced the tower of dirty dishes on the coffee table, and straightens her spine. As she hobbles to her bedroom, she remembers the people who love her. She declares to the empty space that she will not forget to live for them.

Orlando has laid out an outfit for the following day: jeans, a sweater and some walking shoes. In the open diary, he has drawn a diagonal line through the next day. An envelope marks a date two weeks hence and it's circled in red because Rosa wants to accompany her to face her parents at the family home. As she slips into sleep, it is the first time in weeks her mind doesn't fill with images of the scarf around Juanita's neck; instead she visualizes a young toddler, Rosa's son, who she is due to meet next week. He reaches up with his arms to his favourite aunty…

One week of daily outings is all she can take and she complains that she has seen enough local attractions to last her the remainder of the year. Insistent that she is ready to return to the office, she reminds Orlando he has used a week of his holiday allowance already and when she agrees to return on a half-day only basis, he grumbles but accepts the decision.

'Welcome back.'

Everyone speaks as though she will break apart at any moment. All she wants is to get back to normal life but her return is harder than she expected. The walk by the reception desk is the worst; a girl, who she has never met, greets her by name as she enters the building, and she almost gives in to the compulsion to tell her to get out of Juanita's seat. She is unable to look in that direction as she grunts a reply. The raw emotions scald her heart and she stares at the lift door after it has shut her in, aware that she owes an apology when she comes back down.

On automatic, her feet carry her to her desk and leave her free to concentrate on breathing; she controls each respiration and doesn't allow the demons space in her brain. There is a ridiculous sense of pride when she sits down in her chair. Someone has tidied her desk and there are three piles of paperwork, labelled by urgency. Jorge stops by as she flicks through the papers on the urgent stack, with an order to come to his office in five minutes. Everyone else may be on eggshells but he still bullies, not making any allowances for her emotional state.

'Close the door.'

She obeys and he points to the chair facing his desk.

'Sit!'

Plump fingers linked like rows of sausages rest on the top of a folder labelled with her name. There is no sweetener when he speaks. 'I need you at full strength. Are you ready?' His gaze is like a knife, and she tries to outstare him, but he is stronger this time so her eyes fall first. When she raises them again, she knows that he has seen the chink in her confidence. 'If you aren't, you'd better let me know. I'll find a replacement.'

Her hackles rise, *how dare he?* 'I'm here, aren't I? I won't give you any reason for complaint.'

'The article that you were working on before Juanita, well you know…'

'She was murdered.' It infuriates her that he can't say the word.

'Yes, well.' The smoker's cough hasn't improved and she wonders whether she should have remained at home another week as she struggles to sit through his hacking. He clears his throat and continues and she releases her breath. 'The baby thing. No more of that. I've only just managed to get people off my back over that lot.'

'But.'

'No buts. Do what I say for a change. No more missing babies.'

She wins the battle against her fury and remains silent while he is on his grandstand.

'Just concentrate on the assignments that I give you.'

There is no argument as she agrees to all of his demands and his demeanour changes as he softens his tone and tells her that he'll go easy for the first few articles. He keeps his word because she finishes two of them before lunch, and is stuck for something to do in the final half hour until her break. There is none of the usual banter around her area, all of the guys have their heads buried in work; the stillness is eerie but suits her mood. Her eyes sweep the office for something to distract her, then she gives in to the urge and withdraws her notebook. The cover bears a single title, *Carmen*. For the first time since making her acquaintance, she associates the woman's name with the female character that lured a good man into a life of crime as passion took control of his life, reminding Mercedes of the dangers if she falls into a similar trap. If honest, her personal connection with Carmen's story of missing babies has driven her investigation and the time has arrived for a more rigorous approach, so she opens to a blank page with the intention of mapping out a different plan. The objective is sound but, when the pencil is in her hand, she sketches a few random lines and, as something in her memory sharpens focus, the lines become a shape. The cartoon taunts her as she tries to figure it out until she reproduces a reversal of the image so that the two sketches join in the centre. Her drawing is of a bird in flight, a replica of the dove that she first saw on the nun's letter.

From her briefcase, she extracts three sheets of paper and places them side-by-side on her desktop. The one on the left is the confirmation of her fake appointment last month with Doctor Ramón and she scrutinises it with a magnifying glass. Her tutor taught that the importance is in the detail and, when she spots it, she exclaims in triumph. Although smudged, the black ink is legible – the mark below the hospital crest where someone, an administrator perhaps, has stamped the letter. Its purpose could be to identify Doctor Ramón's patients; following his initials are the letters representing his medical qualifications. Everything is intertwined in swirls with a tiny dove in the centre.

She leans back in her chair with her eyes closed as she considers possible meanings but is no wiser by the time she transfers her attention to the middle paper, a photocopy of the agreement that Robby's parents signed prior to his adoption. The official's signature is an illegible scribble but it is of no interest anyway because she doesn't have the time to search for the owner. Instead, the faded trace of a stamp captures her interest: a circle the size of a large coin, divided into four sections by a lopsided cross. Inside each section is a circle and each circle contains a drawing. Much of the detail is gone, making it hard to discern individual elements, but the image in the upper right-hand corner looks like it could be an animal; there is a head, body, and what looks like four legs. Inside of the neighbouring section, a tiny dove is clear to see.

'Premeditated.'

Her arm covers the papers as she glances up at Jaime. 'What?'

'My contact says that Juanita had a stalker. He was seen following her into the park.'

The blood drains from her face, everything goes numb and, for a second, Mercedes expects to slide from the chair onto the floor. Fingers grasp her arm and shake it. From a distance, a man's voice shouts for someone to bring a glass of water. Then something forces her head between her knees until the need for some air takes over and she surfaces, gasping. A crowd of men surrounds her desk with Jorge in the middle and he fails to mask a strange hint of delight when he orders her to leave. His expression remains with her as she slides into the taxi and instructs the driver to take her home.

When she closes the door of her flat, she heaves a sigh of relief. That first day back at work is over, she handled the pain of Juanita's absence and tomorrow should be tolerable. If it hadn't been for Jaime's revelation hardly any of her colleagues would have acknowledged her. While he waited with her for the taxi to arrive, Orlando made a joke about her tidy desk and tried to melt her icy covering.

She grabs a shawl from a cupboard and tries to rub some warmth back into her body. The answerphone is flashing, she promised to call Orlando as soon as she arrived home but he will have to wait five minutes while she changes into warmer clothes. One day she will have to tell him that he is taking his role as her guardian too seriously but for now, she is glad he is concerned.

Her heavy arms have just enough strength to peel off her work clothes and, when she bends to slide a leg into her jogging trousers, the room swims so she sinks onto her side and stares at the silver frame at her bedside. Juanita is in the middle of a laugh with her mouth wide open and her head tipped back. The winds blew strong that day and her hand can't hold the hair that sweeps across both of their faces. Their cheeks press against each other, distorting the features, but her eyes are unmistakeable. Juanita's brother took the snapshot at the top of a hill climb behind the family home and afterwards they had all helped her friend's mother with the meal. It was nothing special but she can still recall the feeling when she sat at the family table, surrounded by their love. Juanita's dad had teased her that she was becoming more like his daughter every time he saw her. As she stares into her friend's face, it strikes her that they were more alike than she had realised; similar physiques, dark eyes, there were a few likenesses, even their dark curls when Juanita didn't use that stupid red rinse. Her heart swells and she starts to talk to her friend.

'I'm going to see my family soon.' Juanita encourages her from the photo. 'My sister came to me. I wish you could have met her. She is beautiful and clever. And I have a nephew. Named after my father, but with a better temper, she says.' Mercedes jabbers, telling the spirit about her return to work, the funny moments, how much she misses her. The phone interrupts her confession; she sighs and answers Orlando's call. She doesn't mention that she forgot to phone him because she was caught up in an imaginary conversation with a ghost because he is threatening to stop in and make sure she is all right. Eventually he settles for her excuse that she was too tired and agrees to leave her in peace until the next day. As she climbs into bed, Juanita gives her a knowing grin.

Chapter 20

'It was meant for me. For my neck.' Her eyes focus on her hands, which twist and turn around each other. 'It was the photo that reminded me. Strangers often asked if we were sisters.'

'But you didn't look like each other.'

'You saw us every day so you know our differences.' When Orlando shakes his head in disbelief, she leans closer, rests her fingers on his forearm, and implores him to consider the possibility. The only look in his eyes is one of concern and she breathes deeply as she tries to persuade him she is not paranoid.

'She was wearing an old jacket I gave her. That scarf, it was mine. I bought it the last time we went shopping. She liked it.' Her throat balloons, nearly choking her. 'I gave it to her.' Her hand covers her lips, and she muffles the sob and her words. 'If I had kept it, she'd still be alive.'

After he unpeels her fingers from his arm, he rubs the four white stripes that mark his skin until pink returns. 'Did you notice anyone watching you when you bought the scarf?'

She tries to picture the concession stall but all she can recall is the display of colours and the miserable woman who served them; otherwise, her memory is blank and she shakes her head.

Orlando misunderstands. 'If no one saw you, how would the murderer know that scarf was yours? Did you ever wear it?'

'I did. In the shop. We were outside when I put it around her neck.' When she realises what she just said, it makes her nauseous. 'Think about it. It makes sense.'

It is important he believes her. She is convinced the scarf is the clue to why Juanita died. Her knees draw to her chest as a barrier to keep him at a distance and Mercedes squirrels into the corner of the settee, trying to clear her head. It is hard to make sense of it all. Lost in the past, her eyes don't see anything as she stares at his chest, then she detects a tear in his T-shirt where a few strands of dark hair poke through. His heart lies beneath and she lowers her gaze; it halts at the coffee stain on his joggers. Every day her mind reels with thoughts of Juanita, and her arrival at his front door before dawn had caught him unawares. She had waited as long as she could through the long night with her conviction growing, but now she wonders if she is promoting a flawed case, based on supposition.

'Okay.' Air puffs from the cushion as he sits back. 'Let's assume that you're right. Why does someone want to kill you?'

The secret detail of her investigation spills out; she doesn't hold anything back as she explains about Burgos, the Americans and the man with odd eyes who appears too often for coincidence. The sentences jumble into each other without pause, until he holds up a palm and pleads with her to calm down and breathe. For a short time, her words are more measured, but she has held back for too long and the facts battle with each other to come out. The torrent continues with no break for his interruptions.

There is one secret she isn't prepared to reveal, as the loss of his love would destroy her and she won't take that risk. When the gush ebbs, Mercedes is spent, and neither of them speaks. The silence breaks with a birdsong that heralds the rise of the sun and start of a new day. A trickle of salty fluid runs onto her lip, her efforts have made her sweat despite the coolness of the room. He speaks, surprising her as she was at the point of giving up on him.

'What about the police?'

'Of course not.' The space between his eyebrows disappears and she butts in before he gives his opinion. 'Can you imagine what they'd say? I can hear it already: hmm, a conspiracy of stolen babies, nuns, and one of the most esteemed doctors in Madrid. I must obtain more proof.'

A thaw flows through her body when his eyes change and she can tell that he is beginning to trust her story; he chews the inside of his cheek, then gathers her under his arm and clutches her to his chest. 'If you're right, the most important thing is your safety.' The refuge of his protection tempts her and she wants to shelter there forever. A stray gust catches the window so that it slams against the frame and the sound hauls her back to reality. There is much at stake and she eases away, aware that she must push forward with her investigation to the end.

'Too many lives have been affected. Mothers and their lost children. And my precious Juanita. I won't rest until I find out why she died.' She stands and spins around to look down at his face. 'I will expose the truth.' Taking his cheeks between her hands, she bends and presses her lips onto his. The farewell falters when his lips move and all of her determination vanishes as she slumps onto his body. A mirror breaks in her bag when she drops it to the ground but she doesn't care because he is pulling her on top of him. Their bodies join and, as one, they slide onto the floor. Her exposed skin touches the cold tiles and she gasps, and then again, as he flips her to trap her body beneath his. He is consumed by their passion, and she tries to tell him that she needs more air, but he misunderstands and seals their lips together while his knee levers her thighs apart. A dark void pulls her in, and the cloud in her mind dissipates when he rolls onto his side, taking her with him and creating room for her lungs to expand. Her heart races until his hand cups her breast and searches for her nipple, then it misses a beat. Similar to the drum in a band, the sound fills her head until the clapping of their bodies becomes the dominant rhythm.

Cat-like movements allow her to wiggle out of his embrace without disturbing him. Her bra hangs from the lampshade and it is impossible to hold onto the giggle until a groan from the man deep in slumber on the floor warns her to strive for silence. While she pulls on her blouse, her final piece of clothing to replace, she tiptoes to his side. On his back, he exhales through lips that are swollen and red; she touches a finger to her own, they probably look the same. Then she kisses the tip and blows, whispering as she turns away. 'Sleep tight my love. I can't rest any longer.' Despite her care, there is a click as she opens the door and before it closes, she hears his reply.

'Be careful. You are too precious to lose.'

Chapter 21

At any minute her stride will have to change, forcing her into a run; Doctor Ramón walks fast and she struggles to keep him in sight. The man appears oblivious to her pursuit. He hasn't looked behind once but she doesn't take any chances and keeps well back with several pedestrians between them. His routine never varies and she is beginning to think that her intuition is off; he has done nothing out of the ordinary during the days she has been his shadow.

It is the start of another working day as they progress along his route towards Atocha Train Station. His apartment occupies the entire top floor of a baroque building in a neighbourhood teeming with designer shops and fancy cars. On Sunday mornings, he attends Mass at the local church, his wife invariably on his heels with her eyes inspecting the ground. Even at a distance, Mercedes is aware of the special welcome given by the priest. Local rumour states that the doctor is a major benefactor of the church and that the priest's enthusiasm multiplies before each fund-raising event. Some question the doctor's Christian spirit; as one of his neighbours put it, 'his view of good and evil can be a bit rigid', and someone else pointed out that he had no scruples when evicting a single mother from one of his rental flats. A creature of habit, every morning without fail he buys a copy of the same newspaper at the local kiosk and pops into the tobacconist to purchase three cigars. She now knows where he likes to eat, what he drinks and who his friends are, and has even found out which cigars he likes to smoke during the day and the more expensive ones he saves for holidays and special occasions. A few coins can purchase a lot of information when a man isn't well-liked.

Seven adults visit every Wednesday night, two of them with his grandchildren in tow; how the one flat accommodates them all, she fails to imagine, but they turn up without fail. There is talk of a beachfront villa in Gandia, that the sceptics say cost more than most of them would earn in a lifetime. The amount of his salary is still a mystery to solve; he lives the lifestyle of a rich man and, according to local records, the inheritance from his parents didn't amount to much.

The most interesting thing she has observed about the man is his unusual choice of friends. One of them, Javier Calixto, a local politician, is known to be susceptible to back-handers and has a growing influence in his party. He was a teenage colleague of the doctor when they were supporters of the Franco's right-wing and a widow with an old grudge recited tales of the two young men, who had such little tolerance for the opposition that they betrayed their families and friends. They vanished from the neighbourhood, she said, at the time that suspicious attitudes began to diminish and friends started to speak to each other again. Javier reappeared a few years later, with a new suit and smooth words, and a rise to prominence that was meteoric. It was several years, on the other hand, before Doctor Ramón came back to the area with a medical qualification (she has since found out that it originates from Berlin) and enough money to open a maternity unit in Madrid. Her informant couldn't wait to tell Mercedes that within a year the doctor had courted and married the daughter of the military police's second-in-command. The event of that year, it attracted all of society's elite including foreign diplomats and others of influence.

An entire notebook is full of facts and it is hard to separate out those that are relevant, but one thing she feels certain of; the doctor holds the key to what has happened to the babies in his clinic. The crowd on the pavement thins as employees deviate into workplaces and the strike of the hour nears. Cover is more difficult to find so she steps into an alcove while she waits for the gap to lengthen between them. The white hair of the man is her beacon and she doesn't release her fix on its movement, so when he abandons his customary route she is vigilant. He deviates to the right through a crevice that is a route between the buildings, and she darts forward to where he vanished. Her palm rests against the rough surface of the concrete wall as she eases her head little by little around the corner until she is able to peer along the dark alley. Ramshackle entrances and discarded rubbish line the narrow path, cluttering it so that she struggles to make out the features in the distance. When she is about to step closer, something moves in the shadows and she catches sight of him disappearing through an open door to the left. The 'b' is long gone from the sign outside but she guesses the letter as the odour of burning tobacco and the stink of ale waft in her direction. A group of workers, reeking of coffee and brandy, exit the bar and walk in her direction. She retreats, sheltering inside a doorway until they have passed.

While she deliberates her next move, a door opens with a loud bang that echoes to her end of the alleyway and she flattens her body against the wall and gets ready to flee, alert to the sound of the doctor's footsteps. Nothing travels in her direction with the exception of a rumble of several low voices; she holds her breath and looks again. Outside of the bar's entrance, two men loiter, deep in conversation. A spiral of smoke floats above their heads and, when the tall one raises a hand to his face, red embers glow at the end of his cigarette and his lips release a white cloud into the air. At this distance, it is impossible to make out his features and she turns her attention to the man she knows; his companion is much shorter and barely stretches to the other's shoulder. The smaller of the two draws shapes in the air with both hands and, as his excitement increases, the gestures speed up. She manages to distinguish a word or two in the midst of the garbled sound.

Absorbed in the actions of the couple, she misses the arrival of a third man until they cluster together in a circle. There is no attempt to pretend that the interloper is welcome and it doesn't take long before she realises that an argument is unfolding within the group. The angry expressions and raised voices are obvious but she is too far away to hear their words, so she drapes her black scarf over her hair and creeps around the corner. She hardly dare breathe, fearful that the sound will give her away, and prays they can't hear the drum pounding inside her chest.

Their drama unfolds and the tall man moves in front of Doctor Ramón, as though protecting his shorter colleague; light glistens when it reflects on the metal surface of the knife that the bodyguard holds in his hand. The doctor raises his voice and wags a finger under the nose of the gate-crasher and, at the same time, he signals to his wingman because the blade slices through the air and comes to a halt at the side of the interloper's neck. Too far away to see if the weapon draws blood, the words of the doctor banish any worry she has about the man's fate.

'… and make sure you get the right woman this time.'

Bile rises into her mouth and she stifles her cry. Her eyes glue onto the blade and she waits for the moment his life ends. Although she presses her back hard, it won't dissolve into the wall.

'Give it to me… another one in the next week or so… Burgos.' As quickly as it emerged, the knife disappears into a pocket in the trousers of the bodyguard and some kind of envelope or packet exchanges between Doctor Ramón and the reprieved man. The doctor inspects the contents before he slips it into his inside pocket and, amongst the mumbles, there is a word that she hears and understands, '*dinero*'. With his money secure, the doctor steps out of the circle and puts distance between himself and the other two men. Her lids squeeze together so that she isn't a witness to the man's demise, but they spring open as she quakes with the knowledge that she could be next to feel the edge of the knife. Thus far, the men are not aware of her presence and she hunts for a visible escape route. When she moves her foot back, a stone crumbles with noise that sounds like a rock fall in the silent alley. Three sets of eyes turn in her direction, but the doctor's dark pair fails to hold her attention; the green ones turn her legs to lead and root her to the spot.

Doctor Ramón roars, breaking the spell and she obeys the order to run, even though it's not intended for her. An opportunity of sanctuary is 200 metres away if she can reach the main avenue, and Mercedes runs the race of her life. She listens for the sound of footfall behind, which could close in at any moment, and when she enters the intersection, she turns right; there is no time to deliberate the choice, but she mumbles a thank you to God when she sees people ahead and believes she may be able to hide in the crowd. As she weaves her way through the throng, she tears off her scarf and jacket and stuffs them under her shirt.

The automatic glass doors of the Dia supermarket open for a customer and, without pause, she follows her in and hides amongst the housewares as she maintains a lookout. A store employee watches her for a minute, disappears and then returns with a man wearing a suit, a walkie-talkie ready in his hand; it is obvious that she has to move but she struggles to decide which direction to go. Her mind whirls and she tries to work out the connection between the three men: the doctor, the politician and the green-eyed man. There is also the matter of the photo of Orlando's father and his relationship with the group, there hasn't been a right moment to ask Orlando about it, but now things seem more urgent. The puzzle needs reconstruction; there was no friendship in the blade held against the politician's throat.

Two women act as her cover when she sneaks out of the shop and nips into the alcove to monitor the surroundings before resuming her flight. A thought teases the edge of her conscious but she can't capture the impression and a passer-by jostles her out of the way, shattering the daydream. She looks for a familiar landmark, this is unknown territory and she has no idea of where she should aim for. Not one face is familiar but she knows that eyes monitor her every move as she scans around for the perpetrator until her eyes alight on a small girl hopping on one foot, too close to the curb. The miniature ballerina performs a pirouette when she sees she has Mercedes' attention, and her heart melts as she obliges with a similar turn, complete with a shallow curtsy. Tiny palms clap in appreciation and, when the mother takes hold of one hand to pull her in the opposite direction, the girl's lower lip trembles. The dancer waves goodbye with her free hand and Mercedes does the same until the girl is out of sight, then sighs and looks around for a street sign to inform her of her whereabouts. When she spots it on the wall, it doesn't help her because there is a *Calle de Alexander Fleming* in most of the city's neighbourhoods.

No wiser, she tags onto the small crowd that waits until the green-man signal indicates it is safe to cross. While the timer counts down the seconds, a woman at her side confirms that a bus to the centre goes by every 20 minutes from the stop down the road. A car passes close to the curb, brushing her leg, and she shifts back from the danger. As the light changes to slow the traffic, someone moves in from behind and applies pressure to the middle of her back.

From that moment, everything happens in slow motion; she turns her head to ask him to give her room, the pressure increases, she plunges forward, a woman screams, and tyres screech. In those final seconds, while the sound of the vehicle grows louder and the voices of the crowd cry out, she identifies that the loudest scream is hers. There is a sickening thud as everything goes silent and darkness descends.

Chapter 22

A weight presses down on her eyelids and they can't obey her instructions, they will not open. Strange noises infiltrate the dark space: high-pitched beeps, repetitive swishes of fluid, mumbled voices. No matter how much effort she uses, her eyelids remain closed and she isn't able to see where the noises originate. Once more she tries, but has to surrender to the darkness that infuses her mind.

A new sound has joined the others the next time she wakes: two voices, a man, and a woman.

Where am I?

Her lips refuse to act and, although her brain asks the question, her mouth doesn't produce the sound.

Water.

Nothing. She is mute. She is blind. Her limbs can't move and are held down by invisible straps. She screams for help to rescue her from her nightmare, but the cries fill her head and not the room. The couple speak over her, without noticing her distress and, voiceless, she pleads with them to help her.

'Look. I think there's movement.'

Light diminishes and a shadow falls over her face. The scent of mint overwhelms her senses as someone's breath caresses her cheek.

'Can you hear me?'

She doesn't recognise the woman's voice.

'Aghh.'

Mercedes fights to answer, and this time she manages a gurgle in her throat. Another body looms over her, a man she thinks; the smell of aftershave doesn't disguise the odour of stale cigar smoke.

'She's coming around.' There is a note of excitement in the rasp. '*Señorita. Hola.*' Leathery skin covers the palm that slips into her hand and tightens around her fingers. 'Squeeze if you feel my hand. Excellent.' Something presses on her right eye and the sear of pain makes her scream for it to stop. No one hears but the pressure releases and the man issues instructions. Then the pain returns, intensifies as a bright light blinds her. 'Her reactions are improving. Keep up the observations through the night and let me know the minute there is any change.'

Any change in what? There is no reply to her silent question but as the shadows pull away, she overhears his query.

'Do we know her…?'

The squelch of their footsteps dwindles and she is alone, surrounded by the sounds of machines; regular beeps keep time with the efforts of her heart. A pungent smell of disinfectant doesn't mask the cloying aroma of blood. The cover lying across her body is rough and irritates her legs, but her fingers won't stretch out to scratch. Underneath her pelvis, she feels dampness and a ruched edge of the sheet fold digs into a sore patch on the cheek of her bottom. She fights against the sinking sensation but her lips become numb as the dark shadow re-invades her mind.

Joy replaces pain and his cry substitutes her screams as his head emerges from her body; she lifts onto her elbows and looks for her son in the space between her legs but the baby has vanished. Dressed from head to feet in a black sheet, a ghost carries him in her arms out through the door. It closes. 'Noooo.'

★

'Hello Mother. I've been searching for you.' Robby reaches for her hand. Then he starts laughing, hysterical guffaws that mock, and she screams for the noise to stop.

There is a man nearby and she hears the urgency in his voice as he questions someone. A false note of platitude taints the woman's reassurances. She knows the man's voice and it comforts her. He will help her. If she can just open her eyes. Nothing happens and she tries to dig into her memory. *Who is he?* Her mind is in a muddle and thoughts flutter, tantalise, and then fly out of touch. The effort exhausts her and she welcomes the darkness when it descends.

This time she is determined to make her eyes obey. Mechanical noises still fill the air around where she lay. There is an ache in her arm, inside of her elbow, but when she tries to shift into a more comfortable position, she can't; it is held fast, fixed against a hard, flat board. Someone forces icy fluid into the back of her hand and she reaches with her other to push him away so that she can stop the agony.

'Oh, thank God. Mercedes, can you hear me?'

His face is near hers, a man she knows. His breath warms her lips.

'Come on, darling, open your eyes. Please.'

She is too tired and wishes that he would shut up so she can drift back into sleep.

'Mercedes, just for a minute. Look at me.'

He doesn't give up. His voice serenades her with pleas and enticement, but she hasn't the energy to listen and tries to turn her face from the smell of coffee and peppermint so she can return to the peace of the dark world. Someone shakes her shoulder. *Who is this persistent person? Leave.* She will order him to go. The brightness stings.

'That's it. Come on. Open them.'

There is a whiff of musk and a sense of peace fills her; it's the smell of safety. Her eyelids separate a little. There is a squashed man at her side.

'Good. It's Orlando. See, it's me.'

Orlando. That name makes her happy. Is he family?

The white light scorches, but she wants to reward his encouragement and, when he wills her to try again, she obeys. The sky above is an expanse of white, which becomes a ceiling. Her eyes travel to the right, the side of his voice, but two metal rods block her view. She follows the poles upwards to plastic bags that hang from hooks; one contains clear fluid, the other a thick red jam. Inside a balloon, partway along one of the tubes, water drips in time with the bleeps. The man speaks and her gaze moves towards his voice. The face is wet and she wishes that she could reach out to dry the rivers on his cheeks. His smile extends into his eyes.

'Thank God. I thought I'd lost you.'

Yes, she knows him. He's the man who will help her find the lost baby. It's... the dark lake claims her.

He sleeps in a chair at her bedside and, even in his dreams, he keeps her hand wrapped in his. Dim light illuminates the room, the night shift has taken over. Reddish light glows against the white sheet and she twists her head slightly until she identifies the source – a ruby light to the left of her bedhead. Her eyes continue to explore the room; at the bedside a display of glowing numbers illuminate the machine as they change every second. They hypnotise, 64, 68, 62, 56, as they flash in time with the beeps that invaded her dreams. In another display, an inky line spikes and falls to the same beat. The figures mean something but her memory won't dig out the fact. She wants to lift her arm and knock some sense into her head.

'Mercedes. Are you awake?'

She wills him to be quiet; it is hard to think. The numbers need her attention. They are important.

'Look at me.'

It is no good, the man won't relent and she allows her eyes to move towards his voice. When she sees the features of his face, her insides melt, and she doesn't feel alone anymore.

'Hello.'

'My baby.'

'What is it, my darling? What do you want?'

'Where's baby?'

The voice soothes. 'No, it's not your baby. That's what you were working on.'

The words confuse her. He's the one helping her, isn't he? She is about to ask more, but then she remembers. *Orlando.* His smell, his hand in hers. A pain stabs her side as she tries to inhale more of him when he leans over her with his lips close to hers. The contact is fleeting and she feels a different pain when he pulls back. A teardrop lands on her cheek and his fingers tickle her skin as he wipes it away.

'Where am I?'

'In hospital, my love.'

'What happened?'

'A car ran into you. You fell into his path. He couldn't avoid you. I thought I'd lost you.' His grip tightens and brings tears to her eyes, but when she tries to loosen her fingers, he won't release.

'My hand.'

Her fingers throb with the return of pulsating blood. Phrases such as 'never wanting her to hurt again' and 'too much pain for one woman to bear' mean nothing for the moment because she wants to find out more about how she came to be lying in the hospital bed.

'When?'

For days in a coma while no one knew her identity, the staff knew her as *una persona no identificada* until someone found a handbag stuffed in a rubbish bin near the scene. One pocket inside contained her press pass and, once it was returned to the paper, they had the first clue in the puzzle of their missing colleague. As soon as the police made the connection, they were close to discovering the name of the accident victim. Orlando rushed to the hospital as soon as Jorge made the announcement.

'And he's been here ever since.' The nurse arrives without a sound and, as she does something to the bags of fluid, she bends down to whisper in Mercedes' ear. 'What a dish! Does he have a brother?' The comment makes him laugh and the nurse's face turns pink, her freckles more pronounced against the extra colour. Mercedes wants to share his happiness, but she can't fight the blanket of sleep and drifts off to the sound of his mirth.

'The police believe that you attempted suicide.'

Her memory is not that sketchy and she attempts to shout a denial but has to settle for a groan accompanied by a careful shake of her head.

'Your friend, Juanita. Do you remember what happened to her?'

In her head appears the image of a young woman tossing a blue scarf over her shoulder, and hot tears trickle down her cheeks. Unable to form the words, she uses her free hand to cover her eyes and block out the image. It doesn't disappear and a piece of her heart ruptures. He pushes gently, repeating the question until she nods. How she could forget her best friend?

His focus changes to the day of her accident. 'Do you remember why you were in that area of the city? The police told me it's not an area women visit, unless they're the working kind.'

There is one exception in her otherwise blank memory, the sensation of falling into an abyss to the accompaniment of a blood-curdling scream. She tries to escape the terror every time she closes her eyes but the tangled sheets need unravelling whenever the nurses come to change her. His disappointment makes her sad and she diverts his attention when she asks if he can fill in some of the gaps for her.

'You left for work as normal, someone saw you walk out of the flat. Jaime says you told him about an important meeting, but there wasn't anything in your diary. A security guard saw you in the train station and the man who serves in the kiosk remembers you purchasing some gum. After that, you vanished. None of the conductors remembers seeing you and you aren't on the security camera tapes, so we don't know what happened next; maybe you caught a train or maybe you went somewhere by bus. Who knows?'

Squeezing her eyes, she ignores the sounds in the room and digs deep into her memory. A kiosk, he said. The impression of a small wooden hut flashes under her lids. Something happened near the kiosk. There was the usual colourful array of magazines displayed outside and a stand stacked with newspapers of different sizes. Strung across the top of the hatch was tattered red and yellow bunting.

'The hut needed repair.'

'Excellent. Any more?' She wants to do better to keep the smile on his face. Splintered wood forms deep cracks along the joints of the hut and, in her mind's eye, she watches a man take her money; he wears a flat cap with a half-moon shaped peak. The material is faded and the pattern is hard to detect. The hat appears old, like its owner. Elated with triumph as the detail returns, she struggles harder. *What else is in the kiosk?*

When she opens her eyes to fill him in, Orlando's face goes fuzzy. There is an important fact to tell him and a flash of green eyes flickers in the darkness of her mind, but it is too late as she plummets into dreamland.

Green eyes follow every move she makes; they are impossible to escape. Her chest will explode if she pushes any harder, but as she turns every corner, the monster emerges from the ground and forces her to change her direction. A different man's voice instructs the eyes where to follow; its owner terrorises her as he reads the intention in her mind. If she pauses for rest it will be the end for her, but her legs are heavy and each step takes strenuous effort, her reserves are running out. The eyes close in behind and heavy breathing ruffles her hair. She twists and turns to avoid his hand as it hovers above her shoulder. Fear threatens to paralyse her and she opens her mouth to scream before it takes over.

'Shhh. You're safe. Easy, my dear.'

Unable to locate the woman's face behind the beam of light, Mercedes is caught in the nowhere land between nightmare and reality. Her teeth clatter and the woman instructs her to take time to breathe. A coil of damp sheet twists in a shackle around her legs and holds her prisoner; she thrashes about, driven by a compulsion to break free. The woman traps her legs under firm hands and continues to murmur reassurances until her words placate her patient and the flailing ceases.

'Do you need another cover?' The woollen edge of a blanket scratches the side of Mercedes' neck. 'There, now you should feel warmer.' Her shivering diminishes as finally, she leaves the horrors of the dream-life behind. Her eyes track the actions of the gowned woman who glides around the room like an angel. While she checks the machines and writes on the charts that hang at the end of the bed, the saint carries on with her encouragement.

'Every hour you're improving. We'll have you up and about in no time.' She returns to the bedside and peeks under the sheets. 'You're soaked. Time to get rid of this wet linen.'

The caregiver washes her from head to toe with a hot sponge and negotiates the masses of tubing as she draws a clean nightgown over her head. Exhausted by the activity, Mercedes protests that she is too tired to get out of bed. The woman performs a miracle as a pair of strong arms flips her body from one side to the other and replaces the soiled sheet with a crisp one. Before leaving the room, she places the call button between Mercedes' fingers, stands in the doorway and looks at her with a smile. 'You'll do'.

Through the crack of the door, Mercedes hears her speak to someone in the corridor and issue a warning to treat her gently. The man's body fills the doorway and the memory of her nightmares disappears. The cracks in her lips split as she smiles.

'You're looking better.' Orlando drags the chair close to the bed until it catches on the frame but he doesn't sit straight away. He devours her with his eyes, takes her hand and presses his lips to the inside of her palm; her stomach somersaults.

'Come closer.' For a moment, she shuts her lids and inhales him and then, she whispers in his ear. 'I've remembered. I was pushed.' He punches his fist into the mattress and she flinches at his reaction so he links his fingers and remains still as his knuckles turn white. 'I think I'm getting too close. They want to stop me.' He collapses into the chair, searching for something in her eyes, and she tries to disguise her fear. 'It may be about the money. The day of my accident, I witnessed some kind of meeting. They must think I'm a threat.' She tries to squeeze his fingers. 'You've got to help me.'

Chapter 23

The plaster cast has developed a grey tinge and the signatures, which decorated it when glaring white, appear tired and faded now. She counts the days until her six weeks of imprisonment ends. *Halfway there*, she sighs, reaching down to her side to capture hold of one of the rubber-tipped poles. There is a technique she uses when she manoeuvers it into position so her weight doesn't fall onto her bad leg. God forbid that should happen; as it is, she gets plenty of grief from Orlando about staying at home to get more rest.

Why do people say 'hop like a rabbit'? Her movement is nowhere near that level of agility as she hauls her body towards the lift. The plastic carrier, draped over the handle of her crutch, clinks in time with each spring; the noise drives her crazy but she hasn't found a better way to carry her things. The raw areas under her arms haven't improved with the cream and there are calluses across both of her palms. Three weeks of inactivity made her demented and last week she hobbled into the office to talk to Jorge. He was happy to have her back, with half of the staff absent for holidays. Working mornings suits her and the return journey more than once a day would kill her, even if she pretends to Orlando that the trip is a piece of cake.

Jaime calls out a comment about hop-along as she limps past his desk and she throws a quip over her shoulder, taking care that she doesn't stagger and draw further banter. The lift doors shut her in and, allowing her mouth to grimace with the pain, Mercedes rests against the metal wall, glad she can abandon her mask for a minute. When near the ground floor, she pinches her cheeks and forces a smile back to her lips. It takes an hour to complete the journey to the flat and, by that time, her good leg shakes with exhaustion and threatens to give way while she extracts the keys from the bag. She hooks the ring over her finger so she doesn't have to rescue them from the floor yet another time; she doesn't have the energy to bend down and get back up. Pushing the door open with her bottom a little too hard, it hits the wall with a bang, but she is too exhausted to care. She rests against the frame and gathers momentum for the final few metres.

'Is that you?'

'No. It's a burglar.' The minute she opens her mouth and the words tumble out, she knows they sound unreasonable. His care has helped her to survive the past few weeks, and she attempts to soften her sarcasm with an excuse that she is tired.

'Do you need help?'

'No. You have to let me learn to manage on my own. It's this dysfunctional walk, it wears me out.' Her bag stays where she's dropped it by the entrance, she performs a final sprint to the lounge, falls onto the settee with a groan and closes her eyes. The aroma of fried garlic and onions produces saliva as her stomach growls and Orlando pokes his head out of the kitchen to blow her a kiss. He sets out the cutlery for three places on the table and hands her a glass of wine.

'Scrambled eggs okay? I didn't have time to pick up anything fresh.'

'Fine.' When she nods at the table and asks what's going on, a gleam appears in his eye and his grin widens.

'There's a surprise arriving for you in a few minutes. A visitor.'

Although it has been lovely to catch up, by the time Rosa walks out of the flat, Mercedes can barely keep her eyes open. Since the accident, she has needed space for her double-sized leg, and the sofa has become her bed; Orlando thinks she should take his bed and she doesn't want to give him another excuse to put the pressure on. It has taken all of her wiles to persuade him she's comfortable with the makeshift arrangement.

'It was nice to see Rosa.'

'Hmm.' *Enthusiasm takes effort.*

'Your family want to look after you.'

Furious that he has discussed her with them behind her back, she clenches her teeth and bites back the reprimand; thereafter, her responses to him are one word until he gives up with an observation that she seems tired as he disappears to his bedroom. Cursing her bad temper, she finds it difficult to relax. He has done everything possible to keep her safe and comfortable and she repays him with complaints. The repairs to the lift in her building should soon be finished and she will be able to go home. Certain that she is capable of managing in her own flat, it will give them space. Her accident has caused their relationship to evolve with an intensity that frightens her and she fears that if she doesn't stand on her own soon, she'll reach a point where she won't want to leave.

There is another reason she must get away from Orlando; his worry about the green-eyed man drives her mad. Whenever she leaves the flat he interrogates her, wanting to know where she is going, for how long, so that she feels like she is his prisoner. He can't hide his relief when she returns in one piece.

The guilt itches so she is unable to drift off and she gives up, extending a crutch to catch the newspaper on the coffee table under the rubber tip and drag it in her direction. The front pages she reviewed at work, but there wasn't time to read the inside pages and she skips to the middle section to scan the columns for items of interest. Few headlines grab her attention and she disregards the majority of the articles, but her eyes latch onto an unusual piece in one corner of a page. The advertisement is set in a box and contains a photo of a youngish man; he holds a handwritten sign in front of his chest. *Are you my mother?* Scanty lines of text explain that he grew up in Chile with his adoptive family of German descent. The recent discovery that he is not their biological child has prompted a search to locate his natural family. He believes they may be Spanish.

Born in the 1960s, the man is too old to be her son, but she touches the face with her forefinger and tries to imagine a boy with her features in his place. She screws up the page into a ball, throws it at the fireplace and closes her eyes to ease the ache in her head. It has been torture to abandon the investigation while she is immobile and her mind fills with images of grieving mothers and children. She blinks them away and concentrates on a crack that winds across the ceiling to the white light cable. Her gaze travels to the far wall, descending until it reaches the two spiral bars of an electric fire, the elements thick with dust, as Orlando prefers a natural flame. Stretching between the elements is the pattern of a spider's web. A fly moves and struggles to break free but she knows that it doesn't stand a chance within its adversary's trap. Their situations are strangely similar, the fly and her; she also feels caught in a web, from which there is little hope of escape, but in her case the spider has a name: Doctor Ramón.

The log fire nestles in an alcove, decorated with ceramic tiles that originate from the time the building underwent a conversion two decades back. Two columns of contrasting tiles run up the sides until they reach the stone ledge that is the mantelpiece. She has never met a man so taken with photographs and they compete with each other to be on view. Some of the faces she knows well, they have observed her recovery, but today she studies them in more detail. In one print, Orlando's feet disappear into the sand and he stands with his arms around his two younger sisters; the family resemblance is undeniable in that mid-laughter moment caught by the photographer. An older woman hovers at the edge of the shot, bent over with one arm across her belly and her mouth open with laughter as she points to a mystery item not in the frame. Mercedes hops across the room to scrutinise her younger lover. Taken while he was a teenager, his shoulders are scrawny and his features immature. *Cute all the same*, she decides as she replaces it, and picks up a heavy baroque silver affair that could do with a polish. Clad in high-waisted jeans and Julio Iglesias T-shirts, two couples pose alongside a poster of the singer. She recognises his parents and the other couple could be his godparents, now aged but still the best of friends. Even today, Orlando's father is a good-looking man, but in this younger version he is more like his son. The scars of hard times now line his face, but his mother still looks great, with more subtle beauty than when she was the heavily made up girl in the photo.

Mercedes yawns, ready for sleep, but as she returns the frame to its position, she notices a photo leaning against the wall, tucked behind the others. Undetected during her time in the flat, a knot grows in her stomach as disbelief sets in. The three subjects have their arms around each other and each face holds a place in her memory. Two are his father and Orlando, the boy young with his chest puffed out and on his toes so that his height matches that of the older men. The adoration can't be misinterpreted in his expression as he looks at the man on his right. The recipient of his gaze causes questions to clutter her brain, and her heart to crack. The shorn man holds a photo of the Dictator; the image of the three men is in black and white but she knows his features and the eyes will always be green to Mercedes. She brings the photo close and tries to imagine beyond the print, but it doesn't reveal the connection between them, leaving her to wonder if she has been hasty to invest her trust in Orlando. Her eyes sweep over to the coffee table and she tries to locate the photo of his father with the doctor.

Two arms imprison her from behind and the distress of her cry shocks them both; the crutch drops and bounces onto the floor in a series of vibrations that resound through the plaster casing around her leg.

'What're you looking at that old thing for?'

Her answer is measured and doesn't betray the mayhem in her head.

'You look so young. Your dad, as well. He could be your brother.'

'Those were the days. This must have been taken more than twenty years ago.' He touches his dad's face. 'Life's been hard. It shows, doesn't it?'

Mercedes grunts and strives for nonchalance when she points to the other man. 'Friend of your family?'

'Not now. He was one of Dad's colleagues, but they fell out years ago. I don't know why I keep this.' Before she can prevent him, he removes it from the frame and rips the image into shreds. After he tosses it into the bin, he catches sight of her expression and explains. 'He betrayed us all. I hate him.' Pain colours his voice, at odds with the awe in his young face, and she puts aside further questions; that would be cruel. 'I don't know where he is now, hopefully in the ground.'

There is no time to delve into the past as her feet leave the ground and he carries her to the settee. He issues an order to stay with her leg up and complains that she will never improve if she refuses to do as her doctor instructed. His expression is unreadable but his body is as tight as a spring, and she dare not refuse so she looks up at him with a mask of meekness. When he goes through to his bedroom, she thinks through these new developments but finds it hard to establish the clarity in the connections. A torn piece of the photo is lying upside down at the side of the bin and tempts her. If she is quick, she may get to it before he returns, so she scoots across the floor on her bottom, slips it into her pocket, and returns the minute before he walks through the door. A fit of pretend coughing disguises her breathlessness and she asks for a glass of water, giving her time to recover.

It's after midnight when he finally leaves her tucked up on the sofa bed with the night light casting a soft glow on her face, and she waits ten minutes before she withdraws the piece of photo. When he was destroying it earlier, she kept silent, her curiosity on hold about the printed information on its reverse side. Now she inspects the numbers and, underneath them, detects the letters 'b' and 'c'; a press photo, what luck. Tomorrow she will look into the paper's archives of '75 and she crosses her fingers, aware that there's a slim chance this photo is from one of their sources.

'What the hell?'

She is applying the last touches to her make up when Orlando's yell penetrates the bathroom door. His curse is directed at the leather holdall at the side of the front door; it contains her belongings and is ready for the journey home tomorrow. There has been a chill between them ever since she tried to explain that it is time for her to regain her independence.

'But I thought you were happy here?'

The plaintive tone has her emotions in turmoil, and she nearly caves in, but she hardens her resolve, aware that she needs privacy. She finds it impossible to think about the significance of her discoveries when he distracts her with his every move and it's time to step up her investigation. 'The agent told me that the lift's back to normal now, so there won't be any problem getting up to the flat.'

His body arrives in front of her and he takes her hands. 'Tomorrow it is then.'

Aware of his tactics, she avoids his eyes and remains steadfast. 'Tomorrow. I'll go back there after work.'

Tonight she tries to make amends, wearing an outfit he likes, with special attention to her make-up. She distracts his efforts with a kiss, without betraying the trepidation inside.

The chilly atmosphere has not thawed completely as they head for work the following morning and Mercedes grips his arm, willing him to smile at her, but his expression is grim and his body stiff like marble. She holds him back, links her arms around his neck and nuzzles the area that pulses below his jawline.

'It's time. You know I can't stay with you forever.' He is unrelenting, unravels her arms, and carries on without speaking. She feels ill; her brave words are a front for the dread that soon she will be on her own. The icy man at her side makes her fear she may have blown her chance of love.

Chapter 24

'Oh hell.'

One of her crutches tumbles down the stairs while she struggles to balance against her door, her arms laden with her keys, handbag and food shopping. Maybe Orlando was right when he said she isn't ready to cope on her own. The metal stick is on the landing, down one flight of stairs. She stares at it, tempted to leave it there; the prospect that she may lose the deposit held by the clinic changes her mind. On her bottom, she lumbers down each step to make the rescue and, by the time she crawls back up to her flat and collapses on the settee, she has no energy left. The unpacking will have to wait and, when she stops panting, she surveys the living room, looking for damage. Reluctant to admit he knew of the break-in, Orlando was forced to tell her about it when she did not falter in her determination to return home; a neighbour had noticed the open door and reported it to the police on the day following her accident. A kind person has tried to tidy things and, apart from a broken cabinet and a few new marks on the wall, it is hard to tell that invaders have been through her flat.

A draft reminds her that the front door lies wide open and she gets to it as quickly as she can. She secures it, then reaches for the pile of post stacked on the entrance table, throws it into a carrier and takes it with her to dump on the coffee table; she intends to deal with it later. The display of her answerphone indicates that the memory is full, but she decides it can wait until she's had some refreshment.

'Two more weeks and you'll be free.' The leg doesn't answer, of course, and it occurs to her that talking to it could be a sign her head injury hasn't fully recovered, but the sound of her voice breaks the silence. It has been a long time since she hasn't been surrounded by hospital noises or Orlando's presence. She feels less lonely when she enters her kitchen and its familiarity and, as she puts the groceries away, she hums until she spies the radio and selects a pop station. The sound of Oasis blasts into the room and lightens her spirit.

Replete with food and drink, she is ready to tackle the correspondence and, with paper and a pen, she listens to the phone messages.

'Hi. This is Isabel. Rosa told me about your accident. I'll call later.'

Half of the callers echo a similar sentiment and she lists the people to call back. One message pricks her interest; an anonymous woman requests that Mercedes contact her about an important personal matter. The telephone number she leaves isn't a local one and the prefix, which would give her a clue, isn't one she recognises. The bag of post waits for her attack but, intrigued by the message, she knows she won't be able to concentrate until she dials that number. The ringing goes on forever and she is about to hang up when there is a rustle in the speaker as someone lifts the handset.

'*Digame.*' Speak to me.

The voice doesn't give her any clues. It belongs to a stranger and, no wiser, she clarifies her identity and mentions the strange message.

'Yes, I left it.' The woman's voice sounds distorted, as though her hand covers the mouthpiece when she speaks. 'I have a message for you, from one of the sisters. She needs to see you.'

'Who?'

'I can't tell you.'

'Who are you?'

'I help at the convent.'

'Can't it wait? I've broken my leg and it's difficult to get around.' Mercedes is about to tell her it's impossible when the woman dangles an enticement.

'I don't know how much longer she'll last. I read the paper to her and, when she heard about your accident, she was insistent that I phone you.'

The woman has piqued her interest but refuses to give her further information until Mercedes agrees to come to the convent on the following Tuesday. It is in an area of Madrid she doesn't know, she has no hint to the name of the nun, and it may be a wasted journey. Nevertheless, her intuition spurs her to look forward to the visit with growing interest.

Another surprise awaits Mercedes; amongst the free marketing papers and bills is an envelope with an American postmark. In his four-page letter, Robby describes his return to the United States and the semblance of reconciliation with his father; he says that everything remains peaceful if he avoids mentioning his adoption.

I have some exciting news for you. I met a guy in Georgia during an open day at the university. Something in his looks reminded me of some of the people I met when I was in Spain, so I introduced myself. Here's the thing. While we were talking about the courses we were signing up for, his mother joined us. I must have looked surprised because, when she saw my confusion at their different colours, she told me that she adopted my new friend when he was a baby. Of course, I was eager to tell him of the co-incidence and he asked if I knew about the support group that helps children to find their birth families. He gave me the number and I made contact with them and, although it is the early stages, they are hopeful that they may be able to obtain more information for me about my origins.

This fact will interest you; I am not the only child who they think comes from Spain. Apparently, many adopted children also came here from China and some from South America. It makes me wonder how many of us there are.

It would be easy to drown in the optimism that her child is one of them and she clutches the letter to her breast as she tries to quell her excitement. She isn't familiar with the organisations he refers to and hasn't heard of any locally, but the people of her country incline towards secrecy about such things. On her list, she notes a reminder to seek the adoption stats for other parts of Spain, trying to keep her enthusiasm in check as Robby warns her near the end of his letter that the co-ordinator told him the search might take years.

The journey across the city is arduous on crutches and she is not in a generous mood as she trails a black waddling tent through the dimly lit corridor. A life of devotion has not spared the woman's figure and Mercedes has to turn sideways to squeeze past the bulk into the cell. The room is not as big as her bathroom, and yet it contains a single cot, a chair, a bedside table and two shelves. One wall-shelf is positioned halfway between the ceiling and floor; balanced on top are several books, one of them a leather Bible, and a wooden cross. The other shelf is a few millimetres off the floor and the padded material that covers it is threadbare, evidence of knees that have lowered onto it for many years. An icon of Mary hangs from a hook on the wall, adorned with fresh lavender, but the smell of decay that permeates the air of the room can't be masked by the scent.

On her first inspection of the cell, she misses the rise in the sheets, a pimple not a mound, and she turns back to ask the guide to take her to the correct room. Then, in the corner of her eye, she catches sight of a stirring beneath the white parachute and there is the sound of rasping breath that ends in a stifled moan. Her escort raises a black wing and points to a chair with a crooked digit, maintaining her silence. The atmosphere seems to lift a little when the old nun trudges out of the room; no words were necessary to signal her disapproval of the visit to her dying sister.

Outside of the cloisters, the weather is perfect with summery warmth so she didn't bother to bring a cardigan. Here, inside the dark building with its tiny windows, the air is dank and cool, and she buffs her arms to get rid of the goose bumps while she watches the rise and fall of the white outline. Not a word interrupts the silence and she searches for clues to the identity of the nun; a beaded cross that lay diagonally over a prayer book is the only item of a personal nature. When her last breath expires and the bed linen is changed, all traces of this woman will be erased, a sad legacy in Mercedes' opinion.

The song of a lark invites her to step near the window and, when she leans out, she discovers a courtyard full of surprises. There is colour everywhere, in stark contrast to the stone building. Purple bougainvillea and red roses climb the trellis on two of the walls and a variety of plants cover the ground: Aloe Vera, cacti and, her favourite, Birds of Paradise. The centrepiece of this sanctuary is an empty marble fountain. A large crack fractures the base and the descent into dereliction probably began when it would no longer hold fluid. A layer of scum doesn't completely obliterate the original pink; it must have been a beautiful sight when the waters flowed.

A creature wails with a pitiful noise that breaks her contemplation and she looks towards the bed, from where it originates; a white cap, a piece of ear shaped skin and a crepe cheek are visible on the swell of the pillow. No features of the face tweak her memory and Mercedes steps closer to search for something that she recognises. Pale eyes point in her direction from the quicksand supporting the distinguishing features of the woman's face. Her lips try to say something, but they are stuck together, interlinked along the dry cracks. There is neither a glass nor water in the room and she is at a loss as to what she can offer the invalid. About to put her head out of the door and call for help, she notices a damp flannel hanging over the side of a bowl of water tucked under the bed. Condensation drips down the outside of the metal container and wets her hands when she lifts it. She soaks a corner of the cloth in the cold fluid and offers it to her parched lips. The old woman sucks like a baby on its blanket and Mercedes puts aside her disgust at the skin sliding over the bones when she strokes the ancient hand. The patient spits out the cloth, racked with a coughing fit that goes on and on and, worried the strain will be too much for that frail body, Mercedes eases an arm behind her bony back and helps the feather-light woman to sit upright. While she battles with her silent hacking, white fuzz escapes from the cap and forms a decorative collar around the neck's bony contours. Distracted by the wispy curls, Mercedes almost misses the signal of her hand. She lowers the bones back onto the pillow, her ancient eyes shut, and her mouth falls open. There is nothing here to discover and Mercedes gathers her things and assumes a starting position on her crutches. A voice hisses.

'Fest.'

It stills her, and she turns her head and stares in amazement; *that voice is too strong for her frail body*. She limps back to the bedside, lowers into the chair and leans across to take her hand as she encourages her with a soothing voice. A foul smell emanates from the open mouth and Mercedes pulls back, but the sounds are incomprehensible and she needs to be near. She edges forward, breathing through her mouth, until the words are audible. Something pierces her hand and she jerks it back with a cry. She has to use her other hand to unwind the woman's grip and loosen her jagged fingernails. The scratches are tinged with blood; she can't believe the nun has the strength to inflict so much damage with those talons.

'Fest.'

There is no such word stored in her brain and she remains silent until, with a judder in her breath, the nun tries again.

'Confest.'

Her leg is killing her and she is reluctant to make any more trips to the door, so her heart sinks as she puts weight onto her arms to push herself up again. 'Okay, I'll call for the priest.'

'No,' the old woman gasps. 'You.'

Her head yanks around and she glares at the bed. 'I don't think so. You've got the wrong person.' Mercedes has had enough but, as she collects her things, the woman begins to thrash in the bed. Contorted fingers beckon her near.

'I. Confess.'

The voice holds her stationary as she studies the withered flesh and looks for the structures of cheeks, chin and the distinctive parts that define a person's face; her effort is to no avail and she struggles to drag up a memory. Finally, it comes to her in an image against her eyelids – the black and white witch carrying her baby from the room and closing the door on her son forever. Her lids fly up as she examines the woman's eyes again to be certain. For now, curtains of blue-tinged skin hide them and she reaches a hand to shake the woman to consciousness. Before making contact, she snatches back her fingers and traps them under her thigh; the other hand presses on her knee to control the frantic tap of her good leg. It is five minutes, or could be five hours, before her eyelids lift, confirming the nun's identity for Mercedes. Her hands clench together, leaving the knee to resume its frenetic movement; if she doesn't control them, they will create a noose around the woman's neck.

'Where's my son?'

Her tired eyes don't reveal fear until Mercedes morphs into a bully. There is hardly any space between their noses and her growl results from an animal instinct.

'I know you. You took my child. How dare you call yourself a woman of God. You're evil.'

The sleeping cap remains empty on the pillow when the sister turns her head away from the menace and unmasks a bald scalp that sports tufts of white fuzz and distended blue veins. The vessels look as though pressure will burst them open at any moment, but Mercedes ignores them; anger eradicates any pity she once felt. She recoils at the thought of touching the woman who has haunted her dreams for more than ten years but madness takes over and murder is a possibility. Then, similar to a wave retreating into the sea, her anger ebbs, leaving emptiness in its wake. Tears navigate the creases in her neck, that has provided the temptation to her hands, and her elderly lips tremble as Mercedes hides her face in her hands.

'Confession. In drawer.'

The eyes no longer appear wicked, only ancient and sad, as they escort hers to the bedside cabinet. Mercedes touches the first drawer with a glance to the bed for confirmation that she is at the correct place. The runners are worn so she has to tip the drawer from side to side to ease it out, taking care that it doesn't stick; halfway out, it refuses to budge and she wiggles the handle of her comb inside. Thin and long, she slides the tool in until she levers the obstruction out of the way and the drawer opens to reveal the guilty object, a tattered cover of a book, curled up at its corners. The comb has made an impression in the surface but it is one of many imperfections. She lifts it over to the bed with both hands to support the binding as it threatens to split and shed the sheets that have detached from the glue. Some of the furrows between Sister Francisco's eyebrows smooth when Mercedes places the book at her side.

'My confession.' The gnarled fingers tap the cover and, with a sigh, she pushes the book towards Mercedes. 'Read.'

While she obeys and turns over the front cover, the voice in the bed murmurs a familiar prayer. The words don't distract her, nor does she notice when they fade into silence.

The nursing sisters who come into the cell to administer care to their patient ignore the outsider who sits in the corner as she digests the contents of the journal. In her private world, Mercedes has no desire for food or drink as the book fulfils her needs. After a decade of mystery, the small notebook that contains the sister's memoirs confirms what she has believed from the beginning; her baby was alive when the sister carried him from the labour room. Her teenage mind did not fabricate a hallucination and her eyes well with gratification. Her feelings change, first with a simmer, and then her blood starts to boil as she finishes reading it for the second time. The journal goes into her bag; it is hers now. In her head, questions clamour for answers and she looks to the bed for signs of life. A gentle rise and fall of the sheet indicates the devil hasn't claimed her yet; Mercedes is prepared to sit through the night if she must and force the woman to admit the name of the town on the border that they used. And where he went after that. And whether her child stayed in France. The first question

218

of the interrogation will be why they chose her child to steal and that is only the beginning.

A feeble groan gives her permission to let the volcano of abuse flow; she has been storing it inside during her vigil at the bedside.

'Forgive…' Her lips struggle to enunciate the word but Mercedes' wrath overflows and her sympathy has vanished.

'Never. You took my son, my life. And what about the other children? In the name of your church, you should burn in hell!'

There is a stutter and a whimper within the sheets that stops her tirade and her hand stifles further abuse. With her confession, the sister has committed a betrayal of her colleagues and of the doctrine she has followed through her entire adult life. The woman needed to find courage in her decision to go against everything she holds dear and, if it were possible to grant forgiveness, Mercedes would. Her tongue won't form the words. As though a heavy load burdens her, she struggles to rise and, before leaving, she contemplates the tiny rise in the white landscape of the bed.

'I guess we are both victims, in our own ways,' she says as she touches the papery skin. 'I will find him.' She tucks the rosary between the woman's digits and whispers words of forgiveness before slipping from the room. Not all of her questions have answers, but she has proof that her son survived, and she hopes that God will forgive even the worst of sinners.

Chapter 25

'I don't need to ask if you're glad to be free.'

Her smile is so wide that it begins to ache and other pedestrians respond to her happiness with cheerful good-day greetings. After months as a prisoner, she is walking on two legs, without a plaster, without a crutch.

'Thanks for coming with me. Who would have thought that doing something this basic would be the best feeling in the world?'

Rosa chuckles and embraces her around the waist, releasing her when Mercedes loses her balance and teeters towards her. 'It's great to see you back to normal.'

'Not quite normal yet, but soon I'll be running races, you'll see.' She looks at the clock tower. 'We have time. Shall we celebrate?'

They enter the first bar they come to and sit down at a table near the window. The waiter thinks he's a Romeo, the type who lowers his voice to seduce any half-decent woman. The effect is over the top and, when he goes to collect their order, the women collapse with laughter.

'You shouldn't lead him on, you naughty married woman.'

Rosa's laughter turns into hiccups and, although Mercedes can't stop them with the usual remedies, they do draw a smile from the sour face of the old man at the next table. While her sister gulps water in a final attempt at a cure, she turns her face to the sun and grins in the knowledge that things are changing for the better. Without the plaster, her leg seems to weigh nothing and she stretches out to inspect it again. It is thinner than its counterpart and her toes have an odd appearance, like little brown sausages poking out at the end of the pale limb. The limp doesn't bother Mercedes as the doctor has reassured her it will improve, and nothing can blight her relief that she is free. Soon, she can take the trip she has been anticipating.

'What're you thinking?' The hiccups and laughter have ended and a cloud passes over the sun. Her sister shivers and reaches for her cardigan.

How does Rosa do that? It's as though she is able to look inside Mercedes' head, although no one knows what happened when she met with the nun; even Orlando thinks she went in pursuit of a different story. Since that visit, the confession has been a plague in her mind and she wonders if this is the time to share her intentions with her sister. Her eyes fix on the scar as she considers the pros and cons of telling Rosa. The doctor warned that the evidence of her accident would mark her leg for the remainder of her life. Until a few months ago, Juanita would have been her confidant; now she is gone and Mercedes has to make a choice about trust. Her recent brush with death has made her fearful that she may not live out her dreams of reuniting with her son and, if she dies, no one knows her child is alive. Her supreme wish is that he learns she had not intended to let him go. At the thought of him, there is no question about what she needs to do and, when Rosa touches her hand, she allays any lingering doubts.

'You can trust me. I won't let you down.'

Their eyes meet and it is as though she looks into her own soul. Their connection is undeniable and Mercedes realises what she says is true. Her sister will never let her down; her heart is too generous.

'Do you have time to stay a while? It is a long story.'

At the end of her tale, Mercedes' body feels different. Her neck moves without restriction, and the weight has lifted from her shoulders. Her secret is out in the open and she has not edited the facts. Her fingers beat the table while she looks for signs of disillusionment in the face of her younger sister. When tears well in Rosa's eyes, she is saddened that she has been the one to mar her sister's happiness. Like a balloon that loses its air, her soul deflates, and she blinks away her tears, missing the moment when Rosa's hand moves; she is first aware of it when she feels lips on the inside of her palm. The touch reminds her of another's lips on the same spot.

'I knew. About the baby.' Her head snaps up and Rosa nods. 'I've always known. The doors couldn't contain Father's words.' When she notices her expression, Rosa is quick to reassure Mercedes. 'Don't worry. No one else was with me and, of course, our parents never discussed it. I don't think anyone else in the family knows.'

Mercedes can't shed the shame of her teenage self. She is thankful her sin isn't common knowledge.

Rosa nods sadly. 'You weren't ready to tell me, so I've waited.' Excitement, or fury, causes a glint in her sister's eyes. 'I didn't know he was born alive.'

'So far, I haven't the proof that he still lives but I intend to find out, even it takes forever. His spirit is with me constantly, I feel it in my pores.'

'Can I help? I'll do anything. What's next?'

'In her diary, the sister who I went to see mentions a convent near the border. According to the map, there is a mountain village close by. I've checked the timetables and can get there in a day. That's my next stop.'

'But will you be safe? You told me people have tried to stop you.' Rosa stares at the scar and Mercedes pulls at her skirt as she tries to hide the reminder, but she fails to allay her sister's concern. Fear grips her as she anticipates their next attempt to stop her but she can't admit to anyone that she lies awake for hours and worries about how far they will go.

'Why doesn't Orlando go with you?'

She can't explain the breathlessness and the walls that are closing in on her, and how the speed and intensity of their relationship stifles her. Her excuse splutters until it fades into silence and she is free to focus on her knees.

'What's that, at the corner of your mouth?'

Rosa passes her a paper serviette and she pats the area. There is a red blot on the white tissue and she crumples it as the gnawed hole begins to sting.

'He doesn't know about my baby.'

'Why not tell him? He's a good man. And he loves you.'

'Do you think so? Maybe one day soon. I can't lose him yet.'

While she travels north on the train, Mercedes replays the conversation but she can't imagine that her sister has predicted Orlando's reaction correctly. It is impossible to know how he will view her past but he has an old-fashioned side to his personality that reminds Mercedes of her father. If his reaction is similar, it will split her heart into pieces. The debate rages in her head and tablets don't dull the pain. She sighs with relief when the conductor announces her station. A sharp pain shoots from her hip to her toes when her weight goes onto her weak leg; stiff to move, it aches after hours seated on the train. This town is the end of the train line and she has to catch a bus for the remainder of the journey but when she checks at the ticket office, the afternoon bus has been cancelled and there isn't another until dawn the following day.

Her first task is to find a bed for the night. The town doesn't look very different from others she has visited in the north; it is hardly more than a large village and seems to have a disproportionate number of churches to bars. Chair-rooted residents line the street outside their houses and heads turn to follow her when she walks past their front doors. There is an atmosphere of suspicion – maybe they think she will walk into their homes and steal their valuables – and she keeps her chin high as she walks the gauntlet. Thousands of invisible daggers lodge themselves in her back and the few responses to her *'buenos dias'* are grudging. It is difficult to understand the mash of Spanish, French and another language she can't recognise.

Young men gather in gangs in the Plaza Major, the central square, and she breathes in and quickens her stride to cross. Concerns that she has mistimed her visit and arrived at the start of a demonstration are unfounded when she discovers they are not troublemakers, simply friends meeting for fun. Two carry a banner bearing the name of a football team and the group moves as one towards a coach at the edge of the square. With the disappearance of the threat, she pauses in the public space to look around. Unlike the ornate plazas of Madrid and Salamanca with their ancient buildings and monuments, this one centres on a dry fountain painted with graffiti. The artwork is almost professional and makes her laugh out loud with its caricatures: political heavyweights holding weighty bags of money, the same political scoundrels squeezing the prominent assets of curvaceous ladies, and other well-known officials with euro signs in their eyes as they steer bulldozers over houses. To ensure the meaning is clear, explicit words (rude but effective) encourage a break from the central government control.

Underneath an ancient tree, she glimpses a wooden structure, a table made up of a pallet balanced on stones. Surrounding it are half a dozen men who sit on all kinds of dilapidated chairs and stools. Each man wears the same uniform: faded trousers that fasten well below his protruding stomach and an open-neck shirt with sleeves rolled midway up weathered arms. The circle of black berets slants downwards as they focus on their game and no one looks up to check out her arrival, she is of less interest than the cards in their hands. Near her destination, the bell tower erupts from one corner of the square and the air cools as she moves under its shadow. The girl in the station directed her to a *hosteleria* near the end of the alley behind.

Music permeates the plaza, spilling through the church doors as they open; the voices that sing praises and the organ all need tuning. A man sings a closing prayer and she peeks through the gap for a glimpse of the altar. The musician has her nose pressed against the sheet music, which accounts for the frequent miscalculation of the keys she pounds. The organist is not the only ancient thing inside of the building; stone crumbles in the arch above her head and light beams through cracks in the wooden door. A haze of incense blurs the golden apparition behind the altar table, gilt covering everything from candlesticks to ceiling. Uneasy when she takes out her camera inside the holy place, Mercedes tries to be quick but before she presses the button, a black widow carrying a bucket of cleaning items shuffles into the edge of the frame. The woman ignores the service as she tends the flowers along the side aisle. She throws dead blooms onto the floor and hums a hymn, increasing the volume after the priest finishes his final blessing. The half-dozen members of the congregation file out and Mercedes ducks a knee and makes the sign of the cross as she slides along one of the pews. Even as a young girl, during weekly visits to the local church with her mother she polished the silverware and swept the tiles. The atmosphere bathes her with reminders of childhood and her enthrallment with the pageantry of the celebrations.

'I am going to be a priest when I am old,' she announced at five, not grasping the reason for everyone's laughter when she wore a collar made of white paper around her neck. Not much older, she understood their hilarity and announced that she was destined for a convent, but her parents had laughed at that as well; Mama had mumbled some words about her rebellious spirit.

Metal clangs as the woman drops a platter and returns Mercedes to the present. She needs somewhere to sleep the night and reluctantly leaves the solitude of the sanctuary. Twilight has descended and she hurries to the inn without detour, crossing her fingers until the proprietor confirms she has a bed.

Several passengers are already at the bus stop for the dawn departure and when she alights, she claims an empty seat at the back and takes out her bread roll; it was too early for breakfast in the inn. Eyes fixed forward, she dare not look out of the window as the bus winds a way that shadows the river. No barriers separate the gulley from the edge of the road and every so often she spots a rotting mound of metal where the driver of a vehicle miscalculated the drop. Her driver takes his hands off the wheel as he chats with the passenger behind his seat; she closes her eyes and prays. When they reach the village, she is the first to disembark, heading for the bar across the road and ordering a strong coffee. After she gulps it down, she orders another and carries it to a small window that opens onto the main road. It is the only road and houses a few derelict buildings, a church and this bar, all with pitched roofs, built of stone and finished with red and white decoration. The sign for the end of the village is visible to her left and the one that marks the beginning is immediately outside of the building where she drinks. Her sprit deflates as she realises she should have made enquiries by telephone before the tedious journey.

The proprietor is old and worn, similar to his bar, and argues in a loud voice with the only other person around: a man of similar age who perches on a stool and leans on the counter with a tray of spent cigarette butts between his elbows. When she comes near to hand over coins to the landlord, a stench from the man's clothing warns her to breathe through her mouth.

Outside the air is considerably cooler than in the city and she gathers her cardigan to her body while deliberating her next move. With little choice, she walks across the road towards the church. Mercedes wonders where the congregation comes from; she counts six houses and, when she tries the door and the handle won't budge, it occurs to her that she is standing outside a relic of the past. A bird calls and she turns her face to the sky. The soloist can't be seen but a crane's nest protrudes through the alcoves of the bell tower. The chirp she heard sounded too delicate for those giants, and the sun appears from behind a cloud and blinds her at the exact moment a man speaks into her ear. She flinches.

'Can I help?'

He is tall, that is the first thing she notices when the spots in front of her eyes fade. His robes are too short and she grins, certain that the red socks are not part of the regulation dress. The man of God is wide and the folds of his neck spill over the edge of his white band; it is so tight that she is amazed he is able to breathe. An aura, almost a halo, illuminates the area above his head and she rubs her eyes but it doesn't disappear until another cloud covers the sun. Creases radiate to his hairline from the edges of his eyes and they match those at the sides of his mouth; his smile crumples most of the features of his face. She senses that she will like this man even as the disappointment takes over.

'You can't be Father Emanuel, you're too young.'

Laughter booms in the barren space, everything about him is big. The barman and his companion have moved outside under the shade of a pine tree and, at the sound of the merriment, they glare at the priest before returning to their contest.

With a twinkle in his eye, the priest holds a finger to his lips and speaks in a loud whisper. 'We mustn't upset the daily game of the locals, people have been expelled from this village for less.'

She gets the impression that his jest holds some truth and asks him, 'Aren't you from here?'

'Goodness no. I'm from a small mountain town near Teruel. I came here three years ago to replace your Father Emanuel. My superiors hoped I would understand the local needs, as I come from a similar village, but I think they were deluding themselves.'

Friendliness oozes out of him, but she chooses her words with care to avoid giving offence. 'The men do seem a little standoffish.'

The folds deepen at the sides of his eyes and his mouth turns down. 'Strangers make them nervous, with just cause. This village has lost more than its fair share of men during the last century.' She expects more, an explanation perhaps, but he changes the topic. 'Why are you looking for the infamous Father?' He scrutinises her eyes but she remains mute. His note of sarcasm shocks her and signposts that his relationship with his predecessor might have had difficulties.

'Someone gave me his name.' She skirts around his question and asks one of her own. 'What was he like? Did you know him?'

'He handed things over to me, with reluctance and little grace; he felt bitter because he was pushed out of his job. The man ruled by fear and gloried in his power, two qualities that do not belong in any man of the church, as far as I am concerned.' Mercedes suspects that if he didn't wear the church uniform, the priest would elaborate, and she tilts her head to one side and studies him.

'I hate to besmirch the man, but let's just say he hated to part with information. Too often, my mistakes occur because he didn't fill me in with the background knowledge I needed. My job is to gain the trust of my flock and insensitive speech can have lasting consequences.'

A greeting interrupts the gloom and he twists around to wave to an elderly woman in her doorway. They shout their conversation about the church flowers at full volume until he reassures her that he will see her later and mumbles out of the side of his mouth that he wishes the woman would wear her hearing aids as he turns back to Mercedes. The robe doesn't hide the wobbles of his stomach beneath his hand as he chuckles. 'The past is the past, and I can't change anything that's happened. I am making progress and one or two of the locals like me now.' *More than one or two*, she bets as she wishes her childhood priest had been as approachable.

Indicating a bench in a gravel area overlooking the churchyard, she requests a few minutes to chat. His bulk fills most of the seat and squeezes her into the corner; she holds her breath as he makes himself comfortable, certain that the slats are going to give way under his weight. When he settles, she remains alert for indications in his demeanour that a subject is taboo and asks for his opinion about the changes in how modern individuals view religion. His intelligent eyes glisten as they embark on a lively debate until she thinks he is off guard and deviates with questions about relationships with neighbouring France and fluidity of movement across the border.

'It's there.' He points out a hillside less than half a kilometre away and, when she covers her eyes to block the sun, she detects a faint white scar that zigzags up the face of the slope until it disappears at a rocky summit. 'That's how close we are, and yet, we speak different languages and have our own cultural idiosyncrasies. Some locals here speak as many as four languages, but many of the elders can't read or write. A few refuse to speak Castellano with me; it's not their native tongue.'

The words flow but his eyes assess her, and she assumes she passes his appraisal because he offers her a carrot. 'Borders, they aren't real, just imaginary lines that separate our towns, our departments and our countries. Yet, they're easy to slip across, like phantom fences. I suspect many people cross them when they want to disappear.'

The statement comes from nowhere, and she flusters. Sharp eyes stare and strip away her pretence as he cocks his head and hardens his tone. 'Maybe it's time that you explain who you are and what you want with the old priest.'

Not certain if she can trust a man who wears the mantle of the same organisation as the nun that stole her baby, she stares up at the church tower and touches the stolen journal. Having come this far, she decides to take her chances. 'A nun gave me information that brought me to this place.' Hopefully, God won't punish her for the white lie.

'Why you?'

She shakes her head before answering; she had expected him to ask about the information. Her upbringing takes over and her words spill out as though she is in the confessional. She holds nothing back as she explains about her own baby and her commitment to the investigation.

'I believe that babies were separated from their mothers so they could be sent to families in other countries.' Her raised hand silences his attempt to interrupt. 'I don't know why, maybe it's for money. I do know that at least one convent was involved; there may be more.' Speaking the words aloud for the first time, she is convinced it is the truth. When she read what Sister Francisco had written in her journal, that a Father Emanuel collected babies from the clinic, Mercedes searched everywhere until she discovered the whereabouts of the priest. The unearthing of his location near the border helped her to make sense of how transporting the babies might work.

Awaiting a response to her theories, she nibbles the dry skin at the edge of a fingernail. His face discloses nothing and when his words dash her expectations, she understands that she misjudged him as an ally.

'It's a fascinating theory, but I can't help you.'

Hatred for him and his kind surges through her and she jumps to her feet, holding back her frustration with clamped teeth and shut lips. She refuses to disgrace herself with a torrent of abuse but it is on the verge of pouring out and there will be no stopping it once under way. Her own stupidity makes her angrier; she has always known they protect their own.

He catches her hand with an unrelenting grip and unnerves her as he tugs her around so she has to look down into his face. 'This is more than a story for you, I know that. If I had information, I would help. The thought of stealing a child makes me want to call upon the wrath of God to punish those responsible. I can only tell you what I hear through local gossip, there are plenty to pass it around a village like this. It's one of local past times, I'm afraid; people talk amongst themselves and don't realise I understand their words.'

As he speaks, her eyes focus on the bare skin at the crown of his head. He will be bald before much longer. She shakes the fluff out of her head, like a wet dog ridding his fur of water, before she asks about the rumours.

'One legend is founded on the sightings of lights that travel along the mountain tracks, like glow-worms in the night, and another describes apparitions that haunt the mountains, ghosts of lost children. Not one of the village women will go there, their name for it is Spirit Mountain.' Her eyes follow the direction of his fingertip to a peak across the gorge. 'Parents lock their doors at night. They say it's to stop the bogey man taking their children. Bizarre, isn't it? What could happen in a place that has few visitors and no place to hide?'

Something crawls up the back of her neck and makes her shudder. He looks at the bumps on her arms and attempts to lighten the gloom that descended with the talk of ghouls.

'Join us for next Sunday's service. You'd enjoy it; the church can be quite full.' At her raised eyebrows, he laughs. 'The village has more than these few buildings, there are homes that you can't see. Lots of smallholdings hold positions in those hills.'

Of course there are; a full-time priest is an expensive indulgence for half a dozen houses and she smiles, pleased he has a decent congregation. He pats the bench at his side and waits for her to sit down again, then he speaks, just above a whisper, with his eyes directed at the men. 'There is a convent, but with few sisters. Young girls don't choose a life of seclusion anymore.' He leans back and inspects the clouds, and she hears the splitting of the wooden seat as showers of splinters fall onto the ground. 'Maybe there is an element of truth in the folklore, a Pied Piper of the mountains. Who shall we consult? Not the old man, he won't help.'

No response is expected, he is rambling aloud as he thinks. She asks him which old man he means.

'Father Emanuel, weren't you searching for him?' The robed man nearly receives the impact of her palm and she reminds him that he said the old priest was gone.

'Yes, gone, not dead. No, even heaven is reluctant to open its gates for him.' Palms together, he raises his eyes to the heavens. 'Sorry, Father.' A hint of a naughty youth of days gone by shows in his expression and, for a second, she wishes he worked in a different world; then she could cherish him as her friend.

'Three nuns from the old convent look after him at a farmhouse. It's out in the wild but they are self-sufficient with chickens, pigs and a vegetable garden. There isn't a lot of money, but they seem to manage. Once a month, I venture out to offer them spiritual support. There's a history with the locals and they aren't welcome in the church, so I do what I can to give my services; it is easier to keep them apart. The sisters used to work in the local school and I think they may have been hard on their pupils; those children are adults now and grudges against cruel teachers last.'

Worried he is ready to go off on a tangent, she breaks in and asks about the location of the farmhouse. The wave of his hand indicates an area of rough land nearby and she stares until she spots the rocky foundations of an overgrown path, which disappears into a pine forest.

As she looks at her leg, her enthusiasm wanes. 'Is it far?'

'A few kilometres but it's steep at times.' A request for help is on her lips, but her determination sets in when he continues, 'You won't do it in those. I'll ask Gustavo, the man over there, to take you.'

Gustavo has poured himself a large brandy for each of her coffees and brought another outside, so she grabs her bag and stands, hoping that her throbbing limb won't fail the test.

'Thanks. I prefer to get there without further injuries. I'm stronger than I look.'

Together they amble to the edge of the village while the inhabitants of the few houses step out of their doorways to watch their progress. Silent suspicion burns through her clothes but the waddling priest pays no attention, droning trivia while nodding his head and smiling at each person they pass. Upon reaching the open countryside, he turns, places his hand on her head and blesses her before she has time to step away. The rubble track disappears down the slope ahead and he advises her to avoid straying from the main path.

'Don't worry about the villagers, they're harmless. You won't miss the turning you need to take, the post marking it is rather special.'

He acts cagey when she probes the remark and the only comment he will add is that it is worth the wait. After a few steps along her route, she returns to embrace him in a tight hug. She kisses his cheeks and sets off again.

He blushes as he issues a final warning. 'Don't expect much from the old tyrant. Use your brain, and some of that womanly persuasion.' He tries to give a lewd wink, but it looks so out of place that she dissolves into laughter.

'I don't know that I've got much of that.'

'My dear, if I was available, you'd be the first on my list.'

Her mouth stretches into a delighted grin that remains in place as she disappears into the pine forest. Now she has escaped the suppressive atmosphere of the village, she starts to hum a happy tune.

In the distance, his voice shouts out another warning. 'You may run into travellers. It's a section of the *Camino*.'

Her hands create a megaphone as she calls back to him. 'The what?'

'The *Camino de Santiago*. For the pilgrims.'

She unfolds the map she carries in her pocket and looks for the line that designates the French border. When her eyes follow its path, she spots a dotted line that comes over the border from France and extends across northern Spain to the city of Santiago, near the west coast. The route shadows the line of the mountains; some men in her office are weekend walkers and discuss their dreams of walking *El Camino* upon retirement. She hadn't realised she was so close to the subject of their ambitions.

The name of the route inspires a headline for the next article of her series, *The Innocent Pilgrims*. As she mulls over the structure to the piece, her shoe slips on loose stones and the jolt sends a shooting pain up her leg. Gingerly she takes another step, relieved to discover she hasn't caused any damage. Not about to take further chances, she pulls the stray twigs from a branch she finds on the ground and fabricates a walking stick.

Less than an hour later, her blouse sticks to a damp back and an intense ache in the recently healed bones cripples her. She refuses to turn around and grits her teeth as she leans more of her weight onto the aid and moves on. The worn stones and dirt grooves contain evidence that many feet have trodden the path and she wonders if she walks in the footsteps of the thief who carried her son from his birthright. Although she doesn't believe in the ghosts of the village fables, she has a feeling some spirits of stolen babies travel beside her, urging her to continue her fight.

Chapter 26

Green slopes give way to a stony pinnacle shrouded in cotton wool, and she is gasping, nearly beaten by the task. The skin on her left heel is in shreds and a paper tissue protects it from the rough seam of her shoe. Maybe the dodgy driver would have been better than this walk; it never seems to end. Her water bottle is almost empty and there are frequent growls from her tummy, reminding her and the world that she hasn't eaten for hours. According to the priest's instructions, she should have reached her destination by now, but the metres continue to stretch out with no buildings in sight. As she stops and catches her breath, she takes time to survey the land ahead; a yellowish slide weaves in hairpins down the face of the mountain. Perched on a boulder, she watches a trail of ants emerge over the summit and move in convoy down the path. When they come closer, their misshapen heads morph into backpacks with legs and before long, the group whoop and wave. She grimaces as she returns the greeting, bewildered that any sane person would tackle the 800 kilometres for pleasure. They disappear into the trees and she sighs, replacing the bloodstained tissue over her heel, and forces her legs into action.

Less than one hundred metres on, she happens upon the post of which the priest spoke. The sound of a wind chime warns her of its proximity before it comes into sight. The makeshift monument is instantly recognisable; an ordinary wooden plank spears the earth and countless scallop shells suspend from strings on all sides. The shells knock against each other in the breeze and create a haunting tune. She had speculated about the shell-like markings stamped along the dotted line on her map and now realises that they are the symbols of the pilgrim's route.

The shells bring her luck. Within minutes, her goal appears to the left; a stone building clings in a precarious manner to the slope, convincing her that a good shake of the earth would cause it to slide down the incline. A sheepdog dashes across the landscape, criss-crossing the fields as he rounds up his strays and, when his fluffy flock is complete, he herds it towards a collection of outbuildings. As she closes in on the smallholding, Mercedes hears the garbled chatter of hens and the call of a rooster. The state of the building was not noticeable at a distance but, as she comes near, the neglect becomes clear – walls of collapsed stones, holes in the roof, and the earth littered with broken tiles. The miracle is that the house remains standing, albeit with wooden replacements for the broken glass of some windows. She suspects money isn't available to do the repairs.

The sound of someone singing, the voice of an angel, stops her in her tracks, and she rests on her stick while she listens to the unexpected entertainment. The pitch is perfect, the tune suits the majesty of the surrounds, and she stands motionless, reluctant to destroy the moment. Then the long black skirt of a nun materialises from around the end of the building and the music loses its charm. Her mood alters with the reminder that evil wears all types of disguise; she will never forget a nun destroyed her life. The song halts mid-phrase and the nun's face remains impassive as she waits and watches Mercedes cross the final hundred metres. Her gaze remains on the nun's face and she disguises her limp as she crosses to a stone, the ancient mark of the boundary. She waits there but the nun extends no welcome, no hand offered to a stranger, only silence. There is no sign of surprise in the face of the old woman, and Mercedes suspects a phone call warned of her visit. The nun regards her with eyes that are navy and swollen with fatigue.

Before she has time to introduce herself and state the purpose of her visit, the nun motions for her to follow and moves towards the front door. They enter and travel through the house in an eerie silence, passing closed doors as they pursue barren corridors until the robed woman halts and bows her head at a partially open door. When Mercedes questions if Father Emanuel lies behind, the nun half-nods, keeping her eyes lowered to the ground.

The man is invisible when she steps through the door, camouflaged by the pillows and cushions stuffed into the chair, so that it takes a second glance to detect his sunken form. A tartan rug drapes over him from his chest to the floor, a curtain that hides the lower two thirds of his body. His chin collapses onto his chest and a saliva trail begins at the corner of his mouth, disappearing under the collar of his shirt. His fingers interlace; they rest, without movement, upon the open book on his lap. The chair could hold two of him and his arms look too frail to be human. A spluttering sound escapes through his blue-tinged lips, and his chest rises and falls to a crackling accompaniment. She turns away, refusing to feel any pity for the creature but, at the same time, she realises the person who can attest to her son's whereabouts doesn't lie amongst those cushions. Before she leaves, she steals a final glance. The eyes appear to be made of wax. Nevertheless, they burn her face.

'Who are you?' The voice of one used to issuing commands rings out clear. 'Come closer. I can't see you.'

The years peter away and, for a moment, Mercedes

regresses to an impotent teenager and obeys the order as she takes a step. Then she remembers that the men of the church no longer hold their power over her and, if she desires, she can walk out of the door. That won't fulfil her quest so she places her handbag on the table and her eyes defy him as she searches through its contents. Once she has the item in her hand, she approaches him and his eyes widen until she stops and looms above his chair. The photo of the dead baby dangles in front of his face.

'Did God teach you to steal children from their mothers? How do you live with yourself?'

Coughs torment his body and his eyes plead for help. She does nothing but watch his labours, relieved when the horrible sound finally tails away. Someone's footsteps approach on the other side of the door, so she pushes it shut, turns the iron key and holds it in front of his eyes to demonstrate that she is in control. 'You are going to talk.'

A gnarled claw trembles on his book but the nervous drumming sparks no sympathy. His eyes monitor her face and he searches with his fingers for the bell. She lets him try for a while, then moves it out of reach. Alerted by the twist of his head towards the open window, she lowers the blind.

'We don't want anyone eavesdropping, do we?'

The invalid sinks further into the padding of his chair and begs her to put him out of his misery and explain what she wants, but the feeling of power is a gag until her glance brushes the photo.

'You've never met me but I have cursed you for many years.'

The stale smell expelled with his breath isn't fear. Something inside of his old body is rotting.

'I am a childless mother. Someone played God and took my baby, snatched him, before I had a chance to hold him.'

Understanding dawns and his eyes return to her fingers. They strangle a paper tissue while she speaks. One hand goes to his throat as the other feels around for his bell.

'Do you want help? Why should I show you mercy?' She spits out the words. 'You are a thief, the worst kind.'

All of a sudden, her body slumps, depleted of its anger but full of emotion, and she flutters to the ground. Mercedes kneels, holds her chest, and asks, 'What did you do with the babies? I want my child.'

Tap, tap, tap.

Her chest swells with oxygen as she regains composure, and she grabs the book from his lap. 'That noise drives me crazy.' When she is near him, the odour of fresh urine is overpowering. She probes. 'Was it your plan, or was Doctor Ramón the man in charge?' He jerks his head away from her bitterness. 'You know that name, don't you?' Certain that he will confess, she pushes. 'Was it you who decided to move the children through France?'

His cheeks turn purple and she suspects she has hit on the truth but it gives her no satisfaction. Once they went over the border, the children could have been sent anywhere in the world. To find them in Spain would be miraculous, but in the vast globe, unlikely. For the first time, she is aware of the flaws in her steely intention. Grief paralyses her for a minute, she yearns for escape and grabs her handbag. It falls open, scattering items onto the floor and tears fall as she kneels to retrieve them. She stands and turns to berate him a final time, but the words catch mid-flow.

'You haven't got away with it. I'm going to the police and will expose you all…'

His head has disappeared under a white cloud and her hand shakes as she lifts the pillow away. All signs of life have gone and the eyes are blank. Her hand stifles a scream as she backs away from the colourless face, crumples of flesh and blue lips dangle to one side. Clutching her abdomen, she shuffles backwards towards the door but there is a noise nearby and her head whips around. She doesn't breathe when the handle turns, then the metal returns to its starting place. The spirit of the dead man mocks her as she tries to make a sensible decision about what she should do next.

The cell doesn't offer inspiration but her glance alights on the bedside cupboard. Aware that the countdown has already started to when she will be kicked out, she pillages the drawers until she finds gold. Once again, she has possession of a journal, bound with brown glue and shreds of fibre and decorated with an emblem on its spine. The meaning of the Latin words embossed on the front is a mystery but she does recognise some of the letters. The sight of the tiny dove, the emblem, rewards her for her efforts.

'Help!'

Mercedes steps to one side as the nun squeezes through the door. While the woman calls for the other sister, she mumbles her condolences and takes leave of the two old women as they prepare to grieve at his bedside. With her, she carries the journal and an envelope of photos she discovered tucked under a pile of handkerchiefs in the bottom drawer.

Chapter 27

The crest of the final hill is at her back and the first house of the village is in sight when the pain returns and her thoughts return to the present from those of the dead man and the lost secrets of his past. Every centimetre of the last few hundred metres tests her endurance and she limps through the door of the bar as the last vestige of strength ebbs from her body. Local men huddle around the four tables but there is an empty chair close to the entrance, and she sinks into it with her eyes closed as she tries to ignore the agony of the electric shocks that shoot through her limb.

The bartender arrives at her side. She smells the stale smoke and peels open an eyelid to acknowledge him; her smile hardly touches her lips but, when he mentions homemade stew, it is no longer an effort. She overhears a woman's voice respond to the order in the kitchen, followed by a clatter of pans. Unasked, the man slips a glass of beer into her hand with a command to drink. At first she sips, as she has never been fond of the taste, but the fluid revives her. The smell from the kitchen makes her stomach growl and, when the man arrives with a bowl, she holds a spoon ready to attack the food. He wishes her good appetite and before he turns away she asks the time of the next bus down the mountain. Her appetite disappears when his answer sends her stomach into free-fall.

'There isn't one until tomorrow morning.' There is no hint of humour in his face, even though she prays this is a practical joke. 'The last one left over an hour ago.' His gaze lingers on the walking stick as she pushes the food around the bowl and considers her options. She is about to ask him about a public telephone when he nods and barks. 'Eat. It looks like you need it. You can stay here. We have a room. It was my daughter's, before she married and moved down the hill.'

'Your wife won't mind?'

The question sets off a series of whinges about the wife, Isabella, who is in tears every morning since their daughter left home. 'She'll enjoy the female company,' he remarks as he goes out through the back door. The bowl is clean when he returns minutes later, dragging his wife in his wake. He orders the woman to sit with Mercedes, mumbles that his name is Pablo, and then vanishes. The women incline their heads to each other, but sit in awkward silence until Mercedes suppresses a yawn and tries to initiate a conversation. Whenever Isabella responds, she looks at the bar first, and the single-word answers encourage Mercedes to abandon her efforts. A final question about their daughter breaks open the shell and Isabella tells her about her daughter's expertise in hairdressing, her children (more beautiful than most), and her brute of a husband. The woman goes on and on, and Mercedes fights exhaustion and feigns interest.

An abrupt change of subject, enquiring about the nuns and the old goat in the mountains, wakes her up. An invisible collar tightens around her neck as she considers whether to leave the truth to some other messenger, but then she sighs and tries to convey regret when she tells of the death. Instead of the sorrow she expects, her companion shocks her when she releases a cackle of mirth, saying under her breath something that sounds like 'long overdue'. Isabella catches her eye and grins like an imp, a wicked glint in her eye. Mercedes snaps her mouth shut and tries to hide her shock at the reaction as she skirts around the subject of the dead man. She need not worry about being discrete; the woman cannot wait to talk about the priest's faults.

'Even as a young man, he had a cruel streak. When I was a tiny girl, he used to lead prayers with a pious look on his face, but we little ones were terrified of him. Many of my childhood friends carry the scars of his punishment on their behinds; he never aimed his belt at an area that would show.'

'Why does a person like him enter the church?'

It is only a thought but Mercedes voices it aloud and Isabella responds. 'For him, it was the power. He was no saint. I know I shouldn't speak ill of the dead, but I lost any love for him on the day I discovered the true extent of his evil, the day my father told me of how he betrayed my uncle.'

The desire for sleep fades as Isabella's story commands her attention.

'Papa's brother was a teenager when he became one of Franco's bodyguards. He was young, but determined to protect his leader. According to Papa, something changed his loyalty overnight and the role became a chore he despised.' Isabella shakes her head in answer to the query. 'No, we never knew but it was soon after he was a witness to a meeting during the war, the big one when that monster murdered the Jews.' Starved of conversation, now that she has begun, Isabella's sentences run into one another. 'No one spoke about it. You know how it is, there's no point in raking up the past. Some arguments I overheard between my parents when I was little I do remember. Franco met with that man on a train somewhere near the French border. Papa said he had to remind his brother that if the Generalissimo hadn't refused to offer support, Europe would have fallen and Spain would have ended up a different country.'

'There was compromise.' Mercedes thinks back to the

history lessons she endured as a youngster and spews out some facts. 'Some of their spies were allowed to base themselves here in Spain.' Blank eyes meet hers and she blushes; education was a luxury for Isabella's generation.

'My father was angry with my mother, she never could hold her tongue. His brother had told him it would lead to his execution if anyone found out he had spoken about the meeting. It wasn't long before they found their reason to shoot him.'

'Why was it important?'

'I don't think Papa knew but he and his friends were angry about a big plan to take children away from unfit parents. He said no family was more suitable than a child's own.'

Mercedes had read about this concept of creating compliant generations, a population that wouldn't go against their ideals.

'Mama said the new order of nuns moved into an old monastery, near here on this side of the border, around that time. They were in seclusion and another uncle of mine received orders to do the heavy work for them. Later, he led groups of refugees from the monastery across the peaks into France. He thought it was to move rebels out of the country.'

'What are you two discussing?'

Pablo arrives with a bottle of wine and three glasses, killing the conversation. Isabella turns voiceless and can hardly manage any response to her spouse. When Mercedes tries to return to the subject, the woman shakes her head with a nervous glance at Pablo. The effects of the beer and wine cloud her mind until her hosts finally notice her tiredness and lead her to a bedroom. Someone has made the room ready; fresh towels, twisted into the shape of a fan, lie on top of the bedcover, and an aroma of lavender seeps around the room. A vase of the freshly picked purple flowers stands on a bedside table, beside it rests a copy of the Bible. She pulls the sheet over her head and enters a dreamland filled with baby pilgrims who toddle behind a Pied Piper and climb a mountain along a trail made of scallop shells.

Payment for her board causes an argument with Pablo the next morning.

'You made my wife smile again, she misses Marie Terese.'

'At least let me give you something for the food.'

His strength forces her fingers to close over the notes, and he shakes his head as he hands her a cheese roll.

'Isabella made this for your trip.'

He pushes her out of the door and the bolt slides into place before she can thank him. She looks for Isabella in the windows but can't see any sign of her and turns towards the bus stop. After crossing the road, she pauses at the church but the priest isn't around and the door is locked, so she scribbles a few words of appreciation on a scrap torn from her notebook and slides it under the door.

She is the only passenger on the bus and arrives at the station with minutes to spare, where she hobbles along the platform to the 9:30 train for Madrid. The seat at her side is empty and she withdraws the items she took from the old priest's room. Her guilt disappears as she surveys her treasures and opens the cover of the journal to the first page, saving the photos for later.

Indigo scrawl crams the unlined pages and the paper crackles as she leafs through. At the top right-hand corner of the first page, a handwritten date notes the period, *Octubre 1940*, and she labours through the illegible writing in anticipation of a bolt of inspiration. Daily reports of a young boy's prayers and his spiritual journey quell her excitement and by the end of an hour of mundane revelations Mercedes is fed-up and no wiser about why the nun directed her to the priest for information.

Lines of columns divide the blankness of the final half-dozen pages, lists in which each number contains six digits followed by two letters, completed with another six digits. These are a code, but without the key she has little hope of understanding its significance.

The photos are also worthless and her spirits plummet. She closes her eyes but is unable to nap as the trail over the mountains fills her thoughts. Her heart aches with the thought that she may have stepped in the footprints of her child's abductor.

Chapter 28

Her intention was to tell Orlando about everything that happened in the mountains, including the visit to the priest and Isabella's tales. The words were on her tongue when he met her train at Atocha Station. And later in his flat, when he poured the wine to drink with the meal he had ready. But they fell upon each other, rendered desperate by the time apart, and love interfered. The opportune moment had never arisen and, together again, he distracted her with kisses, his touch wiped her mind of other thoughts. Now the journal and photos remain in her bag and she saves her story for another time.

Everything changes when she enters her own flat the next afternoon. The minute she opens the front door, she is aware someone has violated her home. The lamp illuminates the corner of the room – since her accident, she makes sure it is on every time she leaves her flat. New wood lies in the fireplace, she prepared it before she headed north because a weatherman forecast cooler nights and she didn't want to be caught out. Those things hold no interest, as they have not been disturbed, and something else puts her on guard. A musky odour permeates the room, not a smell that she recognises. Holding her bag against her chest, she is ready to run while she looks at every corner of the room. A gasp breaks the silence when her eyes alight on an effigy that hangs in front of the window.

A doll, a plastic baby in blue clothes with a red ribbon tied in a bow around his neck, swings in the air, one end of the red hangman's noose twisting around the scroll fixing at the end of the curtain rail. Red letters deface the forehead, but she is unable to make out the detail at this distance and the thought of stepping near horrifies her. Rooted in the doorway, she waits for a villain to materialise. No one responds to her call, not even the neighbour to suss out who needs help. Conscious that she must act, she heaves a foot forward, and then the next, inching towards the figurine. She lifts one of the crutches in the entrance area, there to remind her to return them to the clinic, and holds it as a sword in front of her body.

The silence unnerves her and she holds her breath while she checks behind every door, in each cupboard and under the furniture, the crutch held ready for attack. Nothing else has been disturbed and, now reassured that she is alone, she juts the bolt into its catch and slumps against the wall, the jelly in her legs no longer able to support her. The blank eyes in the cherubic expression on the puppet's face mock and torment her whenever she looks up, then a fire ignites inside and her eyes blaze as she approaches the demon, snapping up a pair of scissors. She obeys the instruction across the forehead when it becomes clear. 'STOP'. Imaginary insects crawl up her spine and she shudders as she takes another step, the scissor blades slice through the fabric and the mannequin plummets to the floor.

There is no mistaking the warning – whoever came into her flat wants her to stop investigating the stolen babies. Her worry is whether the doll indicates her son is in danger, and her heart skips beats as she slides into a heap on the floor. She remains caved-in, with her face hidden in her hands, until the ring of the telephone disrupts the nightmare.

'What kind of sicko has this sense of humour?'
Rosa hurls the doll onto the fire and the plastic toy knocks

the un-cooked logs so they fall like bowling pins out of the fireplace, rolling across the floor. Her sister stomps across the room until she stands over Mercedes, who reclines on the settee with a wet towel across her eyes.

'Drink this.'

Lifting one edge of the compress, she avoids the narrowed eyes of her sister but obeys the order and pretends to sip. She is about to replace the blindfold when Rosa clutches her arm.

'You do realise you can't stay here.'

A hammer pounds the inside of her head and, when she opens her eyes to answer, the pain worsens. Pinching her eyelids shut, she collapses against the cushion. She clings to the wet handkerchief in her palm.

'Go to Orlando's if you won't come to my place.' Rosa squats so she is level with her face and waits until she relents and opens her eyes. 'And, this time, you have got to tell him everything.'

She shakes her head no; the thought makes her feel nauseous.

'The man loves you. Believe me, you'll be okay. Why didn't you call him when you found this?'

Rosa doesn't understand their relationship is new and fragile, and it may not survive a full confession. Her sister ignores her protests and takes control, working her way around the flat, emptying the fridge and choosing clothes for Mercedes' suitcase; she packs for a long trip. Afterwards, Rosa approaches with a change of clothes in her arms, and her words are gentle but firm, in the tone that she would use with her child.

'Come on. You'll feel stronger once you've had a shower.'

She steers Mercedes, hands on her shoulders, into the shower cubicle. The hot water defrosts the ice in Mercedes' bones and she tilts her face so the fluid washes over her face.

The tension in her head eases. Rosa holds a towel open as she steps out of the shower and rubs Mercedes all over until she is dry, then she helps her to dress and combs through her wet hair. By the time she finishes with the hairdryer, Mercedes' headache is a dull niggle and her sister takes her hand and leads her through the lounge. Her legs quake and her heart vibrates. She doesn't see any sign of the doll and shuffles through the room with her head bent. As they leave the flat, Rosa checks the lock and places the keys in Mercedes' handbag, telling her she will let the police know. When she passes the rubbish collection bin at the corner of the road, she tosses a tied carrier bag into the cavern. The lid hisses shut but, before it closes fully, Mercedes hears the mew of a baby doll.

There is no time to ring the bell as the door yanks open and he pulls her into the shelter of his arms; the rhythm beneath her ear lulls her until she fills with calm. They embrace until her sister coughs and he leans back to inspect her face. Fingers stroke her skin and tuck a lock of hair behind her ear. She can't speak for the lump in her throat. Keeping her gathered tight to his side, as one they move into the lounge and sit down. He begins scolding them both, unable to understand the delay in calling the police. When he questions her, every word is measured but she does not have doubts about the magnitude of his anger.

'And you threw away the evidence. What were you thinking?'

Mercedes mumbles an excuse about trust and police while Rosa stares at her knees.

'Don't dare blame your sister. You are capable of making your own decisions.'

Nothing controls her trembling, nor is she able to explain why the doll sapped her courage; that disappeared when her son seemed to come under threat. His expression softens and he clutches her to him and strokes her hair. Rosa mimes at her as she leaves but Mercedes delays her full confession for a few more moments, in case his love is only a memory after the truth comes out.

Her fingers pull at a thread in her skirt and the shadow of his tennis trophy plays on the floor as she waits for him to comment. When the seconds turn into minutes and he is still silent, her heart shatters. She would take the words back in a second so his fantasy of her remained untarnished.

'Thank goodness you've admitted it. You finally trust me.'

The thread rips and her eyes swerve to his. 'How did you know?'

'Not everything. I did guess about the child. There is a look in your eyes whenever you see a baby and you have a few lines here.' His finger follows the curve at the side of her breast and a tingle in her pelvis matches the one beneath her blouse. 'I thought it was adopted.' Before she has time to protest, he places her palm on his chest. 'I should've known you better.' His kiss muffles his words. 'What shall we do next?'

The clock hands point to twelve, a chill has descended in the room, and they haven't finalised an action plan. Orlando stands at one side of the flipchart he created from brown paper discovered in the storage cupboard behind boxes of memorabilia. His stance reminds her of her professors in university and she disguises a grin as he waves his hand at the random words from their brainstorm.

'We need structure, perhaps then we'll get an idea of where to look next. Let's put these in lists together.'

As the columns of related words fill the page, more facts and ideas spark in her mind. When he writes them in large black letters, the significance of some increases and Orlando uses a coloured marker to connect items with red arrows. The gaps in their knowledge are clear and he marks them with his pen.

'Look here, and here. We know someone removes the babies from the mothers soon after they are born and that they never return. Is Doctor Ramón in control?'

'In the clinic, yes. There is also some connection with the church. A nursing sister carried my baby out of the room. And, that old priest in the mountains was hiding something.' She punches the cushion. 'Why did he have to die?'

'It's too late to worry about that. We need to discover how they dealt with the records.'

'And where they sent the children.'

'And whether the politician is involved. Most importantly, why are they trying to stop you? Is it the money?'

Before they retire, they divide the questions into two lists. She picks up the one she prefers, but Orlando immediately swaps it and insists he will make the enquiries about the green-eyed man.

'He nearly killed you last time. It's too dangerous.'

'But they already know about me, what if they come after you?' She tries to cajole him with her arms linked around his neck, but he unhooks them with a stubborn expression and, eventually, she has to agree with his decision.

'You won't change my mind with a few kisses. It's settled.'

The understanding that he puts her safety first whittles away another layer of her armour.

She shrugs off the digs from the others when they arrive at work together the following morning, and ignores the hoots when he escorts her to her desk and kisses the top of her head before he leaves. While the computer grinds through its start-up, she scans through the list, numbers each task in order of importance and, when she is satisfied, she shoves it into her drawer and brings a document onto the screen. Jorge approaches her workstation with papers clutched in his hand. A cloying smell of his overgenerous application of aftershave turns the toast in her stomach and she waits, but he is silent while he stares at the page on her computer. He scans to the bottom and then looks at her with tightly controlled rage.

'What's this? I don't remember asking for a series about…' He tilts his head to the side, squints, and asks what information she has about her 'stolen baby saga'. Before she has to think of a reply, Jaime's voice booms across the room and asks for Jorge's help. The editor nods, but his mouth tightens as he removes his eyes from her computer and orders her to his office later so she can bring him up to speed. When he steps away, she turns her attention to the work on her screen; it is the first of a series about regional cooking. She abandoned the idea after the meeting with Carmen and, on impulse, returned to it today, hoping it proves useful to explain her absences from the office. Her distaste for any cookery related items is no secret amongst her colleagues, so she is not surprised that her ruse puzzles Jorge but he will scupper her baby investigation if she doesn't produce facts, and she needs more time to get them.

It is a struggle to inject any spark into her writing about the difference between stews in various parts of the country. Distracting her is the briefcase her foot plays with under the desk; the folder inside contains items that tempt her interest. A familiar voice nearby makes her shift in her chair and she tries not to look up.

'Are you blushing?' Jaime grins, and his eyes bounce between her face and Orlando's, who winks at her as he makes his way through the desks in her direction. She pretends to concentrate on her work but she is blind to the screen. Her face grows hot with fire spreading into her neck and chest. As he comes near, the hairs on her arms jump to attention and the awareness that his head was in between her legs earlier that morning turns the warmth into a burn.

'Really? Orlando?'

The taunts continue and, when she thinks he has lost steam, Jaime adds another smart observation about her, Orlando, and office relationships until she can't stand it any longer and escapes to the water dispenser. There is a rustle in her pocket when she moves; the to-do list reminds her of its presence and distracts her so that when she returns to her work, she struggles to focus on food. Abandoning her attempts, she leaves a note to say she will return to her desk in an hour. She knows Orlando's eyes follow her when she limps out of the office.

At the central library, she finds a vacant table towards the rear of the main room and spreads her papers over the empty surface to discourage others from claiming the nearby space. She lays out the photographs, those that she pilfered from the priest's drawer, side by side, so she can study them with a magnifying glass. She hasn't been able to identify any of the faces as yet. A dozen men feature in the images; they stand around a fountain in a square and in the background are the arches of a church entrance. The architecture is similar to some of the buildings she has seen in Segovia, but she concludes that it may be co-incidence as many old churches were constructed in that style. In several photos, a man towers above the others and she feels that she knows his face. His skin fell in layers and his eyes were dull when she saw him last, swamped by cushions, but these images are of a young Father Emanuel. Black robes brush the ground and each man wears a white collar and holds a book in his hands. The young features could be of her fellow students when she was at university and she jots down some assumptions:

1. Ages between 22 to 25, exceptions are two 50+, and one man who is possibly in late 60's.
2. Young ones may be study colleagues. Similar books in their hands.
3. Assuming 2 is correct, are they recently ordained?
4. Two young men are dressed in suits with no books.
5. One of number 4 could be Father Emanuel's brother or cousin – similar features.
6. Do I know one of number 4? Looks familiar.

'Jorge is looking for you.' Jaime's expression warns her of impending trouble, but she portrays nonchalance as she enquires if he knows anything about seminaries.

'They don't accept women, you know.'

When he finishes sniggering at his own joke, she assures him she isn't planning to change her sex but needs to identify the location of a photo, and points out the church behind the men.

'I don't recognise it, but leave it with me and I'll see what I can do. Now get to Jorge before he bursts a blood vessel.'

She grimaces and begins the expedition that leads to her boss, then she pivots to ask Jaime whether he knows anything about a dove emblem. He shakes his head but scribbles down the name of a contact he knows, an expert in graphology. Jorge puts his head out of his office at that moment and shouts her name until the entire building seems to rumble with his annoyance.

Chapter 29

'Okay?'

Soft skin nestles in her palm, not Orlando's, his is blemished with calluses. Rosa's grip tightens around her hand and Mercedes thanks her sister again for accompanying her on this ordeal. The countryside has not changed since her last sight of it ten years ago, and Señor García behind the ticket counter as they walk through the station has grey hair, but she still wears the same jumper. Mercedes brushes imaginary dust off her skirt and prays her parents will approve of the changes in her. The platform is empty and ten years vanish in a second as a blow punches her in her stomach.

'Did you tell them I am coming?'

'Yes, don't you remember? We decided they should wait at the house.' Her sister pulls on her arm until she forces her to budge. 'Don't worry. They can't wait to see you.'

The scrubland that used to be in front of the station is now a car park and some drivers have left vehicles blocking the exit. She passes a comment and Rosa explains that the owners leave them unlocked, with the brake off, so others are able to push them out of the way.

'Things are different in Madrid. You would never leave anything unlocked.' Mercedes notices other changes as well. 'Where are all the dilapidated buildings? Everything looks scrubbed and modern.'

'A few years back, a foreigner renovated one of the houses; it started a trend.'

Despite the affluent appearance of the main road, she misses the old town and is relieved when she sees her friend's house hasn't become one of the whitewashed chain. The balcony draws her eyes and, as they pass under it, Rosa whispers in her ear. 'She married the butcher the year after you left for university. He's a breeder and has three by her, and two others she doesn't know about.'

As she rotates her head to look back, Mercedes comments that her old friend didn't deserve that fate but Rosa reassures her. 'Marie Luis is happy with her family and has the security she wanted. She had to marry someone local if she wanted to stay in this town.'

This world, once her everything, is alien now; it is likely she will remain an outsider forever. Her escape may have been by choice, but she has a momentary yearning for the uncomplicated life. Rosa doesn't speak, allowing Mercedes to revisit her past in peace. Their hands remain clasped and, before they step over the threshold of the family home, Rosa kisses her cheek and gives her hand a final squeeze. Suddenly, everything is okay as the door opens to her mother's outstretched arms and her father's smile, evidence that the past no longer divides them.

The nonstop talk lasts all day, she has forgotten how her family are when they are all in the same room, and Mercedes is glad Rosa decided to stay in the village to catch up with a friend, giving her some peace for the return journey. If they are ready to listen during the next visit, she may share her investigation into the missing babies, but today she kept to the safe topics, such as descriptions of her life in Madrid. Rosa is due for a scolding – after she opened her mouth about

Orlando, her parents' questions about him never stopped, and she suspects her mother is planning a wedding now she knows the relationship is serious. When she imagines the mayhem she has left behind in the family home, she smiles. The smile remains as she gives in to the soporific rocking motion.

A change of track jolts the train and jerks her awake. She glances at her watch; there are only twenty minutes before they arrive in the city. Their plan is to meet at Orlando's flat but she has an hour available, which gives her time to stop in at her own place to collect spare clothes. It crosses her mind to wait and she knows Orlando will be angry if she disobeys his orders to stay away from her home. The police haven't made headway in discovering who broke into her flat and, so far, Orlando has been unsuccessful in his attempts to discover the identity of her pursuer. The green-eyed man hasn't been around for days and she decides that two minutes to get her things is worth the risk. Nevertheless, when she walks out of the station, Mercedes is on guard and checks for followers. At the front of her building, she waits for several minutes before entering, until she is sure she is safe. No one lurks so she dashes inside to gather the clothes she needs and back out again to hail a cab. The whole visit only takes five minutes but half a dozen taxis pass her by, and by the time she reaches Orlando's flat, he is anxious.

'What's that?'

Her heart sinks and she knows she can't pretend the overnight bag, full of clothes, contains new purchases; she tries to explain that she only was in her flat for a minute but he rants for hours until she expects a knock on the door from neighbours investigating the noise. Like a chastised child, she stands in his lounge, silent while the reprimands rain over her. When he pauses for a breath, she murmurs an apology, escapes into the bedroom and leans against the door as she tries to stifle a bubble of laughter. When he hears her snorting, the tirade begins again, this time including digs about irresponsible behaviour.

'What do you want to eat tonight?'

He stands to the side of the window and ignores her question while he stares at the road below. When she steps forward, he reaches out with his arm to block her shoulder and hold her away from the glass; his jaw contorts as he chews the edge of his lip. There is an odd colour to his face when he pulls down the blind, turns and pushes her further into the room, away from the window.

'What colour hair does your green-eyed man have?'

His tone causes her throat to thicken and chokes her answer. 'Brown, I guess. Dark.'

'Long or short?'

'Longish. Past his collar anyway.'

The room darkens as he releases the rest of the blinds and his eyes narrow so his eyebrows crease together in a single row of hair. He orders her to collect any items she needs for the night. Her glance keeps straying to the front door as she shoves a change of clothes and some toiletries into a travel bag; her heart pummels like a hammer against her chest. Orlando ends his telephone conversation with a curt goodbye when she comes back into the lounge and she notices new creases at the edges of his eyes.

'We're sorted. You'll be safe tonight.'

A flicker of resentment arises at the way he treats her like a child, and she drops her bag and plants her feet with her arms crossed over her chest. 'If you don't explain, I'm not going anywhere.'

'Oh yes you are.' The grip is unforgiving when he grabs

her upper arms and manhandles her towards the front door with anxiety stifling his voice. 'You don't know who you're dealing with.' With a twist of her body, she escapes his hold but when she turns to argue, the sight of his colour melts her bravado.

'What have you found out?'

'Later. We must get you away from here first.'

The back door is a little-used entrance so it takes some time before Orlando can disengage the rusty lock. Piles of discarded items such as broken chairs and abandoned building materials block the alley and he kicks them out of the way to clear their route as they hurry through the unlit passage; dark creatures scurry across their path and she tries to ignore thoughts of cockroaches and rats. He squeezes her ring into the flesh of her next finger but she remains mute about the pain and pushes herself to shadow his pace. When the light from the main road comes into view the clamp in her chest eases a fraction, but Orlando comes to a sudden stop not far from where the alley emerges so she collides with his back.

He spins around, folds her against his chest and whispers in her ear. 'Walk quickly. Keep your head down. If I say run, get going. Don't wait for me. Go to this address. Make sure no one follows you.' His lips touch her forehead as he presses a piece of paper in her hand. 'Be careful, my love.'

They merge with a few pedestrians and there is no crowd in which to hide, so they link their hands and keep up a quick pace. He frequently checks behind and she perceives the moment he panics.

'Hell!'

Her heart misses a beat as their hands separate, he stops, and his words urge her to flee so she complies with a sprint towards the metro sign less than 200 metres away. Her fingers fumble in her pocket for her season ticket and she flies down the stairs, weaving in and out of the other passengers. At the gate, she shoves the ticket in the machine and heads for any platform where there is the sound of a train ready to leave. As she jumps aboard, the doors trap a tail of her clothing and, while she attempts to release it, she catches sight of a man on the platform peering through windows. She rips the cloth from the door and slumps into the first vacant seat with her hand over her mouth.

'You only just made it.'

The man's remark doesn't register immediately and her expression is blank as she tries to catch her breath. She inclines her head but when the train glides away from the platform, she ignores him and stares out at the dark walls of the tunnel as they fly by.

It is more than two hours later when she rings the doorbell at the unfamiliar address. There is no reply and she inspects the crumpled piece of paper; the numbers Orlando has written are legible although the paper is now torn and damp. She vets the area but there is not one person nearby. Her zig-zag across the metro network has shaken off her pursuer but she doesn't feel safe, exposed on this strange doorstep, and stabs at the bell as she attempts to come up with an alternative plan.

The door releases, she squeezes through the gap, and pushes against the pressurised hinge until the latch locks into place. Flat B is on the seventh floor, to the right of the lift as she exits, and her knuckles barely hit the door when it flings open and a hand pulls her inside.

'Thank God.'

Her legs give way and Orlando's arms catch her before she hits the floor but by then, she has entered a black realm.

Chapter 30

The poison stings her throat and burns all the way down into her stomach, and Mercedes resurfaces in a fit of coughing. She seals her lips against the glass; no more brandy. A trickle of the cool fluid runs down her chin into her neck and she stops it with a finger before it goes further, opening her eyes. Orlando places the glass of amber fluid on a table at his side when he sees she is conscious. Still in the half-world, she looks down at her skirt; amber spots cover it like raindrops so she rubs the edge of her cardigan over them, too late as the silk has absorbed the alcohol and refuses to let it go. With instructions not to move a muscle, Orlando leaves to fetch her a glass of water and, while he is absent, she raises her head from a cushion to take in her surroundings.

This flat is unlike any home she has ever seen. Light reflects off the high-gloss furniture and projects incomplete rainbows onto the cream walls. Leather settees centre on a coffee table; bigger than her bed, it would also suit the lobby of a designer hotel. Above the mantelpiece, on top of the marble fireplace, a painting hangs. She recognises the artist, a future master her friend informed her of during a recent exhibition. She wonders if it is a copy but, considering the quality of other items around the place, she has her doubts. Every vase and each ornament makes a statement; whoever owns the flat has flair, and money.

Orlando moves around the flat with familiarity. He doesn't

have to hunt for the appropriate kitchen cupboard and when she complains of cold, he goes directly to the thermostat. Through her lashes, she observes as she works out the mystery of why he knows this place so well. He checks the window catches and the door lock, pours a glass of brandy for himself and sits opposite her, his body poised to jump. There are grooves between his eyebrows that did not exist a few weeks ago; she slips across the floor to him and traces the lines with her index finger, wishing that she could smooth them away forever. His head falls back, his eyes closing while she strokes him. In a hoarse whisper, she thanks him for his protection and kisses him, once on each of his closed eyelids and afterwards on his lips. As she settles back down on the floor, he moans, 'Come back.'

'I'm sorry I didn't listen. Do you think he followed me from my place?' The silence is loud with the things he won't say, and she reaches for his hand and tries to force him to meet her eyes. 'Tell me. I need to know. You're worried and it's not fair.' He can't hide the debate going on inside and she keeps her silence, but wills him to trust her and leans her body towards his. When he slumps with a sigh of defeat, she knows he will tell her everything.

'You've made some dangerous enemies. It is the investigation into the baby snatching.' The statement does not surprise her. 'A police contact pulled the records on your green-eyed man; I was able to give your description of him and straight away my friend knew who I meant.' A puzzled look comes over his face. 'When I saw him outside of my flat, I felt certain that I know him. I just can't quite remember from where. Anyway, the man has been under surveillance for years but so far the police have only managed to catch him on a minor charge.' His fingers tap a wild rhythm on his knee and he holds back for a minute before he blurts out the rest. 'He's a hired gun, bought to get rid of people's problems. They call him "The Eel". He's a slippery character.'

'Why will they go to these lengths to stop this story? It seems extreme.'

'That's what we have to figure out. I think we should review everything you know, maybe that will point us in the right direction. You won't be safe until we find a way to stop him. Where are your notes?'

Mercedes passes him her notebook, pulls a package from her handbag and unwraps the padding; it protects a disc, a copy of material she saved from her work computer. 'I've also hidden some photocopies of the relevant papers in a safe place'

'Not at your flat, I hope.'

'At work.' She prevents his interruption with her palm. 'It's perfectly safe. Come on; let's try to work this out.' Writing starts to fill a blank page of her notebook. 'The idea that this involves more than one baby began with that phone call from Carmen.'

Individually, they add their findings and fill pages until they can think of nothing more. Orlando taps the base of his glass against his palm while he thinks and then holds up one finger at a time as he works through their assumptions.

'The green-eyed man either works for Doctor Ramón, or with him. The doctor is involved in some kind of baby trafficking network and it has been going on for at least forty years, if we believe Carmen's information. Is he the person in charge or does someone else give the orders? Who chooses which babies?'

She interrupts to expand that point. 'More recently, single mothers have been targeted but Carmen's experience was quite different. They were married but, as political activists, she describes them as "undesirables" in those days.' The only sound that penetrates the flat is a distant hum of the traffic below and Mercedes muses aloud. 'Is this how it all started? The motive? Look, these are my notes about Isabella's uncle.' She flicks through the pages until she finds the section she wants. 'Here it is. The family heard him say that the two leaders discussed an idea: *it starts with the right family*. Individually, each was obsessed with the creation of a perfect society; we learnt that in history. The difference is what each man considered perfect, for one it was race and for the other, political persuasion. Do you think maybe they had some kind of secret arrangement?'

His nod is hesitant as he points out it is unlikely that the war agreements are in place fifty years later.

'I agree, but maybe they do it for different reasons now. I don't know for sure but I am willing to bet it's connected to the money I saw handed to Doctor Ramón that day in the alley.' Much of the detail of the day is wiped from her mind, and yet the image of the doctor and his envelope has taunted her since the early days of her recovery. No matter how hard she tries, the mouths in her memory don't project sound, so she is unable to recall the words that passed between the men.

'I've interviewed a number of women who responded to my advert and there is a similarity to some of their experiences. Some had babies in the same clinic in Madrid who didn't survive the first few hours and not one mother witnessed that moment when the baby drew his last breath; in every case the new-born was taken out of the room.' In reply to his question, Mercedes explains the reasons varied but, most often, the excuse was to give the baby help to breathe. 'Many of them never had a chance to hold their baby again. Every mother uses the same words to describe the photo they saw of their dead baby: white, wrapped in towels, one hand on view. The few mothers who were able to hold the child mention the icy cold. Not one was given the opportunity to attend a funeral, the clinic always took care of it.' Her voice breaks, and she pauses for control before her own memories overwhelm her. She hardens her heart and asks him, if he was in charge, how he would organise a system to traffic babies.

'Once I decide which babies to take, I have to persuade someone to do the taking. You mentioned the sisters are involved but why would they do such a thing? It seems to go against their beliefs. Plus there's the issue of officialdom; there must be some paperwork.'

Next to *paperwork*, she adds *government official?* to her notes. Some of the connections are clear as she recalls the ancient friendships between the doctor and the politician, and she continues with the expansion of his theory. 'And they have to move the babies before anyone asks questions, maybe to somewhere such as the orphanage in Burgos, where children come and go as a regular occurrence. Señora Ferrer referred to a number of babies who stayed for a day or so before they disappeared.'

'Who is in charge of these orphanages?'

'There are nuns on the staff, and volunteers. Maybe the church. I think the volunteers come from the congregation.' She connects some of the words with arrows and shows him the results.

1. *Identify Baby*
   How? Stolen to order?
2. *Steal Baby*
   Who arranges it? How do they do it? Motivation?
3. *Paperwork*
   Someone at central office changes the records? Look at names on certificates. Is a death certificate issued? Burial records?

4. *Transfer Baby from Hospital*
   What kind of transport? Who does it?
5. *Holding Place*
   Is the church involved?
6. *Move to Destination*
   If taken across the border, where do they go? Do they go to other countries? Do any remain in Spain?
7. *Why?*
   Political, social, or money?

He notices the repeated mention of money and asks whether she has uncovered evidence that babies are sold for cash.

'It's hard to confirm, but statistics reveal over half a million people apply to adopt a child in the US every year, and there aren't enough babies available in their own country, so it isn't uncommon for couples go to other countries to find a child. My sources inform me there are private adoptions of children from South America, China, Ireland, just to name a few. Why not Spain? What would prevent people here from cashing in by selling our babies?' She searches in her bag for some papers and hands them to him. 'These are some figures I found in the office of Doctor Ramón.' While he scans through them, she moves behind the settee and leans over his shoulder to point out what she has discovered. 'These numbers represent the years and this is his income. Everything I've checked shows he can't make this much money from his day job. Also, many of the payments are sporadic, big amounts at odd times.'

'Did you find any receipts?'

'No, but I think this page could be a master list of codes. Look here,' she indicates a column on the right. 'These letters aren't random. They don't make sense how they are written. If we break the code, maybe it will give us a chance of finding out where the money originates, and when.'

He is oblivious to her and his pen scratches on the paper as he juggles numbers, doing sums at a furious pace. Dismissing an offer to fetch him another drink with an impatient wave, his focus locks onto the work. Her curiosity results in irritated responses and so, desperate for something to fill the time while he works, she asks whether the owner of the flat would object if she looks around. Again, his hand dismisses her and she tells herself not to mind as she starts to explore.

The flat is like a Tardis, bigger than it first appears and one room leads into another, followed by another, until she counts six bedrooms in all, each decorated with an individual style in modern elegance. The sumptuous luxury of the bathrooms makes her sigh and she opens a bottle of bath salts simply to enjoy the aroma. Orlando is still engrossed in the figures when she strolls back into the lounge but she can't hold back her curiosity.

'Who owns this place? It must be worth millions.'

Red stains his cheeks and he looks like a child caught with his hand in the sweetie jar when he answers. 'I guess so.'

Suspicion grows in her mind and she lowers onto her knees in front of him so their eyes are at the same level and she can detect the truth. When she sees it in his eyes, she presses her forehead against his jeans. His hand strokes her head, like an owner with his beloved pet, while he tries to explain. 'I don't want money to be a thing between us. That's why I work and live as I do. Believe me; normal life is hard when you are born with all of this.'

The sense of betrayal is impossible to bear. 'You couldn't trust me?' Where her cheek lay against his trousers, a damp area grows under the oozing of her tears. He holds her heart, her secrets; how could he keep this from her? Shrewd Orlando waits for her anger to fade before he mumbles into her hair, descriptions of the difference she has made in his life and his hopes for their future. Finally, she brings his palm to her lips, neither one wanting to be the first to disturb the moment.

Later when they are at the table, having finished their meal but before they clear the dirty plates, he rubs circles over his temples. 'I'll do more work on the code tomorrow, but I warn you, it's like looking for a grain of rice in the sand.'

'I can't understand why they think I'm a threat. As yet, I haven't named anyone in my articles, I don't have enough proof.'

'I agree. It's hardly exposure at this stage, a few columns about babies going missing in one clinic years ago.'

'Yes and, even then, Jorge made sure my article didn't make the front pages.'

Orlando agrees that this response to her exposé is odd; the disclosure of baby trafficking could be the scoop of the year.

'He said he was nervous about potential backlash when I put it in front of him. He couldn't refuse to put it into print as it's newsworthy, but I can tell he wants to suppress the story. There have been all kinds of excuses: it won't appeal to the public; only women are interested in babies; it will affect donations to orphans. Even with the massive response I received to that first short piece, he's reticent and says I'll have to obtain more evidence.'

'How do the people after you know what evidence you have? Who has access to your notes?'

'No one. My notebook is always with me and I close down my computer whenever I'm not working on it.'

'They must have access to something.'

About to shake her head, she remembers what happened the week before she had the accident. 'Jorge was at my desk when I returned after an interview and was reading something on the screen of my computer. He closed it down when I approached, explaining that he needed to ask me something and, because my computer was on, he turned it off. I assumed I'd forgotten to switch it off by mistake.' Her stomach churns as she questions herself as well as Orlando, 'Jorge can't be involved, can he?' Sickened when she realises what it could mean, her brain aches to recall what the editor knows.

The mayhem in her mind is interrupted by Orlando. 'We need to do some digging into his past, and fast. If he is passing on information to those involved, they will know how close you are to exposing them.'

Chapter 31

She does not feel one shred of guilt about the lies she told in order to take the day off work; Jorge seemed to believe the coughing and spluttering when she telephoned first thing this morning. Now she dawdles halfway up the steps and pretends to check her watch, in reality surveying the area to confirm no one has followed her here. When she is confident she is alone, she climbs the remainder of the steps towards the entrance of the *Biblioteca Nacional de España* on Paseo de Recoletos. The blank eyes of the statues that line the borders along the flight stare beyond her efforts and, when she reaches the top, she pauses for a moment to catch her breath and enjoy the ornate façade on the pitched roof of the library. Time is short, so she shakes out of her dream, walks between the massive columns and continues towards the reception desk.

The woman's eyes peer over the plastic rim of her glasses as her smile widens. 'We haven't seen you for a while.' They chat while the librarian renews her membership card and Mercedes blames the pressures of work. Her friend asks about new boyfriends and a blush gives away her secret. 'Too busy with work?'

Now the woman has her teeth into the subject it is difficult to extract herself, but eventually Mercedes tells her second white lie of the day, that she has to return to work within the hour. She sighs with relief and gives thanks when another customer enters, as if on cue. The signs to the area where they store the press archives aren't necessary as she knows exactly where she is heading.

Orlando is working at the office because he says he wants to keep an eye on Jorge while she tackles the largest newspaper and magazine archive in Spain. The editor is the focus of her research and, in less than an hour, she has compiled a biography of her boss; the information is readily available but makes tedious reading. The journalist's career hasn't been meteoric and the appointment as Editor came after a period of longevity as he worked his way up from a humble start. His wife and five children she has met already, the woman is a mouse and, after five minutes in her company, Mercedes wanted to give her a good shake. There doesn't appear to be any scandal in their past, although one of his close friends is the joint owner of a dubious club, where men go for women and drugs, she has heard. His golf handicap is low, not surprising as he gets plenty of practice, two times every week as a member of the same foursome. There aren't many photographs of him in the press, he's an ordinary looking man who has had few moments of fame and, in the few photos she has located, he is usually one person in a group at a fund raising event or awards ceremony. About to abandon this line of investigation, she has a brainwave and checks a local paper's sports pages for golf results; she strikes oil.

'Doctor Ramón and Jorge play golf together. I found this photo in a 1989 publication; they won some competition. The caption refers to them as school friends so I looked into Jorge's school background and it turns out they were at the same college. The pieces of the puzzle are slotting together. Here he is, at the edge of this group, and there in the middle is the doctor. And this one, do you recognise this boy?'

'Isn't he…?'

'Before he went to the seminary, yes, it's the bishop.'

She turns over another photo on the table to show Orlando. They don't have much time before the library closes for the day. They had met as arranged at a bar nearby at midday but returned here straight away so she could show him her findings. He sits with his back to the corner and keeps an eye open for intruders.

She lowers her voice. 'Boyhood friends. Here's the mayor; do you recognise him without his moustache?'

'He's thin, it can't be the same man.'

She stifles her snigger, *the man certainly likes his food*. She adopts a serious tone and speaks of the powerful positions that each holds. 'What if they are all a part of this? The evil may spread further than I first thought.' The sound of footsteps echoes along the aisle and she puts her finger to her lips, but it is only the librarian, who mimes that it is time for them to leave. Mercedes signals one minute and gathers her belongings.

His touch stops her. 'I haven't shown you what I found. You'll love this.' Orlando hands her a buff file but, when she unfolds the cover, he shakes his head. 'Not here. Open it when you reach my place.' There aren't any clues in his eyes to the contents, so she puts it into her bag and tries to ignore its magnetic pull as they walk together to the exit. His arm descends like a level crossing and detains her at the main door.

'Give me a few minutes, then leave. And go straight home! As soon as I can get away, I'll join you.' With a final clench of her hand, he disappears and she watches from the shelter of the alcove as he saunters along the pavement as though he hasn't a care in the world. No one shadows his path and she waits five minutes, draws a breath, then leaves the safety of the building.

★

All the way home she senses something is wrong and when she lets herself in through his front door, she leans against the wall and waits for her heart to slow down. It exasperates her that she can't lose the impression of impending doom and her hand trembles so that she struggles to manipulate the bolt. She takes a breath to steady herself before she tries again. Her legs threaten to fold under the strain and she fights the feeling, aware that before she gives in and slides to the floor she must secure the room. The catch hasn't engaged when a force crashes through the door and knocks her to the ground. In the slow motion during her collapse, she panics when she notices the pictures on the walls of Orlando's flat. Automatic memory brought her here; heedful of his reminder when they parted, her mind was alert to the concerns about who followed. Instinct returned her to the flat, the one she knows well and hasn't visited since their escape a couple of days ago. She wilts when a cold tile touches her side and someone swaddles a cloth against her mouth and nose. The smell of ether intensifies and she falls into empty space.

A gorge divides her head but her hands can't explore the cavern, they won't obey her order to move. Her bones ache with cold and there is an acrid taste in her mouth. Her dry tongue drags across her lips; they feel swollen to twice their normal size and she gags when she tastes the iron of blood. A weight on her eyelids holds them down and she tries to fight but they refuse to open. As her memories return, the all-consuming urge to break free encourages her to thrash against the bindings, holding her wrists together behind her back. She keeps going until she runs out of energy. Later, when she is quiet, she listens. The only sound comes from her breathing and the speed of it indicates she is close to losing control. She calls up her steel, aware that if she is to escape this nightmare, she must forget the terror and concentrate.

When fear has freed its grip around her throat and her heart no longer threatens to burst, she manages a few sane thoughts. In order to warm up, she needs to move away from the damp patch underneath her body, but when she makes the effort, a shackle holds her ankle so she can only move a fraction before the line goes taut. At first she despairs, until she figures out she can wiggle in a snakelike fashion and contorts her body until she has shifted onto her side with dry ground beneath. She utters a yelp but her triumph is short-lived when faced with the reality of her predicament. Although no longer chained to a chair, she is still a prisoner and who knows how long they will keep her alive. She fights the nausea; if she vomits, it may earn her another beating.

How long has she been here? With no windows, it is difficult to hazard a guess but she believes that it is hours, maybe an entire day, since her jailer moved her from the first prison. Some of the blood on her lip may be from his hand; she bit it when she was desperate to resist the effects of the cloth he held but his fist smashed into her face and the battle was lost at the same moment her head felt the crack. Her cheek throbs and her right eye won't open. She persists until the left one finally obeys and makes out shadowy shapes as her sight acclimatises to the dark. It's hard to hear much over the rushing of air in and out through her mouth and the thump of her heart, and she attempts a relaxation technique she learnt in her yoga class. In the distance, water or some other fluid travels through pipes and every so often a gurgle, and then a rumble, breaks the tedium. It reminds her of the noise when there is air in her water pipes at home. The sound disappears, replaced with rushing in her head, and she strives for courage but the judder of sobs breaks through her resolve.

Has Orlando worked it out yet? she wonders. She should have paid attention, maybe then she wouldn't have made the simple, but fatal, error of returning to his old flat. All she can do is pray that he is safe and has not fallen into the hands of her abductors. The possibility that they have found him sets off all kinds of crazy notions in her head, so she forces her imagination to picture something pleasant, a reunion with her child. For a short time, the distraction is successful, then a creature scrambles across her leg. Her screams go on and on until her throat begins to sting and the sound turns hoarse. Even then, she is powerless to control the outburst until she hears the sound of a key turn in the lock. Suddenly, it is as though a hand clenches her throat and hushes her voice. Like a cat, she curls in a ball and tries to hide from the man but his shoe finds its target. Another crack, she realises that it's a rib this time; with each breath, a knife stabs her in the chest.

'You were told to keep quiet. I warned you.'

The man's voice isn't the first one she met during her ordeal; nevertheless, it is all too familiar and her lips try to form a word of apology, but all that comes out is a gurgle, which earns her another kick. There is a pause and a foot scoops under her body, rolling her onto her back. It is impossible to hold onto the initial scream but she cuts it off by clenching her teeth and biting her lips. She refuses to give in, even though the pain intensifies as a toe finds the injury in her chest. Finally it releases and she lies rigid until a hand cups behind her head and lifts it so her nose is in the direct path of his fetid breath.

'You make another sound and I won't wait for them to find your boyfriend. I'll finish you off myself.'

A gunshot fires inside of her skull as he drops her head and it hits the ground. The room spins and, this time, she welcomes the release from pain as oblivion claims her.

The gravel path twists and turns, and his dark hair bounces against the nape of his neck as he runs ahead. Although she pushes until her lungs threaten to burst, the boy remains beyond her reach. She shouts out to him, words of reassurance that she is nearby and will save him soon, but the voice of the doctor drowns hers as he encourages the child to run faster. The edge of the cliff looms near and his baby legs carry him ever closer. Her heart is ready to explode as she reaches out to grab him, but he slips through her fingers and vanishes over the precipice. In the next moment, she follows him in free fall, into a bottomless cavern, pieces of her broken heart scattering in the air around her. Millimetres from the ground, her body jolts and returns her to consciousness but another piece of her heart breaks as she realises that she is still a prisoner.

Paralysed, she listens for the man until certain she is alone, and then eases up her eyelids; the right one won't lift, it feels wet and tender and, when she touches it, it is made of sponge. With that movement, she realises for the first time since her abduction that her hands are tied at the front of her body, not behind her back. The change must have occurred while she was unconscious, a memory of the man's shoe attacking her side flashes through her head. Her teeth grate and she ignores the pain in her eye as she tries again and, this time, it moves a little. The triumph is small and she wants to shout her victory, but it is too soon and the lid collapses and refuses to lift again. Her attempts peter out and she turns her attention to the eye that works. When it adjusts to the dark, she can make out shapes in the shadows. It is the same dungeon; the stench is unforgettable and infiltrates her clothes, skin and soul. A rumble disturbs the silence, it comes from her tummy and reminds her that she last ate and drank before she returned to the library with Orlando. *Is it hours or days since then?* An expert, who she interviewed for an article a few years back, suggested a person could live for weeks without food; without water, the prognosis is much worse. She wishes she hadn't remembered that now, as her tongue is suddenly too big for her mouth and sticks to her parched palate. Everything disappears from her mind and all she can think of is water. She gasps for a drink and tries to find the strength to focus on something apart from fluid.

With her good eye, she scans the black void and learns that a chink in the room is admitting a trickle of light. It allows sight of a shape in the periphery of her vision and, when she stares longer, something glistens on top of the shadow. Twisting her head until it feels as though her neck will snap, more shapes come into her view. She believes they may be tables stored in a line, side by side, and her eye follows the shape of a leg down to the floor. The straight edge gives way to a cylindrical shape and she peers for a long time until she works it out, then utters an exclamation as she recognises the wheel of a hospital trolley. Her neck unwinds and she closes her eye, allowing it to rest while she mulls over the significance of this first clue to her location. If it is a hospital or clinic, her guess is that it is somewhere close to Doctor Ramón. If they have kept her in Madrid, she is convinced they would have brought her to Salvador. Now she can hope. Orlando knows of the connections with the clinic and she whispers a prayer that he will work it out in time, remaining out of danger until he finds her.

Chapter 32

An argument wakes her; men's voices shout accusations of ineptitude at each other. One voice makes her skin crawl, the marks its owner has left on her body are excruciating and she masks all sounds of breathing that might remind him of her presence. The identity of the other man is a mystery and, without any other movement, she eases up her good eyelid. They are on the opposite side of the room so it is difficult to see them clearly, but they left the door ajar when they entered and that opening allows in light, enough so that for the first time she sees her prison properly. Her glance immediately turns towards the stretcher trolleys lined up along the wall, her guess was spot on. One of the men kicks something that makes a loud bang and she returns her gaze in their direction.

'Where the hell is he?'

From her position on the tiles, the men resemble giants and cast shadows that stretch to where they merge into the dark. They appear to have forgotten her in their attempts to allocate blame and the heat of their antagonism fills the room. Their faces come together so their noses almost touch and, for a minute, she believes, and hopes, they will kill each other, and solve one of her problems.

'He's disappeared into thin air. No sign of him at his flat, or hers.'

Mercedes presses her lips together to silence her cry. Orlando is alive. And he is safe. Clothing rustles as one of the men moves closer to where she lies and she shuts her eye, remaining rigid as the smell of his leather shoes wafts across her face. Something hard pushes on her nose until she can no longer ignore it and pretends to surface into semi-consciousness with a groan. Her torturer keeps the toe of that shoe on her face and her heart dives while she waits for him to stamp.

'She's still out. When are we going to deal with her?'

'Doc says to keep her alive till we've got the boyfriend. We may need her as bait.'

'It's ridiculous. The longer she's alive, the more dangerous things are. We should get rid of her now.'

'He says they won't find her, no one's been down here in years.'

United by a common purpose, the two are friends again and one pulls the door wide so they exit together, boasting of what each will do to their prey. If she believes those words, she knows she will lose her mind and instead she chooses to pay heed to the strand of hope. It keeps her sane when the door closes and the light disappears.

So drowsy, her mind struggles to work. Is she starving? Or maybe she is dying due to dehydration. Another live thing climbs onto her leg but she lets it ramble undisturbed; such things no longer frighten her. Her body is shutting down, she hasn't passed urine for hours and her brain is muddled with incoherent thoughts. Just now, she heard a baby's cry – another hallucination, a trick of the devil to torment her final hours. If her hands were loose, she would cover her ears and fade away in peace but the restraint still holds them tied and she turns her head to the side so that at least one ear blocks the sound.

There it is again, a baby's cry, unrelenting torture to mock her at the end.

She listens more intently. This cry is not an otherworldly sound, mustered by her addled brain. With the baby's next wail, she rotates her head in the direction of the sound. The whimpering continues and she deliberates whether she should attempt to snake her body towards the sound but delays, aware of the risk that the jailer with his toe weapon could return at any time. Fear absorbs her energy and her willpower.

An angel sings a haunting sound and, although it comes from a great distance, the lullaby comforts Mercedes. No fight remains inside of her but she wants to hear more of the faint song and manages to wiggle her body towards it. The volume fades slightly and she shifts in the opposite direction following the music, inch by inch, until the chain around her ankle is at its limit. When she stops her efforts, the lullaby has ended and there is only silence. She rests her cheek on the cold tile in wait for another cradle-song and her spirit loosens its hold on life until a puff of cool air blows a hair across her cheek, which tickles her under her nose. That small breeze reawakens her desire to live. She must work out the reason for this new development. A flash of inspiration ignites a storm of excitement when she understands that the air and sound have found a way through an opening somewhere near. She stretches and contracts her body, following the path of the breeze until the restraints don't allow her to move further. Against her forehead there are pulses of cool air that alert her to a vent not far away.

The most beautiful music she has ever heard begins, a baby's whimper soothed by the woman's lullaby. Those words she recalls from her own childhood and had planned to croon to her son. At first her voice is gruff because of its redundancy and doesn't make an impression, but she reaches into the last vestiges of her strength, and sings out her plea for help.

Chapter 33

Bubbles explode around her body and Mercedes counts each one as she watches it stretch to obesity before it bursts. She reaches fifty-nine and Orlando barges through the door and breaks her concentration; all of her effort has been in vain. Deep inside, her anger fizzes and threatens to erupt but when she sees the distress in his eyes, a voice in her head orders her to contain the fury.

'Here, drink this.'

She seals her lips and rejects the rim of the cup that he offers. His voice is tender as he encourages her to sip and persists with his efforts, without complaint, until she relents. When no brandy remains, he eases her head back onto the slope of the bath, and afterwards stands guard as though he expects her to vanish any minute. A large bubble forms in the foam around her and she starts the count again, but when she reaches twenty, her lids close and her body slides into the froth.

The men have her trapped and no matter how hard she fights and screams, her legs can't move. Soon they will kill her.

'Hush now. You're safe.'

A cold, wet blindfold squashes her eyes; demons lurk in the dark and she can sense their presence, so she rips off the obstruction and slings it away from her as far as she can. Panic overcomes her when her eyes refuse to open and she thrashes about in terror. A man's voice attempts to soothe her but she has no trust in his platitudes as he imprisons her hands and replaces the compress. Her head twists and flays as she tries to hold back the tumble into the darkness.

'Leave it my love. It will help the bruises.'

He doesn't understand the danger that lurks in the shadows and she tries to explain but she can't form the words and it is only distressed moans that come out of her mouth. Hands press on her arms as a voice instructs her to remain calm but it is too late because her heart accelerates, moves into her throat, and strangles her as she returns to the world of nightmares.

'Orlando, I am not made of glass. This has to stop. It's been over a week now.'

He ignores her complaints; instead, he scoops her into his arms and lifts her up in the bed as though she is as light as a feather. When she is propped against the pillows to his satisfaction, he retrieves a tray of food from the bedside table and places it on her lap. The pink rose makes her smile, he never forgets, but she turns her face from the sight of the food. He won't listen when she tells him her appetite died at that same moment her abductors stole her freedom.

'Eat.'

As usual, he sits at the bedside and glares until she complies with his instructions and picks up the spoon. Her stomach baulks at the prospect but to please him she sips a spoonful of the thick soup and he murmurs a few words of praise; he supervises while she repeats the action until the bowl is half-empty. Then he raises the window blind and lets in the sunshine. It bewilders her; she has lost all perception of time and the hours have merged into each other. Contentment seeps through her as she turns her face to the glow of the day.

'There is nothing that warms me like the sun. I began to

think I would never feel it again.' Tears wash the sleep from the corners of her eyes and, annoyed that she turns to mush at the slightest provocation, she closes her lids. His finger strokes her wet lashes and initiates a rush of love that chases away the self-pity. A wisecrack about weepy women forms in her mouth but the lips on her forehead distract her and she gives up the attempt to lighten the atmosphere.

'If that mother hadn't heard you…' There is no need for him to continue, their thoughts clutter the silence.

'Thank God she believed me and didn't phone anyone else.'

'It was hard to persuade her I could deal with it. If she hadn't been distracted by the baby, she would have involved the ward staff.'

Every day she tries to get him to fill in some of the blanks in her memory, of those final minutes in the prison, but he insists that she should put it behind her. There will be time in the future, he states as he leaves the room. Seconds after he has left, he pops his head through the door with a warning that he expects the plate to be empty when he returns. She wants to please him but her stomach is full of soup and so she separates the fruit salad with her fork and hopes he will believe she made the effort.

Both of her hands lift the weight of the tray into his hands and afterwards her arms fall onto the bed, deplete of energy. Her foot pushes away the sheet and reveals the mottling that stains her legs; each day it fades a little more. The worst of the bruises are around her ankle and the doctor has informed her she will carry the tattoo forever. In years to come, she hopes she will learn to treasure her scars as reminders of the value of her freedom, but for now the marks embody her terror. A shadow flickers at the edge of her vision, drawing her attention to the open window where two birds dip and dive with graceful sweeps through the sky. The spread wings remind her of the dove emblem and her investigation, in limbo while Orlando has her under his control. The moment renews her fortitude; while she lies in this bed and indulges her damaged psyche, there will be no progress in the search for her child. She promises herself to do everything possible to regain her strength so she can start again.

The plate is clean and not a scrap of food remains, and he rewards her with a smile as he carries away her evening tray.

After breakfast the following morning, she has enough strength to sit out in a chair for half an hour. The small victory is a turning point and she improves with every hour, until the bed becomes a haven she only yearns for at night. Orlando still refuses to answer her questions about the rescue but she pesters without relent, until one day he narrows his eyes and gives in.

'Tomorrow, you'll be ready.'

Eyes fixated on his face, she takes no heed of the folder crammed with papers and notebooks that encumbers her lap. His descriptions of the filth in which he found her renews memories she wishes had been left undisturbed and she scratches at her skin even though the bites have long since disappeared. So close to giving up on her life, now a fire burns in her belly as her mind formulates plans for her revenge.

'You are certain these witnesses will support me when I go public and expose the network?'

'Each has made a promise to me. They understand the implications.'

He has not been idle while nursing her return to health but his news is not positive. A legal contact has warned him that the police will require more proof of culpability before they proceed with action against the doctor and his friends. When she hears her experience was not enough evidence and her captors did not leave behind anything that implicated them, she declaims the justice system and the officials in charge of it.

After she runs out of steam, Orlando asks if she feels better, then describes his plan. 'That's not enough.' He frowns at the folder on her knees. 'These men are experts at covering their tracks, and you know how powerful their friends are. Plus, we have no idea who else is involved.'

'But they've stolen our children! And look at what they've done to me! We must be able to do something.'

The volcano builds inside but bubbles underneath the surface when she notices the twinkle in his eye. He captures her face in his hands and his lips tease hers with feathery touches while he mutters to keep faith. He explains what he has arranged and she throws her arms around his neck and plants kisses all over his face.

The slope of her nose acts a ski run for the spectacles so that, time after time, she has to slide them back up into position. A rash is developing on her neck from the synthetic hair and Orlando slaps at her hand with a reminder to stop her scratching. The urge to pull off her disguise and discard it in the bin grows with each second. She catches sight of her reflection in a shop window; with a few accessories, she has become a middle-aged woman, bulky in her layers of clothing and unlikely to attract unwanted attention. A moment of guilt paralyses her when they arrive outside the offices of a rival newspaper, but she hardens her resolve and the feeling vanishes as she remembers waiting for death on the floor of that hospital basement.

Orlando wears a panama hat, it tilts low on his forehead and a woollen scarf covers the lower half of his face so only his eyes are visible as he follows her through the doorway. She smells his anticipation as he steps forward to her side but she pretends he is a stranger until they are out of danger. His body brushes hers, he caresses her fingers for a brief second, and she feels love in the light touch. A small crowd joins them in the wait for the arrival of the lift and, as they enter it, Orlando pushes the button for the eighth floor while she eases into a corner.

The cane she holds taps out an energetic beat until he lifts an eyebrow to warn her. Nerves pull down the corners of her mouth and an electronic voice announces their destination, the lift doors separating to reveal the man she has come to see. He looks nothing like his photograph on the board downstairs; the editor's smile reminds her of the smug face of her sister's cat when he delivered his kill to her feet. Her fingernails dig into her palms and she tries to suppress the feeling of disloyalty as she greets Jorge's opposition. The no-nonsense man leads them through a door – identified with a brass plate etched with his name and title – into an empty office. Mercedes pauses for a moment; it may be sparse in furniture but there are metres of space and the wide windows allow spectacular views of the city skyline. The editor points to two chairs that face the desk and she sinks into one with a sigh, today has been her first venture out since her rescue and the blood vessel in her neck is pumping at double speed. While the two men discuss the results of the football, she removes her glasses and pulls off her hairpiece; the invisible band around her forehead loosens as she frees her curls with her fingers. A film of sweat moistens her upper lip and she strips off her cardigan and the jacket she borrowed from Orlando's mother. Ready for business, she opens the folder containing her notes and waits for the men to finish their conversation.

Negotiations around the legal issues of their collaboration

develop into a battle of wills but she fights on, determined to hold her ground, as no less than front page will do. There is a new respect in his expression as he finally signs off their agreement. The first article of the series will be in the morning edition and the remaining ones will appear at regular intervals until her information expires.

'Once the paper is on the stands, you should be safe. They won't dare touch you after their names are made public in connection with a baby-kidnapping scandal.'

Beside her, Orlando fidgets and starts to interrupt, but the editor reassures him and hands over some keys. 'I don't think we should take any chances. These belong to my beach house in Cullera. Stay there for a few weeks until the police do something with the information.'

The arrangement doesn't fit in with her plans and she objects, telling him of her intention to travel into France. 'I have a lead into an old smuggling operation there and hope that someone along the route remembers something to do with the babies.'

He grasps her hand to force her to listen and, as the old grump speaks, her confidence fades.

'Go to the house and get out of harm's way. Years ago, Jorge's true nature revealed itself to me. Believe me, the man is clever. He may act dim but he knows how to cover his tracks. Until the police arrest his chums, and him, we can't guarantee you will be completely safe. I'll tell you the full story one day, but for now, I am glad to have a chance to show the public who he truly is.'

There is no choice but to agree to the arrangements and, as she and Orlando take their leave, the editor reminds her that the organisers of the network have eyes everywhere. 'Go straight to Cullera. You can buy what you need in the town. Don't assume they don't know you are planning something.

They aren't naive. I've arranged protection, but that isn't a surety. Once your series is underway, our friends will be more concerned with hiding their money and covering their backs than coming after you; but vengeance, well…'

'I wonder if I will ever feel safe again.'

Wearing their disguises, they take the lift to the ground floor and, for a brief moment before the doors open, Orlando draws her to his chest and rubs her back. The action calms her until she notices the misgivings in his eyes. She tries to allay them with a show of confidence and insists they go in separate directions when they emerge from the building. With a whispered farewell, she turns to the right with her eyes straight ahead.

A hulk steps forward as though to follow her, but he pauses, fixing his attention on a man sheltering in a doorway whose green eyes latched onto the couple when they came out through the glass doors. Their owner hesitates for a short time as he struggles with a decision and, with a final glance at Orlando, the man spins and hurries towards the corner in pursuit of Mercedes. With his attention forward, he doesn't notice that the hulk falls in behind, and the procession of three makes its way towards the metro station beyond the next crossroads. As they draw close to the entrance, the stalker lengthens his stride and reaches out his hand to grab hold of the tail of Mercedes' jacket but, at that final moment before she descends to the underground, she deviates to the edge of the road and jumps into a taxi. Her voice encourages the driver to 'burn rubber' when he pulls away and the door handle escapes the grip of her shadow. The hulk grins as the man stamps his foot and issues a string of curses before he disappears into the dark stairwell that leads to the metro.

The hulk holds his hand up for a taxi. The girl is safe for now, his colleagues will watch and ensure her safety on the train. He instructs the driver to deliver him to the airport; he wants to be waiting in Cullera when she arrives on the evening intercity express.

Chapter 34

The old shirt of Orlando's is threadbare, but it is impregnated with his smell so she pulls it over her head and wanders through to the lounge to wait for his return. When he unlocks the door, she forces herself to remain on the sofa until he delivers the present into her outstretched hands. Twenty minutes ago, when she felt the empty space next to her in the bed, she guessed immediately where he was; he must have been the first customer at the kiosk.

'Here it is.'

The evidence rustles in her hands but she stares at the paper with incredulity; in a dream, she reads the bold letters on the front page, the headline of her article, *The Lost Children of Madrid*. The exposure of the network will run for several weeks, the editor overruled her protests, stating that once they hook the interest of their readers, they won't give up on the story. In addition, it will give the police time to uncover the true breadth of the organisation.

This first article describes the kidnapping of babies from a renowned clinic in Madrid and, although she has not individually named the perpetrators, most locals should recognise the clues. She quotes witnesses when she reports on the involvement of government officials in document forgery. The editor telephoned last night to reassure her that the police are prepared to stop any attempts to extract official documents before they have had an opportunity to investigate.

Tomorrow's article will almost certainly give rise to some public objections as she draws attention to the church's role in carrying the babies away from their mothers; the men were justified in insisting she stay hidden until the furore settles.

The telephone rings while she is reading the inside pages. Orlando picks it up, and beckons her so she can speak. Her lover listens to the conversation with his arm across her shoulders and, every so often, he gives a small squeeze.

'Yes, I've seen it. How many? You're kidding!'

When the conversation with the editor finishes, she is in a daze until the handset buzzes and reminds her it needs replacing.

'Are you okay?'

'Their switchboard can't cope with the phone calls. Women and men from all over the country want to speak with me.' She trembles. 'All of them are parents who want to locate their lost babies.' Orlando brings her into his embrace. 'I've unleashed a monster.' She pulls back and stares into his eyes. 'Have I given them false hope?'

Croissant crumbs adorn the floor of the terrace but she ignores the mess and stares out at the Mediterranean as she sips her coffee. She still wears Orlando's shirt, the only clothes she has with her are the ones she wore to the meeting yesterday. Later in the day, they plan to shop for some basics to last over the next week or so. For now, she wants to mull over the responses to her exposé. The paper phones her with updates every half-hour and, with each call, her heart bleeds a little more; many of the women are elderly and hope their missing children have children of their own.

'I don't know how to help them. I don't even know how to help me.'

'You can't do anything for individuals. The best thing is

to do what you do best and concentrate on the network. Find out where the babies went to after they crossed the border. Why take them there? Did some remain here in Spain? Who was involved? You told me people pay thousands of dollars for a child. Can you find out who they are? Did they know they were buying stolen children?'

The number of unknowns daunts her and she wants to cover her ears. 'It's too much. It would need more resources than I have to research all of that. I speak schoolgirl French, and even less English. How am I supposed to probe?'

'Focus on what you can do. You are the best investigative reporter around, you've proven that. Hire a translator to travel with you.'

'But...'

His faith in her ability inspires her so she starts to come up with solutions and records her thoughts until he extracts the pen from her hand and orders her to take a break.

'We're going shopping. I love my mother but her clothes don't flatter your beautiful figure. I need something to enjoy during our exile.'

As soon as she replaces the handset after another call from the editor, the telephone rings again and a man greets her by name and asks to speak with her boyfriend. Orlando raises his eyebrows as he accepts the receiver, all of the previous requests have been for Mercedes, but upon hearing the caller's identity, he turns his back and curls his hand over the mouthpiece. The unusual behaviour makes her curious so she lingers behind the door to listen. His side of the conversation is crisp with words such as 'where' and 'when', but his palm muffles the remainder until he says goodbye. She creeps around the door; he is staring at nothing with the receiver still in his hand. A sense of imminent doom drapes over her and butterflies come to life in her stomach. The muscles in his back expand with his breath and, as he turns, he collects her in his arms.

'The police have made an arrest.' Her exclamation of relief is premature; it is not the doctor in custody. The butterflies move into her head as he explains. 'A man named Ernesto Marquez. He's been charged with Juanita's murder. They discovered his fingerprints on the material of the scarf.'

The room spins and Mercedes fights for control as she tightens her grip on his arms. 'Why her?'

'They don't know yet. My source tells me he's a hired killer, people pay him to get rid of their problems. As far as they know, he had no contact with her before that day of her death.'

The scarf; it haunts her nightmares, and she doubts she will ever learn to live with the guilt. Orlando forces her to meet his eyes as he speaks about the irony of fate and blame in his attempts to offer comfort. No one could have foreseen the consequences of her investigation, he tells her, but Mercedes knows her culpability exists, all the same.

'It's up to you to make certain that Juanita didn't die in vain. Continue the investigation and find your son.'

After she nods her agreement, he informs her that when a fisherman discovered Ernesto on the river's edge, someone had beaten him to near death. It was difficult to identify him and he will live although he may never recover his sight; his contact lenses cut through his eyes.

There is a saying, which the locals use, that Madrid has nine months of winter and three months of hell but the weather could never reconstruct Mercedes' hell and inspire the terror that she felt in that cellar. Even that hell can't be compared to what she has endured since the theft of her baby. Orlando's fingers play with her palm and she tries to put it from her mind and enjoy their enforced holiday. Their hips bump and they mimic each other's steps as they make their way towards the beach restaurant. Her eyes perform an occasional sweep even though she knows her enemies are hours away. Under armed guard, the beast lays broken in hospital minus the green lenses and she should feel safe, but the sensation of being followed never abandons her.

Tomorrow she intends to catch an early train and head to the mountains; she can't wait any longer to speak with Isabella about her uncle's hikes along the border. Her decision caused an argument with Orlando, he wants to accompany her, but Mercedes dug her heels in and said no. She remembers the single-word answers the woman gave her husband and knows Isabella will speak more freely if they are alone. The remainder of her plan is secret; she is going into France to trace the path of the stolen babies.

The first hint that something extraordinary is about to happen is when a waiter brings two flutes and a bottle of bubbly. Mercedes notices the name on the label and turns to Orlando but his chair is empty. He kneels on the floor in front of her and tenderly takes hold of her fingers.

Chapter 35

The smell of something ripe, an expiry date long past, hits her as soon as she shoves her hip against the door to her apartment. She leaves the door wide open and waits for the smell to disperse a little before she steps in. As she walks through the lounge, she slings her overnight bag onto the settee. The silence rips through her chest, the emptiness so painful it brings her to a sudden halt and her resolve dwindles; she wants to hide and let time heal her wounds. Instead, she draws a shuddering breath and hardens her heart.

The windowpane is chilly to touch, she opens it to release the smell and the cold wind makes her shiver; she may feel dead but the sorrow hasn't killed her yet. In the fridge, she locates the guilty packet of cheese and, pinching it between the ends of her fingertips, carries it to the bin, leaving drips of whey along the path. Then she transfers her bag to the bedroom, flings her body on the empty bed, and stares at the ceiling as she tries to block out the memory of Orlando's stricken expression.

Repeated buzzes of the intercom interrupt her self-pity and she splashes cold water onto her face while Rosa is in the lift. Her sister ignored her protests when they spoke on the telephone and insisted on coming to be with her on this first night home. As she enters, the hug nearly suffocates Mercedes but they avoid the taboo subject. Rosa kicks her out of the kitchen and tells her to change the bed while she cooks something. They eat their scrambled eggs in silence but Mercedes can't tolerate the unspoken disapproval and she tries to explain. Her sister listens, her body stiff, and she doesn't need to speak as there is no hiding her disappointment.

'You do know that Orlando asked Papa.'

Mercedes mumbles an excuse through her fingers but Rosa shows no sympathy.

'You can't blame that. Orlando knows about your baby. Has he suggested that it's a problem?'

'He wants children but,' the knife deepens in her heart, 'how can I go through that again?' Her hands snake over each other, gathering momentum with each pass, until her sister collects them and holds them quiet. 'It haunts me.' The ticking of the antique clock counts the seconds.

New wrinkles show at the edges of Rosa's eyes as she tries to understand. She crumples her mouth, then gives up with a shake of her head. 'You're seeing things that aren't there. He's a good man.'

With each nod, another arrow shoots Mercedes in the chest. The past was an excuse but her response can't be undone and she has decided her fate. She lies about a headache and stumbles to the refuge of her bed.

Voices wake her but she keeps her eyes closed and fights to return to the perfect family home in her dreams. Rosa has washed the bed linen and the fragrance of clean laundry creates a sweet haven until an avenging angel appears at the foot of her bed, who glowers as he commands her to rise. She has never seen this side of him and her fingers fumble with the belt of her dressing gown. He leads the way into the living room and she shuffles behind without speaking. When he points to the settee, she obeys and sits. Rosa picks up the house keys and mumbles an excuse about milk as she leaves. The man in the chair opposite doesn't speak a word until the door has shut and they are alone.

'You're not going to do this to me.' Mercedes opens her mouth, but he won't allow her to interrupt. 'You can't pretend you don't love me. I can see it in your eyes. We're going to marry and live life as a normal family.' At his expression of fury, she clamps her lips and hangs her head. 'I don't intend to forget your boy. We'll do everything we can and search until we find out what happened to him, even if it takes our entire lives. If, and when, we do find him, he'll have step-brothers and sisters and be a member of our loving family. Because, you and I are meant to be together and nothing you say can change that.' His palm covers his heart. 'An eternal flame burns in here.' He slides from the chair and kneels in front of her for the second time in twenty-four hours.

They don't hear the key turn in the lock, or when Rosa enters the room. They do hear her when, on noticing the diamond, she hollers as she dances around the room. Entwined in each other's arms, they laugh at her antics until tears stream down Mercedes' face.

In the middle of talk about a wedding, her sister asks a question, so simple that it astounds them all. It also causes pain and Mercedes looks to her fiancé for help. He kisses her fingers and declares that their concern will always be that her boy is well cared for, happy, and knows that his Spanish family is there for him.

'We could never steal him away from a family that he loves.'

Every fibre of her being wants to deny his words, but she knows he speaks the truth and nods her agreement. All the same, a tiny crack has dented her happiness.

Chapter 36

Typical of the month, heavy clouds mask the sun and cast elongated shadows over the land. The change of the season is palpable now the searing heat has disappeared, and last week locals danced outside in the first rain with songs of thanks to God. Depleted reservoirs and rivers have begun to fill and the monotony of hot days and relentless sun has broken; few country people rue the passing of summer.

A crow perches on the boundary wall, his beady eye appears to monitor the cloud of dust that billows on the horizon, and a car emerges out of the swirl on a journey towards a gated entrance. The driver seems reluctant to arrive in haste; one can't deny the solemnity of the occasion and, by the time the sedan pulls up outside the gate, its movement is barely perceptible. Two men wait inside the metal entrance, they don't speak to each other as they lean on their shovels, and both regard the arrival with suspicion.

Blacked-out windows hide the contents of the car's interior and for a long time nothing happens, but at the same moment that one of the diggers reaches into his pocket to withdraw a partially burnt cigarette, a front door opens. He gives his cold butt a look of regret before pushing it into a secure place behind his ear. A man unravels from the driver's seat and straightens to his full height at the side of the vehicle. He brushes the front of his shirt, reaches into the car for a jacket, puts it on and straightens his tie. When he finishes, he checks his reflection in the window. The man will not see another fifty years and has a stoop that makes him appear older; he blames it on his employment, years at a desk in the judicial service. Before he leans in to speak to the occupants of the back seat, he glances at the sky and extracts a furled umbrella from the boot.

A woman's leg, covered with a black stocking and wearing a low-heeled court shoe, emerges from behind the rear door. One of the men at the gate widens his eyes and leans forward on his shovel; when he notices the grey hair and realises that her shapely definition has fooled him, his interest wanes and his eyes turn up to survey the sky.

Carmen falters when she sees the name on the arch and the court representative steps to her side to offer his arm, but the younger woman gets there first.

'I know it's hard. I'm here.' Mercedes hooks the trembling arm through the crook of her elbow and mumbles words of comfort. 'It will be over soon.'

She catches the eye of the judge and nods, keen for the day to be over, fearful the whole event may be too much for the old woman. At the signal, the workers lead the way and weave between the tombstones. Marble headstones, etched with names and dates, mark the resting places; some are pristine, but the weather of many decades has eroded others. Fancy crypts hold departed family members together, reunited in death, and the dates during the civil war give clues to some of the stories.

The clouds blacken, everything turns grey and the judge checks his watch as he raises an eyebrow at Mercedes. She inclines her head and silently urges him to hurry as she mumbles in Carmen's ear. They follow the men along an ancillary path that is overgrown with scrub plants so they have to fight their way through.

It leads into a section where the undesirables lay at rest; few feet have trodden this route. Neither marble statue nor headstone marks the territory; the men know where to go and move to a flat stone hidden amongst some weeds. It is smaller than a cigarette packet and the sight tugs at Mercedes' heart. Shovels shift dry earth, the slicing through the ground is the only sound and even the birds remain silent, as though they honour the solemnity of the occasion. One shovel hits true with a loud clink. Carmen shrivels, and the clouds discharge warning drops.

One of the men reaches into the cavern and lifts out a box, which he places on the ground with unexpected tenderness. The atmosphere is poignant and no one moves as they contemplate the tiny container. Branded into the wood are letters and a date, hand-carved as though they were a last-minute addition.

'Do you want a priest?'

Carmen's eyes reveal her agony as she shakes her head and the judge orders the worker to go ahead. All eyes remain on him as he pushes the flat edge of a crowbar into the join, levers the lid and steps back so that they can see. The sound of the old woman's pain fills the silence as the others stare, transfixed by the stones inside.

Carmen finally has some colour in her cheeks and Mercedes covers the glass before the barman tops up another brandy. She couldn't decide whether the woman needed a bar or a doctor as they staggered from the graveyard. The judge had paperwork to fill in and dropped them here, with a promise to return within the hour. Words spill from her elderly lips, heavy like the rainfall outside, and Mercedes holds her hand and allows the woman to relive her memories. She has heard them many times before.

Carmen should be home with her husband, but the old woman refused to make the call; it is none of his business, she said. Mercedes understands why she hasn't forgiven him, the man betrayed her when he discussed her past with his friends. They took it upon themselves to watch her after that first meeting between the two women in the café, friends of friends who happened by that day, but it turns out they were friends of the doctor as well. That sighting of Carmen with Mercedes initiated a chain of events that left death in its wake and the old woman remains guilt-ridden. Her back hunched with her chin sunk into her collar, Carmen looks ten years older than she did this morning, and her speech is muffled by cotton wool.

'At least I know I'm not mad.'

'None of us are.'

'Where are they? France, like some of the others?'

So many women have asked that question and it grieves Mercedes that she isn't able to provide an answer. Of them all, this old mother deserves an answer; she never gave up hope.

'Maybe, but it is impossible to be certain. My French colleagues are still trying to find out what happened. The children could be anywhere, maybe other countries, although we know some stayed here in Spain. The doctor's network sent babies to South America and to the United States. I'm beginning to realise the Madrid network is just one of many though.'

Mercedes doesn't want to tell her how many records have been falsified or destroyed and have led her investigators to a dead end. For a long time they sit, each lost in reflection, until Carmen's face brightens and she hugs herself.

'They're alive. Maybe they have children of their own. Even if I never find them, it helps to know that.' Some of the haunted look fades from her face. 'For my niece.' The soft skin of her palm pats Mercedes' cheek. 'And for yours. If you look enough, I know one day you'll find him.'

There seems to be nowhere else to look for him; in her cupboard, Mercedes has boxes full of information but he remains the baby of her memory, not the young man she longs to know. After the publication of her article in an international magazine earlier in the year, daily letters began to arrive from all over the world but not the one she is desperate to receive. Lost children and childless mothers write to her for help and she has learnt she is a minnow in a great ocean.

'We'll ask the support group if they can help, now we know that your baby wasn't buried. There's one in Chile; Father Carlos is amazing and has even convinced a few priests to take the lead in the search for those affected. It's been hard for them, knowing some of their colleagues have been responsible.' From her bag, she withdraws a photo of her portly friend from Isabella's village; he wears a straw hat and sports a bad case of sunburn. 'We received this in the post the other day from Santiago. Look at the colour of his face.'

The concept of developing international support groups occurred to Mercedes after a call from Robby, and with the priest's assistance they have established one in eight countries. There are two more planned later this year. Robby's visits to Spain during the past few years have not identified his birth family but the man refuses to lose hope and works tirelessly to help others. It lifts her spirits to hear his reports of the occasional reunion. She has given up on official help; no one will get involved, the attitude of 'let the past be the past' filters through everything. Her desk drawers overflow with letters from agencies all over the world that specialise in helping parents to reunite with their children. Babies have gone missing from Chinese families to South American ones; the international business is a profitable one.

Mercedes doesn't tell her what she has discovered; the old woman will never rest if she knows that criminal gangs control some of the networks and some of the children do not end up in a family.

Carmen chuckles at the photo of the priest, but her lips are tinged purple and her skin is white, and Mercedes forces her into a taxi with orders to take her home immediately. Before the door closes, gnarled fingers grasp hers and pull her down to the side of the car. Velvet skin nestles her cheek as the old woman whispers in her ear, 'I will never be able to thank you enough.'

Chapter 37

The minute she hears the sound, Mercedes feels around for the box on her bedside table to locate the button and stop the alarm's serenade. Careful not to wake the snoring man at her side, she eases from under the covers and stretches both arms to the ceiling while she perches on the edge of the bed; her eyes feel gritty after a night of counting the seconds. The sun won't appear for another hour and when she leans out to grab the handle to close the window, there isn't any noise from the street below. She leaves a crack for air and stoops to retrieve her dressing gown from the floor. She dropped it there after she got up to check the time, less than an hour ago.

On tiptoes, she creeps into the lounge; Stephen King's words are face down on the coffee table and the lamp bulb smells hot, she forgot to switch it off earlier. A floorboard creaks as she sidles up to a door and puts her ear near the opening. Air vibrates across her infant daughter's lips and, for a second, she wants to go into the room, pick her up from the cot and squeeze the tiny body to her chest. Amongst the building bricks, cars and other mayhem that obscures the bed in the neighbouring room, there is her son, a mini Orlando, curled as if a hamster in the favourite sleeping position of his father, burrowed underneath the covers so that only a few ebony curls show he is there.

When she returns to the lounge, she lifts a passport from the pile of documents on the coffee table and, for the umpteenth time, checks that she has signed it; the photo makes her look like a convict but there wasn't time for another one. A child cries out for mummy and her stomach falls as guilt strikes – only time will show if she is going on another hopeless endeavour.

The shower is lukewarm, she'd forgotten to adjust the timer for the water heater, but once she recovers from the shock the cool liquid washes away the cobwebs in her head. As she rubs herself dry, she surveys her dappled body in the full-length mirror and wonders what he'll make of the middle-aged woman, with folds across her tummy that show through her clothes and lines that have recently begun to take root in her face. Sideways on to the mirror, she holds her breath and sucks in the bulge around her middle, but it bounces out again when lack of air forces her to exhale. The reflection grimaces back at her, it's too late to worry.

The figure in the bed snorts once and turns over before he settles back into his rhythmic warbling; in the early days, his night songs kept her awake but now it's the serenade that soothes her into sleep. While he tosses, she is still and afterwards she creeps to the wardrobe to remove the clothes she has chosen especially for today: the navy skirt and cream blouse, black would appear too mournful and her normal daytime wear of jeans and baggy T-shirts too sloppy. She carries them into the living room and starts to dress but the skirt must have shrunk as she struggles to wiggle her hips into it. As her hips twist and turn, the music of La Bamba replays in her head, it was a favourite on the radio yesterday afternoon.

The last time she flew across the ocean, her feet swelled so much she had to walk through the airport in bare feet, so for this long-haul destination she slips on some trusty flats. Mercedes assesses her appearance one more time in the mirror and tries to see beyond the woman with fine streaks of grey around her temples, highlights in her faded black mane. The ordeal five years ago left marks and her reflection doesn't lie, even though her husband starts each morning with the phrase 'more beautiful every day'.

Dawn is about to break and she sits on the settee to wait, tapping out the seconds with her toe. They never returned to his old flat and it's now rented to a nice young man who works at the paper. It took some time to grow used to the luxury, but since the children came along the flat feels more like a home, finger-marks all over the glass surfaces and paintings decorating the fridge door.

The suitcase is ready by the front door; squashed inside are the items that she needs for a week and Orlando says she can buy more clothes if she runs out. He suggested she include photocopies of her work and a copy of last year's press prize but she hopes it doesn't give the impression that she is boastful. There is also an album inside the case, the spine split with the contents; she wanted to include precious photos of her family and she crosses her fingers that she has a chance to show them off. Packed last month, the case had been ready while she waited for the phone call. In fact, when it came, she had two weeks to prepare, each day a lifetime.

It is the final half hour in her long wait and she removes a tattered envelope from her bag to read the letter one more time.

Dear Mercedes

For years, it has been my greatest desire to write you this letter. You have done much for others in highlighting their plight, and deserve some reward for helping families to reunite.

We may have found your son. Two months ago, a teenager matching the description you gave walked into our office in

Boston. He had recently discovered that as a baby, his parents adopted him in 1985. They paid a go-between, a woman arrested here in the States last December for baby trafficking. When the news broke, they confessed to their son and are now trying to help him find his birth mother.

She checks her watch again, twenty minutes to endure, and switches on the television to the early morning broadcast. The familiar faces of the leader of the government and his opponent fill the screen, which holds her interest until she discovers the announcements are old news. Mercedes mutes the sound and stares at the flicker of the silent images as she waits. A rap on the glass of her watch doesn't make any difference to the minute and she pulls her sleeve down to cover the timekeeper. She sighs and opens her wallet to have another look at the photograph. The boy has dark hair and dark eyes, on the reverse someone has written, *Geoff's school photo, 1999.*

A shockwave disrupts the silence as the telephone rings three times before she manages to reach it. A loud groan bursts forth from behind the door of the master bedroom.

'*Dígame*. Speak to me.'

'It's Rosa. I wanted to wish you luck.'

'It's hard to believe it's finally happening. My taxi will be here in ten minutes.'

In the doorway of their bedroom, Orlando appears, his fingers scratching his chest like a bear. He blows her a kiss and mimics making a cup of coffee. She shakes her head no and looks at the ceiling as she mouths her sister's name and 'no time'.

'Did you sleep? I bet you didn't. I wish Mama could have...'

At a break in the monologue, Mercedes interrupts with a promise to let her know the outcome as soon as possible.

There is a lump in her throat as she says farewell, it appeared when Rosa mentioned her mother, and she sidles over to Orlando on the settee and moulds her body against his, her ear in her favourite place over his heart. He holds her there for a bit and then eases her away, landing a kiss on the tip of her nose as he tucks a lock of hair behind her ear.

'You are like her, you know, your mother.'

'She never knew. All those years she doubted me.'

He cups her chin and scolds her. 'Yes, but she did admit her mistake before she went. That took courage.'

She loves that he always seems to know what to say and is about to kiss him again when the taxi driver presses the buzzer. She tries to act calm but her heart races and her voice shakes as she says goodbye. Suddenly she feels alone and the inclination to pack up the kids and Orlando and take them with her makes her go rigid.

'You'll be fine'. He reads her thoughts. 'Until we know for certain, it's the best thing for the little ones. That's what we agreed.'

Tears blur her vision as she blows a kiss towards the children's bedrooms, but Orlando isn't having any of that and grabs her by the shoulders, kisses her hard, and pushes her out of the apartment.

'Go on. This time, let's hope you find your dream. We'll be waiting here for you, whatever happens.'

The display indicates that Flight IB 763 to Washington will leave on time and, after check-in, Mercedes goes through to the departure lounge and picks up a newspaper. The woman at the adjacent table in the coffee bar points to the photo on the front page, the Duchess and her nephew.

'Too much money, those two.'

She nods to be polite but avoids eye contact, and shifts

around so she is able to concentrate on the inside pages and her article about the trial and sentence of Doctor Ramón. Convicted of conspiracy to commit murder, the penalty seems too short in exchange for the life of Juanita. Bile fills her mouth as she remembers the lawyer rabbiting on about mistaken identity; if the hired man had erased the correct victim, she wonders if the doctor's sentence would have been more severe. Near to the back pages, the editor has included her material about the delay in bringing the criminals to justice. It makes her churn that there is still no date set for the baby trafficking trial and the *Baby Snatcher,* her nickname for Doctor Ramón (also the nickname that most of the reporters use unofficially), hasn't received punishment for those crimes.

A woman's voice breaks into her thoughts – the tannoy with an announcement of the gate and the first call for her flight – and her irritation vanishes as she jumps up and rushes along the corridor. First in the queue to present her passport and enter the holding pen, she balances on the edge of a seat next to the entrance that leads onto the air bridge, ready for when the call comes. A man sits down in the next seat. He stinks of aftershave, she hates that fragrance, it is similar to the smell on the cloth her abductor used to cover her face. About to tell him it is rude to stare, he pre-empts her observation when he asks if he knows her. She shakes her head but he works it out and his voice grows louder.

'I've seen you on the telly. You're that reporter, the one who writes about the babies. My wife thinks you're a hero. She's joined one of those groups, wants to find her brother.'

By now, every pair of eyes along the rows of seats watches the exchange with interest and her complexion burns as she tries to demur, but the man makes things worse when he asks for her autograph. This kind of attention feels like an assault and her mind goes blank when she takes hold of the pen. His eyes gleam with admiration so she tries to swallow the lump in her throat and come up with something for him. As she signs her message, a member of the crew asks that she accompany her to a separate area.

'We've upgraded you to first class; it will be more comfortable for the trip over.' She lowers her voice. 'You moved me in that article about your son, I pray that you will find him one day.'

Mercedes flinches, until she understands that the woman doesn't know the purpose of her trip, and mumbles that she hopes so too. When the woman escorts her to a seat near the front of the plane and hands her a plastic glass of champagne, she drains it in one gulp and relaxes back into the leather seat; she can't believe she is on her way and her fingers clutch the end of the armrests as she tries to remain calm. The plane thrusts into the sky above Madrid and, as her city disappears beneath the clouds, she releases her grip and places her hand flat on the cold window, a final wave to her family below. She finishes a second glass of champagne before she has the courage to deal with the other letter in her bag. No one knows about it, and Orlando would have never let her walk out of the flat this morning if he had read the threat that arrived on her desk yesterday.

The phrasebook is open in one hand on the greetings and travel section, and she holds her passport in the other while she waits in the queue for immigration. The noise of the crowd deafens her and the English lessons seem to have been in vain, as she can't understand a single word people say. The words run into each other and no one speaks like Peter, the voice on her compact disc. Bodies push her from behind and the warning from a friend about pickpockets in airports encourages her to clutch her bag to her chest as she waits for a uniformed man with an angry face to direct her to a counter.

'Business or pleasure?'

The phrase isn't in her book so she doesn't know how to answer and the official intimidates her with his glare when he asks again. This time, she understands and tries to mimic the way he pronounces 'pleasure'. Although it doesn't sound right to her, he seems to understand.

'How long are you here for, Ma'am?'

Her stomach twists tighter and she tries to recall the numbers; the man takes pity, repeating the question in Spanish and relief washes over her as she answers. If she could step beyond the counter, she would kiss him a thousand times. A rubber stamp puts a mark onto her passport, he wishes her a good trip in Spanish, and her excitement builds as she follows the other passengers to collect her luggage. Two sliding doors, stained glass with the American flag, hide the view of the other side, and she walks through them into chaos. Hundreds of people wait at the side of the barricade and every one of them watches as she walks along the makeshift corridor. Her eyes sweep the throng, on the lookout for a sign.

A woman waves and calls her name. Mercedes recognises her from the photos sent by the American support group, but her glance is cursory and passes over her to the young man at her side; he grins and half-lifts his hand. She gasps. There is no need for the result of a blood test; the boy is the image of her father.

Mrs. Smith, a random name and not the one written in her real passport, watches Mercedes' hands cartwheel through the air. The Spanish woman sobs as she grabs hold of the boy and kisses the teenager's cheeks, repeatedly until the poor kid is as red as a beetroot. Finally, they link arms and follow the lead of the agency woman towards the car park.

When they pass Mrs. Smith, she falls in behind. A handgun bumps against her hipbone, hidden in her jacket pocket for now, as her employers have instructed her to keep watch and do nothing yet to harm the reporter. They will let her know when they want her to act, but first they want to uncover the name of the mole in their organisation; that person cost them millions last year.

A dog arrives at her feet, sits and growls with his teeth bared. She is about to nudge him out of her way but her expression changes when she realises the dog's owner wears a police uniform and is reaching for his weapon.

Acknowledgements

Alan, Rachael, Barbara, and Rick

The BBC Documentary 'The World: Spain's Stolen Babies'

Margaret and Alistair

S J Watson

Carmen

My Faber Academy contacts

About the Author

L A Berry has written short stories and poetry for pleasure since childhood. Silencio is her first published novel. She left her NHS career as a nurse/midwife to sail across the Atlantic and after two years on the boat, returned to live in England in 2001. She has a home in Spain and travels extensively throughout the country.

If you want to read some of the background information to *Silencio*, baby trafficking or her other works, please visit her website

www.laberrynovels.org